Warlords of the Stars

A Space Merchants Novel
By Wendie Nordgren

www.wendienordgren.com[1]

---

1.   http://www.wendienordgren.com

Cover Design by: Christopher M. Coyle Dark & Stormy Knight Design www.darkandstormyknight.com[2]

---

2. http://www.darkandstormyknight.com

Books by Wendie Nordgren:

The Wendigo Redemption Series

Wendigo Uprising Book One

Wendigo Hunting Book Two

Wendigo Conjuring Book Three

The Space Merchants Series

The Space Merchants Book One

The Space Merchants of Arachne Book Two

The Parvac Emperor's Daughter Book Three

Omnes Videntes Book Four

The Spider Queen Book Five

The Inquisitors Book Six

Thunderdrop A Space Merchants Novella

Materfamilias Book Seven

Ensign Probus Book Eight

The Cosmos Coalition Book Nine

Omnes Videntes Series

Xavier

Jazon

Clue Taylor Series

Clue and The Shrine of the Widowed Bride Book One

Clue and the Sea Dragon Book Two

Clue and the Tree Spirits Book Three

Clue and the Curse of Gashadokuro Book Four

Clue and the Mystery of Bake-kujira Book Five

Standalone

Temporal Locum

Novella

Death's Providence

Chapter One

"Someone, please tell me what exactly it is that we hope to accomplish while sitting uselessly here whilst this young female tends to her most recent offspring?" Ambassador Ness of Sinope paced angrily along the edges of the conference room.

Ignoring the misogynistic asshole, I smiled down at Marielle Galerius, my infant daughter. She was sucking loudly at my breast while playing with her foot. I cooed to her and smoothed her soft, dark-black hair, which grew like a baby swan's fluff about her sweet head. Her twin sister had hair of a lighter shade, a brown to match that of her father. Tabitha Jiri slept beside me in her pram with a belly full of milk.

Inquisitor Eli Beck adjusted the pink Arachnean Silk blanket covering her which drew my lips into a smile. Aside from being a beloved husband, he was an exceptional father and protector. Before I'd accepted him as one of my husbands, he'd been one of my most trusted friends and allies.

In a dangerous tone of voice meant only for Ambassador Ness to hear, Ambassador Edvard Stig, the Galaxic Government's elected representative for our new security endeavor, said, "Calm yourself, Ambassador Ness." I observed Eddie with a sardonically raised eyebrow. He sat across the highly-polished wood conference table from me. His champagne-blond hair fell to his shoulders like a golden waterfall. He stared at Ness with cold, calculating eyes.

Why Stig sounded so worried, I didn't know. The soft weight of Marielle in my arms had me filled with contentment. I wasn't going hurl anything at Ness, at least not in my current mood. I sensed Quaid intended to speak before I heard the sound of his voice. Glancing over at him, I smiled as the lighting caused his blond hair to shine. He kept it short and neat in the preferred style of Galaxic Militia captains.

"Through our cooperative efforts, we have accomplished our first goal," stated Captain Quaid Bosh, formerly of Epopeus.

The lights in the conference room were too bright in my opinion, too bright for a mommy who was trying to get her baby to sleep. Ever present in my mind, Quaid walked over to the room's control panel and dimmed the lights a fraction. He'd accepted his captaincy and position within the Cosmos Coalition at the cost of serving aboard the *Hadrian*, the ship of my cousin, Captain Eric Alaric. However, it was the opportunity to serve for which he'd longed, and his new position had the added benefit of allowing us, for the first time since I'd accepted him, to live together as husband and wife. The long-distance relationship we'd endured had been a strain on our relationship. Ours had begun as a political marriage but had grown into something far deeper and more meaningful. Observing him, I noticed his eyes and those of Ambassador Ness of Sinope appeared solid-black in the now more dimly lit room. It was probably nothing to worry about. Natives of Epopeus, with her two brilliant suns, were accustomed to intense light. Those of us who visited their planet required the use of protective glasses. However, when on their home world, their eyes no longer appeared solid-black where sclera finally became visible. The only other times I'd seen sclera around Quaid's eyes were when he'd become love-drunk. I grinned at those memories.

The other Laconian race, the Enyo, like Yukihyo Alaric Montgomery Lee, my first husband and the love of my life, had eyes of solid-white whose surfaces, if one were to pay close attention, hinted at their emotions through subtle changes occurring to their capillaries. Though their eyes were different, Enyo and Eriopis males had an evolutionary trait in common. They were overprotective of their females. Enyo males were empaths. Able to sense my emotions, Yukihyo would charge to my defense if I felt any fear or soothe my emotions if I felt any sadness. In return, our symbiotic bond provided him with the ability to control his rage and need to fight.

A native of the frozen planet, Chione, Yukihyo had learned to thrive in a hostile environment and had been happy there until Parvac soldiers had slaughtered his family and stolen their women. At the moment, he was with his mother and sisters. He'd taken Neema, Niklos, and Peter to visit their grandmother, aunts, and cousins. When he'd learned of their survival, a deep-seated jagged rawness had left him. His fury over his father and uncles still burned, and he'd never accept Mrs. Tereas' husband, a Parvac General, as his stepfather. However, he had managed to be in the same room with the male a time or two.

While the Laconians had an abundance of females and practiced polygamy, the Parvac Empire had suffered for centuries with low female birthrates. As a polyandrous society, females were encouraged to accept all of the husbands they wished. Having accepted twelve husbands, one sadly of whom I'd untimely lost to the stars, I felt I'd done my part as a Parvac Princess and should be left in peace. Unfortunately, males still vied for my attention. While Parvac males of pure lineage had no empathic or telepathic abilities, they were obsessively protective, ad nauseum.

Some, like Ambassador Ness, would be better off avoiding both my attention and that of the males who sought my affection. The male glared at Eddie. "Don't tell me to calm down, Stig." A vein had begun to pulse in his temple, and his coloring darkened, heated with anger. "I know you for what you are. You are nothing more than a generational criminal and charlatan, using wealth, threats, blackmail, and intimidation to elevate yourself into a position of power within the Galaxic Government."

Stig smiled at him in such a way as to make me shiver. I added, "You're leaving out torture and murder."

Amused, Stig lifted his cup to me.

Patiently, I tried to diffuse the situation. "Ambassador Ness, we have been using our time to collect information about the Pariea, the all-seeing ancient ones. We have shared our intelligence reports about the being we discovered on Earth." The alien, a being who appeared almost as a gelatinous conglomeration of shifting light, had led me to its location with sentient fragments of itself. Even in its weakened state, the alien had been so telepathically powerful as to be able to control and manipulate the minds of the Mad Ones, hybrid Enyo and Eriopis creations of Dr. Stanley Crispus, who Stig employed. Eddie was keeping them under control somehow. So, for now, my Omnes Videntes were allowing their brothers to live. Currently, the hybrids were being treated on a medical station in Earth's orbit. I was relieved for them to be so far away. They'd begun to lose their battle with their own sanity. However, their other brothers had not. I'd bound Zared to myself in a moment of terror and had taken his brothers with him. They'd eagerly fallen under my control.

Of Arachnean lineage, I'd had enough Enyo heritage to form a natural empathic bond with Yukihyo, or so we'd thought. We'd later learned that as an infant, I'd fallen prey to Dr. Crispus and his experimentation just like Zared and his brothers had. He had altered the supramarginal gyrus in my brain. He'd intended to keep me, as the future clan mother of his biologically engineered hybrid progeny, to stabilize them. However, my mother's captor thwarted his plans by disappearing back into hiding with us. Being himself a fugitive, Dr. Crispus never told the authorities about us. I didn't believe I'd ever be able to forgive him for it. I'd suffered abuse at the hands of Nathan Green for eighteen years. Then, Eli had caught him.

Ambassador Ness turned to face me. Having bonded with Yukihyo, Quaid, Zared, and Izaac, my empathic and telepathic abilities had strengthened. From Ness, I could sense he thought my place was in my wing with my children. He thought I should be pampered and protected and not in charge of shared responsibility for the security of Laconian, Galaxic, and Parvac space from alien aggressions. If I were to tell him how much he had in common with the average Parvac male, he'd be offended. However, like theirs, his thoughts and opinions were of no consequence, not when Emperor Tavere Probus had invested me with the responsibility as a boon to please me. I smiled and thought of the new laser cannons which had been affixed to my warship.

Marielle had finally had her fill and dozed off. My nipple popped out of her mouth drawing the attention of every male eye in the room. Quaid came to my side. Carefully, I transferred her into his arms. He held her lovingly at his shoulder until she burped in her sleep before laying her in the pram at her twin sister's side. Eli fussed again with the blanket. I tucked my boob away into my pretty pink, V-necked wrap dress. The long sleeves had ruffled cuffs which matched the ruffled hem. Choji, my stylist, had put my long, dirty-blonde hair up into an intricate bun to add a touch of professionalism to my look. Apparently, it wasn't working.

Ness exploded. "For the stars' sake! Researching bedtime stories won't save us from the Alux when they return for vengeance! It's truly commendable for Emperor Probus to entrust you with matters of consequence, but perhaps for all our sakes, you might find an activity better befitting to one such as yourself." He gave me an apologetic look. "A delicate young woman with past experiences such as yours and a growing family might be better suited to...."

"To what?" I asked. Placing my elbows on the table, I steepled my index fingers and observed the man.

Stig had gone pale, as had Ambassador Stein. Both males had experienced my temper at one time or another. Seated at Stein's side, the Lady Gina Montgomery of Arachne eyed Ness as if he were a rat that she was about to have processed into a can of spider food.

"Oh, enough of this," Ness exclaimed. "Now is not the time for us to be catering to the whims of an uneducated princess playing at universal security." He gestured wildly. "We've all seen her nipple for the stars' sakes."

A blur of black gracefully danced between Ambassador Ness and the conference table. There was a gurgling sound. When Ness became visible to me once more, his eyes were wide, and he clutched at his mouth where blood poured out from between his fingers and down his neck and chest. At his feet, was his severed tongue. My bodyguard once again resumed his silent position behind me.

Eli pressed a button on his vid-screen. Dryly, he said, "Dr. Fotri, report to the conference room. Ambassador Ness has lost his tongue."

Everyone who wasn't Parvacian sat in stunned silence. Dr. Fotri, the Palace physician, rushed in with a team, collecting Ambassador Ness and his severed tongue.

Stig said in a bored tone to Ness, "I warned you." He'd had to learn the hard way to guard his own tongue around me.

Unlike Kaoti, who had become more patient through fatherhood, Inquisitor Cormac Gordian was quick to take offense on my behalf. Cormac had been filling in for the Captain of my Imperial Guard, Kaoti Aegisthus, so that he could spend more time with Violet and their children. Poppy and her new little brother, Kado, needed quality time with their daddy. Cormac had proven himself to both Kaoti and my Papa in his defense of me against the Alux.

Rising from my seat, I broke the stunned silence. "We will adjourn until Ambassador Ness is able to rejoin us."

Edvard and Ambassador Stein quickly left the room.

Sighing heavily, I turned to Inquisitor Cormac Gordian. "You've got to stop doing that."

Eli said, "No, you don't. He was being rude. In the future, perhaps he will better mind his tongue."

Gina snickered and covered her face with her hands. I gaped at her. She said, "Look, he was being an asshole." Turning her attention to Eli and Cormac, she added, "However, if you really want to support her, you have to let her stand up for herself and take charge. It's the only way some of these males will ever allow her to earn their respect." She was staring pointedly at Cormac while trying not to smile.

"She shouldn't need to earn their respect or anyone else's for that matter. She is Princess Teagan of House Probus," Captain Merick Carus stated. My Military Advisory Committee was in attendance. He and the others had thought nothing of the whole slicing out a tongue thing. To them, it seemed completely socially acceptable behavior, but that was Parvac.

Noticing servants in the hall waiting to clean up the blood, I got everyone to leave. On the way to my wing, I asked, "Where is Sherman?"

Pushing the pram at my side, Gina replied, "He and Kitty Stig went sightseeing. Parvac truly is a beautiful planet."

Rolf and Otto, my butlers, held open the doors to my wing and bowed to us.

"Will you help me put them down?"

Gina didn't need any coaxing. She bent to pick up Marielle, who she cradled in her arms. Closing her eyes, she stood still for a moment to luxuriate in the cuddliness. With Tabitha in my own arms, I understood the feeling. There was a comforting relaxation which accompanied holding a sleeping baby in one's arms. In their matching pink gowns, my daughters were the most adorable twin babies on Parvac. They were currently the only ones. Twin daughters were a rare blessing in the Parvac Empire. I led the way to their nursery.

After several conversations, Fitz, Dario, and I had decided to let Marielle and Tabitha sleep in a bed together until they outgrew it. Having been in my tummy together for so long, I thought it would be more comforting for them. Out of the corner of my eye, a long black leg and blue-grey abdomen caught my attention. Thunderdrop, my bonded Arachnean Silk spider and best friend, was ever vigilantly protecting each of my little spiderlings. In fact, one of his favorite places to reside was in his elaborate web above the twin's crib.

While I checked to make sure that my babies would be comfortable, Gina stroked Thunderdrop's abdomen. "Have you checked on your turtles as of yet today?"

"Clack." The sound meant that he had not.

"May I accompany you when you do so?"

"Chirp!" Thunderdrop dropped to the floor and led Gina away.

They would be going out to the Palace gardens and to the pond which had become the turtles' habitat. Thunderdrop had enlisted Neema for help in his rescue of the turtles from Thalassa. While not indigenous to Parvac, Tracy, my sister-in-law through Jazon, had helped us to go about properly relocating them with the help of one of her professors. The girls were all tucked into the swan bed they'd inherited from their older sister, their safe habitat. With a soft sigh, I realized I'd have to go to the infirmary to check on Ambassador Ness, not that I wanted to do so.

Turning toward the door, I gave Cormac an exasperated look. "When you do things like that, you make my life more difficult. You can't simply cut out the tongues of everyone who says something which you consider to be rude."

"Yes, I can. If you need another demonstration, Dr. Fotri has probably reattached it by now." The dead, expressionless tone told me that he wasn't joking. Unlike Kaoti, it wasn't his usual tone. It told me that Cormac had acted out of anger.

"Cormac," I began.

"Eli was close to killing him, Princess. You may believe I was too brutal. However, had Eli killed him, it would have caused us considerably more aggravation than the reparations which Ambassador Ness may demand."

Scowling, I went off in search of Eli and found him in the Palace kitchens with Inquisitor Drex Licinius. I'd married Drex as a ruse to trick my Uncle Kagan into letting me leave Parvac. We'd been on a mission which had resulted in the rescue of my mother, Empress Neema. We'd all believed her to have been dead. Even Nathan Green had believed it. He'd thought he'd stabbed her to death during one of his rages. However, she'd been put into stasis and kept hidden by Ambassador Jiri, a traitorous bastard whom we'd all trusted. Papa had killed him with his bare hands, and I'd watched. I'd almost killed the bastard myself in defense of General Nico Cassian, my second husband and father of my son, Niklos Tavere Cassian, the future Parvac Emperor.

"Eli?" I strode purposefully toward him.

"Dearest one!" Drex exclaimed. Catching my fingers, he brought them to his lips while wrapping his other arm around my waist. "The chefs are outdoing themselves for lunch." Releasing my fingers, he carefully shoved a meat pie into my mouth. It was spicy enough to be delicious but not so much as to make the twins gassy from my milk. I had to be careful since they ate what I ate.

"These are good. I'll take eight. No, make it twelve." Turning in Drex's one-armed embrace, I said, "Eli, will you speak to Cormac about his behavior?"

My Inquisitor approached me and placed another meat pie to my lips. "As you wish." His eyes roamed over me like a caress. Then, while gazing into my eyes, he spoke to the ever-lingering shadow behind me. "You were far too merciful, Cormac. I'd thought to split each of his fingers from tip to knuckle to start."

Cormac's reply was no more than a whisper. "There were ladies present, and the little princesses had just gone to sleep." Picking up a rag, he began cleaning his blade.

After chewing angrily, I shook my finger at Eli. He caught it gently in his teeth while his eyes dared me to punish him. I could see naughty fantasies in their depths.

Drex said, "Word has reached the Galaxic Government and Laconian Sector about Ambassador Ness and his slip of the tongue so to speak."

I groaned. "This is horrible. Aside from cutting out a man's tongue, which is atrocious, you did it in front of Gina, our allies, and my Military Advisory Committee." Inward reflection told me that I wasn't as upset about it as I might once have been. The Inquisitors Academy tended to desensitize its students to violence and torture, not to say its ranks didn't attract inherently sick little fuckers anyway. My team, along with that of Ensign Clark Flavian, my most recent and youngest husband, had roughly a year remaining in our training before we were unleashed upon the universe. Well, I'd be unleashed upon a desk job. Yippee. "I need to check on Ness and try to avert inevitable disaster."

A small huff of air left Eli. He looked at me in puzzlement.

"What?" I scrunched my face up at him. Everything had been going so well until the tongue incident.

"Nothing. Nothing at all. In fact, I'll be happy to accompany you." Eli offered me his arm.

"As would I," Drex said.

Finished with cleaning Ness' blood from his blade, Cormac slid it into the sheath and followed us from the kitchens.

As we walked along the palace halls, the sounds of voices raised in anger reached us. Drawing closer to the noise, I recognized Papa's furious tirade and moved closer toward his office to better hear. The palace hall in this wing was lined with formally uniformed officers whose serious but excited countenances read as a premonition of war. "Oh, no. See what you've done?" I bit my nail and paced. "We worked so hard for peace. Now, you've gone and thrown it all away over someone expressing a personal opinion." Lifting my chin, I entered Papa's office.

He was purple with rage. On the main viewer were several members of the Galaxic Government along with the rulers of the Laconian Sector. At Papa's conference table, Edvard Stig and Ambassador Stein sat rigidly as if awaiting orders to board ships leaving the Empire. "How dare he insult my Princess in whom I have invested my power? Shall I replay for you his words, words that he spoke which her ears might hear?"

My forehead scrunched up. Conspicuously absent was Gina. What was going on in here? Papa held out his hand to me. Taking it, I went to his side.

Consul Bosh said, "I am as disturbed as you are by Ness' outburst."

Blushing, I said, "I apologize for my bodyguard's actions."

Papa looked at me in shock. "My darling, his restraint was admirable. Your Advisory Committee felt such offense at his treatment of you as to formally petition me to declare war upon Sinope and the Laconian Sector."

Shit. I rolled my eyes. "Papa."

"Yes, I know it is out of the question." He turned hard eyes onto Consul Dano. "We have family on Epopeus and honorary princesses residing there, not to mention the Ponidi Clan home on Chione."

"Yes," I nodded enthusiastically. "We have many loved ones in the Laconian Sector. Let's make reparations and put this terrible experience behind us that we might instead strengthen our resolve to protect ourselves against the threat which is the Alux."

Taking my hand and lifting it to his heart, he said, "As a boon to you, I will order my fleets to stand down."

My empathic abilities made my pulse begin a hard fast tick that I could feel in my neck. He wasn't humoring me. He was giving into my wishes even though a livid fury burned him from within. Sinope had been close to annihilation.

Turning his head, he gave a nod to General Lucian Braga. My former father-in-law turned on his heel and left.

Addressing those present, I said, "Please, allow me to take this time to assure you that our primary goal is in securing efficient means of protecting our allied worlds from Alux aggression. This is where our focus should remain. Divisive petty squabbles will do nothing other than to weaken our resolve."

"Well said," Consul Dano agreed with a nod of his head.

Papa, placated, returned to his seat.

Quaid moved to stand at my side. "Why again did you feel it would be of benefit to send Ness along with the diplomatic envoy?"

Consul Dano replied, "He is our system's leading xenobiologist. If we are successful in locating the Pariea, he might be able to offer some insights as to their physiology."

Edvard turned his attention to Consul Bosh. "Should he enter into diplomatic negotiations with the Pariea on our behalf, I fear the result would be two alien species intent upon our destruction. Perhaps, if I may be so bold as to make the suggestion, it might be better for our endeavors if his tongue were not reattached."

My hand flew to my mouth to hide the sardonic laugh which had almost undiplomatically escaped. However, Edvard noticed and gave me a very small but genuine smile.

"I will speak to Ness and remind him of his purpose, study of the Alux and Pariea, not security or diplomacy," Consul Bosh said.

Quaid shook his head at his father. Something unsaid passed between them.

"Captain Bosh, you have the authority to remove Galaxic and Laconian citizens who behave irrationally."

Quaid gave a nod of his head.

Consul Dano said, "Princess Teagan, I offer my sincerest apologies for Ness' uncouth behavior and slanderous remarks."

I gave what I hoped turned out as a gracious and regal bow of my head. "Captain Bosh, will you accompany me? I wish to check on Ambassador Ness and offer my apologies."

Quaid offered me his arm. Curtseying to the room, I held onto Quaid eager to leave. When we were somewhat alone, he said, "Father knows how close I was to challenging Ness. In insulting you, he insulted me and the entire Bosh Clan. Did he forget that he was speaking to my wife?"

"The man is an idiot. I suggest leaving him on his home world." Edvard spoke from behind us.

Perturbed at not being alone, I turned my head to look at him.

His expression was one of boredom. He raised an eyebrow at me.

"You know what? I agree. Ness is a fucking asshole. He doesn't respect any of us, and we're in charge of the Cosmos Coalition. We don't have to put up with him. Eddie is right. Let's drop the fucker off on Sinope. He is easily replaced. Let's find a xenobiologist who respects the investment we've made in protecting our galaxies from hostile alien intrusions." Shaking my head, I thought of the weapons the captured alien had been forced to produce on Earth. "If only those weapons hadn't been destroyed."

Edvard said, "If only Parvac and the Militia hadn't interfered."

Quaid said, "If only you hadn't falsely imprisoned a member of an advanced alien race. Look. The aliens, Pariea, or whatever they are, won't trust you, but they might trust Teagan and Eli since they helped rescue one of their own. Without the two of them along, any attempts at negotiation will most certainly fail if we should even manage to locate them." Something caught his attention, someone rather. It was Ness as he was leaving the infirmary.

Quaid and Ness stood like statues. I could sense they spoke telepathically. However, they blocked me from listening. After a few moments, Quaid said, "Lady Bosh, Ness offers his deepest apologies. The freedoms of the Empire's Materfamilias Caste and the powers of an Imperial Princess are sociological factors which he failed to consider. As a xenobiologist, it was a critical error in judgement and a lesson from which he vows to learn. Should we make contact with the Pariea, he would not want a cultural misunderstanding or outright insult to destroy our chances of eliciting their help in defending our civilizations from the Alux."

My cheeks began to burn. Ness had been cleaned up while in the infirmary. However, his face and neck were swollen from the ordeal. His lips were dry and cracked even under the sheen of ointment which had been applied to them. Dr. Fotri had reattached his tongue, injected him with nanites, and administered pain patches. However, blood stained his shirt, jacket, pants, and shoes.

"I am so terribly sorry for my bodyguard's gruesome attack."

"Teagan, it happened. It is over. Ness is going to his room to rest. He understands that your bodyguard was performing his duty, and that amongst the Warrior Caste, and to Emperor Probus, his words were verbally abusive and punishable by death." Turning solid-black eyes on Ness, he added, "And they were not the only ones to take deep insult to his disparaging words."

Ness bowed.

Quaid said, "Go and rest."

To me, Ness bowed yet again. Then, he walked nervously past Parvac officers who watched him eagerly for an excuse to fight him.

I yelled, "Quit it! He's a scientist for fuck's sake! There is nothing fair or honorable in challenging him." Under my breath, I mumbled, "I could kick his ass."

Edvard made a scoffing sound.

I narrowed my eyes. "I can kick your ass."

The smile he gave me was probably meant to chill my blood, and it probably worked on Kitty Stig. She'd probably like it. My surveillance of the couple had revealed some rather odd bedroom games. In fact, Fitz, Eli, and Drex had offered to play Kitty's role should I ever wish to experiment. Tying them up and blindfolding them might be fun, but I could never do anything to purposefully hurt any of them, even if they might find it thrilling. It was a turn-off for me which might be due to my childhood traumas. I couldn't fathom hurting someone I loved. It was wrong. I sighed. I'd married a few kinky fuckers.

Quaid chuckled at my thoughts.

I glared at Edvard. "Go change. We'll go to the sparring mat right now."

"No," he said in chagrin.

"Scared? Are you a coward? I thought you enjoyed torturing women. Are you afraid of women who can kick your ass?"

He sighed and looked at the ceiling.

Angrily, I stared at his laryngeal prominence.

"My wife is adept at martial arts and quite capable of bettering me while sparring. I don't doubt your abilities. However, after seeing you nurse your infants, there is no possible way I could spar with you. I don't believe you want an opponent who simply stands immobile while you attack."

"Teagan, what do you think you're doing?"

I recognized the sound of his voice at once. Rolling my eyes, I mumbled, "Fucking hell."

Quaid grinned, reached out, and clasped forearms with Ensign Clark Flavian. They were on friendly terms now, but they'd gotten off to a rough start. Quaid had tortured Inquisitor Cory Flavian and cut off his arm. He was fine now. He'd had a new one cloned and attached. Currently, while he recuperated, he taught at the

Inquisitors Academy. Quaid treated Clark more like a younger brother than a co-husband, but at least they were getting along.

Addressing Edvard, Clark said, "My wife doesn't have my permission to spar or fight. I fight for her."

I glared up at him. He was almost as large as Nico, my blond giant. Clark kept growing. He was a foot taller now than when I'd married him. "Don't listen to him!" I wedged myself between Clark and Eddie. "I kicked Clark's ass about a year ago. Ask any cadet or ensign at the Academy!"

Edvard looked from me to Clark's bicep which now exceeded the circumference of my thigh.

"It's true!" Frustrated, I stomped my foot and glared at Clark. "Tell him!"

Clark obeyed me. "I was younger, not as strong as I am now, and she cheated."

Shocked and insulted, I defended my honor. "I did not cheat, and you didn't hold back your punches!"

"You wrapped your legs around my neck."

"I didn't use my pheromones on you."

"You didn't need to." He bent, scooped me up into a bridal hold, and carried me away.

I heard Quaid say, "We will reconvene tomorrow."

"Did he actually forbid her from fighting?"

"Indeed, he did. In doing so, he ingratiated himself with Emperor Probus. She still trains and learns to defend herself. However, we have no intentions of allowing her to be placed in a situation in which she would be forced to defend herself. Please, don't let her goad your wife into a match. Teagan is eager to test her limits, but everyone, and I do mean everyone, is opposed to it."

Edvard simply stated, "Understood. Until tomorrow," and took his leave.

Chapter Two

"Stop pouting."

"No, you ruined it. I was about to kick Eddie's ass and record it to play later for anyone who doubts my abilities."

He turned his head and gave me an exasperated look.

I smiled and kissed him on the nose. "Did you see Eddie checking you out from head to fists? I thought he was going to piss himself."

Clark grinned. He was adorably cute when he did so because his grin was a bit lopsided. Laughing, I kissed his cheek. He carried me to the Palace kitchens where the informal table we preferred had been set. Eli gestured at my plate which he'd stacked with tasty little meat pies. Clark lowered me to my chair.

Eli asked, "What trouble had she gotten herself into?"

I flipped him off and then took a sip of my pineapple fizzy water before attacking my food.

Joining us, Quaid answered. "She was trying to make Stig spar with her in the ring."

"Teagan," Gina admonished as she joined us. Thunderdrop followed behind her, chasing after the swirling yellow silk skirt of her gown. "You command a fleet of Parvac warships. You can captain your own ship when it pleases you. You can shoot all manner of weapons. Why do you feel the need to practice hand-to-hand combat?"

I scowled at her. "They don't believe I'm a badass. It seems only females who regularly beat their adversaries bloody are deemed strong by popular society." I ate a nifty meat pie.

"That is preposterous. A woman needn't be brutal to be strong. Take me for example." She sat and focused her attention on Eli. She stared at him with such intensity that he sat upright. A darkness entered his eyes. "Would you dare oppose me?" she asked quietly.

Diplomatically, he replied, "I would prefer to keep our interests aligned, Lady Montgomery."

Primly, she picked up her utensils, cut a meat pie in half, and ate a bite. "Do you see? Did I need to punch him?"

I threw my hands up. "Well, no! You're scary!"

Thunderdrop chirped in agreement.

"Why?" she asked. "I assure you. I can't beat him or even Neema Alaric Montgomery Lee in a physical altercation."

"No, but there's all sorts of horrid legal shit you would do."

"Precisely." She gave a nod of her head. "Watch your language."

"I enjoy using foul language. It fills me with joy." I checked around to make sure Yukihyo and the kids weren't within earshot.

"Yukihyo would never harm you. Why do you fear for him to overhear you?"

"Ugh. Alright, Gina. I get the point. Assholes like Ness and Stig can either fear the political fallout should they offend me or else be like Dano or Chorgh trying to please me and garner my favor." I rolled my eyes. "I don't need to beat anyone into submission."

Gina smiled and speared the other half of her meat pie. "It's funny you mention Governor Chorgh. Quite some time ago, you gave him a painting."

I shrugged. "We've given him a few paintings over the years. When Hiroshi visits Carmanor, he gives him paintings from Thalassa from us. I like him, his wives, and his children." I took a sip of my drink. "We should take the kids to see the Salt Plains and the ocean."

Quaid made a face. He didn't care for Carmanor's monkey population. They had a tendency of behaving like a maniacal, food-stealing gang of hairy hoodlums.

Gina delicately shrugged her shoulder. "A while back, he was targeted by a thief who stole a painting from him."

Quaid sighed. He'd known about it.

Eli said, "Governor Chorgh's security was impressive."

Quaid laid his fork across his plate. "The crime has been investigated. Attempts were even made to recreate the crime. They failed. No one has been able to solve how the theft was accomplished."

Eli gave the conversation his attention with the same intensity that Phillip gave the viewer when he was watching porn.

Gina said, "I'm surprised you haven't heard of it."

"Lady Gina, a petty crime on a Laconian world wouldn't be reported to the Empire." Eli made a show of studying his nail. I narrowed my eyes at him.

Gina's hands went down to her lap, and she sat a bit straighter. "Petty? The painting is worth a fortune because Teagan touched it and gave it as a gift." She waved her hands in dismissal. "The interesting part is that recently it was returned back to Chorgh's office as if it had never been missing."

Now, Quaid was intrigued. "Was the thief caught?"

She shook her head. "Not an alarm or sensor was tripped. Here. See for yourself. He allowed his security team to release their footage." Pulling out her vid-screen, she found the report and played it for us. One minute, the wall beneath a lighting sconce was bare. The next moment, the painting hung there. It was of a beach scene from Thalassa.

"No shadows, heat signatures, depressions on the rugs, or anything," Eli observed.

Quaid leaned back from the table. "It couldn't have been visual displacement shielding, or it would have set off the bio-scanners."

Almost rhetorically, Drex asked, "How did the thief pull it off?"

"Freaking badass," I mumbled around a meat pie.

They made various sounds of displeasure when she switched to a different report. A cargo crate addressed to Consul Bosh sat inside of a bomb detection scanner. Once it cleared, it was placed into a biogenetic medical decontamination unit. After several additional standard security scans were performed, a guard opened it.

"Is that what I think it is?" Quaid incredulously exclaimed.

Gina nodded. "It has been authenticated."

"Who found it?"

"It wasn't found. It was returned. Rumor has it that the same thief who stole from Chorgh stole this piece from the Bosh archives at the Museum of Paleontological History."

"The theft happened years ago under the heaviest security measures instituted. Father was livid."

"It's ugly." I frowned at the short, fat, heavily-breasted, big-bellied statue and pushed away my plate.

Gina snorted at me in amusement.

"She's beautiful," Quaid argued. "She's an ancient fertility goddess and was worshipped on my planet thousands of years ago. She is a priceless relic from Epopeus' history."

"So, can I have more nanite patches?"

"What?" Even privy as he was to my thoughts, he sometimes had trouble keeping up.

Making a face, I looked down at my stomach.

"You are perfect."

Clark helped himself to my plate. "He's right, and you're fertile."

My upper lip lifted in a sneer. "You sound like Nico."

"Mommy! Mommy! Mommy!" Neema screamed as she ran through the palace and straight to me. Her empathic senses continued to strengthen. Her new favorite game was Hide and Seek. She could find me, Yukihyo, Niklos, Peter, Zared, Quaid, and Izaac with her eyes closed. Gina and Sherman were more challenging for her.

Thunderdrop jumped to the countertop and examined the cookware. When Neema was excited, it tended to make him nervous, especially around food. He'd never gotten over the carrot incident. I tossed a meat pie to him which he caught with his pedipalps.

Neema climbed onto my lap and put her arms around my neck so she could whisper in my ear. I waited while she caught her breath. She'd outrun her brothers but not Flake. The snow fox cocked her grey-tipped ears at Quaid. He held a meat pie up. Once Flake sat, Quaid tossed it. Snapping it out of the air, she quickly gobbled it up.

"Daddy said a bad word! Whew! Daddy said a whole bunches of bad words!" Getting herself more comfortable on my lap, she started counting on her fingers.

Inexplicable joy sprang up in my chest. "Oh? Which ones?"

She gazed at me adoringly. "You so pretty when you smile, Mommy." Trained by her father to tattle on me any time a bad word left my lips in exchange for toys, she now tattled on him. "Shit, damn, fuck, and a bunch of them real fast in other languages, but Ma covered my ears." She shrugged. The Ma to whom she referred was Mrs. Tereas, Yukihyo's mother.

I rubbed my nose to hers. "Excellent, my love. Shall we visit the toy store?" Deep down, I knew it was terrible to bribe my child to tattle on her father, but he'd started this shit. My smile was big and genuine.

"No, I want to go to school with you. Please? I'll be good!" She had been begging to go to the Academy with Clark and me, but Instructor Rovek had been a dick about it saying it was against the rules.

"Alright, you can come with me in the morning." Fuck Rovek. My baby was a good little spy and deserved to be rewarded. I'd deal with him later.

"Oh!" Her voice had gone high-pitched and squeaky which meant she was super excited.

"However," I held up a finger to still her. "You have to get up and ready when I tell you, no sleeping late."

Nodding her head, she slid from my lap and ran from the kitchens. Her smile dwindled to be replaced by a blush because her daddy could sense she'd told on him.

My smile broadened as he walked in. Swirls of orange and grey made his eyes appear crazed. Quaid asked, "What happened?"

I could sense Niklos and Peter in our wing of the Palace. They'd left tattling on Yukihyo to Neema. Yukihyo paced across the kitchen. Being empathetic, I decided not to tease him about cussing in front of the children until he was feeling better.

"Seismic activity combined with avalanches brought about by the spring thaw have caused considerable damage to our clan home! Our home!" He raked his fingers through his hair.

Quaid said, "Let me see the reports."

With a shaking hand, Yukihyo pulled his vid-screen from his pocket and passed it over to him. Hurrying over to Quaid, I read over his shoulder and gasped. The front entrance of the Ponidi fortress appeared unchanged. However, part of the mountain had crumbled inward. An aerial view and topographical overlay showed the devastation in clearer detail. "I must go to Chione at once and see what of our ancestral home can be salvaged."

Eli said, "You'll need a structural engineering team."

Drex added, "Subterranean architects and crews," while tapping away at his vid-screen.

Yukihyo faltered in his agitated pacing and stared at each of them. "What are you doing?"

"Tackling the problem. What else?" Drex answered. "This crew from Daphoene is reputable and eager to serve the Imperial family in any capacity, even if it means a journey to a distant, frozen planet."

"But, it's spring," Yukihyo said sounding confused.

Drex asked, "Do you approve of their hire?" He walked over to show him the details.

Quaid spoke up. "Yukihyo, we're family. We are co-husbands. While the two of us have worked to become friends, it is different for Parvac males. They are our brothers now, something which is natural in Parvacian society."

Dryly, Drex said to Eli, "We need stronger neural blockers."

"Neema wouldn't like it," Eli replied.

"I wouldn't like it, Sweetie."

Drex focused on me, his eyes darkening with passion. Turning to Yukihyo, he asked, "Well?"

He nodded. "For many years, Hiroshi and Phillip were the only family I had." His emotions hit me like a wave. Laconians preferred large families and for generations to stay together. Such was true among the Enyo and Eriopis. The Bosh compound on Epopeus was a further example of it. Empathically or telepathically bonded families strengthened each of its members. From my own experience, I knew I was better for having my family close.

"Oh, and Yukihyo," Drex said, "Chione is frozen even in spring."

Standing straight, he retorted, "It is not. Grass grows and flowers bloom."

Taking his hand, I said, "Please, continue researching what we will need." Eli and Drex glanced up at me and kept doing what they'd been doing. "Quaid, how do we take our security efforts and personnel along to Chione?"

"Easily," he answered.

"Excellent. Come along, husband." I tugged Yukihyo's hand.

"Where are we going?"

I'd never before witnessed him being so unfocused and frazzled. "We are going to go out and get you calm and centered."

He shook his head. "I do not have time to waste. Too much must be done. What heirlooms have been destroyed? How many cherished memories now lay buried under a mountain of stone?"

I tugged harder until he relented and came along with me. Going out a back door, we walked from the kitchen and down to where the boats were docked for our use on the lake. Coming out to greet us, a soldier on duty saluted. Shielding my eyes with my free hand, I scanned the dock. Pointing out a small boat with a roof, I asked, "Can we take that one?"

"Princess Teagan, your pleasure barge is at your disposal."

I waved my hand at him in dismissal. "It's too much trouble at the moment. Anyway, if the kids look out over the lake and see it, they'll have fits wanting to know why we didn't take them with us. We just want some alone time."

The soldier looked over his shoulder and gave a nod of his head. A team hurried to bring my selection from her berth. He spoke quietly into his earpiece. "Your captain will be here in a moment. He will sail the cabin cruiser away from your wing."

"Teagan, it's all right. I'll be fine." The level of tension in his voice was making the opposite argument.

Twining our fingers together, I concentrated on sending him empathic comfort in what I imagined as being a poufy cloud. It worked because the muscles in his neck and shoulders became less bunched. He didn't resist when I tugged him along to the boat which was being made ready for us. The captain must have been nearby and very bored because he boarded as we watched. Yukihyo sighed. He could refuse me nothing. Deciding to relent, he swept me up into his arms and carried me aboard. Holding my arms around his neck, I laughed as one of my sandals slid from my foot and hit the deck.

Having already been told our goal of hiding from our children during what was supposed to be naptime anyway, the captain sailed us along the lake behind the Imperial Palace and past the emperor's wing, past the kitchens, guest wing, and officers' quarters. The palace gardens did very little to disguise our passage. Several sets of eyes spied upon us as we floated by.

Yukihyo sighed again as he placed me on my feet. He noticed the males who watched us the same as did I. "They will be upon you like ice bears upon *ceshoosh* roots in the Spring. You've birthed three daughters which is a rarity. They fight amongst themselves over you even now." He rested his arms on the railing and scowled across the lake toward the grounds where soldiers dressed in black exercise clothes jogged or sparred.

The Parvac Empire was a society at whose apex was the Warrior Caste. The only thing males of the Empire loved more than fighting was finding females of any race to accept them. Once accepted as a husband, a Parvac male would give her all of his wealth and lands, spoiling her as extravagantly as he was able, just for the opportunity to mate with her once a year. My marriages weren't typical in that manner, and everyone knew it.

Slipping my arms around Yukihyo, I rested my cheek against his strong back. "They can fight over me from afar since we're going to Chione." Slowly, he straightened his posture. Sliding his rough palms over my arms, he turned to face me and wrapped me in his protective embrace. "The female doesn't even determine the sex of the child," I mumbled against his chest.

"They consider you to be a blessing to the Empire." He chuckled and kissed my forehead.

Smiling mischievously up at him, with my chin resting on his heavily muscled chest, I said, "I'd like for your cock to consider me a blessing."

"He already does." He gave me the grin which always caused my insides to melt. Leaving the warm comfort of his arms, I took off my other sandal and backed away from him. "Where do you think to go after having teased me and my cock?" He watched me with eyes that had suddenly filled with tangled capillaries of pink and gold, colors symbolic of his passion and desire.

Willing my Parvac pheromones to further beguile him, I smiled seductively and continued to slowly back away to an alcove and couch under the roof. I pressed a button for the sunscreen to lower, obscuring us from view. He lifted his shirt over his head and let it fall. Even though our bond had eased his once constant need to train and fight to keep his aggression tamed, he continued the activities for sport to which his heavily muscled physique attested. His shoes and pants followed his shirt to the deck. I drank in the sight of him. It had been too long since I'd felt his body joined with mine.

He hunched his back and growled playfully like an ice bear. Surprised, my eyes widened and laughter burst from me. Then, he attacked. I turned, shrieking with laughter, but I had no hope of escape. My hungry ice bear began removing my pretty pink dress with his teeth. His scratchy jaw lightly scraped my arm as he tugged my dress down my shoulder. As I pulled my arm free of the sleeve, he captured my nipple with his lips. Closing my eyes, I sighed with pleasure. My breast and I mourned the loss of his hot mouth as he growled and tugged my gown down past my hips. It fell in a pink puddle at my feet. Standing before me, all hard muscles and naked desire, he lowered me to the couch. In his eyes, there was a devious glint.

"Yukihyo," I whined.

"No, Teagan. I am a hungry bear." Moving down my body without taking his eyes from mine, he bit the waistband of my undies and dragged them down my legs. Pebbles rose on my skin at the feeling of his whiskers against my inner thighs.

After years of practice, he knew exactly how to drive me wild with pleasure. Pressing his tongue between my delicate folds, he licked upward until my sharp intake of breath told him exactly what he wanted to know. That was where he stayed, focusing all of his attention on the spot which had me writhing beneath him. I cried out, swept away with the explosion of sparkling lights that burst from my center, through me, and out of the top of my head. Tingling and relaxed, I was left without a care in the universe. It was then that he entered me. My cares suddenly returned as I worried that I'd feel differently to him. If I did, he didn't seem to mind. He pushed and pulled, filling me with himself while rolling his hips in the way that drove me mad with lust. I lifted my hips in time with his thrusts, moaning frantically as he brought me to pleasure once more. Burying his face to my neck, he surged forward and groaned. He pushed himself farther in as he came deep within me. Then, he shivered in my arms.

Lifting himself up on his forearm, he gazed down into my eyes. "Is it just me, or does it get better between us each time?"

Releasing my legs from where I gripped him around his hips, I said, "It's not just you." He made himself comfortable beside me. Together, we looked through the screen at the snow-capped mountains. Cool, fresh air blew down upon our heated bodies from their icy reaches. Scooting against his side, I rested my cheek on his chest. "Perfect," I whispered.

Yukihyo stroked my hair, but his mind had gone elsewhere. "It's our family home. It has been the seat of the Ponidi Clan ever since there were any Ponidis. They don't even care!" he exclaimed in disbelief.

"Who doesn't care? I care."

"Mother and my sisters do not. They said our homes are here now."

He was hurt. I could feel it. "We have many homes. Our ancestral home is amongst the most important."

He grunted in agreement.

"Look at it in a positive manner. This gives us an opportunity."

He nodded while watching two mountain goats nibbling at the vegetation.

"We can finally remodel the bathrooms."

"Wait. What?" Sitting up, he stared down at me in horror. "Everything must be as it was."

I shrugged. "Fine. It can be exactly as it was but with modern waste units, better lighting, and a few safety upgrades around the fireplaces."

"I can't believe the things I am hearing from your beautiful lips or the things I've allowed you to do to me with your dirty mouth."

My laughter interrupted his tirade.

"Teagan, how can you suggest altering Ponidi history?"

Kissing him with my supposedly dirty mouth, I managed to calm him. "Are you telling me that the fortress on Chione is now exactly as it was originally built?"

Flustered by my question, a blush spread across his cheeks. "Well, no. Improvements have been made to it over the centuries." He had the good sense to appear contrite. "The bathing chamber will be preserved," he firmly stated.

"Agreed." My thoughts rushed to Izaac. I could feel his presence as he joined my mind and relived with me the moment in the aforementioned bathing chamber when we had accepted the bond between us and had consummated our love.

Speaking telepathically to both of us, he said, "The bathing chamber will not be altered in any way. It is my favorite place in the universe other than in our lady's company."

A happy warmth blossomed within me.

Grudgingly, Yukihyo said, "Nico, Quaid, and Phillip seemed to enjoy planning our home on Arachne. I could ask for their input."

"Yes, and don't forget that Sherman is here with Gina. He had a hand in our Arachnean home's design as well." Softly rubbing his chest, I asked, "Can we spend a few days on Arachne? Thunderdrop and Itsy need to play in the trees and spend some time amongst their own kind."

Chuckling, he gave me a gentle squeeze. "I think my lady wife needs to spend time there with her family as well. Do you not?"

I nodded. "I miss Gram, Sydney, Hiroshi, Simon, Eliot...."

Chuckling again, he held a finger to my lips. "You could go on all afternoon listing everyone on Arachne whom you miss. Perhaps, while we are there, we will find some elements which we might incorporate into our Clan home."

"Oh, yes. I'd really like that." Relaxing against him, I watched the scenery as we floated along the lake. Then, like a feather against my senses, I felt Tabitha begin to stir from her nap. Sitting up, I looked around the deck for my clothing.

Yukihyo got up, pulled on his pants, and handed my things to me. "Which one?"

"Tabitha," I answered with a joyous smile. I hadn't been comfortable hiring additional nurses. Pierce and Lorca had earned places in our family along with our trust. While previously they had helped with various household issues, taking care of the children was now their only responsibility. We'd had a household meeting. I'd come to my senses on Earth. My family was large and still growing, and we were a messy bunch. I'd asked Momma for help which she was all too eager to give.

Terre's mother, Lady Dacia, had been all too happy to see that not only her daughter's household, but also those of Sparrow and Tracy were fully staffed and being effectively managed. My ladies and their husbands and children had moved from the Palace and into their own homes in nearby and affluent Warrior Caste neighborhoods. Violet, living as she did with House Aegisthus, was the only one of us to avoid the attentions of their motherly guidance. She had the Lady Aegisthus to see to her sprawling household.

However, as Yukihyo had just grudgingly admitted that I was right about modernizing our mountain fortress, I'd had to admit that Momma's changes had made everyone feel more at ease. She'd been careful in her selections, having input from her own trusted Inquisitors, of staffing additions to each of my households within the Empire. Those additions had of course been hired from amidst retired soldiers, a tradition of the Imperial family. It was a way of rewarding the loyal service of males who eagerly sought such employment simply because they couldn't sit still and enjoy their retirement. Most of those who wanted to work in our household had no families of their own.

From my own earlier life experiences, I understood loneliness and the importance of keeping busy. Momma had taken great care to add to my existing staff. For example, on Coronus, Hugo was our chef, and Rory was my domestic assistant. She had added a launderer, a gardener for the main yard, and a chauffeur as permanent positions to the household in addition to the guards already there.

How many guards now protected us at all times, I didn't know and didn't ask. I'd only thought I'd been guarded before. My husbands were one thing. My Papa was another especially after the Alux attack. They wanted me dead. It really sucked having an entire, advanced, psychotic race of aliens out for your blood. However, if I were to think of it in a positive manner, as I'd suggested Yukihyo do about his ancestral home, their hatred was a strong motivator to find allies and a way to defeat them.

In addition to Papa's security concerns, Dario and Fitz had gone completely mental. Vice Admiral Dario Galerius had impressed me on multiple occasions with his fierce intelligence and his ruthlessness as a warrior, but he'd also shown me his sensitive and caring side. We'd become friends before we'd become lovers. Aside from being devastatingly handsome, with his black hair which tended to curl if he allowed it to grow and his seductive dark eyes, he had a way of breaking through to me during times when I failed to keep my anxiety in check. He didn't see me as many of the Warrior Caste did as a traumatized child who'd grown into womanhood after coming home to the Parvac Empire. No, Dario saw me for my potential. Well, he usually did. Now, he saw me as though I were upon a pedestal, a brilliant light glowing about me, the mother of his child, and with our daughter in my arms.

Fitz was even worse. He'd always had an overwhelmingly protective streak where I was concerned. He'd once even come to blows with Uncle Kagan and at another time Luca Braga, may the stars protect him. Had he lived, Luca would have been a doting father. Dario and Fitz were loving, attentive, and gentle toward the children and me. However, I'd witnessed their combined deadly and vehement rage at a perceived threat a few days ago. A reporting drone had flown too close to us as I'd been strolling through the Palace gardens with the girls in their pink ruffled pram. Fitz had used his body to form a protective cage around us while Dario had run, jumped, and struck the drone to the ground where he'd stomped it. Thunderdrop had chirped sadly over the ruined drone. He'd invented a new game to be played with them.

I'd had to gently scold them and explain that a guard from the Palace was controlling that particular drone. He'd sent it to play with Thunderdrop. He would attach a line of silk to the drone and be flown around the gardens at a sedate pace in front of us. If he perceived a threat, he'd sever his line and hunt the poor rodent down. They'd calmed down by the time the apologetic Inquisitor got there to collect his drone. However, their behavior required no apology. They had behaved naturally according to Parvacian societal norms, and to be fair they weren't the only new fathers providing me with ample amusement.

Jazon, Xavier, and Phillip could concentrate on little other than their wives and new babies. Thinking of the trip to Chione, I sighed. I'd ask Tracy, Sparrow, and Terre what they each wanted to do. My children and I adored space travel. However, my ladies might prefer to remain on Parvac with their infants. I could foist my social obligations off on them. Their mothers would love it. I knew better than to ask Violet. She and her children would accompany us. Aside from enjoying trips to Arachne, her home world, she wouldn't want to see her darling assassin's heart break if I were to leave without him, not to mention Poppy and Milk. Poppy and Neema might as well be sisters for their closeness, and their snow foxes were in fact of the same litter. The only noticeable difference between the girls' pets were their ears. Flake's ears were tipped with grey. Milk was solid-white.

While I dressed, Yukihyo told the captain that we were ready to return. Through Zared, I knew Fitz and Dario were near the nursery listening for any sound from our babies. By the time I'd taken a seat to nurse Tabitha and Marielle, they'd be in clean diapers and ready to be placed in my arms. Unworried, Yukihyo and I watched insects along the riverbank, the fish leaping up to gulp them down, and the birds swooping down to catch the fish in their sharp beaks or talons. Ripples on the water's surface were left behind by the tailfins of the fish who got away as they darted back to cool depths.

Rubbing my shoulders, he said, "You are happier and more content than I have ever know you to be."

"I have everything I ever wanted, you, the children, Thunderdrop, almost a dozen husbands, loving parents, family, friends, and a purpose." He kissed my temple and left me feeling even more happy and content.

Softly, he said, "You should remain here on Parvac. I can see to our Clan home on my own. Perhaps, a few of my co-husbands will accompany me."

"I'm glad you are all finally becoming a real family. It hasn't always been easy."

He snorted. "No, when Parvac males are competing over a female, they can be brutal."

Shrugging, I rubbed my hands over the arms with which he held me.

He chuckled. "Do you ever wonder what it would have been like had we had a traditional Laconian marriage rather than a Parvac one? How do you imagine you would have reacted to my second wife?"

A cold rage drenched my mind.

Yukihyo's laughter echoed back to us from the mountains. I left his arms and scowled at him for having purposefully angered me. Taking me back into his embrace, he cajoled, "Do not be angry with me, Lady Wife. I merely wished for you to understand how far I have come from the perspective of most of your Laconian husbands."

"Most?"

Into my mind, Izaac said, "I never thought the day would come when I'd be able to touch my lips to yours or to hold you in my arms."

Yukihyo said, "Yes, most of your Laconian husbands would prefer not to share you. However, you would grow restless and resentful without having your needs met. Especially, this would be true in the coming weeks or months." His grin broadened.

After pregnancy, as a Parvac female's hormones began to return to a natural balance, she would enter a mating heat. There was nothing to be done about it other than one's husbands. The hormones of Parvac females could be problematic at times. I'd learned as much when I'd tried to take control of my own reproduction. Birth control had made me miserable and irrational putting a strain not only on me, but also on my Omnes Videntes. Later, I'd learned it was the reason why Parvac females didn't use it. Had I been raised in the Palace with my real family rather than by the abusive piece of shit Earth Loyalist, Nathan Green, I'd have known. They had struggled to keep me emotionally and mentally balanced.

Yukihyo asked, "Do you want us to begin taking birth control again?"

It had been the solution to my problem at the time. I'd wanted to have my body to myself. "No," I said with a sigh. I thought of Neema, Niklos, Peter, Marielle, and Tabitha. "I'm a mother. I've accepted my fate. Let's take bets on who knocks me up this time."

Yukihyo's laughter was joyous. Laconians loved large families, the more children the better. From his love of our children, I knew it didn't matter to him whether he sired them himself or not. He loved them equally and limitlessly. Being pregnant wouldn't affect any of my current plans, but I did have other worries. In answer to those worries, a wave of fiercely protective emotion surrounded me and lifted me to safety as my Omnes Videntes offered reassurances.

Telepathically, Zared spoke to both Yukihyo and me. "They will not touch you or our children."

I chose to believe him. However, the concerns that I had were about how to make his promise true not only for myself but for all mothers throughout the universe. How could we protect ourselves from the Alux? The alien species fed on adoration. How they managed to accomplish their metaphysical feeding from non-telepathic species was being studied by the most brilliant scientists the Laconian Sector, Galaxic Expanse, and Parvac Empire had to offer. While we had delegated such research to those most suited to discovering the answers, the Cosmos Coalition now searched for less cerebral means of protecting the citizens of our galaxies from the Alux.

They avoided telepathic civilizations because those peoples were strong enough to fight off their mental assaults. The Alux had learned the hard way to avoid Arachne when they had been defeated by the Silk spiders. Aside from being immune to the telepathic manipulation of the Alux, the spiders' venom was also particularly lethal to them. Weaponized synthetic Silk spider venom gave us a means of protecting ourselves. Added to that, Admiral Galerius had captured one of the warships which was being studied. It was another reason why Sparrow Ponidi might wish to remain on Parvac. She had devised weapons with Arachnean Silk spider venom incapsulated in metal-eating nanites with Alux hemoglobin trackers. Who knew what our weapons expert would invent next? Helpful as they were, those two things weren't enough to put us on even footing with the Alux. Our combined forces were still at a disadvantage. I shuddered at the memory of what had happened on Hawking Station 7. The researchers there had sacrificed themselves to the Alux.

The Alux fed on non-telepathic humanoid species. Farowyn's people had encountered them during their search for a habitable planet. He'd explained to us how the Alux travelled through wormholes and fueled their vessels with radiation. The Eloneave considered them to be evil filth, and I had to agree. They tricked sentient species into believing they were gods and then fed on their worship and sacrifice. I wondered how many civilizations had been used as sources of sustenance for the predators.

While Parvacians weren't originally telepathic or empathic unless, like myself, a mother or grandmother from an alien society changed it, they were not affected in the way typical of non-telepathic races. No, Parvacs reacted in quite the opposite way of what the Alux expected, with rage. Dario had told Papa that he'd hungered for battle and to spill Alux blood. Battle rage had led us to another discovery. While their weapons and invisible body shielding absorbed our weapons blasts and used them to power themselves, making our blasters and shock sticks ineffectual, a blade would cut their flesh the same as ours, and their personal defenses were useless against them.

While our engineers worked to reverse engineer the ship Dario had captured, our xenobiologists conducted autopsies of the Alux specimens who'd attacked Parvac in their failed attempt to assassinate me. We would be better prepared for the next fight, but we weren't ready to take the offensive. I felt more prepared with

Quaid at my side. As a captain whose command was serving within the Cosmos Coalition, he was my counterpart and liaison to the Militia. It was his duty to coordinate Militia forces with those of the Empire. Our chain of command was clear. On our orders, warships and warriors would be deployed where they were needed.

Yukihyo said, "You are feeling smug."

"Yeah, I was just thinking. Gina is right. I'm the Parvac Empire's official administrative director of the Cosmos Coalition. I am a badass, and with the power I wield, I don't need to engage in hand-to-hand combat. I can be powerful while nursing, pregnant, or wearing pretty dresses."

His relief washed over me. He'd spent lots of time teaching me to defend myself but didn't want me fighting. Mostly, those who were vehemently opposed to the sight of me so much as making a fist had Parvac genetics. I decided that it was enough for me to have gained admittance to the Inquisitors Academy, paving the way for our niece, Cadet Galina Treves, and her friend, Cadet Rheanna Verok. It was a bonus that Inquisitor Flavian, Clark's father, served as their instructor. The girls were a handful. I enjoyed his torment.

The dock was within view. Dario was waiting for us there with Marielle in his arms. He'd given her a pacifier. Calling out to us over her furious screams, he said, "I thought being closer to you would placate her." His expression turned doubtful when she smacked the pacifier with her tiny hand and sent it flying into the lake. Then, she began a soul-wrenching cry. Dario looked so helpless.

Yukihyo helped me to disembark. Going to the pair, I took our princess from his arms. It caused a tangible wave of relief to wash over the Parvac Admiral and future Praetor of Daphoene. Even Inquisitors feared Dario's disdain. I laughed at him while freeing my left breast. Marielle was now content. Breastfeeding had become as natural to me as breathing. Cradling her in my arms as she nursed, I set a leisurely pace back to my wing of the Palace.

Dario grumbled at Yukihyo, "You seem relaxed."

Yukihyo grinned at him.

"I had an idea, and I would like your input."

"Go on."

"Thermo-resonator missiles were once used against us. Great effort was made to collect and eradicate the weapons...." He looked over and down at me.

My steps hadn't faltered and neither had my calm demeanor. However, my emotions had gone into a momentary hiccup of terror. Arlo Dano of Aurilius had been a powerfully wealthy madman who had been unchecked and unrestrained. He'd become fixated on me in some sick, twisted way which had become an obsession. Aside from hiring Laconian hybrid mercenaries, now sworn to me as my Omnes Videntes, Arlo had had a strange obsession with his mother and some sort of compulsive disorder. Although, his addiction to cleanliness and order could have been considered a positive trait. It pleased me when things were neat and tidy.

After all of the therapy in which Fitz and I had participated, I knew that my own need for cleanliness and order stemmed from my need to feel a sense of control over my environment. Cleaning comforted me.

Yukihyo asked Dario, "What if we encapsulated a thermo-resonator missile in reflective photonic film and added the bio-chemical delivery nanite spores which Sparrow and Tracy have been testing?"

Shocked, I said, "Hello? They have been outlawed."

Dario's brow crinkled as he considered the application of such a weapon against our enemies. "It would make the missiles faster, which if even by a millisecond might give us an advantage. Develop it, and I'll have it tested."

Yukihyo smiled and dipped his head.

"Has Ponidi Propulsions decided to take a new path?"

"No, Dario. I simply wish to propel our weapons speedily toward their targets that the Alux might die in exquisite torture while cursing our names."

The two of them laughed.

"I truly like you," Dario said as if he'd only just realized it.

Yukihyo grinned at him.

"The Enyo, Lord Yukihyo in particular, are particularly brutal. If not for me, he would spend countless hours engaged in strenuous hand-to-hand combat."

Yukihyo snorted. "You enjoy watching me fight."

I took a moment to imagine him shirtless, sweaty, feral, muscles bulging, and with his opponent bleeding at his feet. "I never said I didn't. Did I? I know that I've been angry at you for having lied to me and gone off to fight in matches without me."

He groaned. "You do not want me fighting out of jealousy because losing you is ridiculous, and I should know it. However, I may fight for exercise or for honor."

"Wow. You've finally figured it out. It's only taken you how many years?"

Loud sounds caught our attention. They were screams and coming from my wing! Yukihyo and Dario sprang into action. Yukihyo ran for the Palace. Dario drew a blaster and put himself between the baby and me and the Palace.

Chapter Three

"It's not what you think, but you're definitely not going to like it," Cormac said from directly behind me.

"Are my lady and babe in danger?" His voice chilled my blood.

Listening to his communications device, his reply was succinct. "No."

Sheathing his weapon, Dario led the way.

My steps slowed the closer we got. My lips parted. My eyes stared in disbelief. I'd slowed to a pace that could barely be considered walking. My lovely windows, which provided stunning views of the gardens and lake, were obscured from the inside with some sort of purplish-pink substance. Yukihyo was furious. I watched as he carried Neema out to the patio and deposited her on a chair. She was crying due to her father's anger. Nico carried out both Niklos and Peter. Both of them were the same color as the windows from head to knees.

"What the hell?" I whispered.

When Papa, covered in the same substance, walked out with a wailing Tabitha in his arms, I rushed forward. Nico put the boys down in chairs beside their sister. Their eyes were wide. "This behavior is reprehensible! It will not be tolerated!" Nico barked with the practiced censure of a general.

With my eyes glued to the patio doors, I walked up from the lawn. "Oh, stars." I looked inside at my sitting room from right to left in disbelief. Dark-pink foam was splattered everywhere.

Yukihyo knelt beside Pierce and Lorca. He was untying the two men. "Who did this?"

Pierce sighed heavily and stared at the formerly plush white carpet. "Itsy did. She's working with the rebels."

Lorca said, "They took us by surprise. We had no idea they had an arsenal. We thought it was all pretend." He shook out his hands once Yukihyo had freed them.

Standing beside me on the patio, Thunderdrop took in the mess with his eight eyes. He didn't so much as make a clack. Instead, he turned and scurried off into the gardens.

"You're leaving me?" I called after him.

"Chirp!"

"Fuck," I grumbled.

Dario took Marielle from me. "I'll take the girls to their grandmothers."

Papa said, "I'll carry Tabitha. We'll both go." He was furious.

The children lowered their heads, not daring to look at their Gapa. Stepping over to the door, I spotted Itsy hiding under a table. "Go to Niklos," I told her. She scurried from a table leg to a wall and escaped outside. Yukihyo continued to pick spider silk from the two men. Aside from it, they were coated in the sticky substance that was coating everything. "What is this?" I dragged my finger across a table to collect a sample of the substance.

"It's used in wargames at the Academies." Lorca ran his fingers through his sticky hair. "The children saw some cadets training the other day. I did not realize they'd become so intrigued as to wish to practice their own form of guerrilla tactics."

"Were they shooting at each other inside?"

"No, Teagan, just everything else." Lorca shook his arms to regain feeling in them.

I groaned. "My beautiful carpet."

"It can be cleaned. I'll see to it immediately!"

"We both will," Pierce said. "I can't believe we fell for it."

"Most children don't have an Arachnean Silk spider for an accomplice," Lorca said.

For the most part, my sitting room was unharmed. However, my couches and the windows overlooking the lake and mountains were coated in the pink foamy shit.

"Mommy, I'm sorry!" Neema wailed.

Rolf and Otto took the nurses outside to berate them.

"How did they manage to procure this shit?" I watched as a glob of pink foam paint slid down the wall toward my plush carpeting.

Striding through the doors to my wing, Zared asked, "How do they get everything they want? Your mother gives in to their teeniest whims as she did with all of this. Even now, she laughs at your father's appearance and calls for a crew to clean your rooms." He threw his hands up into the air. Then, he scowled toward the patio.

Into our minds, Izaac said, "I will dissuade our headstrong princess against the wisdom of running away to Poppy's house." He paused on his way outside long enough to pinch me on the bottom. I scowled at him. How could he pinch my bottom at a time like this? Turning his head, he grinned at me and kept walking.

"In these last few months, Empress Neema has been spoiling the children in excess." Zared had been ineffectual in reining in Momma. A few weeks ago, he'd asked her to check with us before buying presents for the children. His genetic modifications and telepathic abilities had saved him from being the object upon which several expensive vases had broken themselves. Shards had become embedded in the Palace walls. Being intelligent, he'd run. Brow furrowed from the memory, he said, "Perhaps now, Emperor Probus might intercede."

Yukihyo entered and said, "I would not recommend sharing parenting advice with him at the moment."

Zared shrugged. "I may not need to. He will want to know from where the children acquired such age-inappropriate incendiaries, and the answer will be found in his own bed." He had been subtly soothing my emotions since he'd entered the room.

I didn't make a big deal of it. They had finally stopped trying to protect me from my own distressful emotions. Now, they used their abilities to facilitate me as I handled them on my own. It had taken several arguments to get to this point, but when they realized the soft-handed approach was strengthening me emotionally, they'd accepted it. Why was it so difficult to get males to actually listen? Perhaps, they needed four ears, two for sounds and two for comprehending the words spoken to them. Zared snorted at my thoughts.

"Oh, my. What is all of this? And tears?"

The arrogant, droll tone was unmistakable, but I turned my head toward him anyway. Stig raised an aristocratic eyebrow. His champagne-blond hair appeared freshly brushed, the collar of his white shirt crisp, and his suit as black and fathomless as his soul. His eyes overflowed with boredom. His gaze left mine to trail downward. He smirked. Following his path, I realized that I had a breast out from nursing Marielle. While I shoved it safely out of sight, he said, "A male having his tongue cut out arouses no response, but a bit of..." dragging a finger across the table nearest the doors, he examined the pink foamy paint before flicking it off onto an already drenched bouquet of roses, formerly of the orange variety, "mess sets you to tears."

"What do you want, Eddie?"

Holding his hands behind his back, he forced himself not to pace the floor as was his habit. I could tell getting the paint on his shiny black shoes was far more annoying to him than he wanted me to know. "Something needs my attention on Earth. May Kitty and I take our leave of Princess Teagan Probus with her blessing?" She stood in his shadow but leaned to the side enough to smile at me. Then, she cringed at the mess.

Zared had become still. Eddie's eye twitched, and his jaw clenched. I knew why. Zared and Izaac wanted to know why Eddie would leave when he'd been using his stay on Parvac to further his political agenda within the Galaxic Government. They were pushing against Stig's neural blocker just enough to annoy him which was a game that amused them to no end. It was a particularly favorite game amongst my Omnes Videntes. Standing amidst the gooey mess in which I found myself, I could only hope that my children would find activities of a less problematic variety in which to engage, like their uncles. Perhaps, I could find a way for them to annoy Stig.

"Of course, you may have my blessing to leave. Please, speak to Captain Bosh regarding weaponry prior to your departure. We have accomplished what we can." Eddie had been tasked with the delivery of substantial defensive weaponry.

"We shall await your arrival on Earth and from thence carry on with our itinerary. It may take a day or so for our preparations for our departure to be completed." He gave me a greasy smile that didn't reach his eyes.

Kitty said, "I'll say hi to the ladies in the neighborhood for you."

"Bye, Kitty." I liked her even though she had shitty taste in men. We exchanged quick hugs before she followed after her odious mate.

"What is he up to?" I asked after they'd vanished down the hall.

Zared said, "Earth is where he is having the Mad Ones treated."

A shiver of fear slid down my spine. I tried not to think of them. Of those who survived, they were unstable to put it kindly. Teams of scientists worked to stabilize their neural pathways. One of those scientists was their creator, Dr. Stanley Crispus. He'd worked to overcome his own personal issues. The loss of his wife had driven him to the brink of insanity. Now, with all I had to lose, I could better understand the depths of pain and despair which had driven him. He'd lost the love of his life to suicide after she'd lost a child too many to miscarriage. Having suffered such a horrendous loss myself, that of mine and Luca's child, I could ache for them both and understand why he'd been so desperate to give his wife children, even after she'd embraced the stars. It was his warped and twisted act of contrition which had ultimately set the course even for my own life.

I found myself staring once again at Luca's portrait. Zared moved behind me and covered my hands with his. "What is this which I sense?" he whispered. "Do you begin to find forgiveness in your heart for he who has caused you such immutable pain?"

I shrugged. "He wasn't driven by greed or pride. He wanted to give her a reason to live, even though she was already gone. It's tragedy atop tragedy, and his suffering has found ways to endure for decades." Staring down the hall, I wondered at the extent of Stig's involvement with Crispus.

Zared whispered, "We will keep track of him."

As my thoughts returned to the present, unpleasant sensations returned with it. My right breast felt as though a thin layer of my straining flesh covered a dense sack of rocks. Sensing Tabitha in her grandparents' wing, I followed the path along which Stig had just led Kitty. Zared easily kept pace at my side.

Yukihyo called after us, "Do not worry about me. I will be fine here cleaning this wanton destruction."

"The sarcasm in your tone is almost as thick as the pink shit the kids blasted all over my beautiful white fucking sanctuary," I yelled back over my shoulder.

His laughter, rather than a scolding for my use of expletives, followed us along the hall.

Zared again whispered in my ear. "You put him in a good mood."

A pink foam bubble which had been stuck to the hem of my dress popped. I snorted at it. So with the bubble, so with the good moods into which Yukihyo and I had put each other. Not bothering to be announced, I raised an eyebrow at Papa's butlers. They made haste to open the doors for me. Momma was trying to keep Tabitha calm with a pacifier. She wasn't having the same luck with Papa. After taking a comfortable seat, I held open my arms. Momma brought her over to me. She was ravenous and would probably spit up. Momma could be the one to burp her. It would serve her right.

Sitting beside me, Zared crossed an ankle over his knee and grabbed a bowl of dried fruits and nuts from a side table. He quietly munched while paying avid attention to the unfolding drama. The current situation was far more entertaining than our last movie night with the kids. It had been based upon a popular Parvacian comic book character with whom the children were enamored. Inwardly, I groaned. Of course, the kids would want to blast the bad guys. They were fixated on hunting evil alien monsters. Nico and I had taken Niklos to a few therapy sessions after his traumatic experiences with the Alux. It was no wonder that my kids wanted to feel powerful.

Into my mind, Zared said, "The children are not traumatized over the Alux. However, they are attempting to empower themselves through imaginative play."

Telepathically, I asked, "Then, what is it?"

Crunching through a handful of mix while mentally responding, he said, "Your children have violent, bloodthirsty impulses ingrained genetically upon them. They are of a warrior race of the strongest House of the Parvac Empire. If anything, Peter is the voice of reason amongst them." I gaped at him. He fed me a chunk of dried pineapple. "Our children will be brilliant savages, warlords of the stars." He took on a dreamy look.

I popped my nipple from Tabitha's mouth and shot a triple-stream of milk into his ear. Tabitha, upset at having her meal disturbed, latched back on with the aforementioned savagery. Zared stuck a salty finger in his ear in an effort to clear his ear canal of breastmilk.

Aloud, he said, "She sucks savagery from your tit. All you do is make me want you more." He growled at me.

"Oh, shut your mouth," I scolded.

In his grin, there was a promise of what he planned to do to me with his mouth once we managed to have a private moment.

"Darling, don't be cross with me," Momma pleaded. She clutched her soft hands together. As usual, her nails were immaculate and had been painted a mossy-green to match the form-fitting, floor-length dress she wore. Long, reddish-brown hair, akin to that of Sherman and Simon, but muted by Parvac genetics, fell in cascades down to her hips.

"Neema, you can't simply give them everything they want and then turn them loose!" Papa had showered. Now, he stood across from her wearing nothing but a towel around his hips. He wasn't using the tone he used with his soldiers when he was angry. He wasn't using the tone he used when he was irritated with me. No, he was furious but valiantly trying to conceal it.

Zared chuckled under his breath. He was enjoying my Papa's predicament.

In a petulant tone, she said, "I was deprived of my own daughter! Would you have me neglect the desires of my precious grandchildren?" She'd become horrified. I couldn't tell if she was serious or putting on a show to get her way.

"My love, I do not want you to neglect their desires. You should do all within your power to please them. Of course, you should. I'm not saying that at all." He placed his hands gently on her arms and spoke as he might to a frightened kitten.

Clearing my throat, I said, "Hello, hi. Remember me? How about spoiling me? I'm your daughter, but my wing looks like a giant ice bear, who'd been gorging on berries, suffered from gastrointestinal distress resulting in explosive diarrhea all over my fucking sitting room. Have you seen it? Everything is ruined." Both of my parents took note of my fury. "Blasters for cadets? Seriously? They are children! They could have been hurt!"

Affronted, Momma said, "Nonsense, the other children play with those all over the neighborhoods. Ask literally anyone. Kagan and I even played with them." She threw her hands up in the air. "Well, call and ask him! We were their age when we got our first foam blasters."

Papa's expression validated her statement, negating my need to verify anything with my uncle. Glaring at her, I asked, "Did you play with them inside?"

She made a sound of disbelief. "Are you joking? Mother would have whipped us." Horrified, she said, "Don't you dare spank my grandbabies." She sounded as if she'd put herself between my children and me to protect them from corporal punishment.

Clenching my teeth, I stood and left the room.

"Teagan, darling, don't be in a temper. They were just playing!"

Out in the hall, I grumbled to Zared. He'd taken the snack bowl with him. "I need a vacation and to blow some shit up."

"I've got something you can blow." He winked at me.

"I should have told her about the time Uncle Kagan spanked me." Lifting my chin, I puckered my lips. "As if I'd hit my babies after how I was treated!" Shoving vile memories of Nathan Green and my childhood away into the blackest, most secret place in my mind, I tried to prepare myself for the disaster we were fast approaching by taking a deep breath.

A small smile graced Zared's lip. "It pleases you to know she would protect them even from a soft tap from you." He was right. When she'd said the words, I'd felt insulted, but it had been quickly replaced by a deep sense of safety. My children wouldn't suffer as I'd suffered. Already, I'd given them more love, protection, and nurturing than I had received. Momma wasn't to blame and neither was Papa. It was what it was.

Eli stood with his back to the doors to my wing. He was supervising. A crew used bots to eradicate all vestiges of pink, foamy paint from my formerly pristine sitting room. Neema looked up at me with big, sad eyes from where she sat on the floor beside a table. A vase of soggy roses was before her. Gloves covered her hands and arms up to her armpits. One by one, she pulled the stems free and deposited the flowers into a trash bag. It brought back memories.

"Like mother, like daughter," I mumbled under my breath on my way to the nursery with Tabitha. She'd grown heavy in my arms. Carefully, I put her down.

Her sister was napping in her grandmother Galerius' arms. Thunderdrop had silently followed me into the room. A properly chastised Itsy had remained with Niklos in the sitting room.

"Chirp chitter." Thunderdrop lifted a long leg and rubbed it across the top of his head.

Reaching over, I patted his abdomen. "Ambassador Thunderdrop, I understand. Hopefully, your turtles won't one day emulate comic book heroes."

Blinking eight eyes at me, he climbed up to the web above the swan crib and chirped a soft agreement.

"Watch her for me?"

"Chirp."

Leaving Tabitha under Thunderdrop's supervision, I returned to the sitting room where I took up a position at Eli's side. Not a speck of pink paint marred the solid-black that my Inquisitor wore from head to toe, unlike me. Niklos and Peter were busy cleaning the windows which overlooked the lake. A blush covered Niklos' cheeks. My empathic children sensed my emotions. Again, Neema beseeched me with her jade-green discs. Her beautiful eyes failed to work their magic on me. Realizing the extent of my annoyance, she hastened her work on the task before her. An anti-grav scrubber bot swirled through the air in front of us before latching itself to a patch of melting pink foam on the wall.

"All should be put to rights in a few hours. Allow me to offer a distraction." Eli had turned his dark, dangerous eyes from the mess to me. When he offered me his arm, I took it.

"They were supposed to be napping," I grumbled.

He made not a sound as he escorted me quickly along the halls and into the pool room. Making a face, I scowled toward the water. He could feel my annoyance along our bond. The connection between us had grown stronger each day since we'd been home on Parvac. What had started as trust, friendship, and passionate love between us had developed into something even more binding, a shared sense of duty. We felt a need to protect each other, our Empire, and our family, the latter of which the two of us clung with a fathomless desperation having survived our earliest years without one.

A wad of fabric hitting me square in the face snapped me out of my reverie and into the present. Eli kept all expression from his face. "While I can think of nothing that I'd rather have than you alone and both of us naked, we have received a report."

The "we" to whom he'd referred could only mean the Inquisitors. Tossing the black uniform onto a lounge chair, I let my dress fall to pool at my feet. The way Eli subtly clenched his jaw and held his hands behind his back had me grinning. He wanted to fuck me senseless but being not only pressed for time but also uncomfortably pressed against the front of his trousers, he could do nothing for it. My smile turned wicked as I hurried to change. He'd stashed my uniform in the pool room along with my boots. If I wanted to, I could satisfy his sexual tension with a touch, spiraling pleasure along his awareness.

Instead, I made eye contact, stared pointedly down at his bulging manly appendage, straining for its freedom, and walked toward the exit. He knew I was punishing him for tossing my uniform at my face, and he loved it. I'd yet to meet an Inquisitor who didn't have some sort of sexual proclivity which could only politely be described as exotic. Eli liked it rough, and Drex enjoyed being bossed around, but then Nico seemed to find the same things exciting. Frowning to myself, I thought of Fitz. The male never ceased to make me blush. Once, in my wing before my bathroom mirror....

I felt my blood heat at the memory and heard Izaac whisper into my thoughts, "All of your Parvac husbands are perverts."

Silently, I retorted, "That's not true!"

"Name one who isn't." He chuckled while he waited.

Eli led me outside to a black transport. After we'd taken our seats, the driver sped away from the Palace. I didn't bother to ask where we were going. I knew from experience that we'd end up at the Inquisitors Academy. "Are you going to tell me what this is about?" I turned my head, and for a moment, even though I knew he sat beside me, I couldn't see him. A passing shadow from the street had temporarily cast his visage into shadow, causing him to be rendered almost invisible within the transport's solid-black interior.

"No, it's a surprise." He grinned at me. I could sense his eagerness and excitement. He was genuinely looking forward to pleasing me with whatever it was he had either done or discovered.

However, when dealing with one of the most calculating and deadly males in the Parvac Empire, any number of things could be in store for me, a new blaster, special body armor, a listening device planted on Eddie....

Izaac interjected into my thoughts, "The severed heads of your enemies...."

I kept my expression neutral. "Eli wouldn't do that."

Izaac laughed in my mind. "You're right. He'd bring them to you alive so you could torture them first. It would be more fun for you in his estimation that way."

I sighed and gave him the equivalent of a mental eyeroll.

Izaac was right. Parvac males who presented sick, twisted, sociopathic tendencies were sought after as protégées amongst the Inquisitors Branch. Who better to hunt down the Empire's enemies and traitors? I didn't have the stomach for torture. I preferred to torment my adversaries with surprise redecorating of a phallic theme. Immersing those who annoyed me in visual representations of what they were behaving like was appropriately inappropriate. Even Gram had a knack for it. The bedding she'd made Ethan make for Maria had been classic.

The driver pulled to a stop in front of the Academy. Eli hastened to get out and open my door. I'd only taken a step away from the transport when I heard, "Aunt Teagan!" She waited for me in front of the building with her arms wide. She'd been running, and seemed eager to be on her way, but for me, she would make an exception. Her milky eyes were dancing with mischievous striations of color. The hug she gave me was quick. Then, she took off toward the assembly hall.

"Treves!" a furious male voice bellowed.

It was a voice I knew, and it didn't inspire any warm fuzzy feelings within me. Sensing it as he rounded the corner, I stuck out my right booted foot. Upon contact, a devious delight blossomed within me. However, my burgeoning smile withered and died as Inquisitor Flavian shifted his balance to his other leg and glided by without so much as a misstep. He stopped a few steps away from us. It infuriated me which was petty. After all, Quaid had tortured Flavian mercilessly for what he and his team had made me believe. Angered, I stroked Eli's hand bringing him to a pinnacle of pleasure. Then, I withdrew my hand, leaving him to suffer in sexual frustration and with a raging hard-on for all to see, not that it wasn't a magnificent one of which any Parvac male would be proud. Eli had been in on the plan, the fucker, which is why he'd earned his current punishment. If I couldn't take out my random burst of anger on

Flavian, Eli would do. Maybe, I had a sick streak too which might have been the reason I'd accepted Drex, Eli, and Clark. We related to each other in ways the others would never be able to fully understand.

Flavian opened his mouth as if to say something, thought better of it, and closed it. Instead, he bowed to me and hurried away after his target.

"When we leave, I'm seeing if Galina can come with us. I'll drop her off with her grandmother on Chione. She deserves a vacation from that odious...." I struggled to find a word other than an expletive. I thought I'd try to be a sweet princess for the rest of the day. Then, I thought better of it. I was dressed as an Inquisitor at the moment. "She deserves a vacation from that odious fucking sorry cunt of a male." I quickly walked away eager to put distance between Flavian and myself.

"The odious cunt is your father-in-law," Eli reminded me.

"And he's your friend, or you wouldn't be defending him to me. Yeah, yeah. You were acting on Papa's orders." Stopping short before plowing into a male chest, I stared up at Ensign Clark Flavian.

"I heard Father's voice and assume from your expression that you didn't have a pleasant exchange."

Unable to help myself, I reached out to stroke his bicep through the sleeve of his uniform. Clark continued to grow stronger and taller. I was quite pleased with the husband that my Parvac hormones had coaxed me to select. "I stuck my foot out to trip him, and he avoided it. The nerve! Can you imagine it?"

Clark gave me a look. "Are you going to give him a break?"

"I was trying to." I smirked up at him.

"Not his leg, Teagan."

"Whatever." Shoving him to the side, I brushed by him.

Eli said, "This way," and led us into a briefing room where the rest of our team already waited.

Cedrenus, Binder, Ross, Stayton, Levi, and Tyler reminded me of a pack of feral, ravenous wolves. They were eager to get started on something, but I didn't know what. I could tell they knew why we'd been summoned. While I'd been busy at the Palace, they'd been spying on our instructor. Whatever they'd discovered must have been worth the effort. Taking a seat, I waited. Instructor Rovek entered a heartbeat later. What Tracy saw in her newest husband, I couldn't fathom, but he'd saved Jazon. He closed the door and activated a holographic display without preamble.

A star map became the centerpiece of the table around which we'd seated ourselves. Recognizing the Laconian Sector and orienting my awareness, I focused on Chione as it came into view. The holographic image faded and refocused. A distant sector came into view. Eris Space Station, Cassini, and a few other uninteresting locations were bypassed as a dull, isolated, miniscule planetary body became the prominent visual image.

Rovek said, "This is Bondi Prime. To us, and to the nearest governmental power in its proximity, the Laconian Government, it is worthless. However, to a group of intergalactic astronomers, Bondi Prime is an astrological location of what Cory of Earth would refer to as Prime real estate."

Despite the mood seeing Flavian had put me into, I chuckled.

Rovek continued but not in his own voice. No, he flowed into Cory's mannerisms and tone of voice with ease. "What did you want? You wanted a planet where it's prevalent night? Cory's found it for you! Did I tell you I'd find it? Of course, I did! What you've got here is a calm atmosphere and clear visibility!" His hand gestures had us all laughing, even Eli. "It's everything you could want for looking at stars, nebulas, and all of the other cosmological occurrences you're studying, but wait! There's more!" He held his hands up for emphasis and widened his eyes making me laugh even harder. "This baby right here has low thermal turbulence, and it's arid! Did Cory tell you he'd find a perfect planet for your research? Eh?"

Then, in a blink, Rovek was back to his usual bland expression and moderate tone of voice. "Inquisitors often must play a part, and for this mission each of you will practice adopting the mannerisms and speech patterns of the individuals whose identities you will be assuming."

The holographic imaging zoomed in on Bondi Prime. Rovek sent files to each of us. Ignoring the dossier, I concentrated on our instructor and the holographic display. A series of enormous telescopes came into focus.

"Bondi Prime is the location of a deep space scientific observatory frequented by a rotating staff of graduate students in the fields of stellar cartography, astrophysics, engineering, and various support personnel." Rovek's glance moved over each of us like a deadly frost, killing the humorous mood created by his portrayal of Cory. "Like the students running the Bondi Observatory, you will be there for a grade."

Tyler leaned back in his chair. "So, we're just going there to impersonate graduate students? What's the point? We could infiltrate a closer university."

Holding my hands on the table in front of me, I said, "It does seem that our time and resources could be put to better use."

"At this time, shouldn't we be concentrating our efforts on defending ourselves against the Alux?" Stayton seemed as puzzled as Tyler and me. I guess we didn't know what the others knew.

Clark shrugged. He didn't know anything either.

Expressionless, Rovek didn't address our concerns. Instead, he continued. "In order to minimize the financial drain of an astronomical observatory which does little to contribute to its field with the exception of the training opportunities it provides to students such as yourselves, who are so desperate for it, educational fees are supplemented by a religious sect that donates heavily to the observatory in return for the site used for their holiest monastery."

Thoughtful, I made a face. The Alux inspired fanatical worship from those who were misfortunate enough to fall victim to them, and they were sustained by what could only be viewed as ritualistic humanoid sacrifice.

As if reading my thoughts, Rovek said, "The Order of Creation is not a dangerous cult. They are collectors of mythological texts. Bondi Prime is an excellent location for the storage of their sacred documents. The dim lighting, dry atmosphere, and moderate surface temperature make it ideal as a setting for the study of original ancient documents which might otherwise disintegrate in a less delicate climate."

My excitement returned.

Noticing, Rovek inclined his head to me. "If stories of the Pariea exist, I can think of no place more likely than in the extensive library of the Monastery of the Order of Creation."

"Why don't we simply pay them a visit? Why pretend to be students?" Stayton asked.

"They don't allow visitors. They are as secretive as we are and guard their amassed knowledge with sanctioned deadly force." He showed a schematic of the monastery.

Clark said, "The security is tighter than that of a Galaxic Starship."

"Much tighter," Eli said as he studied it.

Biometric scans were required along with security clearance for entry. Then, palm scans were required each time a monk entered a room, even a restroom.

"Misogynistic cunts," I grumbled. No one lacking a Y chromosome was allowed.

"Isn't that an oxymoron?" Binder asked.

Raising an eyebrow, I asked, "Is the phrase woman-hating pussies more to your liking?"

Staring at me, he said, "That's the same thing."

Clark asked, "How do we get inside?"

"We should abduct someone with security clearance and alter our DNA to match," Cedrenus suggested.

"We can't replicate a close enough match to trick their biometric system. They take themselves seriously believing they know the creator of humanoid life, and they will kill to protect their knowledge." Rovek shook his head.

Deadpan, I asked, "So, they are dangerous religious fanatics?"

Rovek sighed in resignation.

Ross asked, "How do we get in?"

Rovek said, "We have a plan to get the eight of you into the Observatory Program with assistance from our new supporters from within the Laconian Sector."

Eli stepped forward. "Finding a lead to the Pariea from within the Monastery's extensive collection of literature will require considerable finesse. We need a master thief, and I know of just the one who won't be traced back to us or the Cosmos Coalition."

"Who?" I asked.

Eli took over from Rovek. "Do you recall the package Consul Bosh received?"

I scowled. I remembered the artifact. The birth of the twins had left me feeling like a life-like model of the ancient, short, fat fertility goddess. I didn't feel as squishy as I'd felt in the first months, not since using my high-end nanite patches from Bosh Technologies. I was happier with my figure than I'd been. Not all of my stretch marks had been eradicated. It would take another patch to do the trick and annihilate them like most wished to do with the Alux. I'd be satisfied with the destruction of their ships, resources, and forcing them out of our galaxies so they'd never again cause the death of another innocent civilian. I pushed away memories of the cadets who'd died in the parking lot the day of the attack. "What makes you think you've positively identified the thief? We only heard about it a few hours ago."

The look in Eli's eyes was disbelieving. "Teagan, my curiosity was roused. Now, if I might direct your attention to the original crime. The security surrounding the artifact at the time of its theft presented no means of access."

Clark asked, "What if someone had managed to disrupt the main and secondary power?"

Eli gave a slight shake of his head. "Note the remotely operated power generators which are modulated to assist, support, or assume control of the security system at the slightest power fluctuation. There are no gaps. I, myself, would not have been able to perform the operation so seamlessly. In fact, I planned ways to do so in order to create a list of suspects, as did the Laconian authorities. Here are those suspected and questioned."

Arrest records of a dozen criminals appeared above the conference table replacing Bondi Prime. Each one rotated ever so slowly so that each of us saw their three-dimensional renderings. Not all of the suspects had the solid-black eyes of Eriopis. A few of them were human.

"Time stamps on facial recognition software maintained by our operatives in Laconian and Galaxic space allowed me to eliminate the following." Profiles began to disappear until each and every suspect had fallen away.

I asked, "Then, who did it if not any of them?"

A slow, delighted grin spread across Eli's face. Tapping a command, he shared security footage from Trambelus Space Station in the Laconian Sector. "After investigating hundreds of individuals and establishing their whereabouts on the day of the artifact's theft, this is what I have learned." Lists of names, itineraries, facial recognition scans, and verifications on planets, at land ports, and space docks scrolled painstakingly by.

In awe, Stayton asked, "How long did this take?" He stared incredulously at the details.

"Not as many hours as I would have liked. I haven't enjoyed myself so much in years." Eli's eyes sparkled with joy.

Cedrenus, Binder, Ross, and I made brief eye-contact with each other. It looked like hours of monotonous boredom, like studying financial records. Faces of suspects fell like green, pixelated dew to the table's surface and vanished until only one remained.

"Oh, my. Who do we have here?" I was interested once more. The male in question was sinfully handsome.

Eli said, "I present to you Colwyn Winks Taylor. He has a reputation amongst frequenters of Eris Space Station as a petty thief with quick fingers."

"Wink or blink, and it's gone?" I asked and then grinned. "The Enforcers must have a lengthy file on him."

"On his home world, they are called Protect and Serves." Eli looked around at each of us in turn. "He has a record, but it is not as detailed as I assumed it would be. His arrests seem as though they have been meticulously planned to establish alibis. However, in this case, of each individual I tracked in the days before and after the artifact's theft, only Taylor's whereabouts are unsubstantiated until he manifests on Trambelus Space Station days later." Clasping his hands behind his back, he paced. "This isn't the only priceless treasure to be returned as of late." The holographic image morphed into a painting of a moon above a quiet ocean. "As you know, it was returned under similar circumstances."

Tyler asked, "Why is someone stealing items only to return them?"

Turning to face him, Eli answered, "For amusement. Why else?"

Rovek asked, "Other than his unaccountability during the theft, what is there to tie him to the crime?"

Eli smiled. "Nothing. That in and of itself intrigues me."

"Why?" Tyler asked.

Stayton said, "Any one of those suspects could be made to appear culpable in the crime to the satisfaction of the Protect and Serves."

Tyler said, "You mean make them look guilty even if they are innocent?" He lifted his chin and squared his shoulders.

"Yes, I know how perverse and disgraceful the idea of failing to pursue the truth is to each of us. It isn't a practice to which we would stoop. However, during an investigation, one must always study every possibility. Colwyn Taylor is too clean. Nothing could be finessed to stick to him."

"How will we learn if he is the master thief behind these crimes?" Stayton asked.

Eli smiled. "As a mysterious unsolved theft enticed me into solving it, so might an impossible heist allure our suspect. Would he be able to resist the challenge posed by Princess Teagan of House Probus of Parvac, with all of her impeccable security, adorned with the Imperial crown of Grand Empress Jorja as she attends a gala hosted by Consul Dano on Aurilius? Dano owes us. The gems in the headpiece are priceless. The crown is a symbol of the power of the Materfamilias Caste. Paired with her security, her Omnes Videntes, and a venue overflowing with telepaths, it is something no thief would dare to attempt." Eli was delighted with himself.

Crossing my arms over my chest, I said, "So, you want to use me as bait."

Eli's eyes twinkled. "I know it will work. He won't be able to resist."

Cedrenus grunted.

"Momma might not allow me to borrow it. She could be planning to wear it to a garden party for all I know."

"After what happened in your wing? Ask her if you may borrow it. Once you have it, I will catalogue it and send our security requests to Consul Dano's security liaison."

"What good will that do?" I didn't get where he was going.

Eli explained, "Criminals monitor channels to learn who travels where, but we will have planned for it. Consul Dano will entice affluent members of Laconian society to attend his gala by teasing them with your expected attendance. While Dano works to secure renewed trade agreements, it will give our thief time to plan. When he strikes, we will catch him."

He made it all sound so simple.

Chapter Four

"Absolutely not," Empress Neema huffed in annoyance. She crossed her delicate arms across her chest and lifted her chin. Fabric so fine as to be almost weightless lifted and fell with her movements. I'd made the silk dressing gown for the woman who'd armed my children and who'd de facto ruined my sitting room, and she was telling me no? Pretending as though she couldn't sense my emotions, she said, "Jorja's crown is lovely, but if you want to wear something which this supposed thief will be unable to resist, wear this."

Surprise sealed my lips. Taking me by the wrist, she drew me along with her into her dressing room and into another room which contained her accessories. Papa spoiled her excessively.

"This diadem has been worn by every empress of the Parvac Empire. I wore it once, but I must warn you it's heavy." Pressing her palm to the scanner, she opened a walk-in jewelry box. There was no other way to describe it.

"Whoa." Wide-eyed, my attention was pulled from one sparkling conglomeration to the next. It took my dazzled senses a moment to concentrate. "Aw...oh...." The sounds I made were similar to those my husbands coaxed from me during intimacy.

Momma's laughter danced like the brilliant prismatic lights of sparkling diamonds around us. It was as though we'd stepped into another world, one of beautifully hypnotic twinkles which never seemed to beguile twice. They left me hopeful for an encore, dazzled by the next performance, and breathlessly awaiting more. Usually, I gravitated to simple pieces. However, the piece before me was a masterfully rendered work of art.

"Stunning, isn't it? Try it on. I'll help you."

I didn't argue. Instead, I gathered my hair out of the way. Lifting the necklace from the bust over which it had been draped, she placed it over my head and arranged it while I watched our reflection in one of the mirrors.

"There," she said as she straightened out one of the diamond strands.

Reaching up, I touched one of the platinum hammered bars resting along the top of my shoulders like thin, narrow epaulets. The two bars held five strands stationary. The first strand of five-carat diamonds sparkled along my collarbone. Beneath it, a slightly longer strand of four-carat diamonds was followed by a strand of three-carat diamonds, a strand of two-carat diamonds, and finally of one-carat diamonds which draped just above my naval.

"Now, this." Momma turned away, lifted a diadem from a black velvet pillow, and set it upon my brow.

Gaping at my reflection, I studied the heavy piece of history above my head. Centered at the top of the hammered band of gold, a large round pink diamond had been set within the sculpted talons of a bird of prey. The bird's wings were raised as if it might take flight. Above its sharp, hooked beak were eyes of yellow diamonds. Its head was turned toward its left wing as if waiting for dangers from without the Empire as if it might see into the deepest reaches of space.

"I love it." My declaration was filled with astonishment. "It's like Parvac, all pink and gold."

"Imagine showing up in this and wearing a simple white, floor-length gown. No one will be able to take their eyes from you." Smiling, Momma arranged my hair with her fingers. "Oh, how I've dreamed of this."

"Of what?"

Wistfully, she said, "Playing dress-up with you."

My heart twisted around within me and splattered at her feet.

Sensing my emotions, she playfully tapped the tip of my nose with her finger and laughed. "Go along. Make your plans. I am bequeathing these things to you, but should you lose them, my Imperial Guards will be cross with yours."

Frowning, I said, "If I lose them, I'll be furious and won't rest until I've caught whoever might dare to steal from me."

"That is the point, isn't it?"

Nodding, I felt the diadem shift and quickly righted my head.

"You'll need to practice wearing it. Keep your neck straight and your chin high to keep it balanced."

Giddy, I clapped. "Wow. I look awesome! Thank you, Momma!"

"It was my pleasure, my sweet."

Happily, I began my return to my wing. Eli was lurking in the Palace halls, waiting for me. I could see the ticking of his pulse in his neck as he watched me with dark eyes. To anyone else, his eyes would be unreadable mysteries. To me, I found more clarity there than I had in the reflective surface of Momma's mirror, and it unsettled me. He felt unworthy of me and of my love in that moment. "I will hunt your mother down and throttle her," I swore.

"Why would you do such a thing?" His tone was horrified.

Getting such a reaction from my Inquisitor sobered me. Slicing screaming criminals into chunks didn't get a reaction from him. Realizing he'd stopped walking, I slowed and carefully turned. Gazing into his eyes from across the white tiles of the Palace floors, I could still feel the diminishing vestiges of his pain. "You deserve me, my love, and that of our family, the family which you have guarded, protected, and done all in your power to preserve, even when it meant...." I left off what I'd almost said, even when it had meant hurting me. "Even when it meant deep personal sacrifice. You are mine. I'll never let you go, and you just need to accept it. Now, come along. After I nurse the twins, we're going shopping."

"Shopping?" He'd gone from depressed to confused.

Rolling my eyes at him, I slowly turned and resumed my previous course. "Eli, hurry up. I need you to hold the strands of diamonds out of the way."

"You aren't taking it off?" He seemed more confused.

"No, I don't want to. Momma gave me these things."

He hurried to catch up with me. Purposefully, I ignored my sitting room and hurried into the hall. Ahead, my wishes had already been conveyed to Pierce and Lorca. Tabitha and Marielle were in their nursery freshly diapered and hungry. With Eli holding my jewels out of the way, I took my girls into my arms and sighed as they slowly drained away the aching pain I'd begun experiencing.

"Lorca, will you get their pram? We're going out." Once the girls were full, I went to my rooms and changed into a pink dress to match the diamond in my new diadem and the girls' pram.

With Eli in charge of pushing the girls, I led the way out through the main entrance of the Palace to where my transport was waiting. Zared got out and opened the doors for us. While I fastened the girls into their safety seats, my brilliant Inquisitor struggled with the pram. Zared and I had been engaged in telepathic communication. While no one wanted me to hunt Eli's mother down and punish her for making him feel so unloved, we had compromised. I wasn't going to punch her in the face, but I was going to rub her nose in some metaphorical shit. My Omnes Videntes wouldn't be carefully evading reporters for this very public outing. This shopping trip was meant to be a display which would be all over the news feeds. Eli's lady mother wouldn't be able to miss seeing what a lovely male he was, the son from whom she'd turned her heart. Let her see her son who she couldn't bring herself to love being smothered in it.

Eli took a seat beside me in the transport and looked pointedly at my diadem. "Are you going to wear it shopping? Won't it get in the way?"

Innocently, I explained to him what Momma had told me about practicing and gave him my sweetest smile. "Eli, isn't this exactly the sort of thing you need?"

Not realizing my double meaning, he considered my question. "Seeing you in footage wearing such priceless imperial treasures so casually must certainly serve as an enticement for our thief."

Smiling at his brilliance, I patted his knee.

Eli raised a dark eyebrow. "It was your idea to wear them out. Why are you patting me as if in approval?"

"Why shouldn't I pat you in approval whenever I please?"

Confused by my reasoning yet again, part of his psyche remained present with me while a compartmentalized portion of his consciousness retreated to speculate. Taking out his vid-screen, he set his plans into motion.

It wouldn't take him long to figure out what I was really up to. I couldn't outsmart Eli. Marielle scrunched up her face and kicked off a pink satin shoe. Eli caught it before it could hit the window and bent to kiss her foot before struggling to replace the little shoe onto her tiny foot. Happiness warmed me. It was like sinking into a warm bubble bath but from within my heart.

Zared drove us to the local luxury shops preferred by the elite of the Materfamilias Caste, those who had taken the most powerful and wealthy males the Empire had to offer. My considerations turned to my children. They would not only be inheriting my amassed wealth, but also the generational wealth of their fathers. I'd once judged Parvac females as being weak and pampered with my own mother-in-law, Lady Galerius, amongst them even with her superior academic education. My assumption had been incorrect. In her own way, Momma taught me the error of my former thinking in her own way a few times a day by example. She didn't use force. She was all refinement and grace but could get me to do as she wished like a hungry Silk spider after a juicy rat with her smiles and affection or with diamonds and a diadem. Not wanting me to be cross with her about the paint blasters which she'd given to my children, she'd distracted me.

Pulling out my vid-screen, I looked up the estimated value of the Imperial jewels that I was wearing. Priceless seemed to be the consensus, but monetarily their worth came close to Rupert Warren's amassed credits. When Momma had said that her Imperial Guards would be cross with mine should anything happen to the diadem and necklace, she hadn't been fucking around.

After parking our transport, Zared joined us inside of the boutique I'd decided to enter. News drones outside were netted and dragged away by guards after their pilots began attacking rival drones to get better footage for themselves. The commotion had upset several window shoppers. Looking up at Eli, I braced my diadem and kissed his cheek. He handed Tabitha the rattle she'd flung from the pram and gave me a look. Okay, so he knew what I was doing.

Quietly, he said, "The treasures you wear today pale in comparison to you."

My vid-screen signaled. The tone belonged to Niklos. Answering it with haste, I saw his serious little face. "Mommy, I need to tell you something." He looked as though he faced a firing squad.

"What is it, my darling? It's alright. You can tell me."

Taking a breath which made his little chest puff out, he turned stoic and lifted his chin. "It was my fault. It was like Dax when he captured the aliens. I talked Neema and Peter into it. I should be the one in trouble, not them."

Smiling, I blew him a kiss. "Oh, my love, I'm proud of you for telling me the truth. However, your sister and brother helped you make the mess. The three of you used teamwork. Your participation was equal. Is the mess cleaned up?"

With wide eyes and a confused stare, he shook his head. "No?"

Smiling, I made a shooing gesture with my free hand. "Go clean. Go. I will forgive the three of you when my sitting room is pristine." I ended the call.

"Ouch," Zared said.

Narrowing my eyes at him, I asked, "Will they ever do any shit like that inside ever again?"

Puckering his lips in thought, he said, "No, I don't believe they will. Upsetting you distresses them. This is a lesson that will stay with them."

"Good." I held a dress out for him to take and carry through the store for me.

Later that night in the Palace dining room, family dinner was a somber affair. The children and Momma were well-behaved. Afterwards, when I retired to my wing with my children and husbands, my sitting room contained no traces of paint. Fresh roses filled my vases. At bedtime, Neema, Niklos, and Peter didn't dare ask for me to read a Jax comic. Instead, I read them a tale from Aurilius about a curious monkey who got into all sorts of trouble while trying to get into a crate of figs. They went to sleep with smiles on their faces and contented emotions.

Unlike how I had been parented as a small child, I'd made my point without raising either my hand or my voice. Had I handled things perfectly? Probably not, but my children and I were unique. I had to learn how to parent my future warlords. It was important to teach them to be firm and fair, and that actions had consequences. Their future actions would affect galaxies. Certain I'd managed things as best I could, I rested my head on Yukihyo's chest and went to sleep with a smile on my own lips.

Chapter Five

"Shh.... No, Daddy. Don't wake her up."

Neema's barely audible whisper had me cracking open an eyelid and closing my mouth.

"She will wake on her own any moment. I sense it," Yukihyo said in his quiet, deep monotone.

I heard the rattle of a cup on a saucer. Opening my other eye, I sat up. Neema stood at attention with a coffee service on the table beside her. She wore a purple shirt tucked into a pair of black pants, black boots, a black jacket, and had her soft, dove-grey hair up in a ponytail. "You look nice."

"Thank you, Mommy."

"Chirp chirp." Thunderdrop's long, black legs preceded him as he climbed up onto the bed. He sent me a mental image of the Academy.

Oh, yes. I'd agreed to allow my little princess to accompany me this morning. She was on her best behavior. Obviously, she'd been coached this morning. Her eyes were wide and innocent as she handed her daddy a cup of coffee to hand to me. Taking it, I closed my eyes and inhaled before taking a sip. My sigh made her drop her guard. Probing gently at her thoughts, I found out who had been advising her this morning. Neema had her Daddy Drex wrapped so tightly around her little finger that it was comical. He'd not only helped her to pick out her attire, but also had assisted in procuring for her the coffee tray. Then, he had assured her that I'd get into no trouble for bringing her along to the assembly this morning.

"Oh, that's right. We have plans this morning. I thought I was the one who was supposed to wake you up." She was studying my expression and my emotions which I pretended not to notice. "Very well. I need to feed your sisters and get dressed."

"Can I.... May I help?"

My jaw cracked on my yawn. Thunderdrop snuggled me under my chin.

Nico gave my butt a soft tap and got out of bed. Phillip had put an end to Nico's snoring, but only breakfast would silence the rumblings of his stomach. He said, "Pancakes." To Neema he said, "At ease. I have a mission for you." She nodded eagerly. "Go tell Rolf or Otto that the household of Princess Teagan desires pancakes on the patio."

Neema ran from my room. Thunderdrop leapt from the bed to the wall before chasing after her. Yawning again, I climbed over Yukihyo and went about my morning motherly duties before seeing to my own personal hygiene. I was in uniform when I joined Yukihyo, Neema, Nico, Niklos, Farowyn, Peter, Dario, and Fitz for breakfast. I had a mouth full of pancakes when Momma and Lady Galerius joined us.

"Mother, you look lovely this morning," Dario said as he stood and kissed his mother's cheek. All of the men stood. I kept chewing.

"Things seem put to rights, my sweet," Momma said in a coddling tone.

"Yes, so far, my day has been lovely." I watched her and waited. She wanted something other than my forgiveness.

"Are you going to the Academy?"

"Yes."

"Then, might we take our grandchildren out and about?"

Neema kept her expression as neutral as possible, but I could tell the request had her close to tears.

"Neema is coming with me, but I have no objections to Tabitha and Marielle accompanying you if their fathers have no plans for them."

Dario asked, "What are your plans?"

"Oh, just some shopping," Lady Galerius replied.

I asked, "What sort of shopping?" Dread filled me.

Momma said, "Oh, Teagan, don't be cranky. The children have grown since the arrival of their sisters. Most of their formal clothing needs to be donated or recycled, and since word has reached us of your impending sojourn to Chione, we thought it would be helpful to you if we were to see to the children's wardrobes."

Speaking up, Lady Galerius said, "Play clothing is also needed. Boys tend to be rather rough on fabrics. When Dario was a boy, I always selected styles with reinforced knees and elbows."

The look on Vice Admiral Dario Galerius' face was adorable. He was blushing. His lady mother was right. It was especially true with Peter. Keeping him out of the trees was impossible. To try would break his heart which was unthinkable. The Eloneave loved nothing more than the trees.

Yukihyo grunted. "While repairs are made to our ancestral home, I will hunt ice bear. Mother will reinforce their play clothes with the hides I take."

A horrified Lady Galerius clutched her throat with a soft, delicate hand. "Oh! Do be careful."

"Mother, the children will be nowhere close to the terrifying beasts." Dario's words didn't put his mother at ease.

I added, "It's too cold for Tabitha and Marielle on Chione. In addition to the climate, the fortress isn't currently stable enough for any of my children. We will remain aboard the *Empress* while we are there but will visit the land port, shops, and our neighboring clans. I'm hoping Adina will allow Galina to join us so that she can visit her grandmother. It has been too long."

With their worries put at ease, our mothers soon left with the twins, Niklos, Peter, and their nurses. The boys had expressions of stoic sailors walking the plank. Momma had insisted on taking them, too. I managed one more bite before Clark and Eli came out to the patio and hurried Neema and me out to the transport, not that she needed any urging. She climbed inside of Clark's transport and fastened her safety harness without being asked. Since she and Niklos had reached a height and weight deemed safe, they no longer had to sit in safety seats. It made Peter jealous, but he was small even by Eloneave standards. I'd tried to improve his spirits by showing him pictures of himself as a newborn and letting him see how much he'd grown. It wasn't until Fitz had given him a doll he'd had made to resemble him as an infant that he'd been able to truly understand how tiny he'd been when I'd become his mommy.

"Tiny," he'd said.

Fitz had nodded. "Your mommy was so careful with you."

Proudly, he'd stood tall. "I big now."

"Yes, you are much bigger and stronger."

Then, they'd gone off to play in the pool.

Eli asked, "Where did you go just now?"

Turning my face from the window, I smiled at him. "I was thinking about our children and how much they've grown."

Neema said, "Gama says you grow, Mommy. Gama says you're about to graduate, and she's real proud of you. I'm gonna be like you when I grow up and be an Inquisitor." She puckered her lips together and nodded her head.

A fierce blush rose up my neck and blossomed on my cheeks. I could feel my eyes growing hot. Then, Zared rushed in to emotionally calm and soothe me so that I wouldn't cry. Tears might confuse my daughter and detract from her enjoyment if only for the seconds it would take for her to empathically read me.

Eli said, "You are right to be proud of your mother. She continues to accomplish each of her goals."

Neema nodded. "We're here! We're here!" She struggled to free herself from her safety harness. "I'll be good, Mommy! Watch!"

Grinning like an idiot, I helped her, and hand-in-hand, we entered the Academy. Neema held her chin high and kept a serious expression on her little face. Keeping a smile from my own face was an impossibility. Dressing up as a princess wasn't of interest to a princess, but dressing up as a ruthless, dangerously intelligent hunter of criminals and traitors was great fun. Hearing the thoughts in my head, Zared chuckled softly.

The assembly had been called, so Clark and I led Neema to our classroom where our team waited for us to join them. Forgetting what she pretended to be, she lifted her hands up to Clark. Once he held her on his hip, she kissed his cheek. She said to the guys, "I'm a cadet today. See Neema's jacket? See Neema's hair? I'm just like Mommy." She raised her grey eyebrows.

Cedrenus said, "I was just about to say how much you look like your mother."

A blush rose in her cheeks.

He said, "Let's go."

We could hear ensigns and cadets making their way to the assembly. I fell in line with the boys. It was a good thing that Clark was carrying Neema. She wouldn't have been able to keep up. Soon, we all stood at attention in front of our seats, and remained standing until everyone was present and silent.

The headmaster took the stage. "You may be seated." Between us, Neema scowled in her seat. She couldn't see over the young men in front of us. Fortunately, she knew better than to make a peep and folded her hands on her lap, mimicking me. "Most of you have either completed your final course work or are in the process of doing so. To complete your training, you have a challenge. Each team called here today is to complete a mission objective. Individually, each of you will be held responsible for a specific element of the mission."

The way he said it made it clear. Don't fuck up on your main job. I wondered what mine would be.

"Whether you pass or fail depends upon your knowledge, training, ability to depend upon each other's strengths, and to compensate for each other's weaknesses." He paused, taking the time to slice each and everyone present with his eyes. "Should you succeed in your missions, you will graduate and be awarded the rights and responsibilities of Inquisitors of the Parvac Empire at which point you will receive further training and missions best suited to your levels of proficiency." I observed Clark and Cedrenus from the corners of my eyes. The headmaster's meaning was clear. Teams who failed their missions would be trapped in desk jobs without hope of ever doing fieldwork. My Papa had insisted on it as being my only option, but the guys didn't have to share in my fate. "Assignments are being delivered now. You are permitted to use any resources personally available to you or to your Houses. Dismissed."

I stood with everyone else, lifted Neema to my hip, and turned to follow Cedrenus as we filed out. No excited chatter filled the halls. Instead, each of us seemed to be deep within our thoughts. Even Neema remained silent until we entered our classroom. "Daddy Eli!" She urged me to let her down so that she could go to him.

Eli's eyes were a printed page where I read what I needed to know. He'd submitted our mission. I was sure of it.

Trying to distract Neema, I directed her over to my work station. "Here, baby."

Offended she said, "I am not a baby! I'm a big girl."

"Neema," Eli said in warning.

She scowled at him before turning the attention of her furious jade-green eyes at me. The sight of those eyes filled my heart with love. "I mean it as a term of endearment, not as a definition. We've been over this," I patiently replied.

Thoughts turning inward, she seemed to recall a previous conversation we'd had on the topic. "Oh, yeah. Okay. I do work now." She climbed onto the chair and began amusing herself with my screen. I pressed a few commands and opened a beginner's flight simulation program for her. Gleefully, she immediately crashed a fighter jet.

Levi said, "We are assigned the capture of Colwyn Winks Taylor of Cassini. We are to coerce him into cooperating with us to procure a rare book of Pariea lore from a monastery on Bondi Prime."

Excitement sprang to life within me. Eli had found the lead for me and was giving us a chance to prove ourselves. Opening the file which had been sent to us, I studied our assignment. Levi, Clark, Tad, and Tyler were specifically tasked with security. They were our muscle. Cedrenus had been assigned as our surveillance expert, and Binder and Ross were in charge of target acquisition. My heart sped up in disbelief at my job. Pilot. "Captain? I'm the fucking captain?" I glanced around at them. Hope, disbelief, and gratitude were like fireworks exploding in my chest.

Ross shrugged. "You are the best pilot of the eight of us."

Eli said, "If we leave in four hours, we will arrive on Aurilius in time for Consul Dano's gala."

Four hours? Children, pets, and husbands.... How would I manage it?

Clark said, "We can take the stealth ship we have docked in berth...."

"Clark," I interrupted as I touched his wrist to get his attention. "We can use anything belonging to our Houses."

He met my gaze.

"I'm assuming control of the *Empress*."

He gave me his cute, lopsided grin.

"We can use the bridge stations for research and planning?" Stayton asked.

After checking the rules, I nodded. "Yes, you will serve as my bridge crew in addition to your mission objectives with our team leader's approval." I glanced up at Clark.

Clark said, "Permission granted."

"Will you serve as my first officer?"

"Nothing would please me more." Clark grinned down at me.

"Captain Ricimer, Commander Genso, and Lieutenant Commander Glous will accompany us, but they must stay off the bridge." I tapped away at my vid-screen. Instructor Rovek would be supervising us. If my captain had to step in and take over for me, I'd fail my assignment. Moving to the side of the room where Neema could still see me, I called Captain Ricimer.

His calm, stern face filled my screen. Papa had assigned him to captain my starship because he trusted the male to keep me safe. Ricimer was experienced, a skilled pilot, dangerously intelligent, and completely loyal to his Emperor. In essence, he was just like every male with whom Papa surrounded me. My thoughts darted to Zared, Izaac, Jazon, and Xavier, the dangerous, ruthless males with whom I'd surrounded myself. I could feel their minds at the edges of my consciousness, determined to allow me to succeed or to fail on my own. It made me love them even more. Returning my full attention to the male on my screen, I noticed a smudge of dirt near one of his brown eyes. He was outside. Puzzled, I asked, "What are you doing?"

"Based upon your confused scowl, I'm going to assume you find my presence in my garden hard to believe."

"Yes, you're always on the bridge or at the land port."

He moved his device farther from his face to show me pink and orange sky above and neat rows of newly planted things below. "Since your confused scowl is now apparent curiosity, allow me to explain. These are tomato plants from Earth."

"Wow. Really?"

Neema sang, "Spaghetti spaghetti spaghetti! Bam! Bam! Bam!" She destroyed another simulated fighter ship.

Forcing my attention back to the task at hand, I toned out Neema and the guys. The latter of which were making their own plans and arrangements. "I'm at the Academy. We've been given our final semester assignments. I need to assume command of the *Empress* and travel to the Laconian Sector and perhaps the outer reaches." His eyes held a hint of something I didn't recognize. Was it amusement? "You and the crew can come, but you can't help us."

"Oh, I understand." Now, he did grin. "When do we depart?"

"In four hours. Will she be ready?"

His chuckle was faint. "I don't know. You tell me, captain. We'll be aboard." He bent, pressed a button, and an automated sprinkler began watering his plants. "Vacationing in the Laconian Sector should be enjoyable." He smirked. "Four hours? Will you be ready?"

"Okay! Bye!" Ending the call, my hand trembled a bit as I searched my vid-screen for links to the *Empress*. Finding what I needed, I sent out the call to the crew to prepare for immediate departure. Next, I made a group call. With the sweetest expression I could muster, I explained the situation to Yukihyo, Nico, Quaid, Fitz, Zared, Drex, Farowyn, Dario, and Izaac. Eli stood at my side before helping Neema to close her flight simulation program. I could hear Clark speaking to my dick-in-law. What surprised me was that there were no arguments about anything I had to say. All I got was cooperation.

"I'll pack for you," Nico offered.

"Thank you. I need the...."

Eli, as if he'd read my mind, interrupted, "I'll secure the jewels."

"Okay."

Fitz had already turned away and was calling to Pierce and Lorca to help him pack for the children. He ended his participation in our group call.

"We have our household under control, Lady Wife," Yukihyo said before signing off to make arrangements.

"We will meet you at the land port. Keep Neema with you. Worry only about your mission." Nico's calm assurance put me completely at ease. He and the others each vanished from my viewer.

Feeling more confident, I stood a little taller. I hadn't married them all for only their good looks. They knew their shit and had my back. "Clark, can you drive us to the land port? I need to conduct a pre-flight check of my ship."

Preparing a starship for a long voyage required far more effort than what a four-crew member shuttle necessitated. Fortunately, I excelled at compartmentalizing and being painstakingly meticulous. Being in control of things empowered me emotionally. After getting ourselves out to the transport and seated, I skimmed the pre-flight reports from the medical bay. My thoughts strayed briefly to my life aboard *Tora*. When I'd been able to buy my own clothing, a basic human requirement, for the first time, I'd spent hours arranging everything. Feeling in control and making order of chaos had been a euphoric experience. Emotionally, I'd been starving for the sense of personal empowerment it had given me. To anyone else, it wouldn't have been of any consequence to get new things and put them away. To me, it had meant freedom from an abusive, poverty-stricken childhood. My thoughts and plans kept me occupied all the way to the land port, to my ship, into the lift, and onto the bridge. Pressing a button on my command chair, I called the medical bay.

"Dr. Savelli here."

"Doctor, I see the antibiotics are not fully stocked." Steadily holding his gaze, I waited.

"A courier will arrive within the hour. In addition to the antibiotics and antivirals, I've ordered an array of pediatric medications. I'll be prepared for any known illnesses the little princesses or princes can throw at me." His reassuring smile had me smiling back at him.

"Excellent. Carry on." Ending our communication, I glanced down at Neema. She was coloring and occupied, so my attention moved to the crew complement, ship stores, fueling, and weapons.

"You gonna blow stuff up, Mommy?" Neema had crayons stuck behind each ear and got up to stand next to me where she peered intently at my weapons manifest.

"Hopefully, not."

Aghast, her mouth dropped open. "Don't you want to make stuff go boom?"

Turning my chair slightly, I lifted her up to my lap.

"You got lots of booms you could make."

"You're right. The *Empress* has an impressive artillery. If we have to defend ourselves, we will do so. I'll do whatever it takes to keep you, your brothers, sisters, and fathers safe. However, it's better if we can solve our problems peacefully by talking about them."

Neema sighed. "Major General Varro said even though Nik, Peter, and me know how to punch and kick, we can't do it for no reason. It's only to protect ourselves."

Ridley Varro hadn't only replaced my beloved Luca Braga on my Military Advisory Committee, but he was also training my children to be Parvac Warriors. "Major General Varro is right." Gently, I twirled the end of her ponytail around my finger.

"What if them Alux show up?"

"Let's hope they don't."

Turning around sideways on my lap, she smirked. "Hoping isn't a good strategy, Mommy. You *needs* a plan."

"I'm working on one."

"Is it blowing them up?"

I answered her with a smile and a kiss to her forehead before gently shoving her from my lap. "Color and do it in your book, not on my carpet."

She snorted at me.

I went back to meticulously checking on ship systems, the crew manifest, weapons, and supplies.

The lift doors opened. "Permission to come aboard?" Cedrenus had an excited twinkle in his eyes. He was asking for all of them. Binder and Ross each had an energetic motivation that practically zapped like static electricity. However, they hid their emotions well as Inquisitors tended to do. To anyone other than an empath, the guys might currently appear coldly bored. I knew differently. They were excited. My own feelings were leaning more toward nervousness. It seemed as though I'd been preparing for this moment for all of my adult life.

"Permission granted." Turning back to what I'd been doing, I listened as they moved to their work stations.

A whisper of touch caressed my senses. It was Zared. The bridge faded and was replaced by what he saw, my sitting room in the Palace. It was filled with packed luggage. "We will arrive in an hour. Are your preparations going well?"

Responding telepathically, I said, "I'm waiting on two supply trucks and all of you." He sensed my nerves but didn't soothe them out of respect. My console alerted me to an incoming message. I read it and scowled. Out loud, I said, "Galina and Rhianna have permission to join us. They can train on Chione while visiting." I narrowed my eyes at Clark. "Sadly, they are bringing your father with them."

Clark had an annoyed look on his face which had me expecting an argument. We were good at arguing with each other. Instead, he said, "He's doing this on purpose." He tapped at his console, checking weapons and defensive shielding.

My tone changed to one of uncertainty. "What?"

Turning around in his seat, he said, "He's coming along to take over in case I mess up. He treats me like a child. I'm a grown male with a wife and children. Soon, I'll hold the title and rank of Inquisitor."

I smirked at him and turned around in my chair.

Wounded, he asked, "Don't you care?"

"Of course, I care! I know exactly how you feel. You aren't alone. My own husbands treat me the same way!" Turning back around to face him, I angrily jabbed my finger in the air at him. Oblivious to what he could have done to annoy me, he stared dumbstruck. Levi, Ross, Cedrenus, and the others, knowing full well what he'd done, tried to make themselves invisible. It didn't work. "You treat me like I'm helpless! I'm going to be an Inquisitor, the same as you! Am I not a grown woman with husbands and children? Am I not capable? Instead of trusting me, you wait for me to mess up so you can take over!"

Turning red in the face, Clark stood only to kneel before me. A crayon crunched under his knee.

Neema made a growly sound of annoyance. "He did it, Mommy. Don't blame me when it has colors in it. It was Daddy Clark, not Neema!" Her tone was full of disdain as she huffed and kept coloring.

There was nothing contrite about Clark's expression. In fact, he was practically fuming with indignation. We were going to argue. However, as Parvac males tended to react to angry females, he had positioned himself in a non-threatening way at my feet. "I do not!" he yelled.

Lifting a foot, I braced it against his chest and shoved with all my might using my chair's support as an assist. It knocked him off balance so I had room to stand. "Oh, yes you fucking do!"

"Oh, no I fucking don't!"

Pacing away and back, I stared in disbelief into his angry eyes. "Our marriage contract, Clark! You've crippled me as a warrior with your clause! I have to come to you to do my fighting for me? Are you fucking serious? I trusted you! You used my trust against me and manipulated me!" Furious, I went to the lift. "I'm going to check on the fueling situation."

Neema jumped up and ran after me.

As the doors of the lift closed, I mumbled, "Just like your fucking father." We glared at each other until they had shut all of the way.

The fresh air off the ship was just what I'd needed to cool my temper. Taking in the sights and sounds, I relaxed as much as was possible. Parvacian land ports were unlike any others which I had ever before experienced. They were order where the others were chaos. I took Neema's hand in mine. The land port bustled with activity. All around, ships were being readied for departure.

Eli appeared at my side as if he'd materialized out of thin air.

Squinting off into the distance, I asked, "Is that Farowyn's ship?"

"Yes, he is taking his own starship as are Bosh, Galerius, Licinius, and I. Likewise, Valen will lead our fleet in the event of an Alux attack. Yukihyo, Nico, Fitz, Zared, Clark, and Izaac will journey with you aboard the *Empress*. It is our consensus that seven warships will deter any aggressions."

It wasn't only my team's mission about which I had to concern myself, but also the weighty concerns of the Cosmos Coalition. We'd thought it prudent to multitask and deliver weaponry to our allies. The protection of innocent civilians was paramount. Standing as we were near the boarding ramp, it wasn't possible for us to pretend like we didn't notice the arrival of the Palace transport. The ambassador with the recently reattached tongue had arrived. Eli turned to give my silent, ever-present bodyguard a questioning look, but Cormac didn't respond in any way. I clenched my teeth together. Seven ships were travelling to the Laconian Sector. Couldn't he seek passage on one of them? "Are my ladies coming with us? I haven't had a moment to ask them." I inclined my head to the Ambassador as his driver drove him aboard. Through the transport's window, I could see that his face was still quite swollen.

"Lady Terre and her small entourage shall arrive shortly."

Hand on hip, I stared at him. "Fuck. Is her mother coming?"

Sunlight caught at Eli's black hair making it shine. "No, why?"

"Why did you say her entourage? What the fuck is that?"

"It's more efficient than listing her husband and son." He shrugged. "Rovek is joining us. However, Tracy and Jazon are not, and neither are Sparrow and Xavier."

"Oh." The word was a quiet, accepting affirmative.

Sensing my disappointment, he said, "Sparrow is needed in her weapons lab and became overly emotional from feared anticipation of Tracy's impending abandonment of her to go off into the Laconian Sector with you and Terre."

"You don't need to explain. I get it. She didn't have much notice."

Sparrow was usually good with taking things in stride, but post-pregnancy hormones had wreaked havoc upon her. She needed Tracy's support and would have it. The four of us had become more than family. We were friends. Naturally, Terre would want to escape her mother and her many male suitors. She'd go with me anywhere at any time with a minute's notice. I loved my friends, and they knew it. Having Terre and Violet along would be all of the female companionship I needed.

Eli's expression hardened. It had settled on Ambassador Ness. The Palace transport had left. Now, Ness walked down the ramp. Even with the Parvac Warrior who'd cut out his tongue standing behind me, he approached me. Either he was brave or stupid. Bowing, he spoke telepathically. "Forgive me." It was simple and direct.

Pulling on Zared's abilities had become second-nature to me, so I replied in kind. "I forgive you." The power of my telepathic response made beads of sweat appear on his upper lip. I vocalized to him where his quarters aboard were located. He probably had already been told, and his luggage had probably already been delivered to his quarters. However, saying it was my polite way of giving him permission to get lost. I was too busy to deal with Ambassador Ness. I had a ship to prepare for departure. Where were those last two deliveries? Ness gave me a polite bow, and a crewman escorted him away.

Telepathically, Zared explained, "For the sake of Parvac and Laconian relations, it was decided that he would forgo the invitation he received from Stig and journey with us. Lady and Lord Montgomery are journeying with Captain Bosh aboard *Teagan's Treasure*."

Hearing the name Quaid had bestowed upon his warship brought a smile to my lips. I could just hear Yukihyo's snide comment the moment we'd first heard it. "*Teagan's Treasure*. He thinks he is your treasure."

Eli said, "The jewels are secure in the vault in your closet."

"The diadem and necklace?" They were so pretty and sparkly. Smiling, I considered wearing them but thought they were too much for the bridge. Neema looked up at me hopefully. "No, Neema, not those. I'll share some other sparkles with you." She scowled at me. "I'll share good stuff. I promise."

Eli touched my cheek to draw my attention to himself. "If I may have leave, I will ready my own ship."

"Not until I get hugs and kisses."

In a swift motion that reminded me of exactly who he was, Eli took me into his arms, dipped me back, and kissed me completely senseless. Breathless and once again upright, I stared up into his eyes with absolutely no idea what he waited to hear. Neema nudged my thigh. "Oh, right. Yes, go ahead and do your thing."

When he turned to walk away, I smacked him hard on his ass. When he turned his head to look at me, there was a passionate fire in his eyes. I grinned at him and winked. Two could play the "fan the sexual fires" game. Luckily, my hormones hadn't yet gone haywire. My Parvac post-delivery hormones were yet another thing I might need to compartmentalize so that I could complete my mission, if I could.

My vid-screen gave an alert. The land port crew had completed fueling my ship. However, rather than the satisfaction which I should have felt at having yet another item checked off of my list of things to do, I felt an odd sensation of trepidation. It was as if the collective emotions of the myriad individuals at the land port had drawn in a steadying breath of nervous anticipation. My own telepathic senses were being bombarded with emphatic yet gentle urgency from every bond I held.

Neema felt it too. Into the sudden hushed stillness, she asked, "Mommy, what's that?" She lifted her face toward the pink and orange sky. The crayons fell from behind her ears to the ground.

Following her gaze upward, my eyes widened, and I drew in a sharp breath. Bending, I snatched her up and ran with all of my might up the ramp. The sky above had begun to churn as if boiling. It was something I'd seen before and had hoped to never see again, but I hadn't gotten my wish. They were back.

Chapter Six

Sirens blared across the land port and all of Parvac. Warships shot up into the sky from as close as a mile away. Cormac's footsteps pounded along behind mine. A piercing sound grew louder. From the already raging battle above Parvac, jagged, twisted metal fragments the size of transports sped heavily down, pelting the ground around us hard enough to make it shake and to send chunks of cement flying. Shielding Neema from debris with my body, I clutched her to my chest and ran to the lift with my bodyguard at my back.

While pushing the command to take us to the bridge, I shouted, "Battle stations!" Red lights flashed around us, and as the lift doors opened, those flashing colors greeted us there as well. My team focused on their work stations' bright screens and on active communications with Fleet command around the bridge.

Adding to the frenetic activity was Stayton as he relayed all incoming orders from Parvac command, specifically those from Admiral Valen. "All warships, prepare to engage the invading Alux forces!"

A loud boom from outside the ship made me cringe and lift a hand to protect Neema's head. She covered her ears with her hands and kept her legs tightly wrapped around my waist. I could feel my artificial heart pounding in my ringing ears. Whatever had struck the ground outside sent more chunks of cement flying up to smash against the viewports. Cedrenus stared at me and waited for my orders. A knot formed in my throat. The Alux fired missiles down like rain on the land port.

"Mommy." The word was filled with true fear, an emotion she'd never before experienced.

Niklos had felt it because of the Alux. Now, they were introducing her to it. The bastards. I'd be damned if I allowed my daughter to cower before anyone. An indignant determination fueled me and eroded the knot in my throat. I wasn't going to be a sitting target. It was time to get the fuck out of here. When I spoke, I barely recognized the cold, calculated tone of my words. "Weapons, I want to see the Alux vessel which fired upon us exploding into pieces so small that they become nothing more than incinerated dust particles falling down through the atmosphere to our home world's surface." Smiling at Neema, I kissed her forehead, took my seat, and sat her amidst her colors and books at my feet. "My Princess will not fear dust. Will she?"

"No, Mommy," she said earnestly.

Shifting my immediate attention from her to my controls, I took the *Empress* up in a spray of weapons fire from Cedrenus and Stayton. Dozens of warships engaged in battle above Parvac. A blast hit our hull, jolting us, and sent Neema sprawling.

"Mommy!" Her surprise and terror raked against my senses.

"It's okay." I took an evasive course and increased speed while the boys fired. "Scooch over here and sit on the carpet between my feet. Hold onto my legs like a harness. That's it. Good girl." My bodyguard moved from station to station eager to offer assistance. "Cormac, go order the crew to ready one of Sparrow's special weapons we were planning to deliver to our allies. Our guests may be uninvited, but it's no reason for us to be inhospitable."

The sound of the lift doors opening and closing as he left to obey my order was the only affirmation I needed. Around the *Empress*, the battle raged. Parvac warships bombarded the Alux ships with synthetic spider venom nanite missiles. Our ships had all been stocked with the weapons. We hadn't been sitting idly by for months. Initially, Thunderdrop had taught us how to fight the Alux, but when the predatory aliens had invaded Arachne, the Silk spiders there had confirmed it. Their neurotoxin was lethal to the Alux. Now, our forces were engaged in vicious battles, and they were leaving devastation in their wake. Properly armed and in our own territory, we were kicking their doll-like fucking asses. They had been courting death when they'd attacked our home world yet again.

"But you knew you courted death."

"What, Captain?" Stayton asked.

Clark answered for me. "This is a distraction."

I ordered, "Scan for environmental and biological weapons." I studied the battle as it raged on the starfield on my viewer. Obeying an order from Admiral Valen, I held my position and anxiously awaited my next incoming order. "What are they after?" Resting my elbows on my armrests, I steepled my fingers and contemplated while watching our missiles tear through the nearest alien ship. Alux were ripped from the hull breaches and sucked out into space where their eyes burst. "Clean up the fucking mess," I ordered.

Cedrenus blanketed the area with laser fire, obliterating the floating alien corpses.

"Our ship is a fire-breathing dragon, Mommy." Neema's eyes were wide as she looked up at me from where she clutched my legs.

"No one frightens you and gets away with it, my sweet." Examining the information as it came in, I searched for answers. Why the sudden attack? The Alux knew we could destroy them. They had to be here for a reason other than trying to assassinate me. An order came allowing me to change our position only if necessary. Expecting to see Cormac, I scowled at the sight of Ambassador Ness. The presence of the odious ambassadorial piece of shit set my mind racing. Immediately, I silently scolded myself. I'd told him he had my forgiveness. He watched the scene through the main viewport as Cedrenus continued to target and incinerate Alux corpses. "Stayton, get me Stig's location."

Seconds later, Stig's ship, besieged by Alux vessels and barely managing to keep them at bay, filled my screen. Taking evasive action, I maneuvered my warship away from the fray at maximum speed. Eli and Kane, captains of the nearest warships, took full advantage of my departure. It was as though the *Empress* had been the bait in a deathtrap. Shrapnel and debris shot around us like spray from a gigantic water hose let loose against our stern, crashing into and ricocheting in the vacuum of the *Empress'* wake.

No, the Empire had wasted no time researching and developing weaponry. Having had captured Alux ships and specimens during our previous encounters had facilitated our efforts. I hailed Stig's ship. Tapping at my screen, I calculated our speed and distance. "Estimated time of arrival is twenty minutes at top speed."

Stig's captain gave a quick nod of his head in acknowledgement. His features hardened. "Brace for impact!"

"Stayton, I've lost communications with Stig's ship. Can you get it back?" My attempts at reestablishing them kept failing.

Tad's brow furrowed in concentration as he tried to bypass the interference. "It's being blocked."

All we could do was watch the attack on our viewers as we raced to intercept. Neema was leaving marks on my legs with her fingernails even though I continuously soothed her. "Everything will be alright," I whispered to her.

Communications suddenly flared to life, but not to Stig's ship. The main viewer filled with Kane's face. "What are you doing, tiny cousin?" His tone was deceptively sweet.

"With you and Eli busily vanquishing our enemies, I deemed it necessary to investigate the purpose of this suicidal diversionary tactic."

The two of them had quickly dispatched of our opponents and now flanked the *Empress*. Their vacated positions were filled by other captains who were eager to fight. Both Kane and Eli managed to surpass my current speed. Neither male required any further explanation. Being several strategic steps ahead of me, they were already coordinating their attack. From each of their flight bays, fighter ships deployed and took formation.

Cedrenus said, "We're being hailed."

Raising an eyebrow, I split my screen and answered the hail. "Uncle Kagan," I greeted.

"Fall back, Ensign Probus."

When I opened my mouth, the expression on his face had me questioning the wisdom of any attempt at verbalization. "Yes, sir."

It had been the correct reply. He vanished from my screen. I dropped speed.

Cedrenus reported, "Eight of ours on our port side."

Two of those eight warships stayed with us. The others sped after Eli and Kane.

"Stig hadn't gotten far before being attacked. They must have had him under surveillance." Clark paced the bridge in front of me like a caged tiger starved for bloody flesh.

An unexpected voice startled me. "Stig was returning to Earth with the stellar targeting system," Ambassador Ness condescendingly supplied. His words sounded as swollen as his face and neck appeared.

We all stared at him.

With snark, I replied, "Yes, I am aware." Had he forgotten my role in the Cosmos Coalition?

Affronted, he said, "I am sharing information above your rather inexperienced crew's security level in order to be of assistance to you, Princess Teagan."

Calmly, I explained, "On the bridge of my ship, please address me as Ensign Probus or Captain if you prefer. Furthermore, security clearance or not, those of us here are a mere assignment away from holding the rank of Inquisitors."

Ness rolled his eyes and huffed.

Tyler stepped over to him and slowly looked him up and down. "Blue," he said.

Clearly unsettled from the attention, Ness asked, "Excuse me?"

"Blue is the color of the underwear you put on this morning," Tyler explained. "You pleasure yourself to holograms of...."

"That's quite enough! You have made your point, young sir! How obvious it is to me now in how the Alux were able to pinpoint Stig's location when students are privy to matters of the highest security." The disdain in his tone, had it been placed on a scale, would have weighed more than I had during my final month of pregnancy with Niklos. He lifted a handkerchief to his lip.

"You arrogant fucker, I'm in command of the Cosmos Coalition." I shook my head at myself, so much for being diplomatic with the male. I couldn't let him goad me.

Tad asked, "Shall I cut out his tongue for you since Inquisitor Gordian is otherwise engaged?"

"No, cousin."

Ness stretched out his neck in an asinine attempt to make himself look taller.

Groaning, I lost my battle. "Don't do that, Ness. It doesn't have the intimidating effect you're hoping for."

"No, it doesn't," Tyler said. "It makes you look like a stretched-out turd that got stuck and is waiting for gravity to help it drop."

"Oh, Mommy," Neema scolded as if I was supposed to make Tyler behave.

"Yes, it sounded harsh, Tyler. She's right. Ness, I can only do so much to protect you and my carpet from the combined anger of my bridge crew who you have just insulted." I gazed down at the pretty white, black, and grey marbleized design and scowled at the crayon marks.

"Sorry, Mommy."

"It's okay, my sweet. We shall give the bridge a good scrubbing once this is all done."

She gazed up at me with her beautiful jade-green eyes. "Can we bake cookies, too?"

"Yes, darling. We shall bake whatever sort you like."

Clark bent and gathered together scattered crayons and books which he returned to her. Smiling once more, she returned her attention to the scene she'd been coloring in the book which she'd convinced Drex to buy for her. The male didn't possess the fortitude to deny her anything. One utterance of "Daddy Drex" was all it took.

Ness looked down at the page and visibly paled, an impressive feat with his bruising and swelling.

Red crayon in hand, Neema hummed to herself as she filled in the blood spray spewed across the page from the neck of a multi-tentacled saber-toothed cartoon alien monster. She'd yet to begin coloring the muscular Parvac warrior on the page. Well, she'd colored his knife blade a sparkly pink.

Clearing his throat, Ness asked, "Are Parvac blades forged of pink metal?"

"You haven't had enough experience with Cormac's blades to know the answer?" Tad snarked.

"No, he is much too quick," Ness quietly responded, fearful he might even now be listening.

Neema answered Ness. "Sparkly pink is my favorite."

"How lovely." His reply sounded more wary than sincere. Then, the sweet smile she gave him had him taking a few steps away.

Sensors blared warning across every station across the bridge. "Brace for impact!" Clark warned.

My star map suddenly appeared as if it was nothing more than a black, inky page dropped suddenly in a shallow pan of water. The inky space seemed as though it was becoming spread out and diluted. Fear for all of those aboard, my daughter, husband, friends, and crew, threatened to choke and cripple me as what I was seeing and what it meant washed over my awareness like a freezing gust of wind.

Spinning the *Empress* away, I engaged maximum speed and followed in the path Eli had taken his warship minutes earlier. "Sorry, Uncle Kagan," I muttered. "I'm getting us the fuck away from whatever the fuck that is." Neema scooted back over to me and clutched my legs. The ships that had been flanking me followed and kept pace.

"It's a wormhole!" Stayton reported.

Eli's image suddenly filled my viewer. "Get to the surface. They planned this."

"Yes, sir," was my immediate reply. His image began to break up. I could see Eli shouting, his eyes hardening as all traces of loving husband vanished, supplanted by the Inquisitor at his core.

"Incoming!" Stayton reported.

"Shields at maximum," Tyler said.

There was no time. The exploded hulls of the two Parvac warships that had been protecting us slammed into the *Empress* and sent her spinning through explosions. My head slammed into my viewer with a loud crack. Ness was hurled across the bridge and skidded to a halt at Neema's feet and mine.

My hands flew over my controls. "Get me something!" I yelled before switching to the main view port on the bridge as my most reliable means of navigation. A jolt of electricity zapped my fingertips. Yanking my hands away, I cautioned everyone. "Power surges!"

"This shouldn't be happening," Tad said, but he kept his body away from the control panels just the same until the sparking electricity dancing across our systems grounded itself out. Our ship sensors had become unreliable. We all knew it.

"Mommy," Neema cried.

Rather than words, I sent her my emotions. They were rage and battle hunger. The Alux would pay for their attack and for the warriors who now died around us, their screams silenced by space as they spilled out of hull breaches. "Binder, rescue operations." The bodies were being pulled backwards as if caught in a current. I was forced to correct our speed to compensate for a powerful drag. We were slowing down.

"Aye, aye, sir." He stood but slammed against our own hull before he could complete a step.

Stig's ship crashed into the *Empress*. My head was forced down to my knees. I couldn't lift it up. "Report!" The bridge lights had blacked out. Now, only the red emergency lighting kept us from utter darkness. They made the deck appear as though I viewed it through a wash of blood.

Silence.

"Report!"

Groaning reached my ears.

Able to move once more, I reached down to Neema, picked her up, and brought her to my lap. Twisting around, she circled my neck with her arms and hid her face against my shoulder. "It's okay, baby," I whispered.

Stig's ship was now adrift after having slammed into us. Most of my ship's systems were down. However, my grapplers still functioned. Deploying them, I locked onto Stig's vessel, securing it from drifting any farther off course.

"Are you alright?" Clark asked as he staggered over to my command chair. He wasn't talking to me which despite everything put a huge grin on my face and filled my heart with joy. He rested his hand on Neema's head.

"I'm okay, Daddy Gravy."

I didn't have it in me to laugh.

The lift doors opened. Dr. Savelli and Cormac summed up what they observed. After checking Neema, the doctor turned his attention to me. Touching my forehead with an antiseptic doused cloth, he drew a hiss from me.

"How many fingers am I holding up?" I asked him as I lifted my middle finger.

"Your humor is not infectious. However, a head wound could become so if not sanitized, sutured, and bandaged."

"Whatever." I held still.

"Be brave, Mommy. You got a bad booboo. Gravy, pick me up."

Cormac helped Binder get himself upright. Tyler, Cedrenus, Ross, Stayton, and Levi looked banged up but managed to return to their work stations from where they'd been tumbled about. Then, he checked my console and then that of Cedrenus, trying to get readings.

Checking my offline star chart was a wasted effort. The main view port didn't provide much help either. Other than Stig's ship, there was lots of wreckage floating around but not much else.

"What happened to the stars?" Ness asked. He struggled up to his knees and lurched over to get a better view. I turned my head to see what he meant.

"Stay still," Dr. Savelli gently ordered.

I couldn't. I had to see for myself. Getting up, I went over and stood beside Ness. We stared out at grey and black smoke-like clouds and the electric strikes that passed between them. A burst of electricity struck Stig's ship and then raced along the grapplers to mine before passing from my hull and back out again into the clouds. Tyler hissed and shook out his hand as our hull was struck by yet another charge that sizzled throughout our systems.

Cormac said, "We are in a wormhole. The Alux opened it a second before we could begin our counter offensive. They forced Stig's ship into it which must have been their plan all along. They meant to destroy us along with the other two warships. However, Stig's ship slammed into us and took us into the wormhole with it."

"How do we get out of it?" Stayton asked.

He shook his head. "I don't know."

I ordered, "Get me a line of communication to Stig's ship." Returning to my seat, I allowed Dr. Savelli to suture the gash in my forehead.

"Unable to comply," Tad reported.

Stayton said, "We have life support and emergency systems only."

Incredulously, I asked, "So, basically, we're just drifting along this wormhole tethered to Stig's ship?"

Binder's expression said it all.

"Alright, get out your vid-screens. Put those calculative skills to work. Based upon where we were, where might we end up?"

"How the fuck should I know?" Binder asked.

Shocked, without having even touched the console, I stared around Dr. Savelli, who still worked on my injury, at Binder.

He ran a hand through his hair. "We're stuck without navigation in a wormhole. There's no way for me to calculate shit."

Cedrenus said, "He's right. The best we can do is collect atmospheric data."

"How? Everything has gone haywire," Binder reminded him.

I gazed down at the wedding ring on my finger. "Put a drone in a collector," I suggested.

The two of them left the bridge.

"How long will we be adrift?" Ness asked.

"I don't know. Is there any way to fly over to Stig's ship to check for survivors?" I asked. Dr. Savelli held my chin still to keep me from turning my head toward Cormac.

The Inquisitor said, "It wouldn't be advisable to attempt it either by fighter ship or space suit in these conditions. All we can do for now is wait."

"Can we make repairs while we wait?" I asked. Dr. Savelli had a firm grip on my chin, but from the corner of my eye, I could see my cracked, blood-smeared command console.

Clark said, "We'll need to check the ship deck by deck."

"Put teams together from whatever crew we have and do it," I ordered. "Cormac, figure out what weapons we still have and get them ready. As soon as power is back online, I want to be able to defend ourselves. I want my fighter ship pilots on alert. We can manually open the flight bay doors if we have to."

He saluted me and left the bridge.

"Mommy, I've got to go pee."

"So do I, baby. Let's go." I held my hand out to her as soon as Dr. Savelli finished suturing my wound.

He said, "I'll be in Medical."

Quietly, I asked, "Any casualties?"

"Thankfully, no. Some broken ribs, abrasions, and a few lacerations have been reported."

I nodded. "Carry on." Standing, I said, "Tyler, you have the bridge."

Dark eyes met mine. He slid into my command chair as I left it. Neema and I joined Dr. Savelli in the lift. We exited the dimly lit lift on Deck Two leaving him to continue alone to Deck Three. Releasing my hand, Neema ran through the central living area to her quarters on the Imperial Deck. The emergency lighting made it seem as though we should be in the middle of a sleep cycle.

Chef somberly watched me from the other side of the room near the dining table. "Coffee?" I asked him as I went to my own quarters. The questions I'd seen in his eyes could wait a moment. I went into my bathroom. I'd only just taken a seat on the waste unit when Neema barged in.

"I'll wash my hands in here with you so you won't be scared." She glanced over at me before sticking her hands in the sink. She washed her hands and face. Then, she picked up my brush.

While she worked on her hair, I washed up. Meeting my own green and gold eyes in the mirror, I sighed. I'd cracked my head hard enough on my console to give myself two black eyes. Also, a goose egg had been forming, but Dr. Savelli had done something to halt the swelling when he'd stitched me up. Taking a cleansing cloth, I gently washed my face. Neema handed the brush to me. Quickly, I swept my hair up into a high ponytail. Neema didn't need to know about my doubts and fears and neither did my crew.

"You're afraid." I crouched to look her in the eyes.

Her embarrassment touched my senses.

"No, it's okay to be afraid. Only stupid people don't feel fear at times like this."

"Really, Mommy?" She tilted her head to the side.

"Really." Standing, I gave her my hand and waited until her fingers gripped mine. "We are on a mission, so we will be brave, strong, and remember our training."

"Is Daddy coming to save us?" she asked in a warbly tone.

She referred to Yukihyo. He was always simply Daddy. "We can rescue ourselves, my sweet. We are, after all, Parvac princesses. Are we not? Are we not Parvac Warrior Princesses as well?"

Pursing her lips, she raised an eyebrow in thought and then nodded. Leading the way into my closet, I found what I had in mind. The box opened with a palm scan. Watching me intently, she exclaimed, "Oh! A shock stick!"

"Yes, this is a special shock stick. It was gifted to me by the Enforcers of Arachne. Now, I am passing it on to you. Never touch it here." I pointed.

"I know, Mommy! I learned how!"

"Excuse me?" The involuntary wrinkling of my brow made my forehead hurt.

"Poppy's daddy taught us how to use shock sticks. He did like this when we caught him." Neema jumped, made an "O" with her mouth, and yowled in fake pain.

"Kaoti," I grumbled under my breath. Of course, the assassin would teach his daughter and mine how to use shock sticks. Sarcastically, I asked, "Did he teach you how to use a blaster?"

"I'm not allowed to tell." Neema held her lips tightly together.

Closing my eyes, I took a deep breath and decided to let it go. I'd have a chat with the captain of my guard later. I looped the weapon belt around her waist twice and fastened it. She holstered the defensive weapon like a professional. Taking down another box, I armed myself with blasters that Sparrow had designed for me. Then, I opened my vault and let Neema pick out a necklace. She chose the priceless heirloom necklace that Fitz had given me. I probably shouldn't be letting her wear it, but the occasion did warrant it. What might yet be in store for us, I didn't know. The necklace dangled down her torso which pleased her to no end. That in and of itself made it worth it in my opinion. For myself, I selected the egg-sized diamond suspended on a simple chain with which my beloved Luca had gifted me on the night I'd accepted him. It was the necklace that Cormac had returned to me when I'd believed it to be forever lost.

"Yeah. We good, Mommy." Her smile reached my heart.

I nodded. "We are definitely Parvac warrior princesses. Now, for some coffee."

Happily, we held hands and walked out of the room in search of Chef. He handed me half a cup of coffee. I downed it and held it out for more. Neema had taken her seat and thirstily slurped down pineapple juice. Chef went to refill my cup. Returning, he handed it to me. Neema and I had both needed a break. Everything had seemed like it had happened so fast, but hours had passed. I started making a mental list of everything I needed to do. First, we needed to help Stig and his crew if we could. Then, what damages needed to be repaired on my ship? How far off course were we?

Lifting the cup to my lips, the anticipation was ruined as I took a sip. "Ew, Chef." Making a face at him in the dimly lighted area, I said, "That's tea. I know it's dark in here with the emergency lighting, but is it really so dark as to make such a mistake as this? Are you okay?"

Apologetically, he replied, "You've just had the last of the coffee."

"The fuck you say?" Appalled, I stared at him.

"Our emergency departure occurred before the last of our non-essential ship's stores had been delivered."

"Non-essential, non-essential?" I shook my head as if it might make it easier to understand him. "Are you telling me there isn't any coffee?"

"Don't cry, Mommy." Neema patted my hip.

Nervously, Chef said, "I'll check the cafeteria on Deck Three," and practically ran from my sight.

Getting up, I went to the beverage dispenser and set the tea to its strongest setting. All the while, under my breath, I whispered, "Stupid fucking Alux mother fuckers." Then, hot leaf water in hand, I went back to the table.

Neema was eating from a platter that Chef had set out for us of fruit, cheese, and nuts. I wasn't in the mood to eat but nibbled anyway. Not knowing what might next befall us, it was wise to take sustenance while we were able. It was so quiet. We could hear ourselves chewing. I sipped my tea and waited while she ate her fill. After she finished, I said, "Go and get a book to read." She ran to her quarters while I placed our dishes in the sink for Chef. When she returned, it was with a bag over her shoulder which she'd stuffed with a blanket and pillow. She held her book clutched to her chest. "Ready?" I asked.

She nodded.

Together, we returned to the bridge.

Chapter Seven

The lift doors opened, and Tyler followed us with his eyes. In a fluid movement, he rose from the command chair and took his seat at weapons.

"Report." I spread out Neema's blanket on the floor between the semi-circular short, white dividing wall and the back of my command chair. She placed her pillow against the dividing wall, sat, and opened her book. I grinned when she pulled out a small camping lantern.

"Pilots are standing by on the flight deck. Manual override is necessary in both fighter ships and in onboard ship's weapons systems. It will be slower and less effective with targeting, but it's something. Communications are still down. Minor crew injuries. No fatalities have been reported. Stellar cartography is offline." He too had blasters holstered at his hips and a blaster rifle down his back.

A heaviness settled over me. If the Alux were to attack, we would be fighting to the death. My sweet baby.... I shook my head. I shouldn't dwell on what I couldn't change. She was with me. That was all. "I want all hands armed for combat."

Tyler nodded and caused the emergency lights to flicker red in a few short bursts. It was probably a redundant command, but under the circumstances I thought it best to follow protocol to the letter. Well, except for having a child on the bridge, but I didn't feel comfortable letting her out of my sight.

Neema shivered and rubbed her arms.

I stared at my Laconian daughter. I knew it wasn't the temperature chilling her. "Prepare for battle!"

Through the view port, swirling black and grey space sped by as we dragged Stig's heavily damaged ship along with us. The forces without increased our inertia causing us to exceed the top speeds at which we were capable of traveling. The *Empress* shook and shuddered. Then, she and the ship anchored to her were flung from the wormhole out into purple and grey space that was almost nebula-like in its appearance. Ship's systems blared to sudden life as functions returned. Neema covered her ears against the sirens. Lights flashed.

"Battle stations! Fighters engage!" I ordered as half a dozen Alux warships advanced on our position.

Stig's ship broke free of my grapplers as it regained power. Its captain took it into a defensive position. Fighter ships poured from my flight deck like angry hornets from a struck nest. The lift doors opened and closed as Clark joined us on the bridge and slid into a command station chair.

"Incoming!" Tyler warned.

Unable to maneuver my ship out of its way, the blast scorched the hull. Stig's ship took two direct hits with such force as to make it dip and spin before the captain could regain control. A team of my fighter pilots targeted an Alux ship and unloaded missiles at it, breaking off and closing formation as the enemy vessel was infiltrated with spider venom bearing nanites. Stig's ship battled two Alux ships at once leaving three for me. The blasts rattled my teeth. Neema scooted under my command chair and held on.

Tyler manually fired a missile. "Direct hit!"

A weird sound seized our attention. "What's that?" Panic raced through my veins.

"It's coming from the Command Quarters!" Clark said as he leapt to his feet and darted toward the disturbance.

Horror left my mouth dry. I evaded a missile from an Alux vessel, taking the *Empress* into a downward spiral while Tyler fired shots at it. Unable to leave our stations, we could only watch as the two smiling Alux strolled from the command quarters and onto the bridge. Their beautiful, doll-like faces belied their predatory evil. My husbands were too far away for me to be able to draw on their abilities. Sensing my choking fear for Neema, the closest Alux licked its lips. The blade flashed out in a blur. Ness, almost forgotten where he stood by the hull, gasped.

"Now, it's the two of us," Clark said. Alien blood dripped from his blade. He moved as if in a fluid dance.

The alien dared not to take its eyes from the Parvac warrior. Their blades clashed and grated together. Clark, twice as tall and strong as his opponent, held the Alux's blade at bay above its head with his own. Then, he slid a second blade into her guts. An expression of surprise was frozen upon the alien's face as it fell to the deck. Clark wiped his blades on the alien's cloak and advanced on the captain's quarters.

A sudden sick, twisted rush of emotion had me gagging and my head spinning. Stig's ship was being rocked by a series of explosions. Escape pods burst from ejectors. Swallowing the sickness and pushing down overwhelming emotions, I ordered, "Flight deck, prepare for evacuees. Medical, prepare for casualties." On my deck, the sightless, frozen stare of the severed head unnerved me. "Ness, get those two off of my bridge." He rushed to get an anti-gravity stretcher.

The smoking, badly damaged ship under Stig's command fought like a berserker fueled by beastly rage. Its captain released its weapons into an enemy vessel causing it to explode.

"Give me something, Tyler!" I flew the *Empress* through wreckage and placed her between the debris and the escape pods. Tyler fired repeatedly at an Alux ship as it tried to pick off the escape pods. My crew worked to bring the survivors aboard.

Ness quickly loaded the corpses onto an anti-gravity stretcher in a professional and detached manner which elevated him in my estimation.

Then, through the viewer, we watched as the unthinkable happened. Stig's ship made a suicide run at the remaining vessel. Hailing them, I yelled, "Stop! We can take them together!"

The captain ignored my hails. Our ships were too close. The explosion would cripple my already heavily damaged ship and put my daughter, crew, and the survivors in danger. I took the *Empress* up and sped to put distance between her and the disaster which was about to occur.

Tyler reported, "They are boarding the Alux vessel. They aren't ramming it."

Incredulously, I asked, "What are they doing?"

A piercing scream punctured my eardrums. It was Neema.

Dropping down from my seat to her, I held and soothed her. "Baby, what's wrong?"

Her screams didn't stop.

Then, I sensed it. Devastating pain, rage, anguish, and disbelief threatened to overpower my mind. It was an inescapable wave. Neema's screams pierced my ears. Her psychic pain was debilitating. Panicked, I rushed over to an emergency kit and raced back to her. Fumbling with the latch, I grabbed a neural blocker and inserted it behind her ear.

Tyler yelled, "Dr. Savelli, to the bridge!"

Neema's eyes fluttered closed. Laying her gently on her blanket, I placed the pillow under her head. I had to leave her there and return to my command chair. Desperately, I maneuvered the ship away from an exploding vessel.

"What are they trying to accomplish? What? Why try to board that ship? If the Alux get their hands on the weapons that Stig is transporting, we're all screwed!" Tyler yelled as he fired on another target.

A dizzy, murderous rage turned my vision momentarily black. Clutching the arms of my command chair, I gritted my teeth and tried to breathe through it. Droplets of saliva escaped with the forcefulness of my breaths.

Cedrenus said, "Something's happening!"

The Alux ship had been boarded. A hatch opened. From it dead aliens spilled out, bits and pieces of them at least. The boarded Alux vessel fired upon the other alien ships.

"What the fuck is going on?" I gritted out.

An anomaly opened in space, and before I could fear the arrival of Alux reinforcements, the commandeered Alux vessel vanished into it. Then, the anomaly winked out of existence. We were left, lights flashing red around us, in some uncharted and unknown alien space, surrounded by destroyed Alux warships, dead, floating corpses, and an incapacitated warship.

"I sealed off Commander Genso's quarters. I need a team to seal the hull breach." Clark's words seemed loud in the wake of all of the violence.

"Where are we?" I asked. Fear and dread settled into my bones. "Where the fuck are we?" Knowing I sounded hysterical, I tried to force a meditative calm over myself. Psychic pain slashed at my mind, and it wasn't from Neema. It took me a few tries. Thanks to my childhood with Nathan Green, I was dead and distant inside after the third attempt to wall myself off.

Dr. Savelli finally made it to the bridge and rushed over to me. Shoving him away, I stabbed a finger down toward my child. "Get off me! My daughter suffered a psychic attack."

Falling back, he turned from me to Neema.

"Teagan," Clark said. "Teagan!" Clark tapped my cheek. My fist tried to connect with his nose before I knew what I was doing. His reflexes saved him. Capturing my wrists, he turned his head back toward me. "Teagan, you don't sound like yourself. What are you experiencing?"

"Rage."

Dr. Savelli picked up Neema and carried her to the lift. "I'm taking her to the Medical Bay for scans."

"I'm coming with you." I turned my eyes back to Clark's. "You have the bridge. Figure out where we are." Pointing toward Stig's ship, I said, "Retrieve that. It must not fall into enemy hands if any weapons or knowledge of them are left on it."

"Understood." Clark stood at attention and saluted me.

It broke through everything I'd done to wall myself off emotionally. "Clark," I softly cried out. Lifting up onto my toes, I kissed his lips before rushing to follow after Dr. Savelli and Neema.

The trip to Medical seemed to take forever. Each beat of my heart was an eternity. She was so still. Around us, the screams and cries of the injured were so loud. Every available crewman had been summoned to assist with survivors. All around us was pain and blood. Dr. Savelli placed her on an available exam bed and hooked her up to beeping machines. He spoke words which I didn't understand. All I could comprehend was my baby lying there, shock stick at her hip, diamonds draped across her torso, and seemingly asleep.

"Ensign Probus!" Cormac barked. I jolted. He was in my face, angrily backing me against a wall and away from my daughter. My blood pounded in my ears, drowning out all but my own breathing as sound slowly returned to my ears and reason to my mind.

Dr. Savelli spoke. Focusing on his gold-flecked brown eyes, I managed to hear him. "She's alright. She fainted. You prevented her from suffering from any permanent damage with your quick thinking. I'm leaving the neural blocker and administering a sedative. This is no place for her. Take her to her room to sleep. I'll check on her in a few hours."

"Yes, sir." Groaning, I got my heavy daughter up into my arms with her head on my shoulder and staggered out of the medical bay and into the lift. He was right. If she were to awaken to the screams and pain in Medical, it would terrify her. Also, he didn't need a healthy patient taking a bed away from someone in need. Terrifying to me were the blankets which covered bodies on the exam beds around us. They'd tried to get away. They'd tried. Cormac followed and pressed the command for Deck Two. She was going to be okay. Thanking the stars, I breathed in the scent of her hair and tried not to shake or cry.

Chef met us at the lift. He stood there wringing his hands. "Let me help."

Carefully transitioning her into his arms, I led the way to her quarters and turned down her bed. After gently putting her down, he promised to stay nearby. At her door, Cormac was giving orders to two guards. He was assigning Neema's protection to them and telling them what had occurred. The door closed behind Chef. Alone with my daughter, I brushed her hair away from her temple. She was alive and medically sound. Closing my eyes, I kissed her forehead. Then, I removed her weapon, her necklace, clothes, shoes, and socks. The bottoms of each of her feet near her toes got kisses. Careful so as not to wake her, I changed her into a nightgown, placed her favorite doll in her arms, and tucked her in.

As I walked toward the door, I looked at the shock stick and belt I held in my hands. Shaking my head at myself, I turned back and left the weapon hanging from her chair where she'd be able to see it upon waking. Brave little princesses deserved their own means of self-protection. Bending over her sleeping form, I kissed her sweet forehead once more. It was more for me than for her.

Cormac and Chef waited in the central living space. The guards stood to either side of her open door. Inspecting them, I approved of the spider-venom laced blades sheathed across their chest harnesses and the wicked blades sheathed down their backs. Walking over to Chef, I asked, "Will you watch her for me, please?"

Nodding, he answered, "Yes, Princess, of course."

"Thank you." I started for the lift but stopped. Turning, I asked, "Coffee?"

Chef looked like I'd gut-punched him. "No, Princess."

Dejected, I entered the lift.

"Escape pods are still being brought aboard. Permission to take a shuttle to Stig's ship?" Cormac stood beside me staring forward.

"Granted." I pressed the command for Deck Five. "I'm going with you."

He'd asked me simply as a formality. He'd already selected a team. They had assembled and waited on the flight deck. Going to my flight locker, I quickly dressed in my own gear and managed to board the shuttle before I could be accidentally left behind. Each warrior aboard was an Inquisitor who had been handpicked by Eli and Drex. There were no doubts in my mind that even the lowliest positions aboard my ship had been given to the deadliest, shrewdest males to be found. The grenade blasters on their belts with neurotoxin pellets made me feel even better. Sparrow was brilliant.

The pilot took us from the flight bay and out into the odd area of space into which the wormhole had spewed us. Purple and grey swirling clouds engulfed our shuttle. There were no stars, no sources of light, and no way to discern our location. I pushed my rising terror away. It took mere minutes afterward before we were boarding Stig's ship. The environment aboard had been compromised by several hull breaches. We activated our gravity boots and lowered our face shields before leaving the shuttle. Debris floated through the ship. Bile rose in my throat as we made our way out of the lift. Dead crewmen floated through the corridors until members of the team sealed off the breached areas and reestablished gravity and atmosphere. The devastation was surreal.

Tears fell from my eyes, and I didn't care who saw them. "How many survivors?"

"Three." Cormac's answer was like a knife in my heart. Out of all of those escape pods, only three people had survived. He took the lead. I followed him to the bridge. "Secure the weapons. Wipe the systems," he ordered the men.

My steps faltered. The captain and his bridge crew had died harnessed to their command chairs. However, their blood had floated. Now, it was like red frozen snow crunching under our boots.

"Kitty?" My question echoed in my helmet.

"You are free to search. Take two men with you." Cormac returned his attention to his task.

She hadn't been one of the survivors. It was hard to make myself believe it. We'd said goodbye to each other such a short time ago. It had been for the last time? How could this be true? How could she be dead? Maybe, Kitty had hidden in an escape pod, and it hadn't deployed. Walking along ravaged corridors, we took a few wrong turns before finding the ambassadorial quarters. Dead Alux scattered the decks of the ship. There were more of them than there were of Stig's crew. Even still, our allies hadn't had a chance. We stopped short, unable to go any farther. The quarters had taken a direct hit.

"Medical," one of my escorts suggested.

We climbed a set of service stairs to get there. Down the corridor, the medical bay doors opened and partially closed over and over again. One of the men went to the wall panel beside them and disconnected the offending circuit so the doors would remain open.

"Oh, stars," I choked out.

Medical was a nightmare. Patients had been strapped to medical beds. Doctors and nurses had not. Their bodies had fallen randomly when we'd reestablished gravity. All of them had been frozen and had turned a blue-grey. Scanning the carnage, I sobbed when I saw the cascade of brown hair. It had floated and fallen along the edge of the exam bed from where it had been covered by the blanket under which she'd been put to rest.

"Oh, Kitty, no." Hot tears fell down my cheeks, and the tip of my nose tingled. I'd liked Edvard's better half. Kitty had been tough and smart, but she'd also had a sweet kindness to her. How would I break the news to Sherman and Gina? They'd taken to Kitty as if she were family. "I'm not leaving her here."

"Princess, Dr. Savelli will bring a team once we have secured the ship." His tone was calm and compassionate.

"I'm not leaving her here. She was my friend." My neck felt tight. My words were forced. "It could have been us. Do you understand?"

"Yes, I understand. Stig was targeted because the Alux have their sights set on Earth as their next buffet. Had they targeted the *Empress*, it might very well have been Parvac blood splattering the corridors." He seemed to consider how his words might affect me a moment too late. "It wasn't us. We live to fight another day. We live to give retribution to the Alux of blood for blood, and they will pay it." The fury in his eyes warmed me.

"Yes, we will avenge them," I whispered. It was all I could choke out. Turning from him, I searched for funeral bags and got to work. A few of the men took over seeing as how my hands shook. Then, they placed Kitty's bagged body onto an anti-gravity stretcher. Navigating the unit down the ladder and through the ruined ship's corridors disheartened me further.

"Teagan, stop. You should see this." Cormac adroitly stepped around lighting that had fallen from the corridor's ceiling. I held back while the men loaded the unit with Kitty's body onto the shuttle. In his gloved hands, he had a vid-screen. "These are the moments leading up to the ship's destruction." His screen provided twelve simultaneous views within the ship. "I can slow it down for you later."

I watched the events he replayed for me at high speed. Explosions rocked the ship. On the bridge, Edvard's face drained of color. His scream was soundless. He ran for the lift. His guards ran before him. Alux appeared in the corridor from breaches they'd created, just like the one on my ship. Edvard's Mad Ones cut through the aliens. Swords went in from gut to chin as they sliced through their enemies like machetes through irksome grass. Edvard pulled Kitty from the wreckage of their quarters. The Mad Ones raged. Cold chills burst all over my flesh.

"Get me back to the *Empress*, now."

While Cormac gave orders to secure the ship, I took a seat in the shuttle and considered what he'd shown me. Had the Mad Ones who Stig had employed bonded in some way to Kitty? Had losing her destroyed their fragile hold on sanity? Thoughts churned in my mind during the jaunt back to the *Empress*. My fighter pilots had set up a floating perimeter around her. Even with all of the fire power those ships had, what good would they actually do us? It was only a matter of time before more Alux warships arrived. They'd find us here, damaged and alone. How were we supposed to get out of here and return to charted space? Where even were we?

Glancing up, I found Cormac watching me. "I'd like for you to oversee repairs to my ship. Tell Clark to replenish our weapons with whatever he can."

His clipped nod of acknowledgement was all I needed. Cormac wouldn't disappoint me. Two crewmen took the unit carrying Kitty's body to the Medical Bay, and I followed behind them at a respectful distance. Dr. Savelli stood at the back of the medical bay in front of a clean room monitoring one of the survivors, a badly burned crewman. During our absence, the bodies of those who hadn't survived had been removed. The survivors had been identified. Stig had been one of them. Looking around, I didn't see him anywhere. Pulling aside a nurse, I asked, "Where is Stig?"

"He's in a holding cell."

"Carry on." I hid my surprise and waited as Dr. Savelli approached, deciding to save my questions for him.

He stopped to take a reading of Kitty Stig before quietly giving the attending nurse instructions concerning her. "Neema is doing well. I'm continuing to monitor her closely."

Relieved, I thanked him. "Why is Stig in a holding cell?"

Dr. Savelli shook his head. "He was irrational and violent."

"Why wasn't he sedated?"

Widening his eyes, he made a helpless gesture with his free hand. Then, he showed me a signed order from Clark on his vid-screen to keep Stig alert for questioning. "Take this with you." He took an injector from his pocket and cast a glance over toward Kitty's body. Gently, he said, "I know she was your friend and Maria's. I'll take care of her."

I didn't hide my sadness from him. With a nod, I turned and headed off toward the holding cells.

Chapter Eight

Edward paced his cell like a caged beast. His shoes and belt had been taken from him. Thinking better of entering his cell armed, I left my weapons with one of the two guards stationed to either side of the door to his cell. Head lowered and shoulders hunched, Stig watched my approach through reddened eyes. He was disheveled. Kitty's blood and his own stained his shirt. His hair was tangled and dark from the burned debris he'd torn through to get to Kitty's body. I typed out instructions to the guards not to interfere. Then, placing my palm to the scanner, I waited for the door to open, clasped my hands behind my back, and entered.

"What do you want?" Disdain, rage, and grief warred for control of his voice. Within him, madness encroached. I could sense Edvard was soon to be lost. He'd bonded to Kitty with whatever Eriopis genetics he had within him.

"I'm here to see if your reason has returned. Shall I come back later?"

Incredulously, he expelled a breath through his lips and stepped within inches of me. "Everything has been taken from me! Everything!" He shook with rage. His volume left my ears ringing, but I didn't move. Digging his fingers into my upper arms, he shook me. "You cold-hearted bitch! Do you feel nothing?"

I met his eyes. "I grieve with you."

Hate hardened his features. "Liar." He lifted me up off my feet and twisted me around, shoving my back against the wall of his cell. "Say something! Speak your words of comfort! Do it! Damn you!"

A small, sad smile formed on my lips. My mind took me back....

I approached Luca in the medical bay. A sheet covered him, but he was cold. I'd asked for blankets....

Shaking my head, I closed my eyes and sobbed. Tears spilled from my eyes, blurring and hiding Edvard and his misery from my sight. I felt his pain, and allowed him to sense mine. He crumbled to the deck, taking me with him. He poured out his grief, and I held him as he did, giving him comfort which I knew from experience wasn't enough. The pain would become manageable, but it would never go away.

"I know. I know. I'm sorry." My whispered words were so quiet that I wasn't sure he could hear them over his anguished cries. I knew his pain, and I'd survived it. It wasn't a feeling I would wish on anyone. I wanted to take the misery and loss from him and from the universe. What good was such agony? How was Kitty's loss fair? His tears were wet against my neck. My soul reached for his, snagging and trapping the flailing golden strands before I could attempt to stop it from happening. Sudden heat pooled between my thighs, and I ached. Frozen, my fingers stilled where I'd threaded them through his silken, champagne-blonde strands. Lifting his chin from my shoulder, he moved his head until we were almost nose to nose. My heart raced. What had I done?

"What have you done?" His voice was ragged velvet.

It was then when I realized that Stig was a far more powerful telepath than he'd allowed anyone to realize. Even through his neural blocker, random thoughts spilled from his mind and into mine. His father had kept his own abilities and genetic history a secret, and he'd taught his son to do the same. Other thoughts slipped through his grief-ravaged control. He felt my rush of hormonally induced desire and answered it with a need to control me and hurt me. It destroyed my hunger. Lifting my feet, I shoved my boots against his chest to push him away. It did nothing more than to entice him. Now, along with the grief, there was a possessive hunger in his eyes. I could feel him in my mind, prodding. Scrambling back, I tried to get away. Grabbing my ankle, he held me still. He slid his other hand up my inner thigh.

"You need time to grieve." My soft words cut through his passion.

He snapped his mind closed against me. Staring at each other as though we were feral cats preparing to attack, we waited for the other to strike. Then, it ended. He let me go, stood, and extended a hand down to me. Taking it, I allowed him to draw me up to my feet. A moment of silent evaluation gave me a sense of ease that I wasn't sure I trusted. However, the riptide of irrational pain which had made him seem suicidal seemed to have let him loose. Moving to the door, I motioned for the guard to let me out. Then, I contacted Dr. Savelli to see if he thought it was safe for Edvard to be released. The doctor approved his release on the condition he remain monitored. I ordered the guards to let him out.

"Follow me." I grabbed my weapons and waited while he collected his own weapons, shoes, and belt. Alone with him in the lift, I could feel my need soaking through my undies. "Fucking great. Absolutely fucking great," I muttered. Stepping from the lift and out onto the Imperial Deck, I waved to Chef that all was well and walked inside of a spare room. "You can stay here. Get some rest. We have a fucking mess to deal with."

He grabbed me before I could turn to leave. Filling my mouth with his tongue, he captured my head in his hands and walked me back toward the bed. His thoughts spilled into my own until his grief for Kitty and mine for Luca became an indistinguishable jumble of fresh and faded misery. He smelled of smoke and weapons fire, along with faint traces of blood and tears. His mind reached for mine like a drowning man for a piece of driftwood, but it was madness rather than fathomless ocean depths dragging him toward endless drowning sorrow. The ache of loss was unbearable. Not fighting his need or my own, I moved my hand down the front of his pants and released the closure, pushing them down his hips while he removed my shirt. Shimmying out of my pants, I moaned as we pressed our bodies close. He was so hard, hot, and thick.

Need blinded me to who he was and what I thought of him. I had a need, and he was here. Sliding my hand down his chest, I reached for him and trailed my fingertips along his shaft. Not pausing our kiss, he slid his hands into my hair, fisting them, and yanking my head back hard. My lips were free of his.

"What the fuck?" Unmindful of my outrage, he twisted my hair painfully around his wrist, capturing me. "Let go! That hurts!"

Coldly, he replied, "Spread your legs."

"I said it hurts and to let go!"

His tone had been cold whereas mine was volcanic lava, smoldering and hissing.

"You will obey me when we are intimate."

Lifting my right foot, I brought my heel down hard on his outer ankle. In shock, he released my hair. Free, I made a fist and swung. Blood gushed from his nose. Shocked pain shone through his eyes. "If you want to fight, we do it in the ring. I'm not into this kinky shit, but I'll order you around if you like."

Clutching his nose, he stared at me. "I don't like being ordered to do anything."

"Nor do I. If you try hurting me again, I will defend myself."

"I was only attempting to find pleasure with you."

"By yanking my hair? Seriously? What the fuck is that? No. I don't like it, not at all."

"Then, why? My wife has not yet been sent to her eternal rest, and you have seduced me, bound me."

Yanking up my pants, I defended my actions. "It wasn't on purpose! You know it! You've been lying to everyone, everywhere about your telepathic abilities."

Furious, he stared down his bloodied aristocratic nose at me. "Now, all who are bound to you will know as well."

Wrinkling my brow, I shook my head. "Whatever, Stig. Look. You're sane. You're welcome. I could have let you suffer, deep-dive off into madness, and have been done with you."

An arrogant sneer manifested on his face. "You got exactly what you wanted from the first time we met, me."

Stepping closer, I reached up and patted his cheek. "Yeah, sorry. You don't do it for me." That knocked him off his pedestal.

"Pardon me?"

"Look. Let's acknowledge this for what it is. You know as well as I do that we're trapped here. To survive, we need each other both physically, not sexually, but as manpower, and mentally. If you were to have begun raving and frothing at the mouth, it would have been detrimental to our objective. Get some rest." Grabbing my things, I left the room.

Carrying most of my clothing clutched in my fist at my side, I trudged across the living space to my quarters. Safely inside, I stripped, tossed everything into the cleaning unit, grabbed a breast pump, and went to my shower. My breasts felt like bags of sharp rocks. Minutes later, as hot jets of water bombarded my flesh, I'd filled four bottles for the freezer. One major ache was gone. However, another raged. My Parvac hormones were the least of my worries. What had the Mad Ones done? Why hadn't they taken Stig with them?

Dressed in a fresh uniform, I stored my milk in the cold storage, checked on Neema, who was still sleeping, and entered the lift for the bridge. Hopefully, now that I'd bound Stig, he'd be able to control his telepathic trauma from spilling over to my daughter. The lift doors opened. It was a momentary shock. Pausing, I stared out at purple and grey fathomless clouds through the main viewport. The lack of stars unnerved me. Stepping over to Clark, I checked the information on his console. A crew was working to repair the hull breach in the command quarters, we still didn't know where we were, Ness was occupied with alien autopsies, and teams worked at various repairs all over the ship. Never before had she sustained such extensive damage.

"What? No update?" Wondering why he hadn't started to catch me up on the latest news, I braced myself for the worst. Then, I saw his face. His pupils were blown, and everything about Ensign Clark Flavian was intently focused on me. "Is it bad? It's bad, isn't it?"

Lifting his hand, he adoringly caressed my cheek. "Nothing of you is bad."

The soft growl in his voice made my lady parts practically vibrate. "Can anyone take the bridge for you for a little while? You look like you could use a... nap." How many hours had passed? We'd lost all concept of time, but it felt as though I'd skipped at least two rest cycles.

Staring at my lips, he nodded. "Stayton, the bridge is yours." Taking my hand, he led me back inside of the lift. As the doors closed, he bent and buried his face to my neck, inhaling and leaving soft kisses along my throat. All feeling left my knees. Catching me in his strong arms, Clark carried me from the lift to our quarters. Hastily removing our clothing, we collapsed onto our bed where an "umph" escaped me. He was a heavy weight covering my body and pressing my thighs wide. Lifting my hips for him, I gasped with pleasure as he entered me and sighed with pleasure as I felt myself stretching to accommodate his girth.

"Oh, Clark," I whispered.

His name on my lips made him wild. His strokes were long and fast. With each thrust, it was as though he was attempting to drive thoughts of the Alux, our damaged vessel, the loss of life, and being trapped in unknown space from my mind. After an unrelenting hour, he managed it. Crying out and clawing at his back, I came with such force that it took me some time before I could recall my own name. Finding his release, he collapsed beside me. He'd been fighting it, not allowing his release until he'd seen to my needs, like a good Parvacian husband. Smiling, I smacked him on the ass, but he was already asleep with a grin on his face. Caught between satisfaction and disappointment that he wasn't ready to go again, I covered him up and curled up beside him. A nap couldn't hurt.

Disoriented, I woke up, unsure of how much time had passed. Red blinking lights and soft alarm blasts had ripped us from our slumber. "What now?" Dread heavy upon us, we dressed and hurried from our quarters. Clark met Stig at the lift. I hesitated. Neema stood in her doorway between her guards rubbing her eyes. "I'll be there in a minute." Clark nodded and closed the lift doors. "Hey. Are you okay?" Striding over to her, I picked her up, and kissed her forehead.

"I'm hungry."

Thinking about it, I nodded. "So am I."

Chef asked, "What would the princesses like for breakfast?"

"Cupcakes," Neema answered.

"No, not for breakfast." I sounded adamant, even though I wondered, why not? What might today hold? What if this was our last breakfast? Shaking those thoughts out of my head, I told her to make an appropriate selection.

"Ugh. Fine. Banana pancakes."

"Yum," I said as I tickled her tummy and got her to giggle.

Once Neema was situated in her chair and had gulped down half of her juice, she dropped her hands to her lap and stared at me. "Mommy, where's Daddy? Where's all the daddies?"

Shrugging, I guessed, "Parvac?"

"They coming here?"

Sighing, I said, "We're on a mission. They can't help us right now."

"Okay." She jabbed a banana slice with her fork and chewed. "Mommy, it doesn't feel right."

She didn't notice how quickly I ate or how I scowled at my cup of tea. I watched as she lifted her hand to touch the neural blocker. "Leave it alone, Neema." Thinking of how to put it so she'd understand, I said, "We're hiding from the Alux. It's there to keep you safe for now."

Her eyes were sad as she stared into mine. "All done." Her fork clanked against her plate.

"You know what to do." I pointed her toward her room.

She ran for her shower. Following after her, I supervised her hair washing and toothbrushing activities before helping her to dress. "Can I wear a new necklace today, Mommy?"

"Yes, but first you must dress." The alarms had stopped, but the red lights continued to flash.

"It's okay. I'll hurry." She sensed my concern from my expression. Wearing a pink jumpsuit and brown boots, she looped her weapons belt around her waist while I braided her hair. She selected a pink diamond bracelet made from her diamond mine on Daphoene.

My thoughts drifted to Dario. What would he do if he were here in my place? Rushing off to my quarters, with Neema following close behind me, I brushed my own teeth. Then, I gave her a necklace to wear, the one Yukihyo had given me, the first one. I hoped it would comfort her. "Chef will watch you today."

"Mommy!" She stomped her feet.

Squatting down, I held her hands. Her pout was prominent. "Ask nicely, and maybe he will help you with your forms. You don't want your brothers excelling more than you during our absence, do you?"

That made her think. Storming from my quarters, she strode up to her guards. "Justin and Gonen, you're both playing with me and Chef today. You got that?"

"Neema, you do not speak to adults in such a manner." Scolding her worked.

She put her hands together and begged. "Please?"

I waggled my fingers at Chef and snuck off into the lift.

The answers I'd been after were evident through the main view port. Luckily, the situation wasn't as dire as I'd feared. We were being bombarded but not with weapons fire.

Clark said, "Shields are holding."

The *Empress* was stuck in a debris storm. It was comprised of shards and fragments from Stig's ship and from Alux vessels we'd combined forces to destroy. Now, the wreckage bombarded us. My fighter pilots protected the *Empress* from the heftier pieces. We weren't just surrounded by a deliberately placed field of space junk as we'd once been thanks to the *Hadrian*. This time, we were immersed in deadly shards of it which were stuck in their own inertia.

"Why not blast them off into another path?" I asked.

Stayton replied, "We thought it prudent to preserve energy and missiles."

They were right. My fancy artificial heart pounded with renewed fear. "How long can we sustain ourselves?"

"As we are, we can survive for two years on rations." His expression said everything. If we held our position without being attacked, we could live for two years and then die.

"Do we have any notion of where we are or how long it might take us to arrive at a planet capable of sustaining life?"

Stig cleared his throat. "We appear to be trapped in a pocket of the wormhole. Attempts at blasting free of it are futile. The anomaly absorbs the power, swallows it as if it were a blackhole. Perhaps, it was the wormhole's way of stabilizing itself from the power fluctuations caused while the Alux attacked us. It siphoned off the excess power, almost like storage."

Gripping the command chair, I stared unfocused and considered what our situation meant for my daughter and my crew. "Unacceptable." I shook my head. "Can they find us here?"

"If we wait here," Stig said coldly, "the Alux will do to this ship, they will do to you, what they did to my wife."

Looking up at him, I shook my head. "We aren't staying here. We are going to do what your demented henchmen did."

Cedrenus asked, "How? Teagan, there aren't any Alux vessels for us to commandeer." His eyes darkened. He was afraid. We all were.

"You're right. However, there are bits and pieces of them. It looks like we are stuck in the middle of an Alux warship junkyard. We need to find the parts of their ships used for opening wormholes and get out of here, where ever here is."

Stig said, "Their technology is incompatible with our own."

Cormac paced the bridge. "It doesn't have to be." He had abandoned his bodyguard garb in favor of his Inquisitors uniform. It was comforting to see him dressed in such a manner. "On the chance we find a functioning Alux drive, we lock onto it with our grapplers and remotely operate the device with a robot."

"Excellent," Stig complimented.

Feeling like we at least had a plan, I felt my anxiety levels decrease, but not by much. "Clark, Stig, and I have the bridge. Go take breaks. Eat, shower, take a nap. We begin six-hour rotations now. Dismissed."

Cormac inclined his head to me and left. He wouldn't be taking a break. He and a team would be searching through the debris for whatever part we needed. If one was found, the crew hopefully would be able to figure out how to engage it. After all, during a previous attack Alux ships had been captured and continued to be studied by the finest Parvacian scientists and engineers we had.

The others had left the bridge. The three of us were alone. Stig asked, "What if we do this and end up even farther from charted space?"

"Then, we try again," Clark answered.

Our shift dragged along. Meanwhile, my hormones raged. It was like a perpetual buzzing under my skin that I couldn't vanquish. Clark knew. Stig knew. Every Parvac male aboard the ship probably knew. Closing my eyes, I shook my head in an effort to clear it and remembered the first time I'd gone through this and what had happened with Quaid. Concentrating, I reached for him.

"Stop." Stig gripped my shoulder. Opening my eyes, I glared up at him. Snidely, he said, "One might consider when attempting to hide from telepathic feeders not to reach out to one's telepathic mates. Mightn't one?"

The color drained from my face. He was absolutely right. I'd made a stupid, thoughtless mistake. "Whatever." I shrugged away from his hand.

Clark watched our exchange. "What's going on here, Teagan?" His focus was wholly on Stig.

"He's right, but this fucking hypocrite couldn't keep his own telepathic shit together without my help."

I could practically hear Clark's thoughts snapping together and sensed he'd like to snap Stig's bones in two. "I knew something had changed. I felt something odd." His face had a hard look to it.

"Oh, you felt something odd alright." I snorted and returned my attention to our sensor readings. My bravado hid something. When Stig had touched my shoulder, he'd done something to strengthen my ability to cope with my hormonal turmoil. It wasn't much, but it had helped.

Stig asked, "What exactly do you mean by odd?" The aristocratic contempt in his tone was so thick that I wondered if it fortified his bones. Maybe, it would protect them from Clark.

"You know exactly what I mean."

Clark chuckled. We'd studied Edvard Stig and knew of his proclivities. Most males on Parvac had made a discrete study of me and knew mine. Stig and I did not get off on the same shit and were not sexually compatible. Sensing my frustration, the competitiveness eased out of Clark, and he grinned.

Sadly, I thought about him naked and realized that I had one husband aboard, and we were stuck on bridge duty together. I knew my place was on the bridge. Hopefully, Clark knew the order to take a nap didn't apply to him because when our shift was over, I intended to pounce. In the interim, we occupied ourselves with reports of work being done and of repairs being made. The hours crept by. Luckily, no further attacks occurred. Then, Tyler, Levi, and Stayton arrived to take the next shift. The way they watched me confirmed my fears. My hormones were out of control, and everyone knew it.

I whispered in Clark's ear, "If all goes well, we'll have twelve hours to ourselves."

Stig got inside of the lift with us and pushed the command to take us to our deck. When the lift doors opened, we saw Neema standing on the back of a couch. Its cushions had been repurposed as the walls of a fort. "Attack!" She held up her shock stick. A swath of pink spider silk had been fashioned into a cape. Neema, her guards, and Chef were engaged in an extensive battle staged with every doll and stuffed animal in her possession. The battling doll army was armed with miniature working cannons which fired grapes instead of cannonballs. Neema kept eating the artillery. Chef was a genius. He knew how to trick her into eating healthy.

"Reinforcements!" Neema jumped off of the sofa, cape billowing behind her, and ran to me throwing her arms around my legs.

Stig raised an eyebrow and excused himself to his quarters.

Joining Neema's team, I helped her battle against Clark. We gave Chef and the guards a break. They were staying in quarters on our deck to protect us should the Alux return.

"Okay, you all dead, Daddy Clark. I win." She placed her hands on her hips and surveyed the destruction with satisfaction.

Stig had ventured from his room for sustenance and stepped on a doll head. He frowned.

"Oops. Toss it?" I held my hands up.

Grimly, he bent, picked up the doll head, and rather than doing as I'd requested, found the body and reattached it. He was thinking about Kitty. Pain threatened to slice him into pieces. Instinctively, I soothed him. I glanced over at Neema. The neural blocker still protected her fragile, young mind.

She had stilled. She stared at him. "I'm sorry about Lady Stig. She was pretty and nice. I liked her."

I froze. Someone had told her about Kitty, but it hadn't been me.

His nostrils flared as he inhaled and tried to steady his emotions, but tears that never fell filled his eyes. "I thank you, Princess Neema."

She tossed him a grape. Her face was sad as if she too might cry. "It's gonna be okay. I'll be your friend, and so will Mommy and Daddy Clark." Edvard forced himself to smile for her sake. Stepping close, she patted his knee and met his eyes. "We will stick together and make the bad aliens pay. They are so bad! We *gots* to blow them to bits! Bam!"

The smile reached his eyes. "Bam, indeed, Princess Neema."

Uncomfortable with all of the grief, Clark suggested, "So, let's eat."

"What are we having?" Neema asked as she followed me into the kitchen.

Opening the cold storage unit, I pulled out what Chef had prepared for us and smiled. "Naxan bison steaks and mashed potatoes. Daddy Nico has made certain that we won't be hungry."

Climbing onto her chair, she said, "Good Daddy Coco."

"May I be of assistance?" Stig asked Neema.

She held a knife in one hand and a fork in the other. "With what?" Glancing around, she became hopeful. "Cleaning?"

"Cutting your meat?"

She scowled at him. "No way. This is the only time Mommy lets me cut." Happily, she sawed away at her steak.

I smiled sweetly at Stig's expression.

"Brother cuts his food with his claws," she told him.

I pushed away the pain it caused me to be separated from Peter, Niklos, Marielle, and Tabitha. My goal was to return to them, not to dwell on my private maternal agony. We all turned our heads toward the lift when it opened. "Join us, Cormac." Quickly, I got up and set another place at the table. He waited to sit until I had done so.

"Got any fudge?" Neema asked.

"Not today, I'm afraid. However, once we return to Parvac, you shall have all of the fudge you desire."

Neema raised her dove-grey eyebrows. "I desire lots of fudge."

Matter-of-factly, he said, "As well you should."

The five of us continued our meal in silence. Afterward, Neema and I cleaned the kitchen for Chef. "Bath time."

"Ugh." She scowled at me.

I pointed toward her room.

"You don't have to come," she whined.

"Yes, I do." I followed, not trusting her.

Once she was clean and tucked into her bed, I read her a story until she fell asleep. She missed her siblings as much as I did. She'd asked for the ancient story about the little boy who never grew up, the one where she'd gotten the inspiration for her brother's name. Some childhoods lasted longer than others. Carefully, I brushed her hair back from the neural blocker and wondered if it was safe to remove it. Quietly, I left her room.

Cormac waited at ease in a chair in the living area reading reports on his vid-screen in the dim emergency lighting. Briefly, he acknowledged me with a glance up before returning his attention to his screen.

"Have you found what we need to get out of here?" Sitting on a couch, I took a purple pillow to hold and sadly looked over at Thunderdrop's tree sculpture. Oh, how I missed him. The loneliness of our situation in being lost in unknown space and the uncertainty of our future were fears which threatened to rise up like a wave and drown me. Pushing the myriad fears down, I focused my attention on Cormac.

"We are conducting searches and marking the debris we have documented. Nothing out there remains in any location for very long." He smirked. "It is a swirling mess." Resting his vid-screen on his knee, he flexed his cramped hand and slid it down his thigh to his knee, moving his head to his opposite shoulder to stretch his neck muscles as he did so. "Manual flight operations are necessary due to widespread power fluctuations." Cormac looked at me. He had nothing more to add.

All I could do was to offer him a nod. I knew he was doing everything he could think of to get us home. "Is there anything else I should know?"

"No, Princess Probus."

My hopes fell. Clark had been sitting quietly in the dimly lit area. Now, he stood and held out his hand to me. Together, we retreated into our quarters. When the door closed behind us, he took my wrist gently in his grasp. "Hey," his soft whisper had me looking up into his eyes. "You don't have to put on a brave face in here with me. Got it?" His eyes were practically mirrors of my own in whose depths were fear, uncertainty, protectiveness, and dutifulness.

"Oh, Clark, what are we going to do?"

Slipping his hand from my wrist, he laced our fingers together and drew me along into the bathroom. "We're going to do what we can each day, even if it doesn't seem like much. We'll keep doing whatever we can until we get through this, and we'll do it together, as a team." Turning on the shower, he let go of my hand so he could undress. "Teagan, no one can see either of us crying in here." He stepped under the spray of water.

Watching his eyes while I fumbled out of my own uniform, I could tell the shower hid his own tears. It wasn't just me. I wasn't weak, not if he felt the same way. Joining him, we held each other and cried while the water swept our tears away. Afterwards, we made love until we fell asleep.

Chapter Nine

My eyelids drifted open. The room was dark and quiet. The lights were no longer blinking red, but we continued to be on alert and would remain so. The Alux could attack at any time. With the return of my awareness was the aching need which I couldn't escape. Turning my head, I watched Clark as he slept. He was exhausted, as was I. Deciding to leave him be, I quietly crept into the bathroom to shower and dress.

Leaving my deck, I roamed the corridors of my ship and surveyed the damage to her with my own eyes. Stopping to speak to each crewman I met gave me a more realistic idea of our current situation. Small crews worked diligently during each shift to repair damages to practically every area of the ship. Everyone was tired. On Deck Three, I visited the cafeteria and made my way around to each table. The crewmembers there appeared more rested now that we'd gone on a rotation schedule, but like me, our situation made it difficult for them to be idle. Rather than getting in line with a tray, I went to the beverage dispenser. Grabbing a cup, I lowered my head in disappointment and proceeded to fill my cup with the strongest tea available.

Under my breath, I mumbled, "Horny and un-caffeinated. Stupid fucking Alux pieces of fucking shit." After a disappointing sip of tea, I got in line figuring that I might as well eat.

"Don't like the tea?" Binder asked from ahead of me in line.

"What's to like?" Frowning down at the cup on my tray, I shook my head. "It's so sad, like the tea leaves had a weak cry, and I'm drinking their tears."

Grinning, he pointed to something he wanted the server to put on his tray.

Squinting at his selection, I grimaced. "Protein paste patties? Did Kaoti put you up to this?"

The server said, "No, Princess Probus, we were in the midst of receiving crates of certain... luxuries when the Alux attacked."

The luxuries to which he referred had been the two delivery trucks that I had been waiting on at the land port. On one of those trucks had been my coffee. Scowling, I pulled out my vid-screen and called Chef. "Did you know that the crew is stuck eating emergency protein rations?"

"Yes, Teagan."

"Put our supplies with theirs. We eat with the crew in the cafeteria until we're out of this mess." I felt a wave of guilt. On my deck, we'd been eating Naxan bison steaks while the crew had been eating this crap. Binder raised an eyebrow at me. "Don't say it. Don't say Papa wouldn't approve."

"I won't! Do you think I want to eat this?" Lifting a patty between two fingers, he shook it at me.

Around us, cheers went up. They were happier at least.

The stares I continued to receive from the males around me had me feeling uncomfortable, so after my meal I left and made my way to the command deck and Captain Ricimer's private office. Sitting there alone, I made some more decisions. One of those was to implement an hour a day of blade battle sparring for everyone aboard. Another order was that everyone aboard be armed at all times with blades in the event of an attack. It was no longer a matter of if but of when.

Two hours later, I brought Neema to the cafeteria. She was not happy. Amongst her complaints was that she'd had to get dressed rather than eating breakfast in her nightgown at the dining table. "Why, Mommy? Why?" She scowled at me with her elbows on the table.

"We will have the same meals as the crew for the time being." I scowled at my cup of tea.

It seemed to make Neema happy to witness my caffeine misery. Picking up a spoon, she ate her oatmeal and eggs. Chef had assumed command of the cafeteria kitchens and had begun meal planning with the staff. "He's happy," she said of him.

Turning my head, I followed her gaze and nodded.

She said, "I guess helping everybody is okay." She kicked her feet back and forth under the table while she ate.

"Ouch." I narrowed my eyes at her and rubbed my shin. She smiled and kept doing as she'd been doing. "You are both aggressive and passive-aggressive."

"So?" She scraped her teeth on her spoon as she pulled it from her mouth.

"You should be nice to me."

"I am. I love you."

"Then, stop kicking me."

"I'm not kicking you. I'm making sure you're still there with my toe." She meant it. I glanced at the neural blocker on her temple and sighed. "Mommy?"

"Yes?"

"What's pass a session mean?"

"Passive aggressive?"

"Yes, that's what I said, pass a session."

"Don't worry about it." Smiling, I scrunched my nose at her.

"Oh, brother." She shoved another spoonful of oatmeal into her mouth.

Cormac and his team strode into the cafeteria looking tired and grimy. It took Cormac a moment to realize what had changed. Passing by a table and looking down at a crewman's plate, he quickened his steps to get in line for a Naxan bison steak. Blushing, I felt guilty.

"What's wrong?" Even with a neural blocker, she could recognize my emotions.

"We were being selfish. We had all of the foods we have grown accustomed to while the crew was doing without."

She scowled. "We didn't know. We fixed it after we found out." She kicked me again after having taken credit for my actions.

"You're right." I smiled and scrunched my nose at her again. My knee was starting to throb. Pulling out my vid-screen, I wrote a message to Dr. Savelli to ask if it might be safe to remove the neural blocker. Stig was stable now, and his Mad Ones were nowhere near us. Then, I checked for any updates. Cormac hadn't had time to report as of yet. He'd taken a seat at a table with his team, and while he hadn't forgone his manners completely, he was cutting his steak and shoving bites into his mouth like he hadn't eaten in a while. It was what happened next that surprised me somewhat. Stig walked into the cafeteria wearing standard Parvac attire like the rest of us. Then, he got in line with everyone else.

"All done! Time for training!" Neema hopped down, kissed my cheek, and ran to her guards. I heard talk of punching and kicking as they walked out and toward the lift.

A crewman started to clear our table before I could do it. I got up so someone else could have the table, and unable to suppress my curiosity, went straight to Cormac's table and pulled up a chair. "Don't stop eating on my account. I'll wait until you're done to find out the latest news."

Stig walked by us with his tray. He paused, sensing it as I soothed his grief. Then, we continued ignoring each other which seemed to be working for us.

Cormac said, "The two of you seem to have called a truce." He shoved a glob of potatoes into his mouth.

"Yep." I got up for a refill of strong tea.

When I returned, Cormac asked, "Has he offered himself to you?"

I rolled my eyes. "He and I are not compatible. However, we are able to work together."

He returned his attention to his plate, and after scraping up every remaining bite, pushed his plate away. "If you will excuse me," he said. Then, he got up and left.

Shocked, I stared after him. Um, what? He'd simply gotten up and left? He hadn't given me any news. His behavior was unbelievable! How could he treat me in such a way? He was so... dismissive! Annoyed and confused, I got up and followed him. He'd practically ignored me. Cormac had been chasing after me for years. Now, he was running away? He'd sounded eager to foist me off on Stig of all people, and I knew how he felt about him. He'd never forgive Stig for the pirate attack on his ship which had resulted in the deaths of seven members of his crew. During that attack, Cormac had treated me like a valuable asset. He'd allowed me to disembark in my fighter ship and enter the battle against the pirates, giving me the chance not only to do what was right but to prove my worth.

Some members of the Warrior Caste still wanted to rip him to shreds, along with the Houses which were politically aligned with House Gordian, because of it. Kaoti had earned redemption for his House with the Warrior Caste through his service to me, and it had been his plan to help Cormac to do the same in serving as my temporary bodyguard. So far, the plan had been working. Thinking farther back, I recalled the box with which he'd presented me containing my first uniform. There had been other gifts. I thought of the beautiful flame diamond. Cormac consistently supported me and treated me with kindness. I felt a wave of guilt. Here I was causing him aggravation and creating more problems for him in return. He was in his quarters by the time I caught up to him.

He allowed his door only partially to open and didn't look me in the face. "Now is not a good time. I will see you shortly on the bridge." He began closing his door.

Pushing my combat boot into the small opening, I pried my way inside. "What's the deal, Cormac?" The door shut with finality behind me. His feet were bare, and he'd removed his jacket before I'd found him.

He turned his back to me and spoke. "We found an Alux device which may be operable after a few repairs."

"Great news, but not what I mean." Moving around to stand in front of him, I looked up at him. He looked away. "What's wrong? Is it something I've done?"

Cormac looked at me then. His pupils were blown, taking over his eyes but for a rim of lighter darkness. A sudden rush of emotion hit me as if a high-rise building had imploded and crashed to the ground. It was need. "Yes, what you have done is to trust me. I won't betray you now by taking advantage of you in your current state. Go. Go, now."

This wasn't the Cormac I'd first grown to know, the one who seemed to have a heavy hand in the inner workings of the Inquisitors Branch of the Parvac Empire, the male who, if he set his mind to it, could quite possibly supplant Kaoti's dangerous reputation. He'd turned his back to me. Without his uniform jacket, the corded muscles of his back were no longer camouflaged. Since I'd met him, he'd made an effort to appear non-threatening. Now, with sudden clarity, I realized he'd kept himself disguised. He was dangerous. He might possibly be the most dangerous of them all. Hot, aching need flooded me. "You're avoiding me to protect me?"

"Yes! Go!" His commands were deep growls rather than shouts and had the opposite effect of what he'd intended.

"You'll have to explain your rationale to me. I'm not getting it." I was getting a good view of his back where it tapered down to his waist.

He moved farther into the room, trying to put distance between us, but I followed as if drawn by his heated skin. "Don't you understand? I want you to want me, to accept me. I've offered myself to you. I am yours, but I want you to want me not out of desperation but out of the desire of your heart and mind. If you allow it, after we are free of this pocket of space and in a navigable sector, I will formally offer myself to you again."

Seizing his waistband, I pulled myself close to him and rested my cheek against his back. I could feel the tremble beneath his skin. "Cormac, I care about your feelings. Oh, truly I do. Let me save us both the agony of waiting. I accept you." He turned in my arms which I hadn't realized that I'd wrapped around him. He was wary of me. I could sense it. "Cormac." Anguish suffused my utterance of his name. Shaking my head, I struggled to admit the truth, a truth everyone in my life had accepted long ago. I hadn't accepted it because I'd been clinging to shreds of cultural beliefs that weren't truly my own. However, the time for punishing myself was over.

"I've been unintentionally cruel to you and to myself. I should have accepted you after Luca died, but I didn't."

He stared at me, daring to lift a hand to push a strand of hair behind my ear. "Losing Braga was difficult for you."

"I felt as though part of me died along with him and with our child." I shook my head. "They could attack at any moment. We may only have hours."

"If we have only minutes, I would have them with you. I've watched other women throughout the years, studying them as if I might find someone to pledge myself to for a chance to share a few moments each year. None of them kept my focus. You, you became a thought-stealing distraction. When you entered my life, I could not force my thoughts from you. No, you remained there, a soft whisper, ever present. You weren't some female to be adored on a pedestal from a distance. You were a capable female who could be my equal, a partner. They didn't see it. They wanted to keep you safe. I want you fighting at my side."

Lacing our fingers together, I stared up into his eyes. He saw me. He didn't see what he expected me to be or what he wanted me to be. "All this time, you've given me the freedom to be myself."

"You are glorious." Bending his head toward mine, he looked into my eyes. Finding there the permission he sought, his lips found mine.

We tore ourselves free of our clothing, struggling and fumbling to be free. My need clawed at me from within. Lifting me up, he encouraged me without words to wrap my legs around his waist as he turned and lowered my back to his bed. He pushed at my entrance with his manly appendage. Feeling my lower lips surround his tip as he pushed and pulled, working his long, hard shaft inside of me, made me frantic. I tried to take over, but he kept me in a submissive position beneath him. More and more, he slowly filled me. He took his time, savoring how our joined bodies came together. When his balls finally came to rest against me, all I could do was pant with pleasure. Of all of my males, he was definitely the longest.

"Do I please my lady?" he whispered against my neck right before he licked it. I came while crying out his name. He began to move. His long, slow strokes were incongruous with the ravenous desire we both experienced. Cormac was in no hurry. He seemed to be content to keep me beneath him forever. He watched my eyes and kept himself lifted above me on one arm as he worked his length in and out of me in slow, steady strokes. Each time I came, he seemed to harden even more. Unable to help it, I counted off my intakes of breath in my head as he began to withdraw and thought I'd made it to thirty but couldn't concentrate very well. It was slow, sensual torture. Whimpering, begging, and clawing at his back didn't speed him up. The pressure built and built to the point of pain until my release sent my eyes rolling back in my head. When my thoughts returned, he was still above me, making love to me in his same slow, unhurried pace, watching my expression and my eyes.

"Don't you need to?" I panted.

"My desire is met by easing your ache and by giving you all of the releases you can manage. I have seen how you have suffered. Never will I add to your suffering. I will work toward your happiness and pleasure for all of my days."

He watched as tears slipped from the corners of my eyes to spill to his pillow. "You have, always." Lifting my hand, I stroked his cheek. "You facilitated my entrance into the Academy. You found the necklace Luca had given me. You protected Niklos and me on Earth. You are a part of me, of my family, Cormac. I could never bear to be parted from you." My words had stolen his control. Seductively, I moved my hips. "You've mastered pleasing me. Now, let me experience what it feels like when you take your own pleasure."

Staring into my eyes, he took my hands in his and held them above my head, pressed into the bed. He moved faster using the strength of his hips and thighs. The weight, feel, and scent of his body pressed against mine became my only focus. He had consistently given me the freedom to reach my own goals and desires, but to find his own release, he needed to be in complete control. I gave in. The oppressive, clawing need under which I'd been toiling shattered as he found his release and brought me along with him on an intense wave of pleasure. I bound him then, reaching for him with golden strands and tying him firmly to myself where he'd never again doubt his place in my heart or in my family.

Moving to the side, he took me into his arms and held me. He pressed kisses against the top of my head.

"Cormac, where is it?"

"To what do you refer?" His words were a soft, satisfied murmur of contentment.

"Where is the marriage contract you wish to present me with?"

He carefully reached over to his bedside table so as not to jostle me. Then, vid-screen in hand and arms around me so that I could watch as he navigated through a plethora of files, he opened the document for me to see and gave it to me to hold. Once he had me settled against his chest, he rested his chin atop my head and gently traced along my thighs with his fingertips. They had a roughness to them produced by hours of weapons and combat training. Returning my attention to his marriage contract, I began reading. Bemused, he asked, "Do you intend to read the entire document?"

"Oh, yes. I've learned my lesson." I shrugged and kept reading. His chest was warm and comforting against my back. I could feel the thumping of his heart as it calmed and returned to a regular rate. Incredulously, I asked, "You are gifting me with a secret observation base in the Laconian Sector? Seriously? I don't know whether to be excited or disturbed." My thoughts raced back in time to a moment in Uncle Kagan's kitchen with Grandmother. She'd jokingly told me not to ask where she'd gotten some of her Laconian produce. Parvac spies really were everywhere.

"Teagan, I have not attempted any subterfuge in this contract."

I made a soft sound of agreement and kept reading. "I'm not taking your word for it." I read carefully. I was done with being tricked and being carelessly trusting. I read every fucking word. Nothing was out of the ordinary. There were no sneaky clauses stipulating my behavior. Satisfied, I pressed my palm to the screen. A hard wedge grew between my back and his chest. I smiled and turned, putting the vid-screen on his table and hitting him softly in the face with my breast as I straddled him.

"Seeing your palm scan next to mine has done something to me," he murmured.

Lifting up onto my knees, I positioned myself above his rigid length and carefully lowered myself, groaning at the delicious soreness I could feel from our previous lovemaking. He shook his hips back and forth in a bouncy, unexpected manner which surprised both of us into finding sudden, intense releases.

"Oh, wow. What did you do?" I asked once my orgasm relinquished to me my ability to string words together.

Eyes closed, he continued to shoot hot spurts of his pleasure deep within me. "Stars. Stars." Soft and relaxed, he said, "I didn't do it. I thought you did."

Our eyes locked as the shaking and bouncing happened again. It wasn't us. It was the *Empress*.

Chapter Ten

We were still fastening our uniform jackets when the lift doors opened onto the bridge. Cedrenus' eyes locked onto mine. Then, I saw something out of the corner of my eye and stared out the viewport. In horror, I watched as the black and grey anomalous, gaseous space in which we'd become ensnared seemed to boil. It was like being trapped in a storm cloud as lightning flashed in chaotic, web-like bursts.

"Report!" I ran to my command chair.

Cedrenus said, "We don't know for sure! We think someone is trying to open the wormhole to rescue us, but it's causing it to collapse! Their efforts are destabilizing this pocket of space!"

Horrified, we all watched as Stig's ship was caught in the wormhole and was subsequently torn to shreds. Cormac took my wrist and pulled me from the command chair.

"What are you doing?"

"Taking over temporarily," he stated. "Avenna, take weapons. Flavian, take Teagan and Neema into their escape pod with the guards."

Clark picked me up, tossed me over his shoulder, and jogged to the lift. I wasn't given a chance to protest. He had us back on the Imperial Deck before I could draw two breaths. "Neema," he barked at guards who didn't need to be told. He placed me on my feet, put Neema into my arms, and moved aside so Chef and the guards could enter the room which served as an escape pod.

"Mommy, what's happening?"

I kissed her forehead and soothed her emotions as the ship shivered and rattled around us. The guards coded the door to seal. Every Parvac warship had the same basic floorplan to make it simple for warriors. It also had the added benefit of making space travel simpler for the Imperial family. On the Imperial Deck aboard every warship, my father's quarters, those of the emperor, were an escape pod and contained a viewer and control panel linked to the bridge. Aboard my ship, my quarters had been modified to serve as one such pod. While I wouldn't be assuming control of my ship under the current circumstances, I could lower the wall panel behind my bed so we could watch what was unfolding. Knowing was better than imagining the worst. Pushing the button, I watched as the scene outside of the ship was revealed.

"Oh," Neema said as she scrunched her forehead. She knelt on the bed and watched with us as outside the wreckage became further warped and twisted. "Is that happening to us?" The terror in her cry of fear amplified my own. She reached for my hand. I took it, sat, and pulled her onto my lap.

One of her guards said, "He's activating the Alux drive we scavenged. It's our only chance."

Neema turned her head to look at him.

There was a loud buzzing. It drowned out all other sounds and made my teeth ache. Throwing herself face-first onto the bed, Neema clutched her ears and hid her face in a pillow while I gripped her ankle. I didn't know why I did it other than as a meaningless gesture of comfort. If the ship were to blow apart, holding onto her wouldn't save her. I couldn't protect her. I couldn't do anything. Clark sat behind me and put his arms around me. A helpless laugh was all I could manage. None of us could do anything. It was all up to Cormac, his men, and the engineers. The buzzing became a piercing scream.

A spinning pinpoint of light manifested and drew the *Empress* toward it like a fish on the end of a line that was being retracted. Gravitational dampeners aboard the ship weren't calibrated to compensate. Nausea swirled in the back of my throat. I fought it. Neema wretched, losing the contents of her stomach on the pillow. Drawing her away from the mess, I held her while she cried against my shoulder. Clark encompassed both of us in his arms. He felt as helpless as I did. All any of us could do was wait. Emergency power flickered.

Clark said, "Breathe. Stay calm." He stroked my hair.

"Are you talking to me or to yourself?" I didn't look up. I kept my cheek pressed to the top of Neema's head while staring at the dizzy stream through which we were being dragged.

The edges of the manufactured wormhole were unstable. Cold sweat dripped down my sides. My uniform clung to me. Holding my lips between my teeth, I didn't let the words out, the words saying we weren't going to make it. Instead, I said, "I love you, Neema. I love you, Clark."

A boom of sound reverberated throughout the ship. The *Empress* shook. Then, it was as if the slip of space spat us out like a giant snake regurgitating a mouse. Into the sudden silence, only Neema's cries and the rugged breaths of Clark, Chef, and the guards could be heard.

I met the guard's eyes who was closest to the door. "Open it and let us out. We're going to the bridge."

No one argued. The six of us left my quarters and entered the lift together.

"Mommy, why is it so dark?"

Stroking my hand down her back, I tried to calm her. "We are using emergency power, baby."

The lift doors opened. Across the bridge, stars were visible through the viewport. Relief broke over me like waters bursting through a dam. "You did it! Cormac, you did it!"

He glanced up at me before quickly returning his attention to the cracked command console. Reaching up to gingerly touch my forehead, I grimaced. He said, "We are free of the anomaly, and the wormhole we used to escape it has collapsed. Our drone sensors are not detecting any alien signals for several parsecs, so for the time being we appear to be safe from attack. No casualties. A few minor injuries are being reported."

Neema approached him and quietly said, "I got sick."

Softly, he replied, "I shall report it to Dr. Savelli immediately."

Nodding her approval, she went to Clark and raised her hands to him to be picked up. Once accomplished, she rested her head on his shoulder.

Cormac said, "You are a brave little princess."

"Yep," she answered.

"Thank you, Cormac," I said.

"Ugh. Thank you," Neema grumbled, thinking that I had been correcting her manners.

When I met his eyes, I could tell he knew what I meant. He'd freed the ship and returned us to navigable space where we had a chance of more than just surviving until our supplies ran out.

Clark asked, "What do we do now?"

I walked over to the main viewport and looked out at stars innumerable. "Our photonic film will be able to charge now. We'll be able to power our ship systems. Where are we?" I turned to Cormac.

"Until repairs are made, stellar cartography won't be able to make a determination. Weapons and shields are our first priorities." His voice seemed to get farther and farther away.

"Teagan, you're alive! You're alive." Izaac took me into a crushing embrace. I could feel the entirety of the emotions of my Omnes Videntes weighing upon me like slabs of granite. Closing my eyes, I clung to Izaac and tried to steady myself against the heavy weight of joyous emotion. Slowly, they calmed and centered their thoughts and emotions.

"We're alive. The *Empress* hasn't suffered any casualties. Stig's crew wasn't so fortunate. His ship seems to have been the target."

Izaac, Xavier, Zared, and Jazon raced through my recent memories while the others strengthened their telepathic efforts. The strain of their exertions to reach me was taking its toll on them all. In seconds, they knew everything that I knew about Kitty, Stig, Cormac, the battles with the Alux, our sojourn in the... they called it a rift. "Emperor Probus ordered a wormhole to be opened and probes to be sent through."

"Big mistake," I responded as they sifted through my knowledge of what had resulted. "We don't know where we are."

Safety, loving assurance, and hope infused me. "You will not worry," Zared said. "We will find you. We sense the direction in which you are located, though you are far."

It felt as though they were floating away from me. "My children?" The terrified thought was a shout.

Comfort was like a mist of light rain through the fading bond. "They miss you. They are safe...." The telepathic link slipped away even with their combined efforts to keep it alive.

"Teagan? Teagan?" Clark knelt above me.

Neema held my hand. "Daddy talking to you?" She stared desperately into my eyes.

I was on my back, staring up at the faces surrounding me along with a bit of the bridge's ceiling. "Izaac, Zared, Jazon, Xavier, and the others were. Everything is fine at home, Neema. They can sense our direction and are on their way to find us."

Fat tears dripped down her cheeks. "Really?"

Lifting a hand to wipe away her tears, I said, "Really. Everything is going to be okay." Room was made for Dr. Savelli, who had been summoned to the bridge. "I'm fine other than what I'm sure will be a horrid headache. Can you take Neema, clean her up, and remove this?" I asked him of the neural blocker.

He nodded, gave me a pain patch, and waited for Neema. She kissed my forehead and looked at Chef. He said, "Come along. We'll go with the doctor, get you fixed up, and then we'll go to the cafeteria. How does that sound?"

"Good," she said as she took his hand. Her guards followed them all into the lift.

Clark offered me his hand. Taking it, I let him pull me to my feet. My nose started to run. Lifting my other arm, I dragged it across my nose. A streak of blood was left behind. The lift doors opened, and for a second I worried that the doctor had been called back. However, it was Stig. Shaken, he stared at me. Through our newly formed bond, he'd sensed everything, and my Omnes Videntes had sensed him. Neither of the involved parties had seemed pleased. Clark said, "Sit down. I'll get you a drink."

Cormac offered me the command chair. My head was already beginning to throb. Quickly, I affixed the pain patch. A crewman handed me a cleansing wipe for my nose. The cool cloth felt lovely against the skin of my face and neck. What I really needed was a shower. The hours I'd spent in bed with Cormac had left me feeling sticky. Feeling steadier, I opened my eyes and found Clark and Cormac both watching me like a pair of ravenous Silk spiders who'd been stalking a deer for a week. However, it wasn't just them. The other Parvac males on the bridge were watching me with hungry eyes and something to prove. It was biology, nothing more. Clearing my throat, I crumpled the cleansing wipe and handed it to Clark to discard for me. "You said nothing was within several parsecs of our location. Are sensors detecting anything?"

Cormac pulled up an incomplete star chart and pointed. "There. We don't know what it is." He was curious about it. All of us were.

"Are we sound enough to limp in that direction?"

"It is unadvisable at present."

"Fine. We'll hold our position, make repairs, let the stars power our photonic film, and get some rest." I took the cup that Clark handed me and took a sip. Of course, it was strong tea. Plastering a sweet smile onto my face, I thanked him. "We survived. This calls for a celebration." I hailed the chef on duty in the cafeteria. "We're out of the anomaly and returned to navigable space. Naxan bison steaks for everyone." We could hear cheers from the kitchens.

"My apologies, Captain. However, there aren't enough for the entire ship's compliment."

I could see the disappointment around the bridge. "What about stew? Is there enough for stew?"

Checking the available supplies, he assured me the crew would have a hearty stew with which to celebrate.

"Cormac, you have the bridge." I downed my tea and left.

The males had been making me feel uncomfortable with their staring. I went straight to my quarters to shower and change, putting my hair up in a ponytail and out of my way. Then, in the cafeteria on Deck Three, I joined Neema, Chef, and her guards. She wasn't eating like a polite princess, so I didn't bother to either. She snorted and wiped cheese from my cheek with a piece of toast which she proceeded to eat. "Momma is going to make us take the manners lessons again when we get home."

Neema shrugged. "She's not here, Mommy. We just have to behave when she can see or find out." With the neural blocker removed, she was behaving more like herself.

Perking up, I smiled at her. "We're having a party tonight."

"We are?" Neema stood on her chair. "Woo Hoo!"

"Yep, do you want to help me bake some treats?"

Plopping back down to her seat, she nodded and hurried to finish eating. A mommy and daughter day of baking was exactly what we both needed.

Rather than taking the supplies we'd been allotted and returning to our own kitchen, we stayed even though we were given a small section of counterspace and a single heating unit. The other cooking stations were being used to prepare meals for the crew. "Cookies or cupcakes?" While Neema pondered my question, I placed my vid-screen on a rack at eye-level so I could monitor what was occurring on my ship while we baked.

"Look!" Neema held up star-shaped chocolate chips.

"Yes," I nodded. The stars were the perfect theme since they were in fact the reason for our celebration.

Together, we measured, mixed, and baked. Then, holding a hot cookie out to her on my fingers, I waited while she ate it.

"Yep. Good. You eat one." She used her spatula to select one from the middle of the baking sheet for me.

"Yes, they're good."

"Can they have some?" Neema whispered of her guards and the kitchen staff.

"Yes, fix a platter. Then, we'll put the next batch in."

Inordinately proud of herself, Neema arranged cookies on the tray and then went around passing them out like a magnanimous little cookie queen. Making myself a cup of tea and scowling about it, I skimmed over the work being done and paused at a message from Dr. Savelli.

Neema and I continued baking cookies until she grew bored with it. Then, I sent her off with her guards to the Imperial Deck where she could play. I arranged a few cookies on a plate and turned the remaining dozens we'd baked over to a capable cook who decided to place two cookies per serving plate. Then, I cleaned our work station, took the plate of cookies, and went to Medical. I'd been dreading it since I'd read the doctor's message.

Chapter Eleven

Dr. Savelli looked up at me from a patient's chart and walked over to me as I entered the medical bay. "How's he doing?"

Guiding me over to the medical berth in which Stig's crewman slept, he said, "He will survive. He finally regained consciousness. They questioned him earlier, and he corroborated Stig's account. What they have told us coincides with data recovered from their ship prior to its destruction. The captain made sure that the Alux wouldn't get the weapon. He did his duty."

I watched the man sleep. He and Stig had been lucky to survive. The Mad Ones had made sure of it before they'd abandoned us and left us all stranded. Narrowing my eyes, I stared at the man. "Wait. Max? Is that Max? I barely recognize him." He was Stig's personal bodyguard and had behaved appropriately with me once on Earth when I'd lost a fight with Stig's lawn. Since then, he hadn't caused any problems that I knew of. From the looks of him, he'd earned his pay. I hoped he was charging Stig out the ass. Absently, I said, "Here. Neema and I baked."

"Thank you." He grinned and took the plate.

"I read your message. What does Stig want to do with Kitty's remains?"

He turned and walked toward his office, beckoning me with a tilt of his head to follow. Placing the plate on his desk, he turned to me. "He wants a funeral on Earth. Keeping her aboard...."

"Is what he wants, so we will do it. I'll order the necessary power to be diverted to medical. It shouldn't be a problem now that we have the stars as a power source. The only thing that man and I understand about each other is the excruciating pain of loss. We will respect and facilitate his wishes." Turning, I stared back out at Max where he slept on his berth. "We should have protected them." A wave of grief for Kitty washed over me. She'd been so vibrant.

"We did everything possible!"

Taken aback by his fervor, I looked back at him.

"Teagan, we rushed to their aid and did all we could. Several warships came to their defense, two of which paid the ultimate price. It was a well-planned coordinated attack in which we were almost destroyed."

A tear slipped down my face followed by another and another. "It wasn't enough to save her." Gesturing helplessly, I shook my head at the unfairness of it all. "She was a family friend. We all liked her. Now, she's gone." I wiped my eyes with my fingertips. "I want to crush those mother fuckers. Do you know that? Why the fuck do they even exist? Is it to destroy what's good in the universe?"

He gave my shoulder a gentle squeeze. "All life serves a purpose. We must remember it especially at times such as this."

"Oh? What good are the Alux?"

With eyes full of anger, he responded, "I don't know yet. Perhaps, we will discover something." He gestured with his head toward the science lab where Ness had been conducting Alux autopsies.

"What? Like medical cures or something? All they do is murder innocents."

"They are corrupt. I don't have the answers. However, I do know that all life has purpose and no entire civilization should be judged by the actions of its military."

Taken aback, I absorbed his words. Parvac had been seen only by the actions of its military for centuries. It had been viewed as pillaging marauders intent on expansion, not as a society desperate for survival with a population suffering from critically low female birth rates. "We are not the answer to their food shortage." My tone chilled him.

"No, but what if an alternative could be found?"

I shrugged and turned to leave. Stig stood near the lift where he'd been observing us. When I walked over to him, he gestured toward the exercise room. It was empty. Assuming he wanted to speak privately about Kitty, I followed him. The dim emergency lighting made it seem like the ship was in a sleep cycle which might end soon, but with a skeleton crew and so many repairs needing to be made, it probably would be like this for the foreseeable future. "Repairs are filling up the crew's time," I mumbled while waiting for him to say what he wanted to say. I was due on the bridge soon for my rotation.

"I wanted to thank you." Turning away, he gazed out of a viewport and clasped his hands behind his back. "Your thoughts about my wife…. I appreciate them."

His grief was a blade between my breasts. It drew me to him. Putting my arms around him, I rested my face against his back and simply held him, doing my best to ease his devastated soul. Turning, he surprised me and pinned my back to the hull. Grabbing my wrists, he squeezed them painfully behind my back. I cried out which ignited his passion. Being trapped, being hurt by my father, no by Nathan Green, he'd grabbed me by my arms. He'd shaken me so many times. He'd broken my arm, broken my bones. Rage suffused me.

Stig ravaged my lips with a bruising kiss and pressed his erection against me. Furious, I drove my knee up into his balls. With a grunt, he released me. Balling up my fist, I hit him in the mouth.

"No! No! I'm not helpless!" I fought with everything I had in a blind rage.

"Break it up! Break it up!" Cedrenus pulled me off of Stig. He held me up and away from himself as if I were an angry, feral, wet cat.

Binder got between Stig and me. However, Stig was flat on his back.

"What happened?" Ross asked. He had the audacity to help Stig to his feet.

"He started it! I will fucking finish it!"

Blood dripped from Stig's lip. He was hunched over with a hand to his thigh. "My apologies. The lady and I are having a difficult time learning to communicate effectively." I glared at him. Then, he was in my mind, calming my thoughts and apologizing. "Forgive me," he whispered into my mind.

Ross escorted him from the room.

Putting my feet on Cedrenus' thighs, I pushed with my legs and freed myself from his hold. Rounding on him, I yelled, "Don't fucking grab me!"

"What was I supposed to do? Let you kill him?" His tone was as angry as mine.

Breathing raggedly, I forced myself to calm down. "I wasn't killing him."

Wide-eyed, he asked, "Do you need the waste unit because you're full of shit. Do you want a security replay? They called us rather than Clark." Walking over to a console, he tapped a command and replayed the security video.

Horrified, but sort of impressed, I watched myself go full Yukihyo on Stig.

"Nice roundhouse kick," Cedrenus complimented.

Sheepishly, I thanked him.

"What the fuck, Teagan?"

Shrugging, I told him what had transpired.

"His sadistic shit isn't compatible with your needs. How will you make a marriage work with him?"

Aghast, I said, "Marriage? I'm not! We are not attracted to each other."

Cedrenus replayed the part where I'd hugged Stig.

"He's mourning the loss of his wife! I know what that's like. I know how much it hurts." Tears filled my eyes. "All I was trying to do was help."

Dryly, he said, "I don't like seeing you cry. I'd be happy to hold you and comfort you if you promise not to beat me bloody."

Narrowing my eyes at him, I stomped away to the lift.

Chuckling under his breath, he joined me.

The moment we stepped onto the bridge, two crewmen left for their rest cycles. Cormac stood and relinquished the command chair to me. He looked pointedly at my fists and then into my eyes. I stared back and took my chair. "He apologized."

"Where is he now?" Cormac asked.

Binder and Ross stepped from the lift. "Medical," Ross answered. Two more members of Cormac's crew left the bridge.

"He'll be fine," I grumbled. Then, I began reading the reports in preparation for my stint on the bridge.

Dr. Savelli made an urgent call.

"Yes?"

With a red, upset face, he asked, "Do you want him healed or killed?"

"Who?"

"Stig!" Behind him, Cormac held Stig against the hull by his throat.

"Healed."

Turning, Dr. Savelli gave Cormac a sedative injection in the back of his neck, grabbed him under his arms as he went limp, and dragged him away from Stig. "Time out, boys. No fighting in my medical bay." He waited while one of his nurses took Cormac's feet. Then, they lifted him onto a medical berth. Meanwhile, Stig gasped and choked while trying to drag oxygen into his lungs. Ending the call, I closed my eyes and rubbed my temples.

Cedrenus, Binder, and Ross laughed harder than I'd ever before heard them laugh.

Finding a medical kit, I cleaned my hands and stuck bandages over the ones I'd busted open on Stig.

"Teagan, don't be angry." The cajoling tone and words were spoken through a grinning mouth. Binder said, "Inquisitor Gordian was merely protecting his female."

"Yes, who could blame him?" Cedrenus asked.

"Certainly not Clark. Although, he might very well be upset with you and with good cause. If memory serves, a stipulation he imposed on you was that he was to do your fighting for you. Was it not?" Binder asked.

When it was obvious that their levity was doing nothing to change my mood, Cedrenus nudged my shoulder. "I'm fine. It's complicated with Stig."

Ross said, "No, it's not complicated. It's simple. He hurts females in order to feel pleasure. He should be jettisoned from an airlock. You were right to defend yourself."

Cedrenus nodded. "Let's get him back to Earth and be done with him."

"How long will that take?" I asked.

Cedrenus snorted and handed me a cup of tea. It ended the pointless speculation in which we might otherwise have engaged.

Reading a report from stellar cartography did nothing to improve my mood either. It did enhance the shitty one that I already had going on. "They still don't know where the fuck we are." We all settled into our work stations with the exception of Clark. To be fair, we'd had to switch up our rotations. He and his original team would have their own bridge rotation, but we'd still be able to share rest cycles together. I kept reading reports. One of them was gut wrenching on a personal level. "I'm going to the transport bay. Cedrenus, you have the bridge."

The lift took me to Deck Five. Observing my exit, the crewman in charge approached me. He knew why I'd come. His request had been straight forward enough. Luxury items were needed for scrap to make repairs. The *Empress* had suffered considerable battle damage prior to being buffeted by debris from within the anomaly and later by the complete destruction of Stig's ship. The struggle now was to keep her space worthy long enough for us to be rescued, and that would require sacrifices on all of our parts. Walking over to my transport, I ran my hand over the roof and hood.

With remorse heavy in my words, I said, "Yukihyo bought this for me. It was a symbol of my freedom and his trust in me." Opening the door, I sat on my pretty blue seat. "Do me a favor?"

He nodded.

"Put any personal stuff you find in a crate for me."

"Yes, Captain."

I grabbed a rattle from the floor. It was Tabitha's. Refusing to cry over my transport or my babies, I hurried back to the lift. That was the last time I'd see my transport in one piece, but hopefully it wouldn't be the last time I'd see my children. Cedrenus got up from my command chair the moment I stepped onto the bridge. The rest of our shift was quiet. Well, it was quiet until Cormac's sedative wore off. Then, I'd had to run for medical, pull him off of Stig, and order him not to kill Stig or initiate an attack. It had taken hours, but now they were talking out their issues. Okay, it wasn't that exactly.

Now, in the lift, the two of them were sniping at each other in the way of aristocratic snobs with high-brow insults. Currently, they were on the topic of education. It was a pissing contest but with brain cells and was so boring. I was grateful when I was released from the lift and out onto my deck. Clark was waiting for me. He sat with Neema on a couch reading a story. Seeing them together took away some of the misery I'd been feeling since finding Tabitha's rattle. Walking over, I kissed the top of her head.

"I'm in a party dress. You go and put one on, too. I already picked out what you're wearing." She sat there looking all clean and pretty.

"Oh, okay." I pretended not to notice how Clark was pointedly looking at my hands. "You know something? You are more and more like Momma every day." I gave her cheek a gentle pinch. "So bossy!"

She rolled her eyes at me.

Going to my quarters, I freshened up and put on the pink, sparkly dress she'd had someone to help her lay out on the bed for me.

Delighted when I came out, she clapped her hands and spun around in a circle which made the skirt of her own pink dress flare out. "Party!" She ran for the lift.

I followed her. Clark and Cormac quickly flanked us leaving Stig to stand in front of us with his back to Cormac. It had to be unnerving to him, but it put a twinkle in Cormac's eyes. Thankfully, they kept their comments to themselves in front of Neema. Stig was quick to exit the lift. There was a celebratory air in the cafeteria. Why wouldn't there be? We'd survived a harrowing ordeal. Also, even with myriad power fluctuations, with our drones, we'd managed to collect considerable data which was being compiled for future scientific study. It was an accomplishment of sorts and worth celebrating. The tantalizing scent of Naxan bison stew wafted toward us. Neema drew me along with her to the closest empty table. Every crewman present stood.

Lifting a hand, I said, "Please, be at ease."

While they did return to their seats, they didn't allow Neema or me to get into line like everyone else. They brought us bowls of the chunky stew along with a basket of rolls. Neema knelt on the seat of her chair, closed her eyes, and gave the rolls a deep sniff. "Oh, Mommy, let's eat."

Before she could attack, I suggested, "We should mind our manners since we're wearing party dresses." I opened my napkin and spread it across my lap while waiting for her to do the same.

We passed the meal in silence until dessert. Then, Neema had to go up to everyone and let them know how she'd made the cookies with her mommy and make sure they noticed how they were cut like stars with star-shaped chocolate chips. "See? We got stars outside again, so we get cookies."

Her culinary skills were praised ad nauseum. Eventually, she was worn out from all of her socializing and ready to return to our quarters. She was asleep the moment I tucked her into her bed. Once I'd left her soundly sleeping, my peaceful evening ended.

Chapter Twelve

"You will not dismiss me to my quarters as though I were a recalcitrant youth!" Stig, vehemently angry, glared at Cormac.

"You heard him. He's showing you mercy." Clark stood at ease, but it was obvious from the bunching of his shoulder muscles how angry he truly was.

"Mercy? Do you dare assume that I fear retribution?" The sneer on his lips seemed to delight Cormac.

Approaching them and what could ultimately result in the destruction of my carpet, I tried to diffuse the situation. "If Clark gets his hands on you, you'd have to be a total moron not to ask for mercy." Suddenly, my head began to pound in time with my pulse. I walked past them toward the kitchen and grabbed a cup. Absentmindedly, I pressed the beverage dispenser's command for coffee. The machine made some pathetic, dry little sputters. Closing my eyes, I squeezed the edge of the countertop, counted to forty, and pushed the command for fucking tea. "This is Naxan bison shit."

"I agree. Let's place him into an escape pod and eject him," Cormac said.

"No, I am talking about the lack of coffee aboard." Sighing, I took a disappointing sip.

"Princess Probus, might I have a private audience?" Stig asked.

"No!" Clark answered for me. "You will not be unsupervised with my wife, not after what you pulled!"

Stig stood arrogantly taller, jutting out his chin ever so much.

Moving over to a couch, I sat holding my cup with both hands. The full pink skirts of my dress fluttered about, and its hem puddled on the carpet around my feet. It was quite lovely. Gina had designed it in Arachne's latest fashion. I forced my attention away from Arachnean Silk so that I wouldn't start thinking about my best eight-legged friend.

"I did not intend to hurt or to frighten her. My purpose was to be affectionate."

Cormac focused his full attention on the male. "For you to display affection, you must give pain. Your late wife understood and even required such attentions. It is my sincerest hope that one day you find someone with whom you might again find mutual regard. However, our wife does not share your inclinations to any extent." He was using a quiet tone, one which sounded far more ominous than I'd ever before heard him use.

He was there in my mind where he'd remained since the moment I'd bound him. Now, he touched upon my thoughts to give himself a better advantage. After learning my thoughts on the matter of Cormac and Clark, Stig stopped talking and took a seat on the couch opposite of me.

I didn't have the energy to deal with any of them. "When was the last time I slept?" Shaking my head at my own rhetorical question, I got up, went to my quarters, changed into a nightgown, and got into bed. Sleep came to me as quickly as it had come to Neema.

My dreams were vivid. In them, I saw sweet images of Marielle, Tabitha, Peter, and Niklos with Itsy, my precious darling ones, sleeping in their beds in the Palace with Thunderdrop watching over them. They were safe. Izaac stroked my hair. "They need you to return safely to them. You are our concern." He placed a gentle kiss on my forehead, waking me.

My body felt heavy. Having slept so deeply, it was almost as though I'd become one with the mattress. Clark was solid warmth beside me. Snuggling close, I kissed his shoulder and ran the sole of my foot along his hairy leg. He was awake and rolling me to my back in an instant. He nibbled at my neck. His stubbly cheek made me giggle. Lifting my legs, I crossed my ankles behind his lower back. Relaxing into the rhythm he set, I floated away with him on waves of ecstasy. He didn't last any longer than I did. Lacing our fingers together, he looked into my eyes. "How are you doing with everything?"

Shrugging, I raised my free hand to his hair and smoothed it down where it was sticking up on top. "It helps knowing we aren't trapped in a weird pocket of space with limited supplies and power. We're alone out here, wherever here is, but they know we're alive. They will come for us." I traced his muscles with my fingers and then kissed his warm skin. "They sent me a dream of the children safely sleeping in their beds last night." My nose started to tingle. The tears and terror which I'd been doing my best to wall away from myself crashed down on me.

Clark pulled me close, holding me and providing me with what comfort he could. "I'm scared, too." He gave me a gentle squeeze.

"You are?" I wiped my eyes on the sheet.

"I think everyone is to some extent."

I mumbled, "Kaoti wouldn't be scared."

Clark snorted. "Nothing scares him."

"His wife scares him." I ran my fingertip around his nipple. Tickled, he caught my hand and held it still. My breasts were painfully full.

"He's not stupid."

I left the comfort of Clark's arms for the shower. He followed me. "Are you scared of me?"

Again, Clark made the snorting noise.

Narrowing my eyes, I turned with my breast pump in hand.

He held up his hands in surrender. "Of course, I'm not stupid either. I realized I was wrong and redacted my stipulation in our marriage contract."

Startled, I almost dropped the breast pump. "What? When? Really?"

Reaching around me, he turned on the shower, making the water hot. "You can fight your own battles. Stig's medical chart can attest to it. You broke his nose, partially ruptured one of his testicles, and cracked two of his ribs."

"Shit. I didn't mean to." My cheeks burned with shame. "I snapped inside." I'd really done that sort of damage to a grown male? He wasn't a weakling either. He was bigger and stronger than me and outweighed me.

"Teagan, he doesn't blame you. No one does. He triggered you, and he should have known better."

"Yes, he had to know my history. Who doesn't know it? Still, I should apologize for the testicle." Cringing, I imagined someone causing such an injury to either of my boys and was horrified. "I was trying to get away."

Clark didn't give his opinion. Instead, he scrubbed my back while I filled the bottle with the assistance of the steamy shower.

Fortified by the scent of my favorite Arachnean shampoo, I got dressed and dried my hair. After putting it into a single braid, I found Clark waiting for me in the main sitting area. Neema was still asleep and drooling all over her pillow, so we went to the cafeteria alone. Ross, Cedrenus, Binder, Levi, Stayton, and Tyler were all seated around two tables. After getting bowls of oatmeal and cups of tea, we joined them. I could tell they were up to something.

Levi nudged Tyler. "Flavian, you reconsidered the clause in your contract?"

Crunching on a slice of toast, Clark looked pointedly at Tyler but kept chewing.

Lifting a boiled egg from his plate, Levi cracked its shell against the table. Quiet snickering came from each of them.

Clark hid his expression behind his toast. Then, he said, "I have. Did you know that my wife is considering apologizing to him?" Binder started to choke. Ross whacked him on the back. "I told her not to apologize for defending herself. There were extenuating circumstances."

Cedrenus held up his fork and used it to emphasize his words. "If he can't control himself around her, he needs to be kept away from her."

An alert came through on my vid-screen. Letting my spoon clatter loudly down into my empty bowl, I checked it and noticed the guys were checking their own alerts. "I'm being ordered to report to the flight deck."

Cedrenus returned his vid-screen to his pocket. "So am I."

Tyler and everyone else gave nods of agreement. Together, we filed out of the cafeteria.

We found Inquisitor Gordian waiting for us. He held himself with the same composure with which he usually reserved for formal assemblies at the Academy. He began giving his orders to us the moment our boots were on the flight deck. "Suit up. Pair up. Fly to the structure our sensors are detecting. There are no life signs. Amass data. Return to the *Empress*." Cormac was tense and displeased with the orders he'd just given. I could see it in his eyes. I was the last person he wanted to send on any mission, let alone this one. However, our teams were available and rested. Turning, he walked toward the lift. He entered it with his jaw held so tightly clenched that I feared it might crack. I knew why. He was struggling to treat me like an Inquisitor and not like his wife and a princess. Grinning, I decided to reward him for his behavior later. Anyway, what was there to worry about? If no life signs had been detected, how dangerous could the mission be?

Opening my locker, I dressed in my flight suit and grabbed my gear. Cedrenus and I took my fighter ship. Quickly, I slid into the pilot's seat before he could. Grinning at his scowl, I shrugged. It was my ship.

Clark and Stayton were taking the lead. I took us out and felt the elation which always accompanied being set free to fly amid the stars. It was like bathing in freedom and purity. My sense of renewed confidence was fleeting. The others surrounded us treating me like a baby bird in a nest. Through my helmet, my co-pilot's voice crackled at me. Checking my audio, I made an adjustment. Nothing aboard any of our fighters was in the sort of condition which we preferred to keep them. During my pre-flight checklist, I had documented every problem.

Cedrenus warned, "Don't bother complaining."

"Whatever," I grumbled into my helmet. He was talking about our team who wasn't making the same effort at equality as Cormac.

An hour passed before the structure became visible. Cormac had decided to keep the *Empress* at a safe distance from it. Ross asked, "What is it?"

"Not a space station," Tyler replied.

"Scanning for docking access," I reported.

The others were compiling information about the structure's dimensions and construction.

"I'm not detecting any life signs." Stayton added, "It might be an unmanned communications relay."

Clark said, "It doesn't look like any type of communications relay which I've ever seen."

Checking my scans, I reported, "There is a docking port. Sending coordinates now."

"Taking lead," Clark said as he piloted his fighter toward the tunnel-shaped docking port. "High alert. Stay tight."

"Understood," Binder confirmed.

Cedrenus and I had to wait before we were allowed to fly inside of the structure, dock, and disembark. I was furious by the time my boots hit the deck. From the illumination provided by my helmet, I could tell the guys didn't give a shit whether or not I was pissed. Unlike Cormac, they weren't particularly inclined to treat me as an equal under our current circumstances. Tyler was holding a scanner to the hull. Clark and Binder held assault blasters at the ready. Levi,

Cedrenus, and I prepared probes and sent them off into different directions.

Tyler spoke. "The hull is comprised of the same alloys used in Alux warship construction."

Each of us looked over at him. Inside of my flight suit, I broke out into a cold sweat.

"Well, this isn't a warship or a vacation spot." Cedrenus watched the progress of his drone on his vid-screen while simultaneously sending the information we gathered to the *Empress*. In situations such as this, it was critical to send every tedious bit of information gathered to command. "I'm picking up a power spike."

We waited for Clark to give the okay for us to investigate. Once it came, I fell in line with my team. Staying alert while checking the readings from my probe, I stayed behind Cedrenus. We began taking readings from a panel which seemed to house the only accessible interface we'd found. Holding up my vid-screen, I scanned the command pad. The Alux symbols upon it were unmistakable. My program deciphered, translated, and read those symbols to us. Clark said, "Those are coordinates. They are locations." Carefully listening, he said, "There! Did you hear that one? It's an area of space several parsecs from Malta!"

Stayton asked, "Can we use this to get home?"

"How? How do we operate it?" I asked. My questions were brimming with desperate hope. I wanted to hold my children, close my eyes, and smell their hair. To feel their arms around my neck had become my most fervent wish.

"The Alux operate this remotely." Levi shook his head. "We don't have the proper interface to operate the wormhole directional device, but maybe scientists aboard could figure something out with this." He didn't sound convinced.

"How many of these things do they have?" I asked. No one guessed an answer.

"At least this proves something," Stayton said. "The capability of their wormhole travel is dependent upon these structures. They can't use their drives without establishing a link. It's why the Empire wasn't successful in getting us back when they tried, and we couldn't use the Alux drive with much success when we escaped the anomaly."

"These revelations are making it seem more daunting to get home," Ross grumbled.

"No, we just need to steal an Alux ship," Stayton countered.

Several of us snorted. Stealing one of their warships was no simple task. A harsh buzzing began to reverberate throughout the structure. I could feel it through my boots and hear it through my helmet's audio. Cedrenus studied his readouts and pointed. The corridor ahead was a straight shot to the energy signature our scans had detected.

Stayton said, "There are no crew quarters. There is the docking bay, but it is most likely used by repair crews. Being so inhospitable, this structure isn't a research base."

The service corridor along which we walked was merely functional. No effort had been put into its appearance. Metal edges had been soldered but left jagged. "It's like a big tool, a machine used for some purpose." My helmet hit Cedrenus in the back. He'd stopped walking while I'd been musing on our surroundings. Everyone had stopped.

"Back to your fighters! Move! Move!" Clark yelled.

Behind me, Levi tugged at my flight suit, turning me and getting me moving.

"Go! Go! Go!" Binder yelled.

Running for all I was worth, I saw my fighter through the opening at the end of the corridor and ran even harder. Scrambling up the ladder, I whacked my knee hard on one of the rungs before getting my foot back on the step and launching myself into my seat. Cedrenus was right behind me. Being the last one to dock, I was the first fighter to disembark. "Shit." Once out into space, I had a clear visual.

Cedrenus saw it too. Around the central formation of the Alux structure, power was amassing and sizzling. "The Alux are creating a wormhole! They're making one right now! They're coming! Back to the *Empress*! Now!"

His terror echoed around in my helmet. It bombarded my mind and magnified my own fear. Panic unlike anything I'd ever known sank its icy claws through my chest and shook me so hard as to tear at my soul. How could we fight off an Alux attack? Stars, worse than that, how would any of us survive being dragged into the formation of a manufactured wormhole in our fighter ships? Giving my ship all of her power, I pushed her harder than I'd ever pushed her before. Our team flanked us.

"The *Empress* is putting distance between us," Stayton reported.

Cormac, currently serving as captain, had come to the same conclusion that we had. The *Empress*, in her current state, would be destroyed within seconds of encountering an enemy vessel. She'd been patched together and had limited weapons. Her best defense was to power down, go dark, and hope to go undetected.

"Neema." Her name sounded of desperation on my lips. I had my baby out here with me, the stars only knew where, and my utmost purpose was to keep her safe. The unfortunate truth was that I could lose her at any moment, at any second now. No, I'd precede her being closer to the forming wormhole. My breathing was ragged in my helmet, sounding like a staticky rasping saw against an unmovable limb. My fighter's engine whined as it strained to continue in the direction in which I flew it.

"The drag from the wormhole is slowing us down!" Cedrenus sounded as panicked as I felt.

My hands shook on the controls. No, they were being shaken. It jarred me to my elbows. Neema. Staring off toward the tiny speck that was the *Empress* in the distance, I envisioned her beautiful eyes and soft hair. "Oh, my baby." My throat felt tight and achy as I choked out those three little words. I tried to blink away at the tears in my eyes, but they fell anyway. Unable to wipe them away, I ignored them and pushed away my pain instead. "The only chance they have is us, and we all know it."

They heard me.

After a moment of silent contemplation, Clark ordered, "Activate all weapons. Standard formation. Follow my lead. Fire on my mark." There was a hard edge to his voice. It rattled me for a moment. Had I not known him better, I'd have thought the orders had come from his father. Taking his fighter up and into a spin, he flew back the way we'd come toward the device and the ever-expanding vortex of energy swirling around its collectors. The amassing energy was being funneled toward a distant pinpoint. Clark yelled, "For the *Empress*! For the Empire! Fire!"

Cedrenus unloaded our missiles and fired our weapons at the collectors along with the others. He fired until he'd depleted our arsenal. If not for the protection of our helmets, we might have been blinded so bright was the energy as it sizzled and drew us ever closer.

"Retreat!" Clark ordered. He took his fighter down into a dive and away.

Following his lead, I fought to stay on course. Caught and pulled back, the nose of my fighter was drawn back which sent us spinning, end over end. Warning alarms blared in our helmets. "I can't stop this!" I shouted while fighting for control of my craft.

Around us, the other pilots struggled as well. All of our fighters had been caught by the preliminary explosion for which we'd served as a catalyst. "Fuck!" Stayton yelled.

On the next spin, I saw what he meant. The beam of collected energy aimed at some distant point in space to which the forming wormhole had been anchored, had transformed into an ignited fiery line of sizzling energy. Staring at the reds and blues, I pondered how such a thing could be possible in the vacuum of space. Was it the last thing I'd ever see? A blinding flash forced me to shut my eyes. Then, my helmet was forced to the back of my chair. Unable to move, barely able to breathe, I opened my eyes and saw spots. Blinking rapidly, I concentrated until I was able to make sense of my fighter's readings. "It imploded and then exploded! We've been caught on its event horizon!"

"Hang on!" Tyler yelled. His spinning fighter clipped my ship.

Grunting from the jarring it caused, I braced myself.

"Shit!" Cedrenus barked out.

"Incoming!" Binder warned. His fighter's viewport faced the destruction as he'd been flung backward.

Debris overcame us. A shard of alien metal scraped against my fighter's skin leaving a jagged gash and setting my teeth on edge with the sound it had made in the cockpit. Thankfully, it didn't slice us in half. "Cabin pressure steady." Staring at the control panels, I kept wondering when we would die. Through my helmet, I could hear the sounds of crying.

Clark said, "We did what we had to do to save the ship and crew. It's been an honor serving with each of you."

Catching my lips firmly between my teeth, I held them firmly closed, not trusting myself to speak. Clumps of metal had begun to pelt our ships while we continued to spin on the paths of our inertia. My neck ached. Unconsciously, I rolled my shoulders to relieve the ache. "I can move!" Once the second of disbelief had passed, I used all of my strength to lift my hands back to my controls. Eventually, I was able to stabilize my fighter.

"We survived the debris field," Stayton announced in blatant shock. "I can't believe we aren't fucking dead."

The others had managed to right their fighters as well. Once again flying in formation, our fighters looked like they belonged in a scrap metal recycling facility. Anguished relief carried my words from my lips. "There she is." The *Empress* was intact and holding position.

An edge to his voice, Ross asked, "What are those?"

Blips had appeared on our sensors. "Ships! And, they are heading for my ship!" Screaming in frustration, I did the only thing I could do. I held my course.

Cormac's voice came through our communications. "Hold position. For the stars' sakes act like you've got weapons."

Cedrenus asked me, "What? All they have to do is scan us and tell we're tapped out."

Levi said, "Those aren't Alux ships."

Clark ordered us into an attack formation. We waited.

"The *Empress* has been hailed by one of the alien ships. That's all I know," Cedrenus informed us.

"Their hulls are patched. Those are old ships," Tyler observed.

We waited. An hour passed. No orders came. Another hour passed. Then, the alien ships reversed course. Cormac's voice filled our helmets. "Return to the ship."

"I don't need to be told twice," Clark said as he took the lead.

Docking my ship on the flight deck was surreal.

Clark said, "I never thought we'd be doing this again."

"Neither did I." My voice didn't break. I managed to keep it together, but Clark knew. He knew the thin threads holding me together were frayed. Releasing the cockpit, I waited while Cedrenus disembarked. Then, I stowed my helmet and ran my hands over my face. Taking a deep breath, I tried to steady my nerves. I had two pressing needs. Climbing down from my fighter, I felt unsteady.

Binder had his hands and arms braced against the hull of his fighter with his head bowed. A deck worker held a hand against his back in support. He'd gotten sick. Pretending not to see the vomit on the deck at Binder's feet, I looked over at Clark. His face was drained of color, and he was walking toward me. Turning, I ran across the deck to him and threw myself into his arms. Burying my face to his chest, I closed my eyes and breathed while he enclosed me in his strong arms. I could feel the trembling in his body.

"Can I get in on that?" Levi asked. His voice held a nervous, uncertain edge.

Looking away from Clark's chest, I glanced at Levi and could tell he wasn't joking. Holding an arm out to him, Clark and I widened our circle. Levi slid his arms around both of us. Footsteps approached. Stayton, Tyler, Binder, Ross, and Cedrenus joined us one by one.

"I thought we were dead. I can't believe we're alive and actually standing here together," Ross quietly whispered for only the team to hear.

My thoughts raced to Neema and how I'd longed to hold her once more before what I'd thought to be my certain death. "Yeah, I need to go see my daughter. I really need to touch her."

Arms loosened. Feet moved back. Clark took my hand and walked at my side to the lift. We didn't leave the guys alone though. They were suddenly surrounded by crewmen who were congratulating them and patting their backs. Well, Binder was being handed a cleaning cloth.

Chapter Thirteen

The lift doors opened onto the Imperial Deck. First, it was her voice that I heard. "You can put her in the dress over there." Scanning, I found her. She was the most beautiful sight upon which I'd grown forlorn of seeing.

"Why that one?" Chef asked.

"Because her hair is green. She *don't* look good in red. She's better in blue, green, or yellow."

"Why does your doll get the red dress?" he asked.

"She has pink hair," she said, as if that explained everything.

My steps took me closer, drawn by the sound of my daughter's voice as she explained her fashion choices to a grown male, a retired Parvac warrior. As I came within a foot of her, my knees lost all feeling as if a force from the deck had drained them and dragged them down. On my knees at her side, I reached out and stroked her soft, dove-grey hair. With my deepest wish fulfilled, my eyes began to fill with tears of gratitude.

Turning her face to me, Neema scowled and wrinkled her nose. "Mommy, I love you so much, too." Leaning closer, she whispered, "You smell like Daddy after he's been fighting." She shook her head and pointed toward my quarters. "Go shower and change."

Tilting my head back, I laughed harder than I'd ever laughed in my life. Wiping my eyes on my flight suit's sleeve, I got to my feet and tugged a grinning Clark along with me to the shower. We tossed our flight suits into the cleaning unit and got inside of the shower where we took turns scrubbing each other's backs.

Eventually, I made my way back to Neema fresh, clean, and dressed in something which I hoped would be more to her liking. I'd paired the long, flowing, vibrant-blue and very expensive Arachnean Silk skirt with an inexpensive long-sleeved white T-shirt on which there was a picture of a purple octopus swimming through blue water around a colorful coral reef. It had been something I'd picked up from a gift shop on Epopeus. On a whim, I'd found some of my coral jewelry from Thalassa and put it on to properly accessorize. Rather than going around barefoot, I'd slipped on some white exercise shoes. Following my lead, Clark had dressed in civilian clothing as well, black pants and a blue silk sweater. Our fashion choices were a statement. We'd both had enough of soldiering for the day.

Getting up and running over to me, she stopped short, narrowed her eyes, and sniffed. After determining with her senses that I was no longer offensive, she proceeded to give me ample hugs and kisses. "Mommy, that was scary! There was a big boom! Then, then, Mommy, then the ship went woo, woo, woo! Like it was on the water getting bumped up and down on big waves! Then, then, it shook and shivered before it stopped. It was so many smacking sounds too, like big rain hitting us! Did you hear it? Did you?"

Kneeling before her, I took her hands. Her perceptions of what it had been like riding the explosion and resultant event horizon eased the anxiety which I'd experienced on her behalf. For her, it had been an exciting ride. She didn't know how close we'd all been to death. Her description of the metal shards striking the ship like rain reminded me so much of her father and how he'd eased my fears so long ago when he'd likened the first meteor storm I'd ever heard to rain. "Yes, I did."

"You look pretty." She tugged her hands away from mine and left me for her dolls.

Completely ignored by my child, I allowed Clark to convince me to go with him to take our clean flight suits back to our lockers on the flight deck. Stepping close enough to nudge him, I asked, "Are you more curious about those alien ships or hungry?" He looked down at me from where he'd been staring at the top of the lift doors, waiting for them to open. "Personally, I'm starving."

His expression turned blatant as he answered, "So hungry."

Quickly, we stowed our gear and went to the cafeteria. Seated around a couple of tables were the other members of our team. They were hunched over their plates and shoveling food into their mouths like they'd never before been fed. Enviously, Clark and I got in line. Thankfully, it was short.

"Looks like meat pies." My observation was made while standing up on my toes and balancing against the counter while pushing my tray along.

"Substantial ones," Clark replied. Unlike me, he wasn't struggling to see past the tall people. He was one of them.

Loaded tray finally in hand, I quickly found an empty table, pulled a chair out with my foot and sat, so that I too could sit hunched over my food like a starving Neanderthal. The meat pie was huge, and the dessert, a vanilla pudding topped with white chocolate shavings, was about two cups' worth. Not allowing myself to completely forgo the manners which the proper ladies in my life had tried to help me foster, I waited with my fork poised above my plate until Clark took his seat opposite of me. Then, I did as our team was doing. Stress had a way of making people hungrier. All other thoughts temporarily vanished. It was me and my meat pie. Inside a fluffy pastry shell were tender ice bear pieces in a deliciously thick brown gravy with peas, carrots, and pearl onions. It was perfection. I tried my best but couldn't finish it, so passed it across the table to Clark. He didn't need to ask why. He'd known I wouldn't be able to eat it all. He'd been counting on it. If I tried, I wouldn't have had room for my dessert. Smiling, I exchanged my fork for a spoon.

A loud burp preceded a chair being pulled out from our table. Stayton plopped himself down into it. "Now what? We saved ourselves from being swarmed by the Alux, but now what?" He gestured vaguely around.

My mouth was full of pudding, so I shrugged.

Clark stacked our empty bowls and then pulled his pudding close in a territorial manner while narrowing his eyes at Stayton in warning. He scooped up a huge bite and ate it. "We did what we had to do to live to fight another day. I stand by my actions if that's what this is about."

Stayton placed his hands on his thighs with his elbows out and rubbed his palms across the fabric absentmindedly. "What if we could have figured out how to operate it and get ourselves home?"

"What if we had ended up even farther into Alux territory or had blown ourselves to shit?" His spoon clattered into his already empty bowl.

Unable to finish my pudding, I slid my bowl over to him.

Stayton intercepted it, snatched it up close to his chest, grabbed my spoon, and began shoveling pudding into his mouth. "Don't look sullenly at me. She may be your wife, but she is my cousin."

Stepping toward us with a raised eyebrow, Tyler admonished, "Children, if you've finished squabbling over pudding, let's go find out about those ships. If we aren't alone out here, we need to be prepared for possible attacks."

Stayton's hand darted out. Hitting the bottom of Tyler's tray, he caused his dinnerware to clatter. I laughed at Tyler's attempts to keep everything from hitting the deck. Then, Stayton hurried off with my tray before Tyler could retaliate.

Clark met my eyes as he stood and picked up his own tray. "How quick of an exit can the *Empress* make?"

Shaking my head, I considered all of the recent damage she'd sustained. "Oh, about as fast as Tyler."

"So, basically, we're fucked."

I shrugged.

Levi, having overheard us, said, "Our fighters took heavy damage. Repair crews have been staying constantly busy keeping the

Empress going since we left Parvac, and she keeps incurring more damage."

Thinking about my fighter, I said, "I can't take mine from the flight deck as she is. Anyway, as far as weapons go, all any of us have are blasters at this point." Rubbing my temples, I walked over to the lift and waited for the guys to join me. We didn't have a lot of options. When the lift doors opened onto the bridge, Cormac's eyes met mine. "Report."

He began to stand, but I quickly waved at him to remain seated in the command chair. I'd had enough for the day. He was welcome to stay in charge and to a longer shift. "The captain of the alien vessel has extended to us an invitation to visit their city."

"Their city?" Glancing over at a star map, I gesticulated wildly. "Where the fuck is it?"

Cormac turned his head to a crewman. "Hail the Durhcu." He stood and walked over to the main viewport and held out his hand for me to join him. Slipping my hand into his, I let him draw me closer and looked where he pointed.

In the distance, space shimmered. My eyes widened, and I gasped as there, at the edge of my sight, a massive structure materialized. Its central portion was about the size of a five-story building but cylindrical in shape. Large spires protruded from its top and bottom. At those spires, life ships were docked, two above and two below. Those ships were each easily four-times the size of the *Empress*. Equidistant around the central structure, were four space docks.

Cormac asked, "Shall we accept their invitation?"

"If you're asking me that question, then you've already come to the conclusion that it can only be beneficial to us to do so. Have you not?"

He inclined his head to me.

"Alright. What have we got to lose?"

A crewman opened communications. Shortly thereafter, Durhcu shuttles were tethering the *Empress* and towing her to the nearest dock. It set my teeth on edge. During the hours it took, I reviewed reports. The ship was in worse shape than I'd realized if she couldn't manage to crawl there on her own. Cormac held his hands behind his back and stared out the view port. He was considering all of our options, and he didn't seem pleased. Lights from the space city sparkled against the viewport. Freeing my hand from Cormac's, I ran for the lift.

He called out after me. "They are a peaceful people, Teagan!"

Turning around in the lift, I grinned at him. "Neema has to see this! Be right back!"

Cormac was the only person who was paying attention to me. The others were practically stuck to the viewport. Bursting from the lift, I yelled, "Neema! Neema! Come quick!"

Shock stick in hand and with a fierce countenance, she took a running jump onto the couch, climbed to its back, scanned the room for danger, and then vaulted off it to run to stand before me. Her brow was furrowed.

"Hey! Want to go see aliens that no Parvac princess has ever before seen?"

Head tilted, she asked, "Not even Gama?"

I shook my head, grabbed her hand, and groaned at her guards wishing they'd hurry. One of them said, "We have already been briefed, Princess Probus."

I asked him, "Are we certain they aren't a threat? Cormac said they were peaceful, but come on. I mean really. How the fuck can we be sure?"

"Oh, Mommy said...."

Interrupting her, I said, "Don't use words you can't define, my darling." I gave her my sweetest smile.

She snorted at me. However, as soon as the lift doors opened, her eyes lit up with excitement, and she ran to the viewport where she pushed her way through the legs in her way as if they were saplings in a forest. Clark bent and picked her up to give her a better view. The male to my right cleared his throat. My nose was even with his bicep. I hadn't ever paid attention to how big and strong her guards were. Goren wasn't big enough to distract me from the aliens though.

As if Goren knew it, he spoke up. "Princess Probus asked how we can be certain they mean us no harm."

"Hey, Justin!" Neema shouted, even though he was only about two feet away from her. "Princess Neema Alaric Montgomery Lee of House Probus of Parvac wants to know, too!"

Her guard bowed. "Yes, Princess Neema."

I waited impatiently for Cormac to put my worries at ease. He didn't make me wait for long. "The Durhcu have assured us that they mean us no harm. They are at war with the Alux. This," he said as he gestured at the alien structure, "is an observation outpost." Cormac's eyes glittered with delight. "As an act of goodwill, they have shared with us their amassed surveillance of our mutual enemy."

"I see." Approaching him cautiously, I considered what exactly he meant.

"Decades," he responded, seeing the question in my eyes.

"What do they want in return?" I asked.

"We already gave them what they wanted. We destroyed the wormhole generator for this sector of space. They would have done so themselves. However, they have been hiding here, trying to avoid annihilation while spying on our mutual enemy." In seconds, the delight left his eyes and was replaced by a cold rage. "The Alux decimated their population. In order to survive, they fled their home world. They escaped in life ships and devoted themselves to the construction of this outpost, saving themselves with this camouflaging technology."

"If they're so advanced, why haven't they destroyed the Alux?" Anger flooded my senses. Gesturing wildly, I said, "They can do all of this? What the fuck, Cormac? They are the most advanced society that I've ever witnessed! What the actual fuck?"

"Hey, Justin!" Neema yelled from her lofty perch in Clark's arms. "What is the define nation of the word fuck?"

Her guard looked at me.

"Don't you dare!" I shouted as I air-jabbed a finger at him. Hands on hips, I turned back to Cormac and waited for an answer.

"We are soon to find out. They have offered to assist with our repairs."

My shoulders dropped, and my thoughts raced. "I want heavily armed guards watching their every move. I don't know them, and I don't trust them. They might want to steal our ship. What if they want to toss us out of airlocks or worse, turn us over to the Alux?" Moving out of the crush of bodies, I sat in my command chair and sent my orders out to the crew.

"I would prefer not to trust them either," Cormac whispered in my ear as he leaned down close. "However, as you well know, our damages are heavy and our resources are few."

Lifting my elbows to the armrests, I clasped my hands before me and lifted my knuckles to my lips where I tapped them against my lips while I thought. "My life aboard *Tora* wasn't just wasted years. If bartering is to be done, I'll do it." What did these aliens want from us? Cormac thought we'd already given them what they wanted. I knew better. They always wanted something else. All of them did.

As the *Empress* was docked, every nuance of the procedure was meticulously documented. Rushing back to our quarters, Neema, Clark, and I changed into more professional attire. In my uniform and boots and armed with every weapon that Sparrow had ever made for me, I felt less powerless. Neema, I had dressed in tightly woven Arachnean Spider silk from head to toe. Her safety was my main priority. My crew and ship came in second. Proudly, she rested her hand on her shock stick.

"Are you seriously going to allow her a weapon? She's a child!" Ness glared at me in outrage as if I were a terrible parent.

"Ambassador Ness, mind your own fucking business." I didn't even want to look at him. As tense as I was and under the circumstances, punching him in the nuts would be a stress reliever.

Edvard raised an eyebrow at him. "Do you need your tongue to ask questions?"

Ness, already sweating in eager anticipation, straightened his shoulders. His face drained of color. "It would help."

"Mommy, I don't like it when Ambassador Ness gets hurt. It's mean."

Holding her hand, I tried to put my own emotions aside to comfort her. "You're right, my sweet. It is a shame that Ambassador Ness is so slow to learn proper respect."

A dozen of us waited on Deck Five near what had been the transport and cargo bays. Now, those areas were so much empty space. Crews continued working on repairs to our fighter ships. However, currently, those crews stood armed and ready to defend us, not that it would do any good. We had nowhere to run, limited resources, and nothing but blasters left to us. Well, at least we had my fancy new blaster cannons. They were good. "Oh, Sparrow," I whispered like a wish.

"Lowering cargo bay ramp," a crewman reported.

For the third time, I checked the emergency respirator around Neema's neck. Leaving their oxygen content to chance wasn't something I was prepared to do, not with my daughter. Chin held high and holding hands with my little princess, I walked from the bay and down the ramp.

"Whoa! Mommy! Mommy, look! They are blue! Mommy! Blue aliens!"

"So much for diplomacy," Edvard dryly stated.

Walking toward the group of Durhcu dignitaries, I kept my expression as calm and pleasant as possible. The Durhcu were huge. It was probably why their ships were so large. Taking a step toward me, a Durhcu extended a hand to me. Surprised, I held my hand out to him. His palm was twice the size of mine. He smiled. His teeth were like giant, flat white marshmallows. "Welcome to you, Princess Probus of Parvac and to your crew." The universal translator at his throat lit up with each word he spoke. His actual words had a lyrical beauty to them in an unfamiliar mix of sounds.

"Thank you on behalf of myself and my crew. Your hospitality is most welcomed. We find ourselves here in space which is unknown to us, pursued by our common enemy." Each of my words caused a piece of translator technology over his ear to light up.

"The Alux will not find you here. I promise. Our veil is in place. Stay. Be at peace. Strengthen your ship and your crew." His eyes were kind. He looked down. Neema was tugging at the corner of the white tunic he wore over black pants and boots. The other individuals in his company wore all black just as we did.

Exasperated with her, I managed to keep my expression serene. I didn't know how he would respond and would have preferred for her to stay closer to me and quiet. My preferences weren't high on Neema's agenda. She was too excited.

"Yes?" He bent his knees and hunched down to her.

"What's your name? I'm Princess Neema. I was with my mommy when the Alux attacked us. We had to go fast!" She raised her right hand straight up and made her eyes big. "I only got one daddy with me. Pierce and Lorca aren't here. Got no Flake." The tone of her voice broke my heart. The tears spilling from her eyes made me cry, too.

"Oh, my baby." Lowering myself to my knees, I wrapped my arms around her.

"Brothers at home," she sobbed.

"All will be well, Princess Neema." His words were like a song.

Taking her face from where she'd hidden it against my shoulder, she looked up at him. His eyes were a rich brown and the size of peaches. "All will be well because I am Khe and will make all well. Yes?" He smiled at her with big marshmallow teeth.

"You can try, but Neema *gots* big problems."

He nodded. "Seeing new sights might free your mind from your problems while we work to solve them." Turning his head, he gestured to one of his entourage. "This is Akha our chief engineer." Akha slowly approached and extended his hand to me. As we shook hands, Khe said, "He will coordinate with you to repair your damage."

"Thank you. Please, allow me to introduce Cormac."

After the two of them had shaken hands, Cormac led Akha over to meet the most experienced of the engineers whom we had with us.

I gave a sigh of relief. Quietly, I said, "It's funny, but I feel better already."

Edvard said, "They are telepathic empaths who read you through the touch of your hand." He held his own hands behind his back.

Khe grinned and nodded. "We do not need to touch." Turning to Ambassador Ness, he said, "Shakhep is like you, a xenobiologist." He motioned toward a large blue male who held a scanner far more advanced than the one which Ness attempted to use in a discreet manner on our hosts. Stepping forward, he eagerly shook hands with his alien counterpart.

"You have Alux aboard?" Shakhep asked.

Ness nodded. "Yes, they attempted to commandeer our ship."

"They're dead. Don't worry," I interjected with a reassuring smile.

The two of them moved aside quickly losing themselves in whatever weird biological shit it was that so interested them.

"Flake is my snow fox. My friend, my friend, her name is Poppy. Her snow fox is named Milk." Neema was chatting up a blizzard with her new friend Khe.

I felt a surprising tug on my soul. Closing my eyes, I took a deep breath and luxuriated in the safety of the empathic bond. Then, opening my eyes, I searched for Yukihyo, but found Stig watching me with his cold eyes and a raised eyebrow.

"Why so shocked?" he quietly asked. "You are the one who bound me." He directed my attention toward Neema. "She is an Enyo who has been deprived of the strong empathic bonds on which she has been nurtured. Khe heals her emotions as we speak. Your debt to these people deepens."

Khe raised an eye ridge. A thin brow of sparse black hair grew there. He was bald, but I couldn't tell if it was from age or by choice. "There is nothing owed for helping a child to feel safe and happy. We find peace through caring for those in need." Khe studied Edvard. Then, he tipped his head in a barely perceptible movement before patting Neema gently on the arm and rising to his full height.

"Princess Probus," Ness, flustered with excitement, spoke quickly, "Shakhep has invited me to his lab on habitat ring four unless of course you have need of my services here."

As I listened to him, I detected no signs of a lisp and was glad his tongue had healed so well. "You will take two guards with you." Lifting my hand, I gestured for warriors, Inquisitors both, to come forward.

Blushing, Ness said, "Certainly, we can trust these kind people."

"Ambassador Ness, trust has nothing to do with my order. We all follow protocol for the purpose in which it is intended, and we will remain on our best behavior for the sake of future relations. Am I clear?"

Listening to me for once, he realized it was logical behavior. "Yes. Forgive me. This is all so terribly exciting."

"Do enjoy yourself, doctor." I kept our conversation as quiet as possible, not that it mattered amongst telepathic empaths who tried to act as though they were ignoring us.

Khe gave a nod of his head to Shakhep confirming my order was to be heeded. The two scientists left our company. The two Inquisitors, which one of my Inquisitor husbands had planted amongst my crew at some point, along with a Durhcu guard accompanied them.

In a blasé tone, Edvard said, "Every last one of them is either an Inquisitor or a retired soldier. The least lethal of your crew, besides Ness, are yourself and your team."

Sneering at him, I asked, "Oh? What about Neema?"

Narrowing his eyes at me, he sneered right back. "I was including her."

"You fucking shit head," I whispered. "How would you like to suck on one of your own nuts for lunch?"

"Thanks to you, I already have and didn't find it appetizing. Perhaps, you might learn some new recipes rather than being so redundantly boring."

Fury had me balling my free hand into a fist.

"Shall we take a walk around the communal ring?"

Clark nudged me to answer Khe.

"Yes, thank you." Turning my back to Edvard, I gave our host my attention and took a few steps in his direction. Under my breath to Clark, I said, "What I really need is some alone time on the exercise mat with good old Eddie." Clark gave me a look but kept his thoughts on the matter to himself.

"Mommy, look!"

The spacious lift into which Khe had led us was transparent and cylindrical in shape. The transport tubes were at intervals throughout the structure. Clinging to the outside of them were flowering vines.

"Oh, flowers!" Neema exclaimed with joy as we were carried away. We went up two decks to the habitat ring at the station's center. As we exited the lift, Khe plucked one of the purple blooms and handed it to Neema after first allowing me to scan it.

Intrigued, I reported, "They're edible."

Clark decided to conduct his own scan.

"Princess Neema, if your mother allows it, I shall have a botanist deliver Vadu vines to your ship. They keep the air clean, and their flowers make a nice..." the translator searched before voicing, "snack."

Neema laughed. "Is it okay, Mommy?"

"It's okay with me if it is okay with Dr. Savelli. What do we say?"

"Thank you." Neema gave him her sweetest smile. Cradling her flower in her hands, she sniffed it and smiled.

Khe gestured. "Here we have entertainments, foods, exercise, and activities."

Clear, plasti, walled enclosures ringed the deck. Hydroponic planters served as partitions in front of the various rooms. Other than on the lifts, I didn't see any doors. Neema watched as a group of people used their fingers to paint on a rough canvas. Going along with her as she tugged at my hand, we stood to the side of the transparent room and watched. A female Durhcu, larger than the males who were with her, smiled and spoke. Khe translated. "Jacu is an artist. She has taught her students to make canvas of plant fibers and paints of flowers and minerals. Now, after years of study, they learn to create images. She offers instruction to young ones in the early hours and extends an invitation."

"Thank you."

With another smile, Jacu returned to her students.

Throughout the extensive habitat ring, Durhcu were engaged in all manner of activity, artistic, athletic, and culinary. Khe pointed out different groups and explained with what they occupied themselves.

Clark nudged Stayton and gestured with his chin toward a group playing a rather violent game with a ball.

Neema gasped. My attention snapped back to her. A Durhcu child, who was almost as tall as me, had materialized in front of her.

Khe placed his hands on the large child's shoulders. "Bhamak, what did we discuss?" Khe's cheeks darkened.

Neema shrugged out of my grip.

"Princess Probus, please forgive my offspring. My people do their best to be respectful. However, we have never encountered your like. In addition, your people have destroyed the Alux wormhole generator, a thing we could not do." Unlike the other words which had a lyrical quality, their word for the Alux was harsh and guttural.

Edvard asked, "Why couldn't you? Your technologies are superior to ours."

"Doing so would have alerted the Alux to our position. They believe they have eradicated us. We survive by hiding here in open visage. We devote our resources to shielding our minds and bodies with our veil."

Edvard smiled. It was a creepy, sinister smile.

I realized he was communicating with Khe telepathically. Khe gave a nod of his head as did the others with him.

Not knowing what had been said, I spoke. "On behalf of the Cosmos Coalition of the Parvac Empire, Laconian Sector, and Galaxic Expanse, perhaps we can come to an agreement."

"This would please us," Khe replied.

"Weapons in exchange for services?" I asked.

Neema was speaking to her new friend, Khe's son. "Blow the fuckers up. That's what my Mommy says about the Alux. They bad." My face was now the one to darken in embarrassment. She took his hand and vanished.

My guts dropped to my feet. "Neema!" Panic engulfed me. I couldn't see her! I couldn't sense her!

"Bhamak!" Khe roared. He pressed a command on his wrist cuff. Bhamak and Neema materialized a few partitions down.

Bhamak stomped his foot. His thoughts rolled clearly through my mind. "We want to play! You have them! Why can't I have her?"

"Mommy! I want this! Bhamak has one! I want one, too! Please! Please?" She pointed at something while staring at me.

Meanwhile, my heart had escaped my chest. The fancy artificial contraption had gone from my chest, to my throat, and felt like it was in my fucking nose. "Neema," I growled.

She gave me the look that I often gave to Clark. It said I'm not a baby. I can take care of myself. "I *needs* something equal for a trade, Mommy!"

Bhamak had brought her to a store. Of course, he had. Only my daughter and I could be stranded in unknown space in enemy territory with alien rebel survivors and manage to find someplace to shop. Closing my eyes, I lifted my face and groaned. Then, I jogged over to her with an arm over my aching boobs. The sudden fright had me leaking. Thoughts of my babies sent a knife-like pain through my soul. "What is it, Neema?" My voice sounded of defeat.

Bhamak was already leading her inside. He was showing her capes, helmets, and gravity boots. I was hoping he couldn't hear my loud mental utterance of the word fuck.

Apologetically, Khe explained, "It started as a means of keeping our offspring safe from the Alux. It has developed into their favorite mode of recreation."

A female was providing Neema with a plasti helmet with a sparkling attached cape and a wrist cuff. To me, she handed a larger adjustable cuff. Already getting telepathic lessons from Bhamak, Neema said, "Mommy, buy this. Gotta go play. I'll be with Mack!"

Before I could pay or even learn how to operate the cuff, the little heifer was gone. "Neema Alaric Montgomery Lee, get back here!"

A pale-faced Khe, now a light-blue shade, met my eyes with evident horror. "My deepest apologies. We can track them."

Edvard started laughing.

I stomped on his foot. "It's not funny! Now, I have to have a talk with her about stealing, along with ditching her guards, and everything else she just did!"

Edvard asked, "How do we pay for the items with which Princess Neema has absconded?"

Clark spoke up. "It is my responsibility." He glared at Stig and moved to speak to the female purveyor of parental torment apparatus.

She asked, "Might I have a scan of that in trade?" She was pointing to Clark's blaster. He looked at me.

I refused to look at Eddie. Instead, I took out my vid-screen and called Cormac. "Inquisitor Gordian," I began so he'd know the call was of the professional and not the sexual variety.

"Allow it," he responded before I could ask.

I shouldn't have been surprised that he knew everything happening around me. I nodded to Clark. Unholstering his weapon, he handed it over. She placed it on a padded mat and pressed an activation button. Her eyes twinkled with pleasure. The pad, upon closer inspection, wasn't made of fabric. Rather, millions of needle-like sensors rose up to encompass the weapon until it looked like it had been dropped in deep grass. Leaving Clark and Stayton to oversee the trade, Khe and I tracked and caught our children where they'd veiled themselves and walked in their gravity boots up the hull, fifteen feet up.

"Stars," Cedrenus muttered.

"I know, right? At least now I can send her off after Peter depending on those boots' settings. Hopefully, they work on trees and ceiling beams."

"Peter?" Khe asked as he began searching my memories. Abruptly, the intrusion stopped.

Stig had placed himself sedately in front of Cedrenus and me. In his cultured tones, he stated, "In our cultures, amongst those forming the Cosmos Coalition, it is considered rude to avail oneself of another's thoughts without invitation. It is a violation."

Fear washed over me before being rapidly squashed.

"It was not my intention!" Khe looked at me from around Stig and apologized with sincerity.

"Of course, in a first contact situation such as the one in which we currently find ourselves, we will need to make allowances for each other in the sake of peace." Without being observed, I nudged Cedrenus and signed a question to him at my right side. "Keep an eye on Stig?"

"Understood," he signed back.

Meanwhile, Neema pouted at me.

Khe said, "You are weary from your battles. Please, accept our hospitality. We have lodgings for you as well as for what crew you will allow. Chief Engineer Akha's teams have begun repairs, and repairs tend to be acoustically unpleasant." He smiled at me with big marshmallow teeth.

"Thank you. We accept. Once we are rested, we can begin negotiations for the repairs."

Khe inclined his head to me. I could see in his eyes that he already had a few ideas. Sensing my thoughts as I'd broadcast them, his smile broadened. He said to his son, "Bhamak, you will lead us to our lodging area. You will walk slowly and unveiled."

The young Durhcu child, having been admonished by his parent, contritely obeyed. Likewise, Neema chose to behave. She knew that I wasn't the only adult in her life who had a few words for her. Reaching out, she took hold of Bhamak's hand. "Don't worry, Mack. I'm not in lots of trouble. Ooh, you should have seen what Nik and

Peter did to Mommy's sitting room. It was a mess!" Then, to my horror, she proceeded to loudly describe all that had happened.

A soft grunt had me looking over at Khe. He said, "For all our differences, our children are so similar."

Sighing, all I could do was nod.

The children led us into one of the lifts. Bhamak showed Neema which command to push. All transgressions forgotten, they laughed and giggled as if they'd never done anything for which they might need to display contrite behavior.

Quietly, Stig asked, "What have they done, really?"

Responding telepathically, I said, "Scared me half to death! And, embarrassed me! For the stars' sakes, we just met these people!"

Khe cleared his throat.

Stig looked down his aristocratic nose at me.

Realizing that I'd broadcasted my thoughts instead of sending them directly to Stig which wasn't exactly easy for someone who hadn't been reared in a telepathic household, I blushed. Who needs a kid to embarrass herself when she can do it all on her own?

We all followed the kids out of the lift. Khe gestured. "This is our section." He referred to what resembled the end of a street. Great aesthetic effort had been made to create a habitat which resembled that which the Durhcu had been forced to flee. Situated along the wide, tan stone path were residences. Rather than brick or stone, the residential structures were constructed of hydroponic plasti walls in which all manner of vegetation grew. Instead of doors, each domicile had an arch built into the plasti through which to come and go. Now, as we walked, glimpses of Durhcu families as they went about their activities could be seen. At intervals along the path of tan stone pavers, water splashed and trickled in large, round, ornate fountains. At the end of the path, Bhamak, who still held Neema's hand, led us through the plasti arch of one of the dwellings. "Want to play?" he asked her hopefully.

"Yeah!" she said with the considerable exuberance of a child left too long to her own solitary devices. The two of them ran off to the right.

Following them with my gaze, I watched as they ran toward a large spherical-shaped room. Three spheres lined the far-back right portion of the dwelling space, and three were along the wall directly to my right.

Seeing our curiosity, Khe explained, "The large pods are sleep spheres. The smaller four there," he pointed, "are for play, learning, medical aid, and exercise. They also serve as protection in the case of an emergency evacuation."

Across from the entrance, along the hull, was the largest viewport wall I'd ever seen. Slowing walking the extensive length of deck toward it, I exclaimed, "The view of the stars is breathtaking." Having become so completely captivated, it was a moment before I realized how far into the living quarters I'd advanced. Now, I stood in the center of the enormous private habitat.

Quietly, Stig said, "Indeed." He'd kept pace at my side and now gestured toward the left and a second viewport wall of slightly narrower dimensions. There were no spheres on the left. Instead, it had a more familiar appearance. A large round table surrounded with comfortable-looking chairs was closest to the entrance. A second, smaller table and chairs occupied the back of the room in what was unmistakably a kitchen.

"You have a lovely home."

"Thank you. We have tried to recreate the appearance of our neighborhoods as they once were on our planet so as to feel more at home." He led us over to the pod in which the children had gone. Inside, the two of them were playing a game.

"Stones?" I asked incredulously.

"You know this game?" Khe was as surprised as I was. Joyously, he exclaimed, "We will play!" Turning away from the sphere in which the children played, he pointed. Then, loping over to the left side of the living space, he touched one of the panels on the floor to ceiling storage compartment located there. The storage compartments had been designed to look like a wooden wall.

I was curious of what sorts of things might fill the storage wall in the kitchen. Wistfully, I asked, "Do you have coffee?"

After placing the box on the table that he pulled from a hidden shelf, he extended his hand to me. His expression quizzical, he obviously had no idea what coffee might be. Giving him permission to read my thoughts on the matter, I gave him my hand. His hand was strong and soft, but he shook his head. His translator had no word for delicious, strong, hot coffee. I didn't get it. They played stones, but they didn't drink coffee? Was not coffee, like hope and love, a universal truth?

Sympathetically, he said, "We have a drink made of leaves which might be similar. I will make some. Just one moment."

As he hurried toward the kitchen, I said, "Tea, yes, we drink tea. Thank you ever so much." I tried to appear happy about the tea. However, it was difficult for me to be happy about boiled leaf tears.

After a few games of stones with our host, some tea, and a meal consisting of a salad made of flowers, a root vegetable soup, and a dense bread, all of which Neema adored, we were sent off to our pods.

"Come along," I said as I coaxed Neema along.

"But, Mommy, can't we play a little longer?" Her tone was whiny and tired.

"Yes, you can play in the morning after breakfast." Hoisting her up onto my hip, I carried her into the sleep sphere which our host had offered to us. Aside from the adult bed, a smaller pod-shaped bed was affixed to the wall much like our bunks aboard our stealth ships. A sliding door in the back of the sleep pod revealed a bathroom. "Do you want to take a bath with me before bed?"

Her expression bland, she said, "Bath? Duh."

The alien tub was shaped like a massive boiled egg that had been sliced in half lengthwise and hollowed out. Filled with water and bubbles, it resembled a whole boiled egg once more.

Eyes closed and reclining in the suds, my daughter said, "Ugh. Yes, this is the life." Her helmet, cape, wristband, and clothing made a disorderly pile on the floor.

I groaned in relief as I ditched my boots. Then, it took me some pondering before I figured out how to use the waste unit. Female users had to pull the hidden seat out. I yawned so hard that my jaw cracked. Looking at Neema, I said, "It's a good thing you know how to swim." Stepping into the tub which was only partially filled for her safety, I lowered myself. How long had it been since I'd had a real bath? Showers were fine, but baths were a true luxury. Neema, who'd let her head fall back, was floating. Durhcu had much larger tubs than did even Parvacs. Except for her face, belly, and toes, she was covered in bubbles. Chuckling to myself, I soaked while keeping an eye on her. We stayed as we were until our fingers and toes had shriveled.

Thankfully, Clark had brought from the ship gowns and changes of clothing. "Everyone is settled for the rest cycle. Stig is talking to Khe about weapons. Inquisitor Gordian reported that our fighters have been repaired and their hulls coated with the plasti veil material which the Durhcu use."

"Will it help to hide us from detection?" I had already dried Neema and dressed her in her gown. She was asleep as soon as she climbed into her bed. Covering her with blankets, I pulled her privacy screen closed.

Clark, having already gone into the bathing chamber, had not heard my question, so I turned down the bed. The blankets were woven of a soft, plant-based fiber. With a final hard yawn, I climbed under the covers. The Durhcu didn't use pillows, but the mattress was soft and cushiony. Snuggling under the covers, I fell asleep.

All was quiet and still. Wiping my mouth on a blanket, I snuggled closer to Clark, so solid and warm. Need clawed at me. Sensing it, he roused from dreams. He slid his strong, battle-calloused palms over my shoulders, back, and thighs. The stubble of his cheeks scratched my lips ever so slightly as I kissed him. Pushing his pajama bottoms down, I straddled him, placed him at my entrance, pushed down, and sighed. Slowly, I rode him, gently rocking my hips forward and back. The ache grew and grew into an agonizing and desperate need. It drove me to ride him harder and at a frenzied pace. Then, the ache shattered, replaced by an incredibly intense wave of pleasure which carried me along, boneless and floating as if on a winding river. Having happily collapsed upon Clark's chest, he groaned. His manly appendage was huge and hard within me. Rolling me to my back, he dug his fingers into my hips and drove himself forward and back at a delicious pace.

While he fought for his release, a male voice, not Clark's, whispered, "Did you know that the reason passionate encounters between Durhcu and the salacious dream-like fantasies of the lonely don't bombard our unshielded psyches during our sleep is thanks to psychic veil technology built into the fabrication of these sleep pods?"

I froze. Disengaging myself from Clark, I scurried out from under him and out of the bed.

"Ignore him," Clark said.

While my fancy, artificial heart tried to beat its way out of my chest, I found a light to activate. Then, I wished once more for darkness as I stared in wide-eyed horror at Stig. He appeared delighted in a smug, asshole sort of way. "What are you doing in our bed? Stars! What is he doing in our sleep pod?"

Clark rubbed a hand over his eyes. "Our host put him in here. Said he was also your mate. Cormac ordered me to comply. You were sleeping."

"Oh, did he? Oh, he fucking did?" My fury made Stig's diabolical grin seem even more desirous of a slap.

"Mommy, what's wrong?" She pushed open her privacy screen.

"We are getting dressed so we can go and have a chat with Cormac."

As Neema and I entered the bathing chamber to dress, I heard Clark ask, "What are you so happy about?"

"It pleases me to see your obvious sexual frustration. It is something of which I am quite familiar. When I found my perfect mate, my beautiful Kitty, I'd believed my lonely, twisted suffering to be at an end. However, after too brief of a moment in time, the Alux have ripped heaven from my grasp and cast me into an existence made far more bitter after having tasted peace and contentment." Into my thoughts, he said, "But you sank a claw into my soul, ripping me up from the oblivion of madness and drawing me once more into an existence of populated isolation, together but apart."

Selfishly, I wanted to throw a mental wall between us to protect myself from his abject misery. As far as self-preservation went, it would have been the intelligent, calculated thing to do. It was what an Inquisitor should do, but I couldn't bring myself to do it, to leave him alone. He was right. I hadn't allowed him to take a deep dive into a pool of madness. I hadn't left him to agonize in his own private grief. No, I hadn't done so. I hadn't done so because of Luca. Neema drew me from my musings. She was searching for her toothbrush in the small overnight bag that had been packed for her.

I quickly washed and dressed, but my surroundings were a blurred, out of focus backdrop to the vibrant memory of Luca's beautiful eyes, and his thickly muscled and hairy arms and legs. He'd been a cuddly bear of a male. The smile the memory of him had evoked vanished as it was replaced with the memory of the gaping hole where his chest had been. Papa had killed the male responsible. He'd killed him with his bare hands.

Into my thoughts, Stig whispered, "All I ask is to hear the Alux draw their last breaths while I watch the lights fade from their eyes."

Dressed in my uniform, I exited the bathroom. Stig sat propped up in bed, watching me. Meeting his eyes, I said, "Then, rather than our worship, let us give them death."

Clark said, "If the two of you are talking about the Alux, I'm in agreement."

I narrowed my eyes at him.

"What did I do?" He shoved his feet into his boots.

"What did you do? What did you do? You did me while he was in bed with us!" Furious, I imagined punching him in the nose.

"As I recall, you're the one who did me!"

"Ugh. Mommy." Neema followed me into the room wearing her helmet, cape, and wrist cuff over her clothing.

I wore my own cuff and had made certain that I knew how to track her. "Let's go show your new gear to Cormac."

Face scrunched up in disappointment, she stomped her foot. "Mommy, no! It's playtime. You promised," she whined as we left the sleep sphere with Clark following behind us. Neema's guards were stationed to either side. Her disappointment immediately vanished. "Yay!" Breaking into a run, she lifted her arms and was caught by Cormac.

He lifted her up and spun her around in his arms. "You appear to have slept well. Chef has prepared pancakes for you and a guest of your choosing."

Eyes wide, she held his face between her hands. "Guest? Neema gets to pick?"

He nodded.

"Mack!" she yelled.

My worry that she might be disappointed vanished. Materializing at Cormac's side, Bhamak smiled up at him. Cormac asked, "Princess Probus, do you have any objections to a pancake breakfast?"

"No, as long as it is okay with Chief Administrator Khe."

The big blue alien smiled and spread his hands wide. "It will give us the opportunity to learn from Chief Engineer Akha what repairs have been made to your vessels. Shall we?"

Falling into step with Stig following us at a sedate pace, we left Khe's residence with the children, who'd rendered themselves invisible, leading the way. I noted that Neema's guards now wore tracking cuffs which were identical to my own. Turning my head to look at Khe, I asked, "What would be acceptable in trade for a few more of those?" I gestured toward my invisible child while making a mental tally of the children who would want to play with them, Niklos, Peter, Poppy, and all of their cousins throughout the Parvac Empire, Laconian Sector, and Galaxic Expanse. Lifting my chin, I imagined myself as the favorite aunt.

"I am certain we can work something out." Khe's tone was very pleasant.

Who did he remind me of in that moment? Oh, yes. He sounded just like Hiroshi Lee when he was about to make himself an excellent deal.

After making our way aboard my ship, we stuffed ourselves with pancakes made with a Durhcu flour which was comparable to our own flours. The difference was barely discernable. Neema certainly didn't notice. She was happier than I'd seen her since we'd departed from Parvac. Since the children were enjoying themselves, we decided to let them remain on the Imperial Deck to play under the supervision of Neema's guards. Then, we went to the flight deck to see the repairs which the Durhcu engineers were overseeing.

As I began my pre-flight check list, the dwindling hope which I'd been experiencing since our debacle's onset slowly started replenishing. I ran my palms over my fighter ship's hull. The worst of the damage had been filled and mended with a clear molecularly bonded resin. Close inspection showed me that the battle scars were much worse than I'd initially accepted. However, now that she was cleaned up and repaired, I could see how close I'd come to not making it back to dock in my berth. I scanned the fighters on the flight deck. Like my own ship, the others had been repaired. The Durhcu crews seemed eager to work. They probably hadn't had much to do before our arrival. Their pent-up energy showed. Our fighters had not only been repaired, but they had been improved. It gave us a chance we hadn't had before. We might actually survive long enough to be rescued after all.

It wasn't only our fighter ships that the Durhcu crews had been repairing. The *Empress* was being outfitted with a plasti sheeting which would when activated veil her and make her virtually undetectable to not only the Alux but everyone. In fact, they would have a hard time detecting the *Empress* or our fighters with their sensors once the work was complete.

"How will I ever be able to repay you for all of this? You've given us a chance to survive." I looked away from the repair crews of Durhcu and Parvac working together and over at Khe.

He grinned, obviously delighted I'd asked.

Chapter Fourteen

On the command deck of my ship seated around a conference table, the question I asked sounded incredulous even to my own ears. "You want us to do what?" A chill ran down my spine and along my limbs.

"It will be a rather simple thing for you, really. You have, after all, destroyed the manner in which the Alux were arriving to this sector of space to begin with. All we ask is that you try to deactivate the biodome encompassing our home world. If the Alux are not alerted to our biochemistry, they will continue to believe in our eradication. By the time they arrive in our system by conventional means, we will have amassed enough resources to ensure our survival for decades." Khe was making every effort to make it sound like a simple mission.

Putting my elbows on the table, I laced my fingers together and rested my chin on my thumbs. The *Empress* continued to replenish power, and the Durhcu had shared more information with us than what they had amassed on the Alux. Now, we had star charts of this sector of space which included a habitable planet, the Durhcu home world. It was a home world which they didn't dare visit. If we triggered the Alux biodome, we were fucked. "Go over the plan and the technology again."

From across the table, Stayton shot me a look.

Focusing on him, I lowered my hands to my lap. My left eyebrow raised, I said, "They have done to them what they plan to do to us."

Stig stood and walked over to a viewport. Hands clasped behind his back, his voice was fueled with hatred when he spoke. "Before they attack Parvac, they will lay siege to Earth, whose majority population is not telepathic or genetically adaptive to strong mental barriers. Unlike the Durhcu and Laconian races, the inhabitants of Earth will be a bountiful feast."

He was right. I looked around the table. On their faces, I could see their worry and fear. It wasn't a surprise since I was experiencing the same emotions. Turning back to Khe, I said, "There is a matter to which we must first attend before my team and I embark on a mission which will further antagonize our mutual enemy."

Khe, sensing he would gain his objective, gave me his undivided attention. Raising both of his sparse black eyebrows, he grunted. "You have already riled the Ripzees by destroying their wormhole generator and likely dozens of their awaiting ships in the process."

I shrugged. "It's what I do. I blow shit up. Whatever. My point is this. On the behalf of the Cosmos Coalition of the Parvac Empire, Laconian Sector, and Galaxic Expanse, I extend to you a formal invitation to join us in our efforts to protect our peoples from destructive forces."

Sitting back in his seat, Khe asked, "What would such an alliance entail?"

When Edvard Stig turned from the viewport, the smile reached his eyes for once. Only, it wasn't a smile inspired by joy or happiness. It was an expression of his expectation of one day seeing for himself, through his machinations, the annihilation of those responsible for his wife's death. Within him, a cosmic storm of vengeance brewed, and other than keeping him on my radar, I didn't know what else to do about him. Stig said, "Let us go over the details of this agreement."

For the next few hours, Stig and I discussed contractual responsibilities with Khe and his advisors. Eventually, after adding certain stipulations, they agreed to our proposed alliance. Khe studied one of his fingernails. "We are in agreement and have affixed our hands to the terms. However, there is a problem."

"What?" I stared at him.

He gave me an innocent look. "You have agreed to give us scans of your weapons so that we may fight our common enemy. Unfortunately, the fabrication of these weapons is dependent on obtaining ores and minerals from our home world where we cannot go."

Forcing myself not to roll my eyes, I gave him my sweetest smile. Sparrow would find satisfaction in arming the Durhcu. She would introduce them to all sorts of hysteria inducing implements. "We have a team aboard preparing a synthetic neurotoxin and remote delivery system for your use so that after our departure, you will have an immediate means of defense. However, now that our alliance is official, we will do our utmost to render our immediate assistance on your proposed mission."

Khe smiled. "The Durhcu wish to facilitate your mission to our planet."

I gave him a nod. Hopefully, we'd both be getting what we wanted out of the deal.

After the Durhcu had departed from aboard the *Empress*, I put Neema down for a nap. Then, my team and I took over our living area and began planning our mission. Levi was seated on a couch with vid-screens and holographic maps spread across the cushions. He noticed something on a screen. "There. Do you see it?"

"No," Binder admitted.

Sending the recorded clip to each of us at a slower speed, he waited while Stayton analyzed it. "I see. There's a twenty-second window every planetary rotation when the power grid fluctuates."

"Why does it fluctuate?" Clark asked.

"A trap?" Levi asked.

Ross squinted at an image. "No, it looks like a fried power relay. They think the Durhcu are extinct, so why fix it?" Raising his eyes from the images he'd collected with long-distance imaging, he said, "Our biology shouldn't trigger any warnings, but I'd prefer not to register at all."

The rest of us agreed.

Stig barged in. Fuming, he said, "Out!"

Looking around at each other, the guys were perplexed, but then so was I. Mimicking his imperious, odious tone, I said, "If this concerns the Durhcu or the mission, you may speak in front of my loyal subjects."

Stig sneered. He'd pulled his hair back into a ponytail at his nape and combined with the uniform of a Parvac warrior, he looked more masculine, but I tried not to notice because he was an asshole. "Very well, Princess. A Durhcu healer asked for an audience with me."

Acting surprised, I lifted my hands to my cheeks. "Can the healer cure you of being a sanctimonious, sadistic asshole?"

Bending at the waist to look me in the eyes, he said, "It seems he wants to try. Apparently, keeping my mind as closed to them as possible makes them more curious as to what is in it. They see only your side of the story. They don't know you the way I do. They imagine you as a selfless, loving female who is intent on saving me from my own grief."

I fluttered my eyelids at him and smiled while lacing my fingers together and holding them under my chin. "Thank you for letting us know you'll be in therapy. See you later." Lowering my hands, I lifted my middle finger and used it to wave goodbye to him.

The smile he gave me as he left frightened me a little.

"Are we ready to do this?" Clark asked.

Each of us answered in the affirmative.

Clark went over the plan. "We fly in taking advantage of the rotation window. Fly low once you're through. Land here. It's an agricultural field long overgrown. Then, we hike to this location." He sent the coordinates to each of us. "This building was transformed into the main biodome hub. We take it out, and the entire thing crashes."

Stayton sent another file to us. "This particular signal must be dampened before we do anything else." He explained to us the required task which would prevent a system failure alert bouncing out to the Alux. Anyway, they'd be coming to investigate the destruction of their wormhole generator soon enough. "Alright, you heard Clark," he said with a clap of his hands. "Get your gear. Let's do this."

The guys all went off to prepare for our mission. If it went well, the big blue aliens would be able to reclaim their planet and regain access to valuable resources. Walking to Neema's quarters, I readjusted her blankets and kissed her forehead.

Sleepily, she asked, "What you doing, Mommy?"

"I'm going on a mission to help our new friends. I love you."

With her blue-haired doll in her arms, she was back asleep in a moment. Quietly leaving her room, I went to make my own preparations. Surprised, I found that Cedrenus, Binder, and Ross had returned to the living area to wait for me. "Ready?" Binder asked.

Glancing down at my attire, I shrugged. I was dressed as they were, like an ensign. Nodding, I followed them into the lift.

Cedrenus cleared his throat. "Repairs seem to be coming along nicely, far quicker than I could have imagined even back home. In addition, the Durhcu have shared provisions with us." He reached for my pack. I yanked it away.

"They are vegetarians," Ross whispered. "They don't even eat fish, not even when they lived on their world. They think it is cruel. Knowing this, how can we fully expect them to assist us in our war against the Alux?"

Binder thought about it. Then, he said, "The Alux are their antitheses. If life is sacred to the Durhcu, they must protect it from the predators of the universe. If they weren't prepared to take lethal action, then why begin the process of weaponizing their society?"

"I just hope we aren't creating a new threat for ourselves." It was a relief to admit my fear. "What's to stop them from turning on us one day?"

"Here's to hoping our new allies remain our allies!" Ross shouted.

I blushed and scowled at him for being so loud when I'd been whispering.

Binder stared at Ross. "Hope is Naxan Bison shit, and you know it. We need a more tangible assurance. The Durhcu aren't stupid. After they have the resources they need, they will hasten their production of defensive weaponry and ships."

"Will they have time?" Cedrenus rhetorically asked as our group stepped from the lift and out onto the flight deck.

A small group of very large Durhcu were speaking to Clark and the guys. They quieted at our approach. Chief of Xenobiology Shakhep and Ambassador Ness were among the group. "I'm sorry, Ness, but we don't have room for you to come." Clark was attempting to sound as diplomatic as possible.

Ness pressed his lips firmly together as if keeping his reply to himself was torture. Shakhep's eyes twinkled in merriment. Narrowing my eyes at Ness, I wondered what sort of shit he was telepathically communicating. Shakhep reached out a thick, beefy hand and gently patted Ness on the shoulder. "I understand your eagerness to visit the planet. I, too, long to walk upon the surface to breathe the air and feel the soil between my toes. Trust in the success of this mission, and we will visit my planet together, you and I." Placated by Shakhep's words, Ness visibly calmed. Turning his attention to us, he said, "We have brought to you uniforms for your mission. They will help to obscure your biological readings."

As the Durhcu passed out bags to each of us, we realized they had the same suspicions that we did, that there might be a few Alux hiding on their home world. "We'll be careful," I assured him.

Chief Engineer Akha handed a case to Stayton and briefed him on the contents. The rest of us excused ourselves. At our lockers, Cedrenus said, "Well, well, well." Holding up the uniform, he scanned it. "It is a superior flight suit, and if it helps to hide us from the Alux long enough for us to take the battle advantage, I'll wear it."

Stayton said, "It needs to touch your skin to be most effective."

Unbothered by nudity in the slightest, my team stripped down. Knowing each and every one of them eagerly wanted to attract my sexual notice, I pointedly turned my back on them. "You're all assholes. I need to concentrate on the mission and not your manly appendages." Anger had entered my tone.

"She's right. Now is not the time. Don't distract my cousin by marriage whom I can no longer pursue due to cultural norms." Stayton let his bitterness infuse his words.

Sighing, I changed into the uniform. It was made of the same plasti fabric as the stuff used to make the children's capes. Soft against the skin, it didn't chafe, but it had the outward appearance of being wet. The form-fitting suit had offset horizontal ruching that looked sort of like wet sand ripples on a beach. The cream, brown, and grey shades of it would blend into the planetary surroundings. After shoving my feet into the boots, I put on the helmet, grabbed my pack, and moved toward my ship.

Cedrenus groaned.

Clark hit him on the arm.

As my fighter ship copilot caught up to me, I realized the problem. Like the plasti film they'd used to repair our ships, the suits had some transparency to them. Cedrenus said, "You should have kept on your undergarments."

Ness snickered.

I said, "Clark, if we survive this mission, I want ring time with Ness."

"Understood," he replied.

Having come to see us off, Cormac explained the former clause in Clark and my marriage contract to Ness. Stig, who had arrived with him, smiled at Ness' fear. Shakhep looked at Stig in concern. Shaking my head at all of them, I centered my thoughts and focused on my mission. After completing a satisfactory pre-flight checklist,

Cedrenus and I boarded my fighter ship and waited for our signal to disembark.

The wait seemed to take forever, but once the flight doors opened, and I flew us free of the ship and the station, a feeling of joy infused me. "Oh, Cedrenus. Look at the stars. It's like we're bathing in them." Calm washed over me. "After our last flight together, I didn't think we'd be doing this again until after a hull refitting on Ephors."

"Try not to hit shit this time, Probus."

Snorting at him, I held formation. It was a long flight. The Durhcu had placed their station at a strategically safe distance, and none of us could blame them for it. Being alone in enemy territory with nothing more powerful than a blaster cannon aboard had us all on edge. For the Durhcu to have the remnants of their entire civilization hanging fragilely to existence, like the edible flowering vines which grew on their station, must be a heavy burden for Chief Administrator Khe. My musings made me grimace. The flowers were just as edible to the Durhcu and to us, as all of us were to the Alux. "Stayton," I called.

The audio in our new helmets was crystal clear. "Probus?"

I smirked at his informal tone. "From the information we have collected from the Durhcu, have we found any mention of our ascended alien friends?"

"The ones we've been trying to find to help us defeat the bad aliens?"

"You sound like a demented toddler. You, stupid fuck. Stop with the shit."

He groaned loudly on purpose to hurt my ears.

Levi retorted, "He can't try to seduce you, so he's trying to tease you."

"Keep teasing me, Stayton, and you won't ever be able to seduce anyone." I made my words sound as menacing as possible. It didn't work. All of them laughed.

Tyler said, "He'd like it. He's twisted like Stig."

"All of you are a bit demented," I grumbled.

"You love it," Clark chided.

Stayton, in a serious tone, said, "No, we have learned nothing of them from the Durhcu. Inquisitor Gordian and Councilman Stig shared our intelligence with them, and the Durhcu were astonished."

"That's disappointing."

Clark signaled the command for silence. The remainder of our flight was spent with only our own thoughts for company. Staying in formation, I matched my speed to Clark's. We had a visual on the Durhcu home world. They had supplied us with ample data in regard to their planet. Lush farmland, forested expanses, desert tundra, and frozen wasteland provided them with a diverse habitat until the Alux had targeted them. They'd adapted to a new way of life in space but longed to resettle on their planet. Taking down the Alux biodome would be a first step toward the realization of that dream.

Clark took us in following the trail of a comet that had circled the Durhcu world since they'd had a written language with which to document it. Using the comet's tail for cover, we waited for just the right moment in the planetary rotation. Then, Clark gave the signal when he tipped the nose of his fighter toward the surface. Taking our fighters into position, we followed his lead and dove in unison.

Exhilaration had my soul soaring. The speed, the freedom, the power, and the control thrilled me to my core. We left the blackness of space behind as we dove. Sunrise fast approached this side of the planet. Flying through the layers of atmosphere, we finally hit brilliant solar illuminated cloud cover and briefly broke formation to avoid a flock of giant, deep-billed birds. Our objective became visible as well. The artificial biodome consisted of a grid made up of orbs which floated at set intervals above the surface. The flock of birds avoided the orbs. Those orbs were our objective. Scattered throughout the lower atmosphere, the biodome grid's purpose was to detect Durhcu life signs and alert the Alux so that they could attack. Our job was to take it down. Our genetics wouldn't register since the Alux hadn't known of our existence at the time of the biodome's invention. The field in which we'd landed had once grown grain. In some sections, wild grain still grew, but other clumps of vegetation had sprung up.

"Clear," Cedrenus reported of the atmospheric surface conditions, not that we intended to remove our helmets.

Clark was taking lead, so we all waited for him to release his cockpit before following. Climbing from my fighter ship, I shouldered my pack and readied my pulse rifle. Long grasses waved around my thighs and crunched under my boots. Gravity was heavier here. Cedrenus' boots made a thud as he landed beside me. He stepped back to guard my back. His boots left deep imprints in the flattened grain stalks and rich brown dirt. I closed the cockpit, not wanting any indigenous surprises greeting us upon our return. Keeping low, we walked.

Cedrenus activated a drone and sent it ahead of us to scout. "We haven't set off any warning sirens which is a good sign."

"Take cover," I hissed.

The team heeded my warning. Sensor readings on my face shield had activated. The upper left corner showed dozens of life forms approaching our location at a run. Pulse rifle hoisted and aimed, I prepared to fire and hoped the Alux would feel it. The tips of vegetation shook in the near distance. Knots formed in my stomach, and sweat beaded on my upper lip. I kept my breathing steady by the force of my will. From the thick underbrush at the edge of the field, a herd of large avian-like creatures burst forth.

"At ease," Clark ordered. "Teagan is protecting us from…. I don't know what those are." Standing, he stared at the big birds who were taking advantage of whatever insects our landing had stirred up.

Ross waved a gloved hand in front of his face shield where a palm-sized moth had alighted.

The birds had long, slender necks. They had brown and black feathers with longer ones growing horizontally from the backs of their heads making them look like models who were having their hair blown back by fans. Their beaks were almost as long as their heads. Their bodies were as large as were their wings. The tips of their wings came close to dragging the ground as they walked on thick legs with chicken-like feet. "Emu or ostrich?" I asked.

"Sort of but not quite," Cedrenus answered as he scanned them with his drone.

One of the birds dropped its head, shook something, and raised its head up once more. In its beak was a still writhing snake of green, yellow, and black speckles. It had to be seven feet long. "Yeah, so let's go." I prodded Cedrenus forward. "Are those birds still watching us? I feel like we're being watched." Lifting my rifle, which I trusted more than the Durhcu visor, I looked through the scope and searched our surroundings. Small life signs appeared as small heat signatures on my visor. There was nothing big like those birds showing up.

The sun had fully risen. All manner of insects filled the air. They landed on our suits and helmets, swarming to us as if they'd forgotten what humanoids were. Ahead, Tyler and Levi were working to gain access to the building in which the main relay we needed was located. The outside of the building had become nothing more than a trellis for indigenous vines. From them, green gourds grew. Levi began removing a panel near the entry point.

Slowly, I turned in a full circle. The strange feeling that I had of being watched wasn't a feeling that I could shake. When the door slid open, I jumped.

"Pull yourself together." Cedrenus raised an eyebrow at me.

"Are you certain there are no sentient lifeforms watching us?"

He checked again. "Nothing appears on any of my scans." Attaching his vid-screen to his wrist, he drew a blade from one of his leg sheaths. Trusting my instincts, he stepped closer to me. "Something has our empath on edge," he reported.

"Noted," Clark responded. "Proceed with caution."

Cedrenus and I crept closer to the building. It was our job to keep the team under our scrutiny. A snake slithered over the toe of my boot. Ignoring it, I kept walking cautiously forward. Clark and Levi had entered the structure. At another point of entry, a side door, Stayton and Tyler were entering. Binder and Ross were covering them. The minutes seemed to stretch off into infinity. Through our helmets we heard Clark. "We have reached the hub." Several minutes lapsed. The sound of his voice made me jump when he spoke again. "Dampener in place and activated."

A loud growl from above forced my eyes and rifle up too late. My shot went wild as a creature dropped onto me from a tree branch from far above and slammed me to the ground. The air was knocked out of me. Grabbing me by the shoulders, it lifted me up and flung me away. I slammed back down to the ground. It hurt, but it saved me because it got me breathing again. The creature had me by the shoulder. Drawing my other arm in and between myself and my attacker, I drove my fist into its inner arm joint to make it release its hold. Pushing down with my left foot, I got it off balance and rolled it off of me. The blade was in my left hand. On my feet, I dodged as the blue, ragged beast lunged. With a mighty swinging fist, the creature knocked my blade from my hand.

"Shit!" I stumbled away.

The creature let forth a furious roar. Spittle flew from its wide maw. Sharp, thick incisors proved this was no vegetarian. The animalistic scream was deafening as it charged me. There was no time to run. It lunged and grabbed me. Caught in its punishing grip, I squirmed trying to free myself. Lifting me high above its head, it flung me through the air. Everything was a blur as I spun out of control. Then, I slammed once more to the surface, crashing into a sturdy bush whose branches cracked as I fell through it. Gravity on the Durhcu home world really was a bitch. Opening my mouth, I panted through the pain. I'd split the bush's trunk. Part of the splintered wood had pierced both my suit and my hip. The pain was excruciating. I'd almost collected myself enough to call out for help when the ground began to shudder. No, it was pounding.

"Fuck," I whimpered. It was the creature running toward me. I screamed as it grabbed me and yanked me up. My flesh tore as the monster ripped me from the impaling I'd suffered.

A heavy paw slammed into the side of my head and knocked off my helmet. It rolled away through the tall grass and left my ears ringing. Reaching behind me, I yanked the blade free from my back scabbard as I prepared to fight till the death. Mouth opened wide, incisors dripping with saliva, the beast roared as it scented my blood. I imagined those teeth piercing my flesh and ripping it free as terror lent me courage.

With a defiant scream of my own, I drove my blade down through the top of its hairy shoulder near its squat, thick neck. The creature yowled. It didn't release its hold. Yanking the blade free, I jabbed it down again. The beast let forth a loud, warbling, plaintive cry as if it was confused as to why I'd be so cruel as to injure it. Dark, purplish-red blood gurgled up from the wounds and down its fur. Finally, it dropped me. Then, it ran away with a bow-legged gait occasionally using the knuckles on the hand of its uninjured side. The alien ape had almost killed me.

Cedrenus was nowhere in sight. Hand on my bleeding hip, I slowly limped over to where my helmet had landed. After shaking the bugs out of it, I put it on. My cracked visor gave me a sketchy outline of his location on a tracking grid, so I followed the sounds of screeching, excited apes. Grabbing up my pulse rifle, I forced myself into a run. I wiped my blood from my hand. Staunching the bleeding would have to wait. Both of my hands required weapons. He wasn't far. The apes surrounding him were smaller than the giant one that had attacked me, but there were more of them.

Setting my rifle to its most powerful setting, I aimed and fired. My shot hit one of the creatures in the chest and slammed it back into a tree with a loud crack. Taking a knee to steady myself, I took aim and fired again. Noticing two of their own dead and not liking the scary loud sounds I was making with my rifle, the rest of them fled into the trees.

"Teagan!" Cedrenus called out.

Getting back up onto my feet was a struggle. Sheathing the blade, I held my hip and limped over to him. He was down with his back against a thick-trunked tree. A few dead apes were scattered around him. Crumbling to the ground beside him, I used my rifle to drag his pack over. Grunting with the pain the movement caused, I said, "I'll do you, if you do me."

"I thought you'd never ask." He grinned at me. His helmet was smashed to pieces a few feet away. Blood smeared the side of his face. I plucked a shard of plasti from his temple which made blood gush from the wound. Opening the pack, I found his emergency kit, cleaned his head wound, and applied a pressure bandage. I stuck a pain patch onto his neck. Then, I got to work on the gashes on his arm.

"Did you get bitten?"

"No, but I can't move it." He was pale.

My vid-screen had been crushed at some point, so I took his and scanned him. Then, I gave it back to him by putting it on his lap. I took his hand, leaned close, and kissed his cheek. "I'm sorry about this." He was too shocked from the kiss to stop me. With a firm hold on his wrist, I pulled his arm forward and straight in front of him. The pain was so much as to rob him of breath, but I did get it back into its socket. Slipping a sling over his head, I got his arm into it and gave him a pain patch before spraying antiseptic over deep claw marks. "There. Now, you won't feel bad about what you're going to have to do to me."

His eyes held a hint of fear when they beheld my hip and the blood soaking the left side of my suit down to my boots. Quickly, he hid his emotions. Leaning against the tree behind him, I kept my rifle ready. Insects buzzed around the apes we'd killed. "Cedrenus to Flavian." He waited for a reply.

My helmet was fried, but I tried contacting our team anyway. It didn't work.

He slipped his arm out of the sling to cut away part of my suit. Blood spilled from the larger opening. "Feeling weak," I admitted. "You know what I need right about now? Cookies and juice."

"Hold still." He was generous with the pain patches. It was nice on one hand, but on the other it made me feel very concerned that whatever was about to happen wasn't going to be good. "I'm sorry about this."

Unlike how he'd reacted after I'd said those words to him, I vocalized my pain. I vocalized it with such feeling as to make birds burst forth from trees. Cedrenus had pulled a sliver of wood from the bloody, gaping wound in my hip. Using the probe he'd recalled to our location, he scanned my hip and withdrew two more slivers. The wound was stinging and throbbing horrendously. By the time he'd started cleaning it, I was using the breathing I'd used for childbirth. At least, he was done digging around in my hip for massive splinters. The pressure bandage was a relief. I wiped a shaking hand over my forehead to keep sweat from dripping into my eyes. The sounds of angry apes riling themselves up to violence in the not-too-distant area forced us to get up and moving. Cedrenus carefully got his arm back into the sling and sent his probe toward the building into which our team had gone.

"Fly it inside, find Clark, and hit him in the head with it repeatedly until he gets really mad. Then, maybe, if we're lucky, he'll follow it back to us." Slowly ambling toward the structure, we watched the visual. Nothing seemed amiss. However, every single step either of us took was misery. "There is no way that I'm making love to Clark tonight, not after abandoning us to mad mega monkeys."

"I seriously doubt you'll be in the mood even if the pain patches don't wear off."

I snorted. "I'm always in the mood."

Nervously, he said, "I'm available and...."

Squatting down and dragging him down with me, I painfully lost my balance and fell on top of him. Our eyes met. His immediate physical reaction was poking me in the stomach. "Cedrenus, I've had enough long, hard pieces of wood impaling me today, not that I'm not flattered."

He blushed. He had hit his shoulder when we'd fallen. Now, he clenched his teeth to keep from crying out. I pointed. Seeing the Alux fighter ship as I did, the hard appendage in his lower anatomy stopped poking me. The fighter had landed directly in front of the structure, the structure in which our team was presently located. I dropped my head to his shoulder, whacking him in the chin with my helmet. Taking it off since the tech no longer worked, I left the ruined thing in the bushes. It had saved me from having my head knocked off by the big blue ape, but it couldn't save me from the Alux. Resting my head on his shoulder again since moving took too much effort, thoughts of what to do raced through my mind. "Can you disable its communications?" My hip was on fire. "Then, render it inoperable?"

"Yes." He had rid himself of his helmet as well.

"Do it." I kept still. Wishing I wasn't about to have to say it, I said it anyway. "I'm going in. Can you help me up?" Standing was a team effort for both of us. He made a face and came in close to sniff me. "I know, right?" Shuddering, I recalled the huge ape's horrific stench and disgusting breath, total halitosis in the extreme. It had gotten its smelliness on me. "Quaid can't stand monkeys. His main complaint is stolen food. Wait until I tell him about this." My tone didn't even sound hopeful to my own ears.

Turning carefully, I limped away. Neither of the entrances our team had used appealed to me. Instead, I trudged around the building while keeping a careful watch for the indigenous wildlife. My body really didn't need another injury. Dread of what I might find inside turned my stomach into knots. Had Clark been unable to come to our aid? What was going on? The ground crunched beneath my boots. At some point, a neat gravel path had surrounded the building. Now, it was overgrown. Aside from making noise, my steps drove bugs from their leafy bowers. One of them found my jawline and bit it. The bug's sting was like fire, and I could feel its bite beginning to swell. It was just one more thing. The Durhcu home world wasn't turning out to be a great vacation location.

From the architectural plans which we had been shown, I thought I knew of a way I could get inside without drawing any notice. The rectangular vent was near the ground and had been used as a chute for fertilizer distribution to fill carts. It hadn't been used in decades. How bad could it be?

Lifting up the metal flap, I used a stick to keep it open. Head and shoulders inside, I took a breath and gagged as quietly as possible. Clearly, decades hadn't been long enough. Reversing course came to mind, but it was only a couple of feet. My hip and side were of the opinion that this short, smelly crawl would be preferable to my other options, like scaling the building and going through a window. The space up ahead was dimly visible. Using my elbows and forearms, I kept my hip up and used my other knee to push myself along. A piece of equipment provided me with cover as I slithered out of the chute and onto the flooring.

Light entered through a series of windows along the roofline. Equipment had been abandoned in a hurry when the Durhcu had fled, and since then the Alux hadn't done much to clear it out. They'd simply repurposed the building and its power source against the former inhabitants whom they had consumed. What use were crops to the Alux? If they weren't stopped, they'd do the same thing to every race they found. Pulse rifle in hand, I crept forward and hoped it would have an effect if fired. If nothing else, I could create a distraction. Blade battle in my current state would have to be my last resort.

Loud sounds came from ahead. Carefully spying around a corner, I saw someone was down. It was Levi. He wasn't moving. Several feet away from him was Stayton. He had an Alux blade skewering his arm, but he'd disabled the device and obtained our objective. It lacked power, and smoke rose up from it. Clark, Ross, and Binder had their hands behind their heads. They were on their knees. Their weapons were piled up near their captor.

A lone Alux, screeching in undecipherable bursts of its language, brandished blades in its hands as if it had gone mad. If given a distraction, they'd be able to get their weapons and fight. How had one alien gotten the upper hand? Oh, there had been two. The body was just out of sight except for a booted foot. What Clark was thinking, I didn't have a clue. Why didn't he act? Distraction time. Lifting my pulse rifle and putting it on the highest setting, which might make its body armor fluctuate long enough for Clark to attack, I took aim and fired. The alien exploded into chunks upon impact. Horrified, I lowered my rifle and stared in shock.

"Ugh. Fuck." Clark wiped wet globs from his face and chest.

"What the actual fuck? Clark, gross. I'm so sorry, babe. Are you okay?"

He flicked the gruesome Alux remnants from his hands onto the floor as he stood.

Shrugging, I said, "I thought it would be using shielding."

Binder scrambled to get out a pressure bandage and had it ready for when Ross pulled the blade free.

Clark said, "Give me some help with Levi."

"Can't." Limping out from behind where I'd taken cover, I let him have a look at the damage. "Cedrenus isn't much better."

Clark's expression was unreadable. "Alux?"

"No, apes."

He stared at me as if he didn't believe me for a second before he bent and picked Levi up in a fireman's carry. Then, he led the way out the door. Cedrenus was painfully making his way toward us. "Sit with Levi," he ordered us. "There are plenty of machines around here. We should be able to find something with transport abilities." He glanced over at the small Alux fighter.

"Disabled," Cedrenus volunteered.

Carefully, I lowered myself to sit beside him but kept my rifle in hand. In the trees, the apes screamed and screeched. The treetops shook. Stayton crouched beside us.

"Binder, you're with me."

Clark and Binder were gone long enough for the four of us to get nervous. The apes had started throwing rocks at us. Then, a rusty, clanking sound drew closer. It frightened the apes. Upon closer reflection, it didn't make me feel all that comfortable either. "A fertilizer cart, great," I muttered.

Cedrenus asked, "Would you rather walk?"

"Go give it a sniff, and you tell me."

Clark didn't care that it was smelly. He rudely picked me up and placed me in the shitty cart between Levi and Cedrenus. He drove with Stayton seated beside him. Balancing around the cart's edges with rifles held ready were Ross, Binder, and Tyler. Looking at us was all the proof they needed as to the ever-present danger posed by the mean, hairy, stinky apes. Soon, our fighter ships came into view in the field where we'd left them, and I was so relieved. As the cart shook and clanked to a stop, Levi groaned.

"Hey, sleepy head!" I gave him a cheerful smile.

"My head," he complained as he clenched his skull between his hands.

Clark made a gesture at me to hurry up.

"What?" I scrunched my face up at him.

He shook his finger at me. "Don't even, Teagan. Don't you fucking start your independent shit with me. Put your arms around my neck. I'll let you be in charge of blasters. Ross, you take Cedrenus. Binder, take Levi. Tyler, take Stayton. Stick to the plan. Go."

Too tired to argue and seeing the logic as well as knowing the protocol for our situation, I gave him his way. He was the mission leader anyway. If I were to lose consciousness during flight, it would be a huge fucking mess. I imagined how long it would take someone aboard the *Empress* to override my commands. It was a safety feature to which my cousin had seen to long ago. Clark helped me into the seat. Taking the helmet, I put it on and fastened my safety harness. It seemed as though I'd done it out of order which wasn't like me. Maybe, he was right. He took us up. It was a relief to be off world and in amongst the stars. "Clark?"

"Yes, Teagan?"

"I'm gonna take a tiny little nap. Wake me up if you need me to shoot something."

He was quiet for a moment before he replied, "Yes, Teagan."

Chapter Fifteen

I squinted. A bright light was shining into my eyes.

"Don't start with the doctors, Teagan. You've still got slivers of wood in your wound. They've got to come out. You also need antibiotics."

I tried to talk. My mouth was swollen.

A Durhcu doctor held up a picture of a flying insect. "Is this what stung you?"

I nodded at the picture of the miserable, nasty bug.

Dr. Savelli was cheerfully cutting off my flight suit.

"Hey! I just got this!" My words were unintelligible. It sounded like I was trying to talk with a mouthful of manly appendages.

A snide asshole said, "Of course, you would be concerned with your clothing."

"Fuck you."

That or the look a Durhcu doctor gave him shut Stig up.

Another voice said, "Fascinating. Absolutely fascinating. In smaller delivery, such as with the merest prick of a needle, this insect toxin could be used to temporarily change the features of those in need of a disguise." It was Cormac postulating.

"Fucking Inquisitors," I grumbled as Dr. Savelli started digging splinters out of my numb hip. A Durhcu doctor applied a cold, medicated compress to my face. The swelling vanished almost simultaneously.

Cormac said, "The Durhcu have begun jaunts to the surface. As per the previous orders which you and Representative Stig had approved, I have allowed the Durhcu to scan our pulse cannons. Also, we have shared with them the formula for synthetic Arachnean Silk spider neurotoxin and a few delivery systems."

Considering his words, I asked, "How long before they can effectively defend themselves?"

"Here? A week, at least." Stepping closer so that I could see him, he said, "They have been sharing their specific knowledge of this region's stellar cartography."

Something about his tone got me excited. "What?" I looked from him to Clark. I looked over at Stig, flipped him off, checked what Savelli was extracting from my hip, and returned my attention to Cormac. Levi groaned. I glanced over at him. "What did the Alux do to Levi?"

Dr. Savelli explained. "The two Alux on the planet had been abandoned there to keep the biodome functioning. They were starving. One of them tried to feed from Levi. Instead of adoration and worship, it got a psychic overload of hate and murderous rage. Levi will be fine. He got free of it and killed it. He'll have a severe headache for a few days, but otherwise he is unharmed."

"Ouch! Stars!" I glared at my doctor.

"More numbing agent?" he asked pointlessly.

A few Durhcu whispered amongst themselves. It was obvious that Stig was their topic. Even I could tell he was enjoying seeing me in pain, the sick fuck.

With the countenance of an ancient devil, he said, "Ambassador Ness requests permission to journey to the Durhcu home world with them on their next jaunt. Shall I allow it?"

Shortly, I answered, "Do what you think is best." If the odious man got himself into trouble, I'd rather the Galaxic Expanse's representative be the one who'd made it permissible.

"All done. You can go." Doctor Savelli helped me up.

Puzzled, I stared at him. "Am I in some alternate universe where you don't make a fuss over my boo-boos?"

He grinned and shook his head.

Cormac offered me his arm. Taking it, I let him help me down from the exam bed and into a robe.

Clark said, "I'll stay with Levi."

Before I could nod, Cormac had lifted me into his arms and was carrying me away to the lift. When the doors opened onto the Imperial Deck, I felt like something was wrong. "It's quiet, too quiet." Every pillow on the sofas was in its place. No toys were strewn about. Chef poked his head out from the kitchen and waved. I waved back. Cormac carried me into my quarters and straight to the shower. He said, "Neema and Bhamak are having a closely supervised playdate on Habitat Ring Three. We are having a quiet evening alone together." Slipping my robe from me, he gestured for me to activate the shower.

"Oh, are we?"

"Yes, we are."

I was surprised when he stripped and joined me. Even more surprising was that he didn't offer to wash my hair or any other part of me. Instead, he left me to my own ablutions while he did the same. Since he wasn't being amorous, I indulged in a thorough scrubbing. Noticing my body hair, I scowled. "I need a spa day." Raising my arm for the jets to rinse, I grimaced. My fingernails were terrible. Looking down at my toenails, I saw another problem. "Even my kitty has gone feral."

After he realized to what I referred, he laughed. Stepping from the shower, he rummaged around and returned with a shaver.

"Thanks." Taking it, I did what I could to put myself to rights. Smiling, I ran a hand over my slippery leg.

"Dry off and put on something comfortable."

"What sort of activity do you have in mind?" I hoped it wouldn't involve moving.

"Would movies and manicures interest you, along with whatever Chef is preparing for us to eat? I took the liberty of asking him to return to your deck from the crew cafeteria since the Durhcu have so generously replenished our ship stores with provisions."

Thinking of being able to eat breakfast in my nightgown once more was more pleasing to me than I was ready to admit. "All of that sounds like a vacation to me."

He dipped his head to me and left with a towel around his hips.

Since he'd suggested dressing for comfort, I opted for a short, pink Arachnean Silk gown and matching robe. Then, I joined him in the living area with my hair still wrapped in a towel. Around the room, Cormac had placed various boxes. "What's all of this?"

"These are items from Choji's arsenal," he answered as he arranged a blanket over the couch. Choji was one of the stylists who Momma had hired for me. My ladies spent more time enjoying his talents than I did. After I sat, Cormac placed a pedicure device at my feet. Chef filled it with warm water and activated it.

Sinking my feet into the water, I rested my sore feet against the kneading foot pads. "Oh, stars. Yes." I opened my eyes when Cormac took my hand and started clipping my nails. When he moved onto filing, I had to ask. "How did you learn to do this?"

"I have made it a point to study the things which give you enjoyment, as have most of your chosen mates. Being able to care for you pleases me."

His sweetness made me blush.

Once he'd trimmed my cuticles, he asked, "What color would you like?"

Choji always made it a point to have the highest quality mineral paints and cosmetics. "Oh, I like this one. It's glittery black like space and the stars. Have I told you how glad I am to be back out in them?" The wormhole had been a nightmare.

Cormac painted my pinky. "Um. I can redo it." He furrowed his brow.

"How about I do the painting?" I smiled and tried not to laugh. Nail painting wasn't one of his many strengths. After removing black sparkly paint from my skin, I painted my nails while he started a movie. Cormac's expression turned horrified. I laughed until tears streamed down my face. "You got that from Philip's quarters." Wiping at my tears with my palms so as not to mess up my nails, I gulped for air. "Put it back. Trust nothing in his room."

"The description was a band of brave women daring the elements to scale a mountain. This is all outdoor sex!"

"I'll put it away for you," Chef offered with far too much bashful innocence.

I sent Cormac in the direction of the movies we'd gotten to amuse Kaoti. My manicure and pedicure complete, I worked on my hair while we watched a spy thriller. Chef brought us individual platters of fried tubers, the Durhcu version of potatoes. He said, "That's the last of the ketchup, so enjoy."

"How are our food stores, really?" I asked as I chewed.

"The Durhcu have been more than generous. We have fruits, vegetables, preserves, freeze-dried produce, sauces, fruit and vegetable jerkies, and all manner of spices. It will take the crew some time to adjust to the lower levels of protein, but none of us will starve." With a grin, he admitted, "It is fun experimenting with the new foods. How are your tubers?"

"They're fabulous." I demonstrated by dipping two at a time and eating them.

Neema and her guards returned. She'd already eaten and was happy and tired from playing all day. "Night, Mommy." After kissing my cheek, she skipped away to her bed without ever realizing anything had been amiss. It made me feel like I'd won the day.

Full, clean, patched-up, and feeling returned to rights in general, I began to doze off. Cormac placed an arm around me. "In my opinion, you should get yourself to bed."

Something in his tone and choice of words gave me pause for concern. "You aren't coming with me?"

He became quiet. "Are you ready for me to? It would do more to proclaim me as yours than our marriage contract has done. Here, there has been no Parvacian Society to make note of our union." He shrugged. "What of Ensign Flavian and Neema's reactions?"

I snorted. "You don't give a shit what Clark thinks." In the depths of his eyes, I could tell I was right. "Cormac, once we are home, everyone will know that I have accepted you. Momma will throw an elaborate party. She adores you and has been hopeful of our marriage for quite some time. The reporters will become absolutely frazzled. Wait and see if I am right."

"You believe so?" He studied me.

"I know so." Surprised that he needed my assurance, I tucked the knowledge away. My steadfast Inquisitor needed to feel special in his own way. He needed our society to know that he was mine. He needed to be shown off, and I would be certain to do it. I smiled thinking of Eli, and how he'd needed his mother's nose rubbed in his own value.

"Perhaps, I am concerned," he admitted.

"Okay. Be concerned while tucked into bed. You can spoon me. Don't touch my hip. Come on." Curled up in bed with Cormac, sleep quickly claimed me.

My arm was asleep by the time I woke again. Cormac was heavy and warm against my back, like a giant heating pad. On his other side, Clark was grinning seductively at his vid-screen while taking pictures. Seeing my quizzical expression, he showed me dozens of pictures he'd taken of himself in bed with Cormac. He'd been sending them off in encrypted files for the last hour or so. It would take Cormac several hours to search out and delete them all.

"Payback for Epopeus?" I asked.

Clark grinned. Then, he puckered up.

Cormac, who looked as though he still slept, threatened, "If you attempt to kiss me, Ensign Flavian, I will adhere your lips to your scrotum. You need to question whether it will be your skin that stretches or whether it will be the breaking of your spine which will make it possible."

"Cormac, you are not allowed to fight with Clark in a manner which causes serious injury. I won't permit it. If it is bravado which you both wish to display, you may have a cock fight once we're home."

"Excuse me?" Clark asked.

"I'll have Nico explain it to you." My stomach growled.

Crawling over Cormac, Clark's knee pressed into his side and made him grunt in discomfort. Careful not to hurt me, Clark wedged a foot between mine and smiled, seductively convincing me to move my legs enough to give him room between them. His ploy worked. Hot need stole all of my thoughts except for those involving him inside of me. "Explain it to me now."

Reaching for the waistband of his bottoms, I said, "Maybe later."

Innocently, he asked, "Later? Why not now?"

"Fuck you, Clark. You know why, and you probably already know the story about what happened." My frustration got him grinning. He tossed his sleep bottoms at Cormac and pushed the thick head of his manly appendage between my folds, filling my ache with his delicious hardness. Moaning, I tried clutching him to me. His hard thrusts were fast and rhythmic. Cormac took advantage of how Clark held himself away from me to capture my nipple in his mouth. I cried out as ecstasy flooded my senses. My undoing was Clark's. He shivered above me and lost his control. Collapsing at my side, he made no argument when I drew Cormac to myself, needing the ache that hadn't dissipated for long to be relieved. He didn't try to show off. Instead, he gave me what I needed, fighting his own release until he'd made certain I was satiated. Once he had, I smiled contentedly and stretched languidly with my husbands laying to each side of me trying to capture their breaths.

"Sharing your toy nicely, I see." The snide statement came from the direction of the door to my quarters. Cormac pressed his foot to the mattress and launched himself at Stig.

Trying to imitate him, I pushed against the mattress with my heels, but it made my hip hurt. Sitting up, I watched Cormac's elbows fly and took a moment to enjoy Stig's grunts of pain. Each one was like a flower in a bouquet. "Enough." My whispered command was all it took.

Cormac rose. The muscles of his arms were taut and rippling as were those in his back. He'd proven to me time and again that he was just as lethal as Kaoti. However, belonging to House Gordian had sent him along a different path. "Do not enter my lady's quarters without her invitation." His tone suggested a desire to grant Stig a slow death.

From where Cormac had put him on the floor, he said, "Princess Neema ordered me to get her Mommy. She is distraught."

Those words had me grabbing my robe and launching from the room.

Neema sat at the breakfast table in tears. If Stig had upset my baby, I'd beat him senseless myself. "Mommy!"

Wrapping her in my arms, I checked her for injuries or fever. "What's wrong? Is it your tummy?"

"No!" She wailed and held out her hand. On her palm was a tooth.

My delighted expression turned her face from tears to annoyance.

"How you gonna be happy about this?" She had a missing top tooth and a cute little lisp.

There was a commotion near the lift. "Lower your weapons! Are you mad?" Stig yelled with his hands raised as if to ward off impending violence. He moved to place himself between us and the guards.

I sensed something, but it wasn't danger. Through ship's communications, a male voice said, "Ensign Probus, Chief Administrator Khe desperately wishes admittance."

"Granted." No sooner had the word left my lips than Bhamak materialized at Neema's side.

His eyes were filled with terror. Neema held her hand out to show the sneaky Durhcu child what tragedy had befallen her. "My *toof* fell out!"

He nodded in sympathy and patted her back. Then, he grinned at her and showed her where his tooth had begun to wiggle.

"Oh," she said. A rational look came across her face. She took her tooth over to the waste disposal and then washed her hands.

It was then that Khe entered. He was flanked by guards and had a look of horror. Seeing Bhamak vanquished it. Dryly, Stig said, "If I may serve as an example, it is never wise to enter the presence of Parvac princesses unannounced." Reaching over to the table, he picked up a napkin, dabbed it in water, and held it to his cheek. "And, I reside here." He gestured toward his quarters.

"You barged in on my husbands and me. Be glad that Cormac didn't actually hurt you." I glared at him, the smug asshole.

Khe said, "Please, forgive my child. He sensed distress from his dear friend and playmate. He got away from me."

Meanwhile, the two children had run to Neema's room for her shielding gear. Then, when they returned dressed alike, she began showing him Parvac Warrior fighting stances and forms. Cormac had quickly dressed in his uniform and was now at my side.

Khe stared quizzically at Stig. "I do not understand. You are her mate as well. They do not accept you. Therefore, she rejects you. Is this why her pain gives you pleasure? This is not healthy. You will speak to the healer. The healer will see you now. It is my gift to you for saving my people." He slapped his hands to his thighs. "Come. Come."

I stared at him. "Wait. What?"

Stig had gone pale with mortification. He said, "Princess Probus requires time to ready herself. Might we meet with you in an hour?"

The big blue alien nodded. "Yes, I will await you on Habitat Ring Three." His son caught his attention.

I said, "Bhamak can stay here and play with Neema. We will be along soon." After he had gone, I picked up a spoon and ate the vegetarian version of yogurt with berries that Chef had put on the table before me. The sounds of the children playing soothed me. Once I'd finished my breakfast, I went to my quarters. Stig followed me.

He cautioned, "When a Durhcu offers a gift, one must accept or risk causing terrible offense."

I turned in the bathroom to face him. "Did you misrepresent yourself to him? Did you claim to be my husband? Did you lie to him for some reason? What game are you playing?" Pulling off my gown, I tossed it to the floor and entered the shower.

Coldly, he watched me. "I have already been coerced into seeing one of their healers. You agreed to it. Have you forgotten?"

Tits out, I looked at him. "Must have." It didn't ring any bells with me.

"The healer and everyone else amongst the Durhcu see us as bonded mates. They deem me as a rejected mate."

"A what?" The shower made his tone difficult to hear.

The shower door opened, and Stig, completely nude, stepped inside with me. The immediate, needy ache of my betraying body made me angry. "They see me as a rejected mate. I am yours. You have bound me. However, you do not want me." His voice was like suds sliding down my heated flesh.

Battling the heat, my tone was as cold as I could make it. "We aren't married."

"In the way of their people, we are." His gaze settled on my nipple, and it was if he had painfully squeezed it with his thoughts.

"So, you made me out to be the villain."

He stepped closer and lowered his chin ever so slightly. Shaking his head, he said, "I want.... I need to learn to touch you without...." He stared into my eyes. It seemed as if a war raged within his mind. He lifted his hand. I flinched back preparing to defend myself. His hand stilled, water dripping from his fingertips. Deciding it was safe for him to do so, he reached for me. Drops of water on his fingertips found a path down along my neck. His gaze followed the droplets down, and his touch followed pausing at my breast. His urge was to grab my nipple and squeeze it until I cried out. Fighting the urge, he sank his fingers into my hair and merged his thoughts fully with my own.

Again, he let his hand trail slowly down my skin to my breast. Sensing the pleasure aroused within me by a soft touch confused him. Kitty would have grown wet and achy had he pinched her nipples painfully which would have in turn aroused him. His length remained flaccid along his thigh. He trailed his hand lower. I gasped when he sank his fingers between my folds and searched my mind to learn how to please me. With one long finger within me, he trapped my folds to either side with his other fingers and rubbed, quickly bringing me to climax. While I clung to him, he spiraled pleasure through me. When he took his hand from me, I could see he hadn't been able to gain an erection.

Knowing my thoughts and seeing the question in my eyes, he answered, "No, it isn't you. You haven't done anything wrong. Being able to give you pleasure without pain is an improvement, so the healer must be helping." Placing his hands to the shower wall to either side of my head, he confided, "This is the first time in my life I've ever given anyone pleasure without first giving either fear or pain." Dropping his hands, he abruptly turned and left. However, I could feel his lingering presence in my mind.

Confused by the encounter, I waited until he'd dried and dressed himself before I got out. "You know, it's okay if I'm the only one who enjoys it. You can be like one of those ancient eunuchs." I gave him my sweetest smile, wrapped my hair in a towel, and dried myself in a provocative manner. His expression was so rigid, stone would have looked soft and cuddly in comparison. "Oh, Eddie, at least your face can get hard for me."

"You are insufferable."

Stepping close to him, I whispered, "And you still have your fingers after having touched me without my permission."

Grey eyes darted over my face. He lifted his hands up behind me and ran them over my butt. "You gave me permission in your mind. You want me so you'll have someone with whom to share your pain." His words grinded like gravel.

It felt as though he'd punched me in the gut.

Taking his hands from me, he turned and left as if I'd scalded him.

Chapter Sixteen

Bhamak and Neema led the way from my ship and out to the large lift which took us up to the third habitat ring on the Durhcu station. I knew that Cormac was on the Bridge and had everything under control. The station was practically empty. Half of the population had gone on jaunts in their rugged vessels to their planet for everything they could gather. Many others, some of my crew included, worked diligently to arm the Durhcu against imminent Alux attack or any other predators who might be lurking in the system. However, it had been insisted upon by Dr. Savelli that my team and I take a day off to recover from our successful mission which had facilitated the flurry of activity.

Khe joined us. Smiling, he took note of my clothing, a loose silk top and wide-legged pants. He couldn't seem to help reading my thoughts. "You like making clothes, yes?"

"Yes, Arachnean Silk and the design and manufacturing of it is the business of my extended family." I tried to project to him a mental image of my beloved Thunderdrop and of my beautiful trees in my forest. "I love it there. It is home."

He looked down into my eyes. His glistened with understanding of the love and the ache filling my heart and mind. "I know this love. One day soon, we will return to our world, and no one will force us from it again."

I inclined my head to him. If the reports were correct, it would be possible to turn the biodome against the Alux. However, the Durhcu would still need a means of defense against the Alux warships. We all did. "Our original mission is of crucial importance to us all. The alien race we encountered may be able to help us. Their technology is far more advanced than ours or yours for that matter."

Khe said, "The Pariea may not wish to be found." He spoke the words sadly. "Why have they not come to our aid? Why allow so much suffering, so much loss?"

Bhamak ran to his father and hugged his leg.

Neema tugged me down and whispered in my ear. "The Alux killed Bhamak's mommy. They don't talk about people no more after they're gone." She hugged my neck, kissed my cheek, and stared into my eyes like she was trying to memorize them.

I wanted to tell her not to worry. I wanted to promise her that I'd never leave her, but we were out here without Marielle, Tabitha, Peter, Niklos, Yukihyo.... I couldn't. I couldn't think of them all. I had to stay strong. It was far too painful. Neema squeezed my hand. Then, she tugged at Bhamak coaxing him to join her in a game of hide and seek. Lifting my arm, I checked that my wrist cuff was on and activated. Khe gestured for Stig and me to follow him to the appointment with the healer. I'd been expecting a nice office with couches and plants. This wasn't it. In a quiet section of the habitat ring, a giant blue Durhcu waited for us. He was wearing a long blue robe. Khe simply bowed and left us.

The healer didn't use words to communicate. Telepathically, he welcomed us inside.

To Stig, I whispered, "You've been here before?"

"Yes," was his hushed response.

"What is this supposed to be?" The room was dimly lit. In the center was a circular pool of water which was partially covered by an opaque dome. My palms started to sweat. This wasn't the sort of therapy I was expecting. I'd been to therapy and lots of it on Parvac. This was totally different. What sort of creepy naked crap were we going to be expected to do?

The healer gestured toward a dais to the left of the anxiety inducing pool. Telepathically, he said, "Please, remove your foot coverings." Each of us bent and did as he'd requested. He led us up to the dais, sat on a huge circular cushion, and gestured for us to join him. Once we were seated, he closed his eyes.

We sat that way for several long minutes. Leaning closer to Stig, I whispered, "What are we supposed to be doing?"

He dryly replied, "I have never before been to couples' therapy. I thought you were the expert."

Rolling my eyes at him, my attention began to wander out of boredom. Stig's toe hair was the same champagne blond as his hair. "I've been to lots and lots of it. It's so helpful. Look. We don't have to be a couple. I've bound my Omnes Videntes to save them from madness. Of them, I only have romantic feelings for Zared and Izaac. I'm clan mother to the others. I can be that for you, and you can one day find a special partner."

"No!"

His vehemence startled me. He stood and paced. What had I said? The Durhcu healer was doing something. It felt as though a partition came between me and the adaptations I'd made to survive emotionally from childhood to present. Those things were set aside. Pulled forth were those wants and needs which would provide me with the most happiness in its purest form. I concentrated on Stig. His father had yearned for power and wealth. He'd needed those things to pursue his fascination with alien discovery. His son had been a tool. All the control had been his and not Edvard's. He'd turned his father's rejection and the forced suppression of his telepathic abilities into a defense against any expression of love or kindness. Too often, his father's expressions of love and acceptance had been ploys in order to achieve a goal. His telepathic abilities had allowed him to see through every attempt at using him. He used others. If they wanted something from him, he made them earn it through their pain. It was the pain they caused him by using him as a means to an end. In time, he could only find pleasure by giving pain.

Even Kitty had lied to him and used him in the beginning, even his beloved Kitty.

"You didn't want anything other than to protect your child and save me from madness." At some point, he'd stopped pacing. "We are opposites, you and I."

Drawn from where I'd spun through revelations of Edvard's trauma, I realized what the healer had done. He'd shielded us each from the painful memories that had shaped us into our current identities and shown them to each other.

The healer stood. He stepped down from the dais. He gestured toward our shoes. Edvard and I avoided looking at each other while we busied ourselves with our respective footwear. The healer returned. "Give me your hands." He held a vine. Edvard held out his hand. Distrustfully, I did the same. With the vine, he tied our hands and wrists together. "Go together. When there are blooms, enjoy them. When there are no blooms, nurture the buds and wait." He smiled and walked us out.

At the doorway to the healer's office or whatever it was, I looked up at Edvard, not knowing what to do or say. He said, "I assume we are supposed to leave this on until it blooms." He fumbled in his pocket with his free hand for his vid-screen. The data the Durhcu had shared with us included ample records on botany. He scanned the vine and found it. "The flowers of this vine can take anywhere from four to eight hours to bloom. So as not to cause offence, I suggest we not remove it."

"Aw, the joys of diplomacy," I grumbled.

"Mommy! Mommy!" Neema and Bhamak came running. Her gap-toothed smile got me grinning. "Come see! Come see!" She turned and ran.

"Come on, Eddie." We followed the children. "Thanks for earlier with the guards and Bhamak. That could have been...."

"Yes, there is no need to mention it."

Contritely, I looked up at him. His mouth was bruised.

"Yes, I will be more careful with Inquisitor Gordian. If it were not for my position within the Galaxic Government, he'd have little use for me."

"He'd find a use. You're brutal. He likes that about you. Look, our mission hasn't changed. We need to return to Laconian space. We're a month behind schedule." Lifting my free hand, I made as though to smooth down my top, but I was checking my breasts. Over the past few days, I'd noticed my milk had been drying up. Despair and longing for my babies would cripple me if I didn't fight against it. Compartmentalizing those feelings was my only option.

"They will pay for what they have done to us. They stole Kitty. They stole precious time from you. They will suffer." His cold hatred for our mutual enemy made me feel better.

We caught up to Neema. She was playing with a group of Durhcu children. She was tiny amongst them. They'd been playing a peaceful game with colorful tubes until she'd shown up. Now, those tubes were being used as swords. She was teaching them to parry and thrust. Khe stepped over to my side. "I'm so sorry." I blushed.

"Don't be. It is not our way, but our ways almost led to our extinction. If a blade might allow one child to survive, we might live on." There was sadness in his big brown eyes, but there was also hope. "You have helped us, and we will help you. We are allies. The Cosmos and Durhcu are one. Enjoy today. I have sent requests to our allies who hide along your path through the stars. I await word if they will help you."

Not sure what they could do, I thanked him anyway. Then, we watched the children play until they were sweaty, bored, and ready to move onto the next thing.

"Mommy, I'm hungry. Let's go find something." She and Bhamak ran toward a café of sorts.

Stig laced our fingers together as we walked.

I narrowed my eyes at him.

"It's less chafing." His tone wasn't as snooty as usual.

The children were already being served beansprout sandwiches. Khe coaxed us into sitting down and sharing one. Between thin slices of a grain-rich bread were mounds of fresh beansprouts and crunchy slices of a fruit similar to tomatoes all drizzled with a green sauce. No sooner had we finished eating than the kids were ready to go exploring the station. Stuck together as we were, we spent the wake cycle following them around the communal ring. They paused long enough to help a botanist plant a few new seeds that had been brought up from the surface. While they worked, something caught my attention. A Durhcu couple, hands bound as ours were, surrounded by friends and family, were being covered with flowers. "Um, Stig."

"Yes, they are blooming. I suppose we are free of each other now."

"No, look." I pointed. "That damn healer bound us. He bound us more cohesively than I did. Can you feel it? And look!" As inner reflection and my words sank in, he saw the couple. Lifting our joined hands, I shook them. However, I didn't expect what happened next. The pollen from the flowers seeped into our skin. Khe and various Durhcu around us cheered. Dizzying need slammed through me.

"Here! Here!" Khe gestured for us to go through an arched doorway. It appeared to be someone's home.

It was quiet inside. I could hear my heartbeat pounding in my ears. My undies were soaked with need. "Oh, no. What have they done?"

"The flowers' pollen must be an aphrodisiac." He pulled me along behind him, searching the domicile. He opened the closest sleep sphere and pulled me inside. "I'm removing your clothing and intend to fuck you. If you object, leave."

I didn't object.

The vine continued to crumble and send more pollen into our skin. A desperate whine escaped me. Stig shoved me back onto the sleeping surface, forced my legs wide, and roughly entered me. He didn't ease his way in but kept pushing. I cried out but took him, needing to feel stretched and full. He paused. "Please." The word was out before I could stop myself. It gave him an odd pleasure, having me pinned beneath him, my legs spread wide, and at his mercy. He grew harder which made me wetter.

"Please what?" He sounded sinister. "Do you want me to kiss you gently?" He held still. "Do you want me to slowly move within you?"

The healer had linked us in some way beneath our egos in a primal way. His needs and mine mingled.

"No, don't make love to me. Fuck me, and don't hold back."

My command set him free. Capturing my wrists above my head, he drove his hips forward and pulled them back at a punishing speed. I teetered between pleasure and pain. He was rough and violent but didn't do anything purposefully to hurt or frighten me. After nearly a hundred thrusts, he calmed enough to enter my mind. I could sense him there, judging what movements did what to me. Moving his body slightly up, he put pressure against my clit with his shaft, dragging it, grinding it hard and fast as he plunged himself in and out of me. I cried out, needing and reaching for my release. He held my wrists firmly, not allowing me to claw needily at his back. He kept his weight against me not letting me move my legs or shift. He drove in and out. He was in control, not me. Helpless, I gave in to him. My womanly center zinged and felt as though it burst with tiny exploding bubbles. I moaned and sighed as they drifted and burst throughout my body. A hot, wet mouth encircled my nipple, sucking. Pleasure burst through me again.

He came in a series of deep, wracking shudders that made his entire body tremble, all with my breast still in his mouth. After the fourth one, he collapsed atop me with his lips at my throat. I laid beneath him with my heart pounding in my chest. "How will this even work? How will I share you?" His voice was cold, possessive. He closed those thoughts away from me. Soft cascades of his hair trailed across my sensitive chest. Lowering his lips, he gave my other breast his attention while spiraling pleasure through me until I was weak with it.

At some point, my brain shorted out from it all. I came to my senses in his arms where I wept softly. He'd relieved me of my intense hormonal urges as only an Eriopis male could.

"Father took pride in our heritage, distant as it was. He hired a physician to treat me with a selective gene therapy when I was young to stimulate my Eriopis' abilities. It was a secret no one was ever to know." He stroked my arm as he held me. "It will be a struggle to hide anything from you."

"You're planning to hide things from me?"

"Oh, most definitely."

I sat up and looked at him.

He was quite serious. "You and I know each other at a deeper, more intimate level now, thanks to the Durhcu healer, than before we even privately knew ourselves. I feel you nestled in my mind and in my soul. You are undoubtably my mate. However, know this. I will not fall in line, fawning at your feet like one of your obedient husbands." He had that smug, aristocratic look on his face, the one I often wanted to slap off.

Seriously, had he met Quaid or Yukihyo? "That's fine, Eddie." I grinned at him. "I sure as fuck won't be taking orders from you. You can't tell me to do shit. You can't control me, not in any way."

His smile was slow, diabolical. Grabbing my ankles, he rolled me to my back and pushed himself deep inside of me. Much later, after having brought me pleasure once more, he cupped my chin in his palm and spoke quietly. "When you come to my bed, come alone."

He took away his hand and the warmth of his body. Sitting on the edge of the bed, he began to dress and handed me my clothing.

When we left the sleep sphere we'd commandeered in our haste, I for one was horrified. The Durhcu were in the midst of a station-wide bonding party which they were throwing in our honor. My team, Clark in particular, watched us from a safe distance. His expression was unreadable. Trapped by intentions of goodwill, Stig and I were forced to accept food, drinks, and congratulations. Neema, in her element, became the center of attention amongst the Durhcu children.

Cormac appeared by my side. "Do try to smile." His expression was calm.

"Are you sure? I didn't think you'd be accepting of this. I don't even know how I feel about this."

Ever watchful, he kept Neema and me in his sight. Stig had edged away from us to speak with a few of the Durhcu hierarchy.

"You did what you had to do for Princess Neema's psychic well-being. The Durhcu wished to repay us in some way for our service to their people. I have learned that it was no simple matter for their most prominent healer to mend the violent sadism of your newest husband." Quietly, he said, "From what I gather, the healer was only able to eradicate those tendencies from him in regard to you and yours. He remains to his core a sadistic, cruel bastard."

Watching Stig, I knew Cormac was right. Stig needed me, but he didn't like it. The man was dangerous, and once he was returned to the Galaxic Expanse, he'd be too powerful to ignore.

"In other news, Stig's henchman, Max, is taking solid food and will soon begin physical therapy."

"Cormac, how long before we are underway? We've done all we can here." My attention shifted to Neema. She was smiling, her missing tooth forgotten, and happily playing.

"We can disembark in a few hours."

Startled, I turned to him. A feeling of excitement and anticipation jolted me. "What have you been able to extrapolate from the star charts?"

"If we journey to the quadrant the Durhcu have proposed, we should end up along Chione's distant outer rim in a few weeks."

I clutched his wrists. "Are you serious? Are you really serious?" Closing my eyes, I shouted, "Thank the stars!"

Loud, joyous shouts from the Durhcu sounded around us.

Chapter Seventeen

Her bottom lip quivered. Tears spilled from her beautiful jade-green eyes. "I will miss you." She wiped away her tears with the back of her hand. Slamming herself into Bhamak, she hugged him fiercely.

He hugged her and patted her back. His eyes were filled with sadness.

"You will see each other again. I promise. Bhamak and his people are our new allies. We will return, and when we do, we will bring them weapons with which to protect themselves against the Alux. We will return." The two children looked at me and knew I spoke the truth.

Neema sniffled. Then she looked up at her friend. "Bye, Mack."

"Bye, Neema." Dejectedly, he walked over to his father and held onto his leg.

Strict protocols had been put into place prior to our departure to ensure that the Durhcu kept all of theirs and we kept ours. Combined, we had the sneakiest children in the universe. With Neema's hand in mine, we walked up the ramp of the *Empress*. She turned her head and watched him until it closed.

I tried to be sensitive to my daughter's emotional state. I really did. She sat with me, squished in at my side, in my command chair. It was a tight fit, even with my legs crossed to give her more room, but it was worth the peace of mind it gave me to know she couldn't sneak off the ship and back to Bhamak.

The happiness I felt was indescribable. My ship was repaired. She had been restocked. She was fully powered. We were going home. Cleared to disembark, I took my ship from the space dock and laid in the course the Durhcu had helped us to chart. I pointed at the station. "Their blaster cannons look nice." I'd explained to Neema that we weren't leaving our new allies defenseless. We had shared scans of our weapons. With access to their home world returned to them, they had the resources to quickly begin manufacturing them. They had reciprocated in their own way. Throughout my ship Vadu vines flowered. Planted in plasti pots with plasti trellises, the edible blooms had been affixed so as not to pose any impediments to the crew. The air aboard already smelled fresher. Also, the Durhcu had gifted us with another new source of sustainable sustenance. The hydroponic garden filled an unused section of the transport bay. The plasti hydroponic towers could be easily relocated at our discretion. None of us would have to rely on protein patties.

"Bye, Mack." Neema sounded so sad.

I didn't know what else to say to her to make it better.

Clark saved me. "You'll see Bhamak again. What do you think of getting him some toys from different planets we visit and bringing them to him when we see him again?"

Neema sadly nodded that it was an acceptable idea. She had her favorite doll clutched in her arms. "We going to Chione?"

"Yes, baby."

Behind us, the Durhcu station shimmered briefly before vanishing. They would be safe. The Durhcu had done far more for us than repairs and restocking. They'd shared their technology. Cedrenus looked at me. I gave him the nod he was waiting to see.

"Activating veil," he reported.

Neema nodded to herself. Then, she climbed down from my command chair and laid on her stomach to look out the main viewer at the stars.

I took the ship out to a safe distance before engaging in maximum speed. Resting my elbows on my armrests, a satisfied smile played about my lips. The Durhcu were promising new allies. They'd repaired my ship, our fighter ships, restocked our supplies, and healed some of our minds and bodies. They'd also given me a greater gift, the ability to hide my ship and crew right under the noses of our enemies.

Stig said, "We have extended to them admittance to the Cosmos Coalition, have weaponized them, and have returned to them their home world. Those are no small gifts." His response had been to my thoughts.

"I'm satisfied with our encounter with the Durhcu."

I watched him as he strolled across the bridge to stand at my side. "As am I."

He was planning something. I could sense it, and it was giving me a stomach ache. His smile made my own wither. "I shall see you at dinner." Hands behind his back, he left the bridge.

When the lift doors had hidden him from sight, Neema said, "Oh, Mommy, new daddy not on the team."

Her tone disturbed me, and it wasn't the only thing. She'd accepted Stig into our family, and I still wasn't sure of my own feelings toward him. Were feelings involved? He'd only ever been a vile villain in every aspect. Cormac had been right. Saving Stig had been necessary in order to save us all. His mental break had been hurting Neema, but it had also served as a mental beacon to the psychic-feeding Alux. "What do you mean, my sweet?"

Getting up, she walked over to me and took my hand. Then, she whispered in my ear, "He has his own plans." She kissed my cheek. "Can I go play with Chef?" She had nothing further to add now that she'd shared her cryptic warning. "We're making cinnamon rolls today. Chef said I could bring some to the bridge."

"Okay. Have fun. May I have a hug from my brave girl?"

She gave my neck a squeeze and then skipped away into the lift with her guards.

"Did I make a huge mistake?" Staring pointedly at Cedrenus, I waited for a reply.

Binder answered for him. "What other option was there?"

Ross said, "He could have been placed in a medical coma, but he still would have had brain activity for the Alux to sense. Anyway, being as short-handed as we were and still are, it would have made protecting the ship that much more difficult."

"You don't seem to mind him so much now that the Durhcu healers have had their go at him." Cedrenus' words were tinged with hurt.

"Don't be like that. I can't accept you, Binder, or Ross. It would change our dynamic, and you know it. Teams at the Academy tend to remain teams for life. Put your sexual fantasies about me out of your minds and start looking for wives elsewhere."

Cedrenus raised an eyebrow at me. "We can make it work." He grinned and blew me a kiss.

"You would no longer see me as an equal. It would change everything."

He sighed.

"She's right," Ross argued on my behalf. "Look at Flavian."

Anger rose in my cheeks. "What's that supposed to mean?"

Ross pursed his lips at me. "It means, he used to want to kick your ass, and now he has other things in mind for it."

Letting out a breath, I tried to keep in mind how Ross was trying to make my argument for me.

Cedrenus, in a completely serious tone, reported, "Alux scout ship, port side, twelve parsecs out."

"Taking us to impulse speed. Let's test our Durhcu veil. Ross, be prepared to fire."

We waited. It was no surprise to encounter the Alux scout ship. We knew they would investigate the destruction of their wormhole generator. They'd want to know what malfunction could have occurred and resulted in the destruction of so many of their warships. We didn't necessarily want them to learn we'd been the cause or that we were out here without backup. The Alux patrol gave no indication of sensing our presence in any form, physical or telepathic. Eventually, it left to search another grid.

"Moving ahead at full speed. I want every instance of Alux activity in this sector recorded. They occupy this sector for now, but not for long. We can't allow them to remain unchecked in what is practically the Laconian Sector's backyard."

"What are we going to do about it?" Binder wasn't being sarcastic. He was ready to formulate a battle plan.

"That is the question. Isn't it?" Cedrenus had the same speculative distance in his eyes.

Our jaunt through Alux territory was one fraught with tension. However, their patrols didn't extend farther than the distance we covered during our shift on the bridge. The four of us were relieved by Clark and his team. My report was ready for him by the time he took the command chair. "Teagan, Chef and Neema have had a minor disagreement. He wouldn't let her bring the rolls to the bridge because of the Alux. He thought distracting the bridge crew at such a time would be ill-advised."

Kissing his cheek on my way to the lift, I agreed. "He was right. May your shift be uneventful. See you in a few hours." Ours had been a stressful shift.

The smell of cinnamon rolls wafted to my nose as I stepped out onto the Imperial Deck. Bending, I took my boots off and left them by the door.

"Mommy!" She ran to me.

"I'm hungry. What do we have to eat?"

"Oh, I'll take care of you, Mommy. I baked and baked." She nodded and feigned exhaustion.

After amply praising her baking and having a cup of tea, we played with her dolls and her starship dollhouse. Then, the lift doors opened, and Dr. Savelli walked over to us. He was agitated.

"What's wrong?"

"It's Dr. Ness."

Hearing the odious male being referred to by a title other than ambassador threw me off for a second. "What about him?" We hadn't left him behind. I'd been careful about checking the ship's attendance.

"I'm concerned about his mental state." With his eyes, he told me he needed to speak to me privately.

Kissing Neema on the forehead, I got up and left her to her play. Lifting my hand, I extended my index finger, a signal to him to give me a moment. I went to my quarters, got a pair of flip flops, and met him at the lift. There was no way I'd be putting those boots back on unless there was an emergency. Dr. Savelli led the way to the lab space he'd given to Dr. Ness, the xenobiologist representative sent to us from the Laconian Sector.

"Dr. Ness, how goes your research?" Dr. Savelli spoke loudly enough to interrupt the other doctor.

The male paused and stared. His pupils were blown. It was probably nothing though. Eriopis pupils often appeared that way in space. They came from a system with twin suns.

"How does it go? How? I'm middle-aged. This is several lifetimes worth of fascinating new discoveries! I'm so far behind! However, I must be meticulous. I've so much to do, so much to do." Clearly, Dr. Ness hadn't slept, bathed, eaten, or changed his clothes.

Of course, Dr. Savelli was well-aware of this which was why he'd come to get me. I grumbled, "Why didn't you get Stig? He could deal with him."

"I did. He said the male would eventually tire himself out." Dr. Savelli sighed. "Stig isn't the one sharing work space with a manic workaholic."

I approached Dr. Ness. "It's time for you to take a break."

He stared at me. "Yes, yes, in a little while." He waved me away with his hand.

"Dr. Ness, that's an order, not a request."

"Excuse me?" His expression was one of disbelief.

"Dr. Savelli, how many hours has Dr. Ness worked without a rest cycle?"

Tapping at his vid-screen, he reported, "Dr. Ness has been working in his lab aboard the *Empress* for the last twenty-one hours straight without a break. I do not know if he rested while aboard the Durhcu station."

Anger darkened Dr. Ness' face. "Now, listen here. I have important work to do."

"Yes, we all do. Your work is critical to the survival of all races belonging to the Cosmos Coalition. Your research is too important for me to allow any harm to befall you under my watch."

Snidely, he retorted, "Oh, indeed? Like having my tongue cut out?"

I gave him my sweetest smile. "Dr. Ness, you don't need your tongue to help me defeat the Alux. Seriously, what would you do, lick them into submission?" My laughter horrified him. "As I was saying, you are my responsibility. I have decided that you will rest. Are you coming with me willingly?" I allowed my expression to turn eager. "Or, do I have to make you?"

He turned pale. His hands trembled. "I suppose I can take a short break."

Smiling, I clapped my hands together. "Excellent. Come along." With Ness obediently following behind me, I returned to my deck. As we exited the lift, I pointed. "Go shower and put on clean clothes." The male seemed confused. I pointed toward the quarters I'd assigned him on my deck and waited until he stumbled away to do my bidding. "Chef, what can you make to send him into a sleepy food stupor?"

Chuckling, he said, "Leave it to me."

I'd been about to sit on the couch when the guys entered the room and stopped me.

"What are you doing? We're back aboard." Ross gestured for me to hurry up. "We have a schedule."

"Teagan, it's time to spar. Aren't you going to change?" Binder was wearing exercise clothes.

My shoulders dropped in defeat. I went to my quarters and hurried to change into stretchy workout clothes. Then, the four of us went to the exercise room where we practiced hand-to-hand combat for an hour. Next, we practiced blade battle with dulled weapons under Cormac's instruction. We'd learned the hard way to fight the Alux with swords and knives when in close quarters. Well, in our sector of space anyway where they'd adapted their armor to absorb our blasts. I cringed remembering the gooey mess I'd created out of the last Alux I'd blasted.

Eventually, I returned to my quarters for a much-needed shower. Like the guys, Neema was ready to fall into our shipboard routine. She was waiting for me at the dinner table. Spread across the table were her learning tablets. At my seat, Chef had placed a vegetarian lunch. Taking my place, I ate while helping Neema with her work.

With such a small crew complement, none of us had much idle time. Between Neema and the ship, my wake rotations were fully occupied. Everyone aboard quickly reacclimated to life aboard the *Empress*, including Dr. Ness. After our initial intervention, he behaved like a rational person and balanced his physical needs with his intellectual pursuits.

We had a long journey back to Laconian space ahead of us. During our morning walk around the ship, Neema said, "Mommy, our ship is fixed. We're on our way home to everybody. So, why do people look sad?"

I sighed. I knew how they felt. "I think we're all bored." I shrugged. "It's sort of good to be bored. It's better than be scared we're about to get attacked."

Scowling, she hit her fist into her palm. "We need more parties."

I began walking again to catch up to her. "What if we had a movie playing each rotation in the Recreation Room on Deck Three?"

"Yea! Movie!"

During the remainder of our walk, we made our plans. Then, we got help setting out a rug and ten chairs in a corner of the Recreation Room. We sent out an invitation to the crew. After a few days, we accepted defeat on the movie night idea. The crew wasn't into it.

Neema and I were sitting at the dining table when an idea on how to improve morale came to me.

"Uh oh. What's that face for, Mommy?"

"I know how to cheer them up."

Skeptically, she asked, "How?" She had a purple Vadu flower tucked behind her ear.

"We'll do what Daddy and Uncle Hiroshi would do."

"What's that?"

"We'll have fighting matches and gambling." Grinning, I started planning.

"Oh, brother." Neema wasn't interested.

However, the males aboard eagerly participated in the new social activity. Since Clark had released me from the stipulation in our contract, I participated in a few matches as well. Morale aboard greatly improved, we settled further into our routine and continued on our long journey home.

By the time we had arrived in the outer reaches of Laconian space, we'd charted a significant expanse of unexplored territory. Chione was still a week away, but knowing it was so close improved the morale of everyone aboard even more.

"Magnify viewer." I'd been on duty for two hours when the structure had come into range. I studied what I saw on the screen.

"It's a fueling station," Ross reported.

"Hail them. Ask if they have any coffee."

Knowing I wasn't joking, he opened communications. The male who answered our hail had given up on personal grooming. His light-brown hair was too long and went off in every direction, and his cheeks were scraggly. Aside from his desperate need for a shave, he wore mismatched civilian clothing. I scrunched my forehead at his completely unprofessional impression. Then, he spoke. "Very funny. You, fucking dimwitted cunts! Stop playing around! This little stunt is getting your credits docked!" He flipped us off.

Appearance aside, I liked him. "Excuse me. I assure you that I am not playing. I'd like to know if you have any coffee with which you'd be willing to part by sale or trade."

The rugged station dweller rolled his eyes. "Bob, fuck off. I know it's you. Enough with the voice modulator. Find some actual work to do. How much time did you waste on this simulation? With talent like yours, you could do promotional work for a waste unit company."

Binder chuckled.

Annoyed, I asked, "What is your name?"

Uncertainty entered his eyes. "This is Andrew...."

"Hello, Andrew. I am Ensign Probus. I'd like to refuel my ship and purchase any coffee you might have. If this is acceptable, please transmit docking procedures."

"We thought you were dead!"

"No, I'm just out of coffee."

There was silence. Then, "Pardon me, Ensign Probus, but how many parsecs are you out? You aren't showing up on my sensors."

I gestured at Cedrenus. He lowered our Durhcu veil.

Eyes wide, Andrew gasped and grabbed his console with both hands. The *Empress* was at a respectful distance. No one from the station would be able to see us through a viewport with the naked eye.

"I don't mean to alarm you, but we've been through an ordeal."

Andrew's mouth moved. No sound came out. "Sending standard docking and fueling guidelines now, Princess, uh... Ensign...." He jumped up and darted from his office.

"I think I've been recognized." Taking us toward the station at a safe speed, I reviewed the procedures and was prepared to dock my ship upon arrival. "This is your Captain speaking. Feel free to enjoy what Fueling Station 149630 has to offer during your rest rotation." Clark and his team had come to relieve us. I kissed his cheek on my way to the lift. "We have dossiers on the stations' crew, but there are a lot of questionable ships using this place. I'm sure you and your team are as bored as we are, so it will give you something to do. I'm taking Neema with me."

"Good. She could use a distraction. I've got the bridge."

I nodded and entered the lift with my team. Neema and I liked a good routine. However, breakfast, walks, study, and playtime had become monotonous for her. Exiting the lift, I watched her where she sat playing with her guards. She needed more. She needed our family. Once we'd safely docked on Chione, we'd use the long-distance communications array to contact them. A sudden wave of dizziness took me to my knees. Someone rushed to my side. With my nose inches from the carpeting, I couldn't quite tell who it was.

"You're hurting her," Stig accused with seething rage. He knelt and took me into his arms. "You won't need to call your Laconian mates or your Laconian hybrid guards. They have found you, my brutal beauty." He combed through my hair with his fingers. "Once the veil dropped, it didn't take them long. How long would we have if the Alux were actively seeking us?"

Neema scrambled over to us. "Is it Daddy?"

Focusing on her, I said, "Daddy knows where we are. He's coming."

"Finally." Her forehead wrinkled with anger.

"It's not his fault." Clutching Stig's arm, I sat up and took a deep breath.

She shrugged. "It's taking him long enough is all I'm saying."

I sighed. "Go get your shock stick. We'll go explore the grimy fueling station for fun. After we refuel, we'll go to Chione to Daddy's fortress."

She shrugged and ran to her room.

"Are you alright?" Cormac asked. "Shall I call Dr. Savelli?"

Stig helped me to my feet. "I'm okay. The important thing is that they know where we are and where we are going. A team will meet us there." He knew what I meant. Inquisitors in the sector were being diverted to our location. There was no telling how many it could be. Looking up at Cormac, though, I had a feeling he knew. Closing my eyes, I held still for a moment. The tsunami of desperate telepathic communication had dissipated enough for me to function. However, Izaac was heavy in my mind, like a solid lump. He'd backed off as much as he was able. When Neema scampered back to me, armed and dangerous, my smile was genuine. She'd quickly changed into a poufy blue skirt and glittery pink boots.

"Hi, Daddy Izaac, Ed, and Cade!"

Stig became still. We realized at the same moment that my husbands weren't seeing only through my eyes. Neema was no longer as alone as she had been either. It made me feel better because if Neema were in danger, her telepathic protectors would gently intercede and do what they could to keep her safe. While it made me feel better, it didn't have the same effect on Stig.

He asked, "Who is Ed?"

Neema was carrying on a conversation with someone, partially out loud and partially telepathically. "We hid in a Durhcu shield so they couldn't find us. It was the longest Hide and Seek game ever. You know what? We won! We're going to look for coffee. Yes, you can come. I *gots* my shock stick."

"Zared," I quietly answered. "Cade is Quaid. Sometimes, she uses the names she called them when she was a toddler. They've been a part of her life since she was an infant." I looked down and realized that Stig was holding my hand. It seemed out of character for him. Having Izaac and Zared once again present in my mind gave me an added layer of protection as well. If I needed assistance in combat, they would take over. A shadow caught my attention. It was Cormac. He'd changed from his Inquisitor's uniform and returned to his former garb, that of my bodyguard. Still dressed all in black, he had blades sheathed at his hips, along his ribs, at his arms, and down his back. It was an incredibly sexy look for him. When I met his eyes, I knew he knew what I thought even if he wasn't telepathic. "Come along, Neema. Now, I must warn you that this station won't be pretty like the Durhcu station."

She shrugged again and led the way into the lift. One of her bodyguards cleared his throat which made her scowl. "Sorry. You or a grownup goes in first to check on the station. Don't run ahead. Yeah, yeah."

I grinned. They had been going over protocols with her.

My crew had the airlocks securely in place by the time we arrived. Cedrenus, Binder, and Ross were coming along with us. The station manager, Andrew, bowed when we stepped onto the deck plating. "Princess Probus, it is a great honor to meet you and to be able to offer assistance in your time of need. Welcome!"

Delighted, I smiled. He'd washed his face, tried to shave but missed a patch on his throat, and had wet his hair back. A station bomber jacket hid his tacky tropical shirt. "Thank you so much for your hospitality."

He gestured for us to walk along a service passage. The station had a compliment of roughly sixty crewmen, so they had us outnumbered. Some kept the fuel flowing. Some kept the station running, and some kept the people going. It was to a few of the latter that Andrew took us. The station had a diner. "This probably isn't what you're used to, but we do have coffee."

I was so pleased by the news as to almost hug the man, almost. "Thank the stars!" I quickened my steps. The station was clean and tidy but still had a grimy, aged patina to it. On what passed as a promenade, we walked by a table outside the diner where a few older men sat and curiously watched us. Filing by them, we entered the diner. I went straight to the counter and took a seat on one of the swiveling stools. The seat was a deep-red faux leather and squeaked when I sat.

"This guy is brand new, but no one has complained," Andrew whispered.

"Welcome, what can I get you?"

The older man looked anything but new. He had a reconstructed jaw and a robotic eye implant.

Neema cried out, "What happened?" Before any of us could stop her, she had climbed onto the counter. Hand gently cupping his jaw, she kissed his eyelid.

Taken aback, a big tear formed and spilled out of his good eye. "Aren't you a little angel," he said gruffly. "It was a mining accident years ago. It doesn't hurt anymore."

Cedrenus helped Neema down from the counter to her stool.

Ross asked, "Do you have any meat?"

"Do you have coffee?" I asked.

"I want scrambled eggs and cheese!" Neema shouted.

"I can make you some breakfast platters," he said as he filled cups and placed them down on the counter in front of us.

Eyes wide, I reached for mine. Could it be? Closing my eyes, I brought the white cup to my lips. Breathing in the intoxicating scent, I drew in air through my mouth as well while slurping up the delicious, hot, strong, black coffee. "Oh, stars, that's good."

Cormac chuckled. Dressed as he was, the sound caused the hairs on the Cook's arms to raise.

"Bodyguard, sit. Have some."

He did not. He was on duty.

I'd finished my second cup when the platters started coming out. Scrambled eggs with melted cheese on top, mounds of hashbrowns, fluffy biscuits smothered in white, peppered gravy, and stacks of....

"I hope ice bear bacon is okay," the Cook said.

"Yeah!" Both of Neema's hands shot out.

Copying her, I had bacon in each hand before the guys could attack it. I gave Cormac a quizzical look, but he remained stoic. He really was tough to be able to resist the tantalizing allure of bacon. I wasn't so impressed as to not eat my bacon though.

"How about some steaks to go with it?"

We all looked at the cook with adoration. Ross and Binder nodded. Their mouths were too full to speak.

He said, "We've got plenty of ice bear."

I reached into my pocket and placed a credit chip on the counter. It had a few thousand credits on it. "This should cover my crew. They will come in rotations and will keep you busy."

Taking my credits, he locked them away. Then, he kept the ice bear bacon coming while he started cooking our steaks.

"Hey, can I buy some coffee from you for my ship's beverage dispensers? Please?" I'd cleared the eggs and biscuits. I had a few bites of salty, greasy hashbrowns left to savor. They were fabulous.

"Sure thing."

"You don't know how happy you've made me."

Neema had demolished her cheesy eggs. "Mommy, can we eat dinner here?"

"Yes, my sweet."

Andrew, the station manager, asked, "What's for dinner?"

"Meatballs, gravy, and mashed *ceshoosh*."

Neema closed her eyes and tilted her head back. She had some eggs in her hair. "Yes, Ma food."

"Pardon?" the cook asked.

I translated. "Her grandmother, rather her Laconian grandmother, makes that meal for us at home on Parvac. She's delighted."

Ross began helping Neema to clean her plate. She couldn't eat another bite. "Oh, Mommy." She burped and rubbed her belly. "I need to walk this off."

"Can I get five orders of this with coffee to go?" I asked. While he prepared my take-out order, Neema and I led Cormac and her guards around the promenade. It was a working station. There was nothing interesting for little girls to look at.

"Okay, food is ready. Let's go," she said as she tugged me back toward the diner.

"How do you know?" I asked.

"Ed told me."

I felt a wave of guilt. "I didn't mean to cause any of you any suffering." I spoke the words out loud.

Izaac whispered into my mind, "Communicating with us would have given away your location."

At the diner, we were loaded down with take-out bags and coffee packets. Andrew escorted us back to our ship's airlock. While Neema and I took the food to the bridge, Binder, Ross, and Cedrenus gave Andrew a brief tour of our ship.

The lift doors opened. "Neema and I have the bridge. Go eat in the conference room."

"Ice bear bacon!" Neema shouted.

Cormac, his stoicism abandoned, grabbed a bag and led the way. Clark, Levi, Tyler, and Stayton were on his heels. We could still hear them. From the conference room, they sounded like starved beasts tearing into their kill. Taking my command chair, I pressed a button.

"Chef to the bridge." When he arrived, I gave him my treasure, a bag of coffee packets for the beverage dispensers.

"Teagan," Chef said only for my ears. "There are willing hands aboard the station, seasonal employees, seeking to earn credits, who are willing to travel and fill low-level positions aboard." He gave a shrug of his shoulder and added, "in the kitchens."

"Understood. Hire who you want. Send me their information for final approval. Anyone coming aboard will be fully vetted."

He nodded, took the coffee, and left.

After each member of my crew had enjoyed a meal from the diner and my ship had been fueled, we were underway. Our brief stint at the station had boosted morale aboard considerably, mine included. I grinned as I looked over the list of temporary hires we'd picked up at the station. Adding one of them into each rotation would give my experienced crewmen the opportunity to return to more specialized roles aboard the ship. It never ceased to amaze me the amount of information an experienced Inquisitor could uncover about any particular individual, but a bored Inquisitor delving into a person's history was something else entirely. So many interesting facts had been revealed about the new crewmen who I had allowed aboard. One of Chef's hires was too good to be true. I doubted that Andrew would feel the same way. Crossing my legs, I happily bobbed my foot and watched the stars zip by along our course to Chione.

Chapter Eighteen

Warm, content, and sound asleep, I snuggled closer and tried to ignore the incessant, intrusive sound trying to wake me up.

"What?" Cormac's voice was deep and rumbly with sleep. "How far out are they?" He listened to someone. "Good. Carry on."

"What is it?" I curled up against his chest and let my fingers trail downward to his manly appendage which was too tired to play with me.

"Two Laconian ships from Chione are joining us to serve as escort and to provide additional security." Putting his vid-screen down, he sleepily patted the back of my head. "Everything is fine. Go back to sleep." He kissed my forehead and immediately took his own advice.

I tried. Every ache, every pain, and every worry made itself know to me as I tried to return to sleep. What would happen if the Alux were to attack Chione? I turned my head on the pillow. Clark was deep in sleep. His eyelids were twitching. Unable to remain still any longer, I crawled from bed, took my robe, and left my quarters.

"Come here."

Shocked, I stubbed my toe on a chair on my way into the kitchen and bit my lip to keep from yelping and waking up Neema. The command had been telepathic. Hand on my aching hip, I scowled in the direction of Stig's quarters and decided to yell at him. Before I could signal for entry, the door opened. He stood right there. He wore nothing. Forgetting to yell at him, my eyes were drawn down from his heated gaze to his lower anatomy which stood achingly firm. The ache was something I understood all too well. Taking my hand, he drew me inside and to his chest. Sliding my robe from my shoulders, he turned my back to his bed, shoved his foot between my legs, and pushed me back. He joined us together with more gentleness than I'd expected of him.

"Stop thinking," he ordered. He entered my mind with the same gentleness in which he'd entered my body. The worries left my mind. Instead, the pleasures of his touch consumed my attention. Lifting my hands, I ran my palms over his lower back and hips. His strokes were long and deep.

"You really are quite beautiful."

He put more force behind his thrusts. "Does it upset you?"

"Oh, no, not at all. You can speed up." My thoughts drifted to Nico and Eli. They had some powerful thrusting action. I couldn't wait to wake up between them.

"No, does it upset you that I'm prettier than you?"

"Ha!" I pushed his silky hair away from my face. "What conditioner do you use?"

"I see," his tone was warm honey. "It isn't my beauty, wealth, or power. It's our shared misery. They took Katherine from me. They robbed you of precious time with your infants." His voice hardened, and his movements within me became punishing. "They will pay for what they have taken from us, Teagan. They will suffer as they have made us suffer."

For what remained of the night, he gave me pleasure twisted with emotional misery, both of which made us feel mutually better. The Durhcu healer had done something alright. He'd switched Stig's preferred sadistic preferences in regard to me to something I could tolerate. If nothing else, my childhood traumas had taught me to survive emotional torture.

I woke up alone. I'd fallen asleep with Stig. The weird thing was that I didn't sense him nearby. He seemed like the type who would be gloating while waiting for me to awaken. Getting up, I pulled on my robe and left his quarters for my own. Cormac and Clark still slept. Trying not to wake them, I went to the bathroom to shower and dress. All the while, I searched for the mind of a male who seemed to be hiding from me. Filling my palm with shampoo, I scrubbed my scalp.

Like a whisper, Izaac's thoughts drifted through my mind. "He has gone. He and Max have taken the body of Katherine Stig along with them."

My hands stilled. Suds dribbled down into my eyes, causing my vision to blur and sting. "How?" It wasn't reasonable to try to hide my surprise and hurt from Izaac.

"He contacted one of his warships from the fueling station. His ship and crew awaited him on Chione."

Sticking my face in front of a jet to rinse my eyes, I tried to process what I was learning. "We're already on Chione?" Hurrying to finish, I dried and dressed.

Izaac had retreated. Cowardice wasn't like him.

On the bridge, I asked, "When did we dock?"

The officer on duty, one of Cormac's, replied, "An hour ago."

"When did Stig leave?"

"As soon as we docked. Should we have prevented his departure?" His tone said he'd retrieve Stig if ordered to do so. He vacated my chair.

"Put me through to his ship."

The officer at communications did so. Stig appeared on my viewer. Seated in the command chair, he'd changed his attire and was no longer dressed as a Parvac soldier. Now, he wore the expensive sort of modern suit preferred by the elite ruling class of the Galaxic Government. The black suit and dark-grey silk shirt appeared solemn. "Before you ask, know that I must lay Katherine to rest as befits her." He wasn't so far away that I couldn't sense his pain.

"You could have said goodbye to me in person."

"No, I could not have done so."

"Have you forgotten against whom the Alux launched their coordinated attack on Parvac?" Modulating my voice was impossible. "What are you thinking going off alone like this after what we have just survived? Aside from that, how can you simply take off in a warship you could use in our defense?"

"I have seen to your safety." The silence stretched between us. "We are in route to Earth. I will await you there and communicate with you regularly." He wasn't alone. It was obvious he didn't want to say anything personal in front of those who were present on his bridge.

"Understood. Safe travels. Probus out." Asshole.

An officer cleared his throat. "Counselor Stig has assigned a warship from his personal fleet to protect the *Empress*." He showed me a visual of it where it had been docked nearby. It wasn't the only one. Several warships from both the Militia and private sectors were docked at the land port. The Alux threat was being taken seriously. "In addition, the *Hadrian* has been diverted to our location."

Perking up, I began to feel better. "Eric is coming?" I smiled. Oh, the fun we could have in our fighter ships!

The lift doors opened. Hair a wild mess and with her clothes on lopsided, Neema spilled out onto the bridge. "Don't leave! I'm ready!"

"Leave? I'm not leaving." Walking over to her, I squatted down to put her clothing to rights. It was Arachnean Silk.

She rolled her eyes. "Of course, we're leaving. Go get some credits, Mommy. We can go eat and shop."

The bridge officers chuckled. Yes, she was mine alright.

"On one condition." I stood and stared down at her.

Freezing, she stared at me with wide eyes and waited.

"I want you to wear you Durhcu helmet, cape, and boots, along with your shock stick. At any threat of danger, I want you to hide. Do you understand?"

She nodded. Then, all seriousness abandoned in favor of conceit, she snorted. "I'm good at hiding." She tugged me into the lift and pressed the command for the Imperial Deck.

While Neema ran off to her quarters for her gear, I went to the kitchen in search of Clark and Cormac. They weren't there. Opening the door to my quarters, I found them both still asleep. "Hey, wake up."

Clark groaned. "Teagan, I can't. I promise I'll see Dr. Savelli and try again in a few hours."

Rolling my eyes, I shook him by his foot and tapped Cormac's leg. "Time to wake up. We've docked on Chione. We are going to visit the shops at the land port because Neema wants to."

Cormac sat up on the side of the bed and combed his fingers through his hair. I wondered if they even realized that I'd spent part of the night in Stig's bed. Cormac stood, grinned at me rather than kissing me, as if he were afraid that I might want more, and went to shower. They were both ridiculous. My libido wasn't that bad.

"Five more minutes," Clark grumbled.

Leaving the room, I went to the kitchen and enjoyed a fabulous cup of coffee while everyone got ready. My vid-screen signaled. "Yes?" A smiling face greeted me. Her hair was a soft dove-grey, and her eyes were purest white.

"Lady Ponidi, welcome home." It was Lady Sidero.

Hearing the familiar voice, Neema ran over to me and climbed up onto my lap. "Lady Sidero, thank you for the escort. It was greatly appreciated. I don't have the words to describe how very relieved we are to have safely returned to Laconian space."

Her eyes met and held mine. "I am glad you have returned. Many fears have been expressed in your absence." Her attention drifted to Neema. "For now, we rejoice. Allow me to serve as your host. Work has begun on your ancestral home, but it is far from complete."

"We want to go to the land port shops," Neema told her.

"Then, you shall," Lady Sidero promised.

A troubling thought occurred to me. It must have shown in my expression because Lady Sidero lifted her hand palm up and motioned for me to explain. "We have our fighters but had to use our transports as scrap to make repairs. Would you be kind enough to send a transport to pick us up?"

"It will be my pleasure. In fact, I will come for you myself." She warned, "Dress warmly." The screen went dark. She wasn't one for flowery goodbyes.

Staying warm wasn't a problem for us, not with all of the ice bear coats and boots with which Yukihyo regularly gifted us. By the time we reached the empty transport bay, Cormac, dressed as my bodyguard, and my team, were waiting for Neema, me, and her guards. When the ramp lowered, snow blew in on a chilly air current. Apparently, having been gone for so long, we'd missed the short Spring and Summer weather on Chione. The heavy roller made a crunching sound on its way up the ramp. Clumps of ice melted and slid from its sides to the deck making a sloshy mess the crew would clean up after our departure.

"Well, what are you waiting for? Get in!" Lady Sidero yelled as one of her clan opened a side hatch and lowered steps for us to climb. Clark and Cedrenus preceded Neema's bodyguards meaning to protect us. Lady Sidero snorted at them from the passenger seat. "No alien predators await you in my roller. If you are eager to hunt something, hunt something we can eat. Our stores are as thin as I imagine yours to be. Now, get in and close the door! Are you trying to melt Chione letting all the heat out?" She stopped fussing once the hatch was closed.

For some reason, Neema decided to take a seat and be on her best behavior.

Lady Sidero gave her a look. It needed no words. It clearly said, "You aren't fooling me."

Mounted in racks along the top of the compartment were heavy ice bear guns. Looking at them, Neema said, "Bears are dangerous."

"So are the wolves," I cautioned. From across the great expanse of space, I could feel Zared trying to soothe my worries, assuring me that he would be with me in battle should I need him.

Lady Sidero swiveled around in her chair to face us while her driver maneuvered the roller from my ship and out into the land port. "Tell me everything." Faint traces of worried orange laced the white sclera of her eyes, but the clan leader didn't show outright fear. The Enyo were confident they could ward off the Alux. She grinned sensing my thoughts. "We'd leave a bitter taste."

No, not much scared her, but I'd seen what they could do.

She huffed at me. "The Alux can fight. I'll give them as much. The Enyo are warriors. If I loosen my hold on the males of my clan, they will show what they truly are. You would be wise to learn to do the same."

Shocked, I stared at her and sat up.

She waggled her finger at me. "You keep your males swaddled in emotional safety. You wrap them in golden strands of love and contentment. Turn those golden strands to blue, red, and purple and see what they do to their enemies." She gestured with her chin at Neema. "You might want to cover her eyes when you do." She waved her hand. "Bah," she exclaimed in frustration. "Tell me everything later. We've arrived."

With permission to put our recollection of events on hold, we waited for the hatch to open and walked through the parking garage and into the structure. Neema kept her gloved hand in mine as we entered. However, moments later, she needed both hands to wave at curious onlookers. Word of our arrival had preceded us. Cormac stared pointedly at a news crew. So much for secrecy.

Catching his attention, Lady Sidero scolded him. "Everyone thought you were dead! What do you expect?"

"It would be safer for Princess Probus for everyone to continue to believe the rumors of her demise."

She snorted. "The bear is out of the trap. There's no getting it to go back into it now."

The delicious scent of seared meat wafted over to us. Our noses led the way over toward the vendors. "Neema, give me your gloves." She yanked them off and handed them to me. Squatting in front of her, I tucked them into the pockets of her coat where she could find them if needed. Clark handed her a meat kabob. Cedrenus had a tray of them which he was carrying over to a table. Stayton was purchasing a tray of meat pies.

Concerned, Lady Sidero asked, "Have you been starving?"

Levi answered her. "We've been vegetarians for days and days. We were managing, but the situation would have been dire had the Durhcu not rendered us aid. I don't think any of us relished the idea of surviving for weeks on protein bar rations. Although, we could have survived on them for another year." He took a huge bite of one of the meat pies.

Neema grimaced. "Pancakes and ice bear bacon are way better than those bars."

The guys nodded in agreement with her.

"The ice bear population has tripled since the Spring. Take down the males in your territory, and we will process them for you."

Clark and the guys were paying attention to her in between bites. Snagging a meat pie, I passed it over to Cormac. He kept his hands behind his back. "Oh, for fuck's sake. Take it and eat it."

Raising an eyebrow, he relented.

I waited until he'd finished eating before taking one for myself.

"Can we go look?" Neema stared at me with barely contained eagerness.

"Yes," wiping off my hands, I stood. Lady Sidero joined us, walking at my side.

Cormac relaxed. He realized that the Sidero Clan had come in force. Each of the ever-watchful males was armed with blades and blasters. Neema's guards kept close. Lady Sidero said, "You are stronger than when we last met. It suits you."

I grinned at her. "Battling alien apes will do that for you." While Neema looked at everything and spoke to everyone, I told Lady Sidero what had befallen us since our forced departure from Parvac. I saw Clark and Stayton leave through a side exit with a stranger. "Cormac, what's that about?"

Neema's guards listened to his instructions to protect us while he went to investigate.

"Mommy! Mommy! Look!" She pointed frantically. We followed her into a shop where she had already made herself at home inside of a small thermal tent. "Can I have this? We can use it inside of Daddy's broken castle!"

Squatting down, I looked inside. I felt the bright-orange fabric. "You can have it. We will set it up in our living space inside of our ship." I handed a credit chip to the shop keeper.

Neema pouted. "Do we have to go back to the ship already? We stay on it all of the time!" Her glare was full of disappointment.

"I agree with you. However, the fortress suffered some damage and isn't safe right now."

Lady Sidero touched my elbow. "Your ancestral home has been under construction for weeks. A renovation crew continues to work on structural improvements. Yukihyo ordered a few modernizations."

I narrowed my eyes wondering if it was safe to pee there.

She grinned at me. "I have checked on the workers myself. The architectural engineer will meet with you at your convenience." Leaning in close so that only I could hear, she warned, "He is...energetic." The discomfort in her tone confused me. Knowing it, she shook her head. "You will see. You will have more patience with him than I."

"What is his contact information?"

She took out her vid-screen and sent it to me.

"Archibald Finnegan of Earth?"

She nodded and rolled her eyes.

I shrugged. His credentials and portfolio were both exceptional.

Neema had moved on from the tent. Now, she pointed at something else. "Mommy, can I have one of those?"

"It's bigger than you are, so no. However, you may buy each of your guards one so they can go hunting for ice bear bacon."

Her eyes got wide. She held her hands to her mouth and turned to her guards. "Will you get me ice bear bacon?" She asked with eager hope.

My attention shifted to Cormac as he returned.

"Anything to please you, Princess Neema," Justin replied. She clapped her hands.

With Cormac at my side, Justin and Gonen were free to examine the guns much to their little charge's delight.

Cormac said, "They are securing purchase of heavy rollers."

A wave of relief lifted my spirits. "Excellent. It is an inconvenience to not have them at our disposal." My thoughts darted back to when I'd been eighteen and riding on public transport to the land port for the first time. Quickly, I updated Cormac on the status of our fortress.

He checked his vid-screen. "If you want to visit, I can arrange security. Then, those who wish to form hunting parties or bivouac on the grounds may do so. Aside from our brief respite with the Durhcu, we've spent considerable time aboard. Fresh air and solid ground are good for the mind." Cormac waited for my approval.

"I agree. Also, if they are successful hunting, it will be good for our cold storage units." Quickly, I typed out a directive on my vid-screen for my crew to remain on our land.

"Mommy, look! Can we get this for Aunt Sparrow?"

"Sure, baby," I replied. My mistake had been in not looking up to see at what she had referred. I learned my lesson while lugging the ancient gun back to the ship. Everyone else carried their own purchases along with the items Neema had selected. After stashing the weapon in Sparrow and Xavier's quarters, it was time to put Neema's tent together. Chef had gone to the land port to secure an order of meat and produce. Clark and I busied ourselves with pleasing Neema. We arranged an ice bear rug under her tent and set up solar lanterns. We darkened the lights and used a projector to cast stars upon the ceiling. Then, the three of us watched a documentary about the wildlife of Chione. A signal from the intercom got me to my feet. "Yes?"

"Captain, sorry to disturb you."

"It's alright. What is it?" I glanced over. Neema was telling Clark where to place her sleeping bag.

"Mr. Finnegan is here to see you."

I sighed. A meeting tonight hadn't been on my agenda. I hadn't even contacted the male yet. He hadn't made an appointment either. "Fine. Take him to the conference room. I'm on my way."

Neema poked her head out of her tent to scowl at me.

"Don't give me that look. Your daddy is the one who hired him, not me."

"Fine. Whatever, Mommy. Hurry up."

I snorted at her and entered the lift. She got her bossiness from her Gama, not from me. Stepping inside of the conference room, I suppressed a wave of shock from showing on my face and managed to keep my expression pleasant. The male's appearance was ghastly.

His choice of attire distracted me from every other thought that had been rolling around in my head.

He stood and extended his hand while walking around the table toward me. He stumbled over his own feet and quickly righted himself. Then, he acted as though it hadn't happened. When he noticed my hands were behind my back, he quickly retracted it, blushed, and bowed. Then, he released the breath he'd been holding when I extended my hand. "Archibald Finnegan at your service, Princess Probus, or shall I say Captain Probus, or maybe something else?" His expression changed from friendly confidence and a smile to perplexed nervousness and a frown in a second. Meanwhile, he kept pumping my hand up and down.

"Call me Teagan."

His smile returned and was larger than before. "Call me Archie!"

I carefully extracted my hand and gestured for him to return to his seat.

Archie managed to get there without tripping. From a leather case, he removed a large, foldable vid-screen. "I've brought damage reports along with progress updates."

While he set things up, I tried to rationalize his fashion decisions which had caused my initial shock upon seeing him. The male had dressed himself in a blue and green plaid sportscoat, a red polka-dot white collared dress shirt, a blue bowtie, denim pants, and knee-high orange snow boots. Yet, his portfolio was impeccable. Oh, well. It was for his architectural prowess and not his interior decorating skills for which Yukihyo had hired him. Archie began showing me images of the damages which had occurred.

"Stars," I groaned.

"The rubble has been removed. I hired local crews," he assured me. His auburn hair added to the color overload. Noticing my scrutiny, he exhaled. "I've done it again. Haven't I?" He shook his head. His hair didn't move. He'd used some sort of setting cream in it which made it stick together and look almost wet in some areas.

"Pardon?"

He gestured at his ensemble. "Do I match?" Archie stared at me with his intense green eyes, waiting for an honest response.

"No, you don't match in the slightest."

He let out another exhalation. "I'm colorblind. It has caused me significant embarrassment over the years."

"Why don't you have it corrected?"

He grinned at me. His green eyes sparkled with mischief. "It sometimes gets me attention from beautiful women."

"Let me guess. You accept their generous offers to help you with your wardrobe?"

Leaning closer, he slathered on the charm. "Sadly, none of them have been able to tame me, or rather my closet."

"Tragic." I shook my head. He reminded me of Phillip prior to Terri. Well, at least he did until he started talking about plans for the fortress. Archibald Finnegan became quite animated while discussing structural integrity and the latest galvanized support beams, mesh layers, and integrated force shields designed to prevent cave-ins. When Cedrenus innocently carried in a coffee service, I beseeched him with my eyes to save me.

Bending to my ear, he whispered, "Accept me, and I will do anything for you."

I narrowed my eyes at him.

He shrugged, put down the coffee tray, and left. Apparently, he hadn't given up on being one of my husbands.

Pouring the coffee, I half listened to Archie while he bored me. Cormac stood against the hull behind us, keeping ever vigilant. It was a good thing that he and most Parvac males weren't overly jealous. Otherwise, Archie wouldn't need the big case for his vid-screen because Cormac would have found a warm, new home for it in Archie's person. The man blatantly undressed me with his eyes and watched my lips every time I took a sip from my cup. However, even in my current hormonal state, there was something other than his atrocious sense of style that felt off to me. "Wait." I tapped the table.

He stopped his chatter and stared at me.

"Go back to the restrooms." I waited while he scrolled. "Did Yukihyo approve of those?"

"Yes, they are new models."

"Right. So, the only update he is willing to make is for the waste units?"

Archie nodded.

"Unbelievable."

"Would you prefer a different model?"

Raising my eyebrows at him, I pointed at the screen. "The waste units are fine, but let's bring the rest of it up to this century, or at least the last hundred years. Stars. The sinks, mirrors, countertops, and hand dryers need replacing. Also, I want half baths added to each bedroom along with built-in storage. There is plenty of space in each room for enclosed waste units and sinks. It's fine if they are of the space-saving variety, but I've had it with stumbling along in the dark during the middle of the night to go and pee." I crossed my arms over my chest.

"Yes, ma'am. I will put together some plans and a budget proposal for your approval."

"Good. Also, when you get to the kitchen, I want a top-of-the line beverage dispenser, cold storage unit, and cleaning unit."

"All while retaining the original charm?" he asked.

I nodded. "Be careful of the dishes."

Once we had concluded our meeting, Cormac and I escorted him to his transport. "Thank you for your valuable time, Teagan. It has been both a pleasure and an honor." He winked, flashed his smile, and managed to drop his satchel. Blushing, he bent to retrieve it while hastily shoving the items which had spilled out of it back inside. He gave me an awkward salute, blushed about having done it in the first place, and got inside of his transport. Luckily, he managed to drive down the ramp without mishap. Finally, I was able to return to Neema and our indoor campground.

"Interesting sense of fashion," Cormac stated. He had a lethally sharp blade sheathed down his back.

"Yep, and he's single."

"Please, don't."

Laughing, I turned and ran for the lift, but Cormac beat me inside. "Let's go see what Neema and Clark are doing."

As soon as she saw us, she said, "Go change! Both of you are dressed wrong."

Gaping at her, Cormac said, "You should see how the man with whom your mommy had a meeting was dressed." He showed her a security image.

Scrunching up her face, she said, "Nik would like it."

She had a point. Her brother often made odd fashion choices. He didn't care much what he wore as long as it was comfortable. The four of us got comfortable. Neema's guards had joined a Parvac hunting party on our lands, so Chef decided it was his duty to watch over us. With the security that Stig and Lady Sidero had provided, my crew was free to enjoy some off-duty time. Most of them had formed hunting parties. They'd earned it. The most recent party to be taking their leave of the ship was comprised of Clark's and my teams. They were following Archie.

Outside, snow fell. It didn't deter the hunting parties, nor did it deter the ships docking and disembarking in a mad rush for supplies. While the land port was all frantic activity which had undoubtably been caused by our arrival, aboard my warship, all was quiet and still. It was so quiet that I could hear Neema breathing. She was sound asleep, but I couldn't manage it. Snug in her sleeping bag, she didn't wake when I activated my vid-screen. She'd made me promise to stay with her in her tent throughout the night. Clark and Cormac had gone to bed over an hour ago.

The signal was erratic. Using a simple technique we'd been taught at the Academy, I attached my signal to the land port for a boost. Then, I attached it to another communications relay near Leucon before it cleared up. Finally, I got a stable link to a Laconian news broadcast and started scrolling. My finger froze as a heading grabbed me. Disbelief washed over me leaving me cold. It quickly metamorphized into heated anger.

Chapter Nineteen

"Why didn't anyone tell me about this?" I was shaking Cormac awake.

"What?" Sitting up, he looked at the screen that I held before his eyes. He was as shocked as I was. There was no faking his reaction.

Turning, I left the room and went directly to the bridge. Stepping from the lift, I approached the communications officer. "Why are our communications being scrambled? On whose orders has this been done?" Fury made my words sound harsh and grating even to my own ears.

"There has been no such order."

I gestured at his controls. "Bring up Earth news then. Fill my ears with all of the celebrity gossip." Plopping down onto my command chair, I called my prime suspect. A staticky view of gorgeous blue eyes, a sparkling white smile, and glossy black hair filled my personal vid-screen.

"Hello, cousin. It's good to have you back. We thought you were dead."

"It's a huge fucking relief to be back. However, some of this shit gets boring. I don't need to be protected or coddled. In fact, as head of the Cosmos Coalition, it's downright criminal to hide such things from me. Did you do this on your own, or were you following orders?"

Captain Eric Alaric gave me a vacant stare. "Did you hit your head?" He was serious.

"Yes, several times, but that's not the point."

Leaning back in his command chair, he said, "I'll have my Chief Medical Officer check your brain as soon as we get there."

I rolled my eyes at him. "Don't bother. I'm leaving for Earth as soon as I can recall my crew to the ship."

Eric sat forward. His eyes narrowed. "Excuse me? Teagan, it's not safe for any of us to travel alone right now. The Alux are stirred up and striking every chance they get."

"Is that what happened to the medical space station orbiting Earth?"

A furrow creased his brow. "What are you talking about?"

"Check the news." I smirked. As if he didn't know. I shrugged. "Whatever, Eric."

Cormac entered the bridge and went straight to the communications officer. Bending to listen, he learned what the officer had been able to discover so far after bypassing the signal scramblers and buffers that had kept us ignorant. He did so with far more skill than I possessed. Meanwhile, I studied my cousin. His face was slowly turning a deep-red as his own communications officer reported to him. Of course, he'd muted me, so I couldn't hear.

"He wasn't behind it," Cormac said. He turned to me from where he'd been hunched over the console.

Eric had himself unmuted. "We weren't behind this. Obviously, you weren't. I'll get to the bottom of it. However, my personal thoughts are that Stig is the only one with the pull or the motive for this."

I blushed. How could Eric already know about Stig and me? Did he have a spy aboard my ship? Stig must have purposefully kept the news from me to keep me relatively safe on Chione since he was on his way to Earth anyway.

Eric said, "Obviously, Stig is involved and wants to cover it up before it's investigated."

My cheeks burned hotter. I'd been off on both points. Eric didn't know about Stig and me, and maybe Stig had been behind it.

Cormac asked, "Why would you suspect Stig's involvement?"

Eric looked up from a report he was only now receiving. "Dr. Stanley Crispus was being held or rehabilitated, however you choose to see it, on that medical space station. It got some of its funding from Stig personally, and Crispus is missing." Eric rubbed his jaw. "Why would he want Crispus?"

Cormac and I locked eyes.

"Eric, when we got drawn into the anomaly with Stig's vessel in Parvac space, Kitty Stig was killed." Closing my eyes, I took a calming breath and went on. "Edvard is far more Laconian than he or his paternal ancestors let on. They hid it for business and political advantages. Kitty stabilized him to a degree, made him less pirate king for a while. Another thing we didn't know was that the Mad Ones in his employ managed to form a fucked-up version of a paternal telepathic bond with him."

Cormac said, "And through him to Katherine Stig."

Eric leaned back in his chair and contemplated what he'd already begun to deduce.

Cormac continued. "Katherine's death shredded what remained of the Mad Ones' grasp on sanity. They were overcome with rage and bloodlust. They attacked an Alux ship within the anomaly, overtook it, and left us all behind, trapped. We can only surmise that they have gone on their own mission of death."

Eric lifted his eyes to stare vacantly as he processed it all. "Stig had Crispus taken so he can help track his insane pseudo sons. He wants revenge as well."

"We have another problem." My voice was too quiet. I cleared my throat and spoke up. "Stig was stranded aboard my ship with his bodyguard, Max, who was grievously injured. Stig's grief was overwhelming. It was hurting Neema." I took a deep breath, let it out in a whoosh, and blurted out, "I bound him to me."

"You what?" Eric shouted. On his feet now, he yelled, "Unbelievable! Does Quaid know?"

Scrunching up my face, I started chewing my fingernail, messing up the black, sparkly paint. I feared I might be getting it on my teeth.

"I can accept as many males as I choose." My words were heavy with petulance.

Hands on his hips, Eric said, "I don't give a fuck about that! He's a danger to everything! He's the domino that could topple your entire Empire!"

"My father-in-law would never allow that to happen. If need be, Consul Bosh will fix everything. He told me so before." I rubbed my temple, not wanting to think of the last batch of Mad Ones with whom I'd had to deal.

"Look. You stay put there. That's an order, not as Captain Alaric, but as your cousin Eric. You got it?"

Reconsidering the wisdom of rushing off to Earth, I shrugged. "Whatever." My reply had some of the tension leaving his jaw, but not enough of it. He looked kind of scary. "You know what? Fine. I won't be the one to deal with Stig. This is all clearly a Galaxic Militia problem. I have my own problems."

"Does that mean you'll stay put?"

"I'll stay in the Laconian Sector."

Eric nodded. "Deal. I'm on my way. Alaric out." The screen, along with its static, went blank.

"Fucking hell. I'm going back to Neema." Getting up, I left the bridge, went to my deck, kicked off my shoes, and crawled back inside of the tent. If Stig and the Mad Ones wanted revenge against the Alux and managed to destroy a few of their warships, who was I to interfere?

The next morning, Neema and I sat at our dining table together and enjoyed steaks and eggs for breakfast. My cup was filled almost to the brim with hot, strong, black coffee. It was a wonderful morning until Yukihyo's architect showed up uninvited. "What does he want?" I scowled at Cormac.

"He wants to give you an opportunity to inspect the repairs and see holographic overlays of his proposed updates to the kitchen."

"Fine. Bring him here. He can wait while I finish eating."

Chef began setting another place at the table.

"Mommy, I'm done. May I be excused?"

"Yes."

She went to her quarters. When she returned, she was dressed for an excursion with her temporary guards to visit the land port. Cormac had approved of the little adventure along with an additional security detail to keep the little princess safe. Lady Sidero had planned a small social event for Neema and a few local children. It involved a traditional storyteller. She hugged my neck, kissed my cheek, and darted off into the lift with an excited smile on her face and her shock stick at her hip.

I closed the mission files I'd been studying and took another bite before tucking my vid-screen away into a jacket pocket. Last night, I'd been too agitated to get quickly to sleep, so I'd laid there thinking. Now that we were here, there really wasn't any reason why we shouldn't return to our original mission to catch our thief, pose as students, and infiltrate the monastic library. Maybe, Stig and the Mad Ones would keep the Alux off of our asses long enough for us to find a lead on the Pariea and convince them to help us. Realizing how hopeless it all sounded, I rubbed my temples.

"Oh, no. Have a headache?" It was Archibald Finnegan. The concern in his voice was tinged with disappointment.

I gave him a smile that I didn't feel and lowered my hands to my lap. "It's nothing. May I offer you some breakfast?" I gestured to the place which Chef had just set on the table.

"Why, I'd be delighted! I'm famished now as I think about it." He took his seat but appeared distracted.

"Something wrong?"

He smiled at Chef who was placing a loaded plate in front of him. "Not at all. I simply don't recall my last actual meal. Most often, I grab something and go." His fork clattered loudly to the table. "Oh, pardon me." He fumbled around a bit more before managing to feed himself.

Taking up my cup, I enjoyed the luxury that was coffee.

"All done! Thank you! It was wonderful." He was wiping his mouth.

"How...." Stopping myself, I realized my coffee had gone cold, and Chef had removed my plate. Time had seemed as though it had stopped for me. And, it didn't seem as if it was the first occurrence of such an event, but I couldn't seem to pinpoint it.

"Ready?" Archie stood and pushed in his chair. Picking up his plate, he walked it to Chef in the kitchen.

"Yes, just let me get my coat." In my quarters, I quietly called Dr. Savelli and told him what had happened.

"Any other symptoms?"

"No, sir."

"It could be stress related. Go see the fortress as you've planned. When you return, we'll do a full exam. From your most recent check-up last week, nothing is wrong. You're perfectly healthy, so don't let it worry you."

I heard someone yelling in the background. It was Ambassador Ness. Dr. Savelli growled low in his throat before ending our consultation. In my closet, I found the coat and boots Yukihyo had made for me and dressed to match Neema. The weather reports we'd been receiving necessitated warm outerwear. Fall on Chione could turn icy in hours which my crew well knew. Coat held before me, I returned to the living area where Archie waited.

With Cormac looking on, Archie helped me with my ice bear coat. Then, in the lift, he chatted away about kinetically heated flooring systems. In the transport bay, he gestured to his roller. "Shall we?"

"No, we'll take a stealth ship. It will be faster. I don't want to be away for long."

Cormac focused his attention on Archie which caused the male to cringe. "Don't worry. We'll return to this ship together."

"Yes, very well. It will save us from dealing with the roads." Gazing out through the lowered transport bay ramp, he watched the wind drafts as they twirled around tiny snowflakes.

"This way," I called back over my shoulder.

A pilot stood ready at the stealth vessel. Once we were seated and had fastened our safety harnesses, he flew us from the ship.

"So, what do you think of the flooring system? Is it something you might wish to integrate into the design of the fortress?"

"The thought does appeal to me. However, there is something special about those fireplaces and how they draw us together to huddle for warmth and company." I shook my head in the negative. "Let's stick with the bathroom and kitchen updates."

He grinned and winked at me. "Keep the charm so to speak? Very well."

It was quiet for the rest of the trip. A warm, fuzzy feeling suffused me as the fortress came into view. It brought Yukihyo to the forefront of my mind along with the safety, love, and acceptance he gave to me. Heavy work transports, crews, and machinery had made a muddy mess of what I considered to be the front yard. Snowflakes strove to conceal the tread marks and tracks. Archie was trying to free himself from his harness. I looked at Cormac. He looked at me. Realizing he would prefer to blast him rather than help him, I got up and freed the bumbling architect.

"Thank you. I'm terribly sorry."

"No worries."

He blushed and hurried from the vessel. Then, for the next hour, Archie showed us what the crews had done to remove the rubble, reinforce, and repair the structural integrity of our home.

"How long before repairs are complete?" I listened absently to his response while imagining how lovely a summer vacation here would be with my entire family. I pushed thoughts of my babies, Tabitha and Marielle, Peter, Niklos, and my best friend, Thunderdrop, from my mind before I could become weepy about them. We would soon be reunited. I had to focus on something or go crazy. I made up my mind then and there. For now, I would concentrate on our original mission, before everything had been blown to shit.

Archie clutched his stomach, made a face, and went rather pale. "If you will excuse me for a moment?" He hurried away.

"He did say that he hadn't been eating full meals lately," Cormac dryly stated.

A slow grin replaced my expression of annoyance. "You know what? I think we're alone. The workers are... somewhere that way from the sound of it." Inching my way closer, I gently touched his lips with my finger and trailed a path down his chest. "We could go inspect the bedrooms and make sure there is no damage."

His tone was low, deep, and hushed. "Which bedroom?"

"The closest one." My whispered reply raised chills on his neck. I laughed as he chased me up the front steps, but let him catch up so he could open the heavy door.

It was sometime later. Laying with my head on Cormac's shoulder, I stared up at the ceiling. The bedsheets hadn't stayed cold for long. "We should go and find him. He's had an hour or so to get himself sorted."

Cormac pulled me a little closer. "Or so, most assuredly."

Smiling against his warm chest, I closed my eyes. "It's so luxurious."

"What?"

"Being here, safe and warm in your arms."

"I couldn't agree more."

Both of our vid-screens alerted at the same time. Groaning, I rolled from his warm embrace and got the device from my pile of clothing.

Cormac read, "Communications are restricted. Citizens are asked to use vid-screens for emergency use only. Government officials and their agents must use encryption protocols. The order is issued by Captain Bosh of the Cosmos Coalition and has approval from the Parvac Empire, the Laconian Sector, and the Galaxic Expanse." Holding perfectly still, my mind raced. Then, we both hurried to dress and raced through the fortress and out to our vessel. Boots pounding down the stone steps, Cormac said over his shoulder, "I'm unable to send a long-range communication to Parvac."

Not quite as coordinated as he was, the only contact that I was currently attempting was that of my boots to the ground as I tried to keep up. All the time I'd been spending in the exercise room had paid off though. He was less than three feet ahead of me. Our pilot, having received the same alert, was lowering the ramp. Cormac, expecting it to happen, hadn't even slowed his pace. I closed the hatch after myself. "Should we get him?" I gestured with my thumb over toward the portable restrooms placed out for the work crews.

"No." He sent an order to our crew to return to the ship. "They can bring him along if they want." The pilot took us up. An urgent call came through our devices. It wasn't the one Cormac had sent. It was far more ominous, and it could only mean one thing. Chione was under attack. "The threat hasn't materialized."

I stared at the incoming encrypted message while simultaneously working to decipher it. "Several anomalous events have been detected. Expect incursion at the following coordinates. There are two anomalies in Laconian space, one near Trambelus Space Station and another a few parsecs from Sinope."

"This close. They can generate their wormhole this close, and we didn't know."

The Galaxic Militia had always been thinly spread out. Galaxic starships patrolled their assigned sectors and travelled from planet to planet much as we merchants had done aboard the *Tora*. The Galaxic Militia didn't have the fleet it would need to defend against the Alux. My guts twisted. "Maybe, we should leave Neema here with the Sidero Clan." When the Alux attacked, we would fight, and the chances were that we wouldn't survive.

The trip back to the land port wasn't long enough for me to make up my mind about what would be best for my daughter's survival. Our vessel hadn't been the only one flying back in all haste. The ships were like angry hornets swarming their nest. Cormac and I were on our way to the bridge when my own crew began boarding. My team, still dressed in warm hunting gear, had arrived on the flight deck. One of Neema's guards waited for us by the lift.

"Is my daughter aboard?"

"Yes, Captain." He saluted and followed us inside.

I guess that settled it. She'd be with me. Stepping onto the bridge, I listened to updates, and relieved the bridge crew when my team arrived.

"What's the plan?" Clark and his team had joined us.

"I'm taking us up. If we are under attack, we'll be better off being in a position where we can maneuver and fight."

Clark pulled off his gloves and heavy coat. "We couldn't locate Mr. Finnegan."

"He might be better off where he is."

I hadn't been the only captain with the idea to take my ship up. It was a ragged assembly. Other than the *Empress*, and the warship Stig had left to protect us, there were the two warships that had escorted us in, and an assortment of vessels with the same defensive capabilities of the *Tora*. I had blaster cannons but little else. We might do well against a couple of Parvac warships, but there wasn't much we'd be able to do against an Alux warship. "Stayton, plan an attack formation for the ships we have. Assign each captain a code."

He tapped away at his console, knowing what I wanted.

"Cedrenus, encrypt an open communication to the captains."

"Ready," he replied.

"Hail them." As they accepted, they appeared on my screen. "This is Teagan Probus of the Cosmos Coalition. We might be facing an Alux attack. Should this occur, you will follow my orders. Your ships have been scanned. You are now receiving codes which contain encrypted battle plans specific to your ships. Watch your orders carefully as plans can change from second to second. Questions?" I made a quick scan of the pairs of eyes watching mine. "Probus out." I entered the command for the formation I wanted and watched as they moved their vessels into position.

The most powerful of our ships were orbiting in positions equidistant from each other to provide the planet with emergency protection. I forced my breathing to slow and reminded myself that Neema was in the safest area aboard my ship. We still had our cannons. The best of our weapons had been used in Parvac space. Breathe. Keep calm. Stay in the moment. Centering my mind, I shielded my thoughts, retreating behind the mental walls I'd learned to erect as an empathic child trapped with an abusive, murderous bastard of a male father figure. The stars vanished. The blackness of space appeared to roll like water in a pot. Reaching a boil, the anomaly spat out Alux pods.

"Track them." My order was quiet, but I knew that I didn't need to shout to be obeyed. Narrowing my eyes, I waited. We all did. The wait wasn't long. Like a metal shard tearing through the flesh of space, the Alux ship screamed into Chione's orbit. Those screams weren't figurative. The ship had been torn apart as if from an internal explosion. Now, sheets of its metal hull scraped against each other as they plummeted toward the planet's surface. "Who did they piss off?"

"Readings suggest sabotage," Stayton reported.

"Survivors?" I pressed a series of commands designed to have the wreckage shot away from the planet. Then, I took the ship in so Cedrenus could use our blasters to slow the wrecked alien ship. Working with the other captains, we finally managed to maneuver it into a mass of space junk. One of the captains placed an order for a garbage scow to clean it up.

Clark reported, "There are no signs of life."

I opened communications with the other captains. "We were fortunate. They were in no condition to engage with us in battle." I'd been expecting to see relief. Rather than engaging in battle, we'd defended Chione from wreckage. Granted, the wreckage could have been quite damaging. Instead, the captains, with the exception of the two from the Galaxic Militia, seemed unnerved.

One of the captains of a Laconian merchant vessel stared at me with his white eyes shot through with orange and grey, the only visible sign of his discomfiture. "What did the damage to their ships?"

Checking a report, I saw that he was right. The mangled metal had been two ships. I shrugged. "I don't know. Let's capture a few survivors and find out."

His answering grin was diabolical.

Another captain roared, "We shall make it a hunting game!"

Now, the Galaxic Militia captains looked unnerved. I thought it might be best if the Alux survivors surrendered to the ice bears. The bears would be nicer to them. "Let me know what you learn. Probus out."

Cedrenus said, "They have already begun setting bounties for live captures."

Cormac said, "I almost feel sorry for the Alux."

I grimaced. Being hunted by a pissed off Enyo would be a nightmare.

"What are you thinking?" Clark asked.

I shivered. "Did I tell you about the time when I was kidnapped by miners on Malta?" I wrinkled my nose at the harsh memory of what Yukihyo had done in retaliation. My team and Clark's were unimpressed.

"We've read the reports," Levi replied.

"Yeah, Eli was watching over you. Yukihyo acted appropriately." Stayton sounded so blasé.

I made eye-contact with each of them. "You're all some demented fuckers. Do you know that?"

"So, you say," Tyler said in an aggrieved tone.

My grin dissolved, and a furrow appeared on my brow. "Clark, Cormac, come with me. It's Neema. Something is wrong!"

Chapter Twenty

"Stayton, you have the bridge!" I said as I ran for the lift. Had the Alux managed to board us? Was the wreckage all a ploy? Why was my baby scared and angry? Blaster drawn and raised, I stepped from the lift flanked by my males.

Chef was down, unconscious with a blaster at his side. Neema's guards were both slumped over the furniture, unconscious like Chef. Neema was nowhere to be seen. I couldn't sense her. My heart had dropped to my feet, but I could hear its pounding beat in my ears. No, she was here, somewhere. She was obeying me, hiding as the Durhcu had taught her to do. The air in front of my quarters seemed to shiver and jerk. The three of us took aim.

"Hold!" Clark warned before Cormac or I could fire upon it.

We heard sounds first, a sort of deep warble. Then, suddenly, it was as if a veil dropped. Neema came into view. She had her feet braced on a branch of Thunderdrop's tree sculpture. She held on with one hand. In her other she held her shock stick, and she had it pushed hard into the suddenly materialized body of the male who had attacked Chef and her guards! Neema's battle cry was a high-pitched accompaniment to her opponent's electrocuted gurgling. Clark raced over to Neema, grabbed her, and brought her over to me where I stood dumbfounded. Cormac had the male down and bound before I could release the breath that I hadn't realized I'd been holding.

"*Him* was trying to steal Mommy's sparkles! The ones Gama let us take! No! No! He *not* getting our pretties! No way!" Neema was a ball of fury.

"You!" Cormac stated in surprise.

On the carpet with his face turned toward us, was the diner cook who we'd taken on from the fueling station. He stared at us through his mechanical eye.

"How dare you frighten my daughter!" I felt the red creeping up my neck to my cheeks.

"I'll cut him into pieces and use him as ice bear bait," Cormac swore. His tone said that he'd enjoy it.

Feeling somewhat vindicated, I knew he would enjoy it.

"Please! Please! Don't kill me! I have a daughter, too! I'd never have hurt Princess Neema. She's had a special place in my heart since we first met."

Neema huffed. "I have never met this person before in my life."

"Baby, what do you mean? You met him in the diner on the station. Don't you remember?" Concerned, I shifted her on my hip so I could see into her eyes. What was wrong with my baby's memory?

Cormac said, "Did you think we wouldn't uncover your true identity? We knew you were our thief, Colwyn Winks Taylor, before you boarded." He hoisted the male to his feet. "My only question is how you managed to plant yourself on the station in anticipation of our arrival when we didn't know for certain where we would be."

"Mommy, that's not my ice bear chef."

"What, my baby? Yes, that's him. We hired him. Don't you recall, my sweet?" A cold sweat began to trickle down my sides. Had he done something to her?

"Mommy. No. Listen." She took my face in her hands. "Feel him. Feel him with your feeling feelers. That is not my ice bear chef. I don't know him."

She was right. He didn't feel like our new cook. "Clark...."

Clark was already scanning the intruder. "She's right."

I took a step away with Neema. "What the fuck?"

"I'm taking him to a holding cell while we figure this out." Cormac moved toward the lift.

"No, Daddy Cormac." Neema narrowed her eyes. "He got happy when you said that. He wants to go to a cell." She rubbed her foot on my thigh. "Cook, come here!"

Moving over to the intercom, I said, "Red alert." Then, deciding to trust Neema's instincts and senses, I ordered the cook to come immediately to my deck along with additional security and Dr. Savelli.

When the grizzled cook entered, he was as surprised as we were. "Who's that?" He pointed at his double.

Dr. Savelli scanned our cook and the male in Cormac's custody. Neema held her hands out to the cook. I let her go to him. Our deck had filled with warriors. They had the lift doors covered.

Cormac said to the intruder, "Please, don't volunteer any information. Let me learn the truth on my own."

Dr. Savelli raised an eyebrow as he watched the intruder's heart rate become dangerously elevated.

"He has Gama's stuff! He hid it in the air! I saw it!"

"So, this is our thief. Set course for Cassini. If he won't talk, perhaps his daughter will."

"No! Please!"

"Oh, I know all about your daughter." I smiled my sweetest smile. I watched as sweat beaded on his upper lip. "Her name is Clue Shimizu. Oh, wait. It's Clue Taylor again. She had a male but discarded him."

"Please," he begged.

"I don't give a fuck about your daughter. You're the one I want, Winks. If you want to keep your home world in one piece, you will do exactly what I want."

"Anything! Anything! I swear it."

Furious, Neema yelled, "Give us back our sparkles!"

Slowly, Cormac released his hold on the thief.

He let his head sway slowly. It was as if he argued with himself. "My secret or my daughter's life?" He looked around the deck. He was caught, and he knew it, but he wouldn't be the only one to pay for his crimes. "Don't shoot. She's right. I hid them in the air. I have to do something to get the gems back."

"Do it then. You know what you risk," Cormac stated.

Dr. Savelli was busy reviving Chef.

At the thief's side, the air shimmered. From the shimmering, he removed a pouch. Puzzled, we stared at it trying to figure out how he'd done it. He handed the pouch to Clark. Inside was the necklace Momma had given me. Clark brought the pouch over to Neema who scowled at the thief.

Stepping from the lift, flanked by Cedrenus and Levi, Stayton said, "It was rather ingenious of you to lure House Ponidi here. You arranged for the damage to the fortress, found a male to incriminate on a fueling station far enough away to buy you some time if you were suspected, and managed to get Yukihyo to hire you while impersonating an architect."

I gasped.

Stayton continued, "It was mere chance that we hired the male you intended to frame. It was also chance that the Princess Neema caught you in the act."

"Wait. The thief is Archie?"

"Yes, way too obvious, isn't it? We thought the thief was Finnegan at first, since he meets the description of Colwyn Taylor, but we dismissed it as being a set-up, just as he wanted."

"Bastard! You rotten bastard, here I am trying to make an honest life for myself, and you go and try and ruin it!" The cook was livid.

"It's okay. Don't be mad. Neema knows you're good. You can be Neema's cook. Mommy has her own cooks. Neema can have her own cook." She nodded to herself.

I shrugged. She could have her own cook as long as he didn't cook unhealthy things for her.

Stayton said, "I assume you hired the woman on Earth who took you shopping for your current wardrobe. After I realized you'd set-up the cook, I decided to concentrate all of my attention on you. You invested considerable time creating Archie Finnegan." He tapped at his vid-screen and showed the thief an image. "I do love the facial recognition technology of Earth and how simple it is to link with it when you work with the head of their interstellar security."

I shook my head. Stayton had just managed to win our private team betting pool on how our target would infiltrate our defenses. "I personally vetted everyone who I allowed onto my ship, and you had me tricked. I thought the thief was our new cook." Turning my head to him, I said, "Sorry." Returning my attention to the thief, I said, "Your timing was excellent, waiting until what could have been a crisis. It worked out in our favor though. It's why Cormac is still allowing you to breathe. You can't get away as easily with us in space."

Cormac said, "You can't escape us. Know that."

"What do you want from me?"

Clark answered. "We need help with a school project."

"You..." He pointed and turned. "You, and I ask this with all due respect along with a healthy dose of fear for my life, my daughter's life, and for our home world, you need my help? You need my help?"

"Yes, we do. Did you think stealing my momma's jewels was your idea? You drew our attention when you returned that ugly statue to my father-in-law. If anyone can help us, it's you."

Clark said, "We need a book from a library."

The thief's eyes grew wide. Then, he bent slightly at the waist and started laughing.

"Look, if we don't complete our mission right now, we won't get to. My cousin, Eric, is on his way, and my husbands, well, most of them, are not far behind."

The thief had finally stopped laughing, realizing that we were serious. "Wait, really?"

I scowled at him. "Get him cleaned up. The eye has got to go. That's really fucked up, using someone's disability for your own selfish reasons."

"You're damn right," Neema's cook seconded.

"Plan this shit out with him and update me. I'll be on the bridge getting our course underway. I'm taking us out to Bondi Prime."

Leaving the surface hadn't been as easy as I'd thought it would be. While Captain Alaric had been fine with me agreeing to remain in the Laconian Sector, the captains who had been assigned to protect the *Empress* were not okay with her even so much as leaving Chione. Getting into a yelling match with them hadn't helped my case in the least as they'd flanked my ship with the intention of following me wherever I decided to travel. Now, I smiled to myself. Getting into a fight with an alien ape hadn't been fun, but activating my ship's Durhcu Veil sure was. I waggled my fingers goodbye at the captains who could no longer find us on their sensors. Feeling happy and empowered, I turned the bridge over to Cormac's men and went to the conference room to strategize for our Academy mission. The first thing I saw was the thief scrunching up his face in disgust.

"No, no, no, no, no! It won't work."

Our captured thief had studied the carefully orchestrated plan devised by Eli and Rovek. He thought it was shit. I took a seat and listened.

Cormac scrutinized the male. He wasn't offended. He was curious. "Why not?"

Winks ran his fingers through his thick, short auburn hair, causing it to stand on end in a roguish fashion. "You've got too many variables. I can use the kids, but not how you've planned."

He really was quite handsome now that he'd removed his disguises, that of both cook and architect. There was a wildness to him. Along with the cybernetic eye, he'd removed a hidden neural blocker. Now, I could sense his thoughts and emotions. The latter came in frenetic bursts of joy, excitement, and intense annoyance. It was no wonder that he used disguises, first as a bumbling architect and secondly as the disabled short-order cook who he'd tried to set up. Without a disguise, he was too memorable, too captivating.

"Captain to the bridge."

Obeying the tiny intercom voice, I scowled, stood, and excused myself from the room. "Just as it was getting good," I grumbled under my breath. Returning to the bridge, I asked, "What?"

A quick glance from the communications officer to his screen gave me my answer.

"What the fuck, Teagan?" Eric scowled right back at me. "You said you'd stay in the Laconian Sector." He leaned forward in his chair and made a sarcastic show of searching all around his bridge. "You lost?"

"No, I'm not lost."

Glaring, he asked, "Why did you break your word?"

A heavy sigh escaped me. "Technically...."

"Technically my ass." His blue eyes were icebergs, seemingly calm and cold while below the surface, they were ready to rip your shit to shreds.

I decided to change tactics and fast. My sweetest smile replaced my scowl. "Oh, Eric, don't be angry. I have permission. Eli and Instructor Rovek know exactly where we are going."

He smirked. Knowing my manipulative trick for what it was, he leaned back in his command chair. "Then, you won't mind if the *Hadrian* follows you."

Shrugging, I raised my eyebrows, "If you can find me. Can I go now?" I knew I sounded like a petulant teenager, but it wasn't my fault. It was Eric's fault.

"Alaric out." He'd sounded like he'd won, like it was a challenge.

"Ugh!"

Stayton had followed me onto the bridge and had heard everything. "He'll ruin whatever plans we make."

"He can't ruin anything if he can't find us."

"Agreed." He stared down at his boots. "Have you looked at the calendar?" It was a worried resignation in his tone. "We have lost so much time. If we don't complete our mission, we will be held back for another year, or worse. They could stick us all in desk jobs."

Heat crept up my neck and infused my cheeks. "It wasn't our fault! Surely, the Academy will make an exception based upon the extreme extenuating circumstances."

"No, it doesn't matter. The only thing that ever matters is completing the mission and not getting caught."

Knowing he was right, I took my chair and increased our speed. "Go back to the meeting." He left, leaving me to my thoughts. Yes, everything we'd been working so hard for depended on the successful completion of our mission, but our mission's success had further implications. The stars streaked past like empty white lines on black paper. Finding the Pariea would dictate what story might fill those blank pages.

Sometime later, Cedrenus came to stand beside my command chair. "You'd better go listen to what Taylor has to say." He gestured with his thumb toward the conference room. His expression said that he didn't much care for whatever it was.

After listening to what had unfolded, my expression was almost identical. "The what?" Horrified, I stared at Colwyn Winks Taylor. Cormac was busy investigating the veracity of the incredulous story he'd related to us.

"It's all true, and I can fabricate a data chip that will fool them." He had the audacity to wink at me.

I closed my mouth but continued to stare at the thief while listening to Cormac verify the details. "A decade ago, a failed priest of the Order of Creation absconded with incriminating information procured during his hiatus on Bondi Prime. What the information was, no one will say. However, the Order has a standing bounty of seven million credits for the priest. He's wanted alive."

Colwyn raised his closed fists and pointed his thumbs at himself. Grinning, he promised, "I can become Priest Goral." His eyes were twinkling. His smile was unsettling. He was attractive and making my thoughts wander to things very un-mission-like. Just as my nipples hardened, he pointed at me. "You can be the bounty hunter. They don't admit girls, but they'll let in whoever captures me."

I crossed my arms over my chest.

Winks continued. "Come on. You as a mousy graduate student? It's not believable. However, you in synthetic leather with a blaster strapped to your thigh is something you can pull off."

Pursing my lips, I turned to Cormac. He said, "I like it. It's simple. You get in. While the Order is distracted with Taylor, you can search for the literature they possess regarding the Pariea, our all-seeing ancient ones."

Colwyn rubbed his hands together. "Great. Now that we've got it settled, where am I bunking?" He looked from me to Cormac, and back again. "Well, you're not leaving me in the brig! Are you?"

Turning on my heel, I left the conference room.

"Princess! Hey! Wait up!" He yelled as he followed me into the lift.

Clenching my jaw, I faced him as the doors closed.

"Where are you going?" He grinned the grin again, the one that caused warmth to pool and the ache to return. "We have work to do. This will require practice and planning. You don't think I use magic to pull off my heists, do you?"

"Now, isn't a good time." Pressing the command for Deck Five, I turned to face the lift doors. He didn't understand that he'd been dismissed. Removing my jacket while I walked, I entered the exercise room and went to the back. He kept pace with me and watched as I took a pair of gloves. He stopped me as I was reaching for one of the training balls I'd been planning to use.

"I'll spar with you."

Surprised, I froze. "You will?"

He lifted a shoulder and let it fall. "Sure." He took a pair of gloves for himself.

We sat and removed our boots. The room was free, so after putting on our gloves, we stepped onto the sparring mat. The way he moved his feet proved to me that he knew what he was doing. Keeping my gloves up, I dodged to the right to avoid his left. Clearing my mind, I centered myself and threw a punch which he easily swiped aside. He wasn't going easy on me which I liked. I decided not to hold back. It wasn't long before we'd both begun to work up a sweat.

"You're pretty good at this."

"Thanks. You aren't like Parvac males. They get upset when females fight."

"Why?" He ducked my left.

"They see it as an affront." I kept my feet moving, letting him hit the air. "They see it as a failure on their part. They think they should do our fighting for us."

He snorted. "I think every individual should be able to defend themselves. In fact, I find strong, powerful women to be extremely sexy."

Surprised, I didn't notice it when he swept out his leg. My back flat to the mat, he crouched above me. "You do?" I stared up into his green eyes.

"Oh, I do. My ex is an absolute demon." He winked at me.

"Your ex?" I tried to seem disinterested, but his scent was wild and earthy.

"Yes, she's on Cassini. She's an absolute terror, can eat a man whole."

I chuckled at his exaggeration.

His eyes drifted from the pulse in my neck down to my nipples. Then, holding a hand down to me, he helped me up. "Say, I don't know where my new quarters are located, somewhere on Deck Two where you can keep an eye on me?"

Turning my back to him, I put my gloves away, grabbed a towel, and went over to where I'd left my boots. He followed me into the lift. When the doors opened to my deck, I stepped out and then turned to block his exit. The puzzled look on his face begged for an explanation. "As captain of my vessel, I get a few perks, like overruling Inquisitor Gordian when I see fit, like now. Your quarters are on Deck Four with the crew, right next door to Cook. Remember Cook, the male you planned to frame for the theft of Momma's jewels that she gave me?" I smiled and shook my head. "You thought you could hide from us in plain sight. Don't worry about being ignored while on Deck Four. We'll be watching you ever so closely." My sweetest smile graced my lips as I closed the door on his ruined plans.

"What's that all about?" Clark asked. "Is he my new co-husband?" He was sitting on a chair with his vid-screen.

Sauntering over to him, I waited for him to lift his hands out of the way so that I could sit on his lap. He was studying the structural layout on Bondi Prime. "We need to have a team meeting."

He grunted and sent out a message to our team.

While we waited, I explained, "Colwyn tried to seduce me. He thought he'd get quarters on my deck and easily get me into his bed." I shook my head. "I just let him win a sparring match. He feels like he's the superior fighter."

Hearing my words as he entered with Stayton, Cormac made a derisive snort. It was a surprising sound coming from him. Hiding my smile, I gazed down at Clark's vid-screen. Cormac had spent years courting me. He'd swooned me with fudge, supported my entry into the Academy, searched parsecs of space for Luca's necklace, and defended me and my family with his very life. I'd fallen for him many months ago but hadn't admitted it to myself, not until now.

"The thief is so manipulative!" Stayton said. Everyone had joined us. "Teagan said he tried to get her to make love to him."

I said, "We need to modify our plan. I don't like his plan one tiny bit, and I definitely don't trust him."

Levi said, "None of us trust him. He is trying to manipulate you specifically. By suggesting that you pose as a badass female bounty hunter, capable of capturing the elusive thief, priest, or whatever, when no one else in the universe has been able to do so, he's obviously inflating your ego."

I nodded. He was right.

"We change the plan on him last minute. Dress him up like we are going along with his plan, However, in the flight bay, half of us, as mercenaries, take him." Levi's suggestion was a good one.

Stayton said, "Taylor's plan was to disguise Teagan as a female bounty hunter and use her fighter ship, which is unrecognizable after the Durhcu repairs and modifications. It would be a simple matter for him to disappear in a stolen fighter with its Durhcu veiling."

Cedrenus said, "We should stick with his idea to dress her as a bounty hunter."

Binder smirked at him. "You just want to see her as a redhead. Don't you?"

Cedrenus nodded enthusiastically.

"Kiki? You all had to be fucking kidding with the name. Kiki the bounty hunter sounds like she enjoys holding hands and eating candy. Fucking Kiki. Even her backstory, complete with arrest records and mugshots by various Enforcers make her look rather bored and arrogant."

Ross suggested studying his possible motives along with every conceivable exit strategy our thief might employ to gain his freedom from us. "He knows we know his true identity and where his home world is located. If I were him, I'd escape, get a head start, evacuate my family, and create new identities."

"Then, we track him." Tyler looked around at each of us.

"Yes, I agree." Clark stared down at the marbled designs in the carpet. "If I were a thief of his caliber, I'd had several contingency plans in place for my possible detection and capture with new identities, hidden credit stashes, and means for extracting my family." He looked up. "He's going to be slippery."

"Yes, he is. You've never before dealt with anyone of his ilk. He's got contingency plan after plan. Thinks about shit like that like you wouldn't believe."

The voice hadn't belonged to any of us. We were on our feet immediately. The guys had me surrounded.

"If I meant any of you any harm, would I have spoken?" Colwyn Winks Taylor grinned at Cormac, the male he rightly perceived as being the greatest threat.

"What?" I gasped. "I mean, how?" Shocked, I realized that I was grasping the back of Clark's jacket with both hands as I hid behind him looking over his shoulder on my tippy toes.

Colwyn winked and shook a finger at me. "Now, now, Princess. You can try and figure out my secrets, but I won't be telling 'em to you." Slowly, he held up both hands. "No one gets injured during my jobs. I'm not in it for the credits anymore. I'm in it for the challenge."

"At ease," I ordered those around me.

Colwyn lowered his hands once Cormac took one of his blades away from where he'd had the tip poking one of his balls. Cormac said, "If your genitals were removed, surgically of course, perhaps it would insure your cooperation."

Unnerved, Colwyn rocked back on his heels. "How about leaving my branch and berries alone?"

Cormac retorted, "How about leaving my wife alone?"

A wide grin spread across the thief's face. He held his hand out to the Inquisitor. "It's a deal." When Cormac stared at him as if he'd prefer to slice him into bits, Colwyn lowered his hand. "Look, I give you my word, and my word is my bond."

Stomping into the sitting area, her hair a crazy mess, a scowl on her face, and dragging a blue-haired doll behind her, Neema glared at Colwyn. "You're the man who tried to steal our sparkles. Bad!"

Stayton picked her up and situated her on his hip where she'd be safe.

Colwyn said, "Don't be mad, baby girl. You have your sparkles back."

"Neema is mad! You pretended to be Neema's friend! You tried to get him in trouble!" She hid her face against Stayton's shoulder.

Colwyn appeared contrite. "Aw, baby girl." The playfulness had left him.

I spoke up. "If you are truly sorry about betraying the Princess Neema's trust, prove it on our mission. You may return to your assigned quarters." I nodded to two guards who saw him out.

"How did he get in here with none of us the wiser?" Cormac asked. We studied security surveillance for the next two hours without discovering how he'd done it.

Stayton cleared his throat. "I think we should return to our original plan." He returned his gaze to the large vid-screen where we'd been studying our mission. "The goal is to get what we need and complete our assignment without anyone ever knowing spies from the Parvac Empire were there. We need to be unmemorable. If it weren't the case, we could simply show up in the *Empress* and threaten to destroy Bondi Prime unless they were to give us what we want."

His words sent my thoughts to Nico and how angry he'd been with the psycho Dano and his secret moon base.

"He's right," Tyler agreed.

Cedrenus nodded. "Inquisitor Rovek and Inquisitor Beck helped us formulate this plan. They know what they are doing, and we can trust them with our lives. I think we need to toss the thief's Bounty Hunter Kiki idea and return to our original plan. It's solid, and our aliases are still viable."

Colwyn sighed. "Fine. I'll be a sight unseen."

Eyes wide, my heart pounded.

Cormac pinned the thief to the wall. "How?" The question wasn't asking how he'd manage to be unseen. After all, he'd just proved it. The question was how he'd managed to get back into the room with us without any of us or the guards for that matter knowing it. There was an edge of respect in Cormac's utterance of that single word, and the thief knew it.

"I'm not telling. It's too cute watching you try to figure it out."

Cormac gave a grunt, or maybe more of a growl, and removed his forearm from across Colwyn's throat.

Shaken, but not wanting the thief to know it, I said, "Alright. Let's go over this again. We'll arrive at Bondi Prime in forty-nine hours. We need to drop speed, board the modified shuttle, and arrive at the observatory during our appointed time. It should appear to any observers that a Militia cruiser gave us a lift. Start the program."

Ross tapped out the command. "Program running. The *Empress* will appear to any scans as a Galaxic vessel."

"Let's do this." Clark began going over our mission details.

After we'd all listened very carefully, the thief spoke up. He was sitting leaned back with his knee bent and his right foot up on the seat of his chair. "You all want to check out a book, all secret like, about some mythological ancient aliens, aliens who make those hybrid Laconian warriors look like junior Enforcers. Is that about right? All this so you can try and track down these telepathic and technologically advanced aliens who may or may not have magnanimous feelings toward you all considering how Princess Teagan's newest mate treated one of their own. He imprisoned one of 'em on Earth, right?" He shook his head, but his eyes twinkled. It was like he was a kid with a stick poised to take a whack at a hornets' nest just to see what would happen to the other unsuspecting kids who were trying to play outside and have fun.

Teeth clenched so hard as to make my jaw hurt, I thought about what he'd said. He didn't care if we got stung. What we'd planned did sound like a dreadful way to worsen our situation, all optimism aside.

Stayton spoke into the sudden quiet in the room. "Without their help, the Alux will systematically decimate every sentient species in our universe. They'll strengthen themselves on the weak first, and then move onto the telepathic species, and then us. To keep it from happening, we need an edge." His quiet speech clarified our position while driving home the hopeless strategic situation in which we'd found ourselves.

"We didn't go looking for the Alux," Binder said.

Colwyn stared at him. "No, you didn't, and I don't want them coming to my neck of the woods. I'm in. You have my word on it. Trust me." He looked at my expression and laughed. "Alright, look at it this way. I'm bored, and this is a challenge."

Groaning, I stood. "I'm going to go and spend some time with my daughter." Leaving the room, I wondered what sort of universe we'd be leaving for the children if we were to fail.

The evening consisted of playing dolls, coloring, checking the safe to see if all the sparkles were still there, having dinner, bathing, and reading stories. After tucking Neema into her bed, I tiredly went to my own quarters. Clark was in the shower. I wasn't sure what Cormac was up to. Already in my gown, I got into bed. The side of my face sank into the pillow. Pulling the covers up over my shoulder and bunching them in my hands, I curled up on my side. As the tension left me, so did consciousness.

Chapter Twenty-One

"Remember. We are not to interfere. Our part is to get Colwyn to Bondi Prime. Once he has the information on the Pariea, we extract him and go." Each of us listened to Clark.

I tried to be mature, but I started laughing. He looked nothing like himself. He had a prosthetic belly, had been given the appearance of thinning hair, sported a scraggly goatee, and had pale-blue eyes. As per our original plan, we were impersonating the real-life graduate students who were supposed to be arriving at the observatory. Poor Levi. He had taken on a rodent-like countenance with pinched nostrils, beady eyes, and an overbite, but had great hair. While he'd taken on a rodent-like appearance, I was the one with the mousy shade of dull brown hair. My skin was pale, my ears poked out through my straight hair, and my timid persona forced me to cringe at loud or sudden noises. I wanted to find the woman who I was impersonating and give her a confidence boost, but doing so would blow my cover. None of the brilliant students whose identities we were temporarily assuming could ever know what we had done. We had the cooperation for this sanctioned mission to make sure of it.

Colwyn was already aboard our shuttle. The gear with which we'd outfitted him had made him virtually undetectable. We all knew he was there, but we wouldn't be breaking character until we again boarded the *Empress* at the conclusion of our mission. Clark was serving as stealth ship captain. He took us from the docking bay. Then, he flew us to the ship from the Laconian Sector with which we were scheduled to rendezvous. It all went off without a hitch.

Our eventual arrival at the observatory on Bondi Prime was met with enthusiasm. As we filed out of the shuttle with our luggage, the graduate students whom we were replacing filed in. They would be boarding the same Laconian vessel on which they'd arrived and never be the wiser that anything was amiss. They seemed eager to be gone from the place. I stared at my shoes, looking shyly up from time to time while pleasantries were exchanged. No one would remember me which was exactly as it should be. Then, they were off.

The observatory station was clean, well-maintained, and with the exception of a few framed space themed posters, was unadorned. Likewise, the planet's surface offered no scenic distractions. Aside from the observatory's massive telescopes and work stations, there was an automated cafeteria that was stocked with pre-made meals, beverage dispensers, tables, and chairs. There was a medical bay in which Ross was supposed to assume his duties. For exercise, there was a small, functional gymnasium.

After a brief tour of the facilities, I went off to find my quarters. Opening the door, I found a bunk, study desk, and small bathroom. How would my Earth realtor describe this place? I imagined him lifting his hands to his face and wiping them tiredly over his eyes at the prospect of finding a buyer. Grinning to myself, I kept in character and stashed my gear. Then, picking up my data pad, I scampered off to begin my assignment.

My work station was equipped with a telescope which would allow the graduate student who I was pretending to be to study her preferred area of concentration, Cosmochemistry, which studied the chemical composition of and changes in the makeup of the universe according to the field's definition. Unlike her, the definition was all I understood on the topic. She and I couldn't be more academically opposite. Chemistry of any sort happened to be my worst subject. My alias had been a necessity. She'd been the only female assigned to the station. I'd been forced to study enough on the subject to pass for looking like I belonged.

I took a seat and tried to look like I knew what I was doing. I began searching until I found an insignificant planetoid with a mixture of dirt and ice ringing it. The analysis program which I began would take several hours to run.

Someone cleared his throat. "Hi." It was Cedrenus which I wouldn't have known if he'd randomly approached me anywhere else. He scratched his thick beard. His cover had a feral appearance.

"May I help you?" My tone was prim.

"Hi. Yeah. Do you want to eat something?"

I stared at him.

"It's late. We're supposed to keep to a solar schedule so our circadian rhythms don't get distorted. You've been in here for hours." He smoothed the front of his lab coat.

Checking the time, I was actually surprised. "I didn't realize how long I'd been working. It's so fascinating to actually be here. You know?" Standing, I consciously hunched my shoulders and looked down.

He rushed over and pushed in my chair.

Instead of rolling my eyes, I tried to feign a blush which was really hard.

"I'd offer you my arm, but the rules about sexual harassment are strict." He cleared his throat.

"Are they?" We walked side-by-side to the cafeteria.

"Yes, to have um... friendlier relationships, people have to submit forms to their universities for approval."

"Is that something you want to do?" Crossing my arms over my chest, I acted awkwardly.

"Yes, I'd like to submit forms with you anytime. I mean if you want."

"I'll think about it."

"Welcome to Bondi Prime." The unfamiliar voice had us both jerking to stops mid-step. The male was unlike any male I'd ever seen. Head shaved and dressed in a red-lined black, hooded robe, the monk, priest, or whatever the fuck they called themselves within their cult, dipped his shiny head to us. Behind him, the others in our team had gathered in the cafeteria.

"Thanks," Cedrenus replied while I looked at my shoes.

"We have come to bid you welcome to Bondi Prime. Should you require emergency assistance, we are not far." The male kept his hands clasped before him and hidden by the wide sleeves of his robe.

Cedrenus thanked him again.

Glancing up, I spotted a second creepy fucker over to my left. He was obviously spying and snooping which had me feeling a tad bit hypocritical. My attention spread across the room. My team had done an excellent job. Their disguises even obscured their actual physiques. Cedrenus wore clothing that was a size too large in the arms and legs, modified to make him look weak and scrawny. Binder wore a bodysuit under his clothing to make him appear chubby. Ross, well, he kept rubbing his ear, a mannerism of the graduate student whose identity he'd assumed. Then, there was Stayton. Pursing my lips in disapproval as my identity tended to do, I stared him up and down. He'd used hair products in his brown wig to make the strands stay combed back. His teeth were overly white, and he smiled too much. His identity was accustomed to being the life of the party.

The creepy monk to my left caught me rolling my eyes. Gliding over to me in what I could only describe as being an ominous manner, he clasped his hands before him as if the gesture might make him appear less sinister. "You don't approve?" he quietly asked.

Raising my eyes, I stared at the monk. "And you are?"

He grinned. His eyebrows were light-brown. Therefore, I assumed, had he not shaved himself bald and shined his head to a high-gloss, his hair must be a similar shade. His eyes were a murky blue as if a storm had stirred up the sand in previously clean, clear ocean water. "I am Father William."

Unimpressed by his appellation, I crossed my arms over my chest. Clearly, he was a nutcase. "No, I don't particularly approve."

As if I'd made a confession, he asked, "Do you resent his leadership role?"

Unable to help it, I snorted. "No, I'm worried those blinding white teeth of his will interfere with the telescopes."

His head involuntarily moved back a fraction. Good. His body language told me that he didn't know what to make of me. He bowed ever so slightly and walked at a sedate pace over to his colleague. I moved away, too. The sound of Binder's voice drew me closer. He was talking to the other priest.

"What we hope to accomplish here is evident." He gestured toward one of the wide, horizontal windows and out at the dark, star-filled view. "What, may I ask, is it that you and your fellows hope to accomplish here, isolated from all other sentient life?"

"Ours is the pursuit of academic religious studies and the preservation of knowledge." The priest smiled.

Ross piped up from the background. "Have you considered scanning it all and going digital?" He was still rubbing his ear.

"Our texts are sacred." The priest sounded scandalized.

"So, no lending library?" Ross looked genuinely puzzled.

Rather than replying to the question, the priest said, "On my next visit, I will bring you a data pad onto which I personally will load materials which might awaken your spirituality."

Ross tried to appear appreciative and not as though he was disappointed. It didn't work.

"Regretfully, it is not within my power to facilitate a tour."

Ross shrugged.

Meanwhile, Binder had ventured off to the beverage dispenser. His cup clattered to the floor and spilled a sticky orange soda across it. My sigh was loud enough to make Father William turn his head toward me. A cleaning bot hummed from a wall compartment and rolled itself over to the mess. A loud sucking noise followed. My knees went sideways, and I compensated by shifting my torso to keep from falling before managing to right myself. Temporary shock made a blank of my mind. Realizing that some outward force had acted upon my equilibrium, I regained my balance and tried to figure out what had transpired. I wasn't the only one.

"What was that?" Stayton asked.

Ross asked, "A meteor strike?"

I jogged over to a window just as a second strike caused the ground to shift beneath us. Alarms blared around the station.

Father William lifted the sleeve of his robe and checked the vid-screen which he wore on a wristband. "We're under attack!" His warning sounded as though he didn't believe it himself. "Come on!" he ordered as he grabbed me by the wrist and Ross by the shoulder. He urged us toward the nearest exit.

"What are you doing? We're safer inside!" Ross exclaimed. His question was ignored.

The priests were too busy arguing with each other.

"We can't take them!"

"We must, Carter! To abandon them here will mean their deaths!"

Relenting, Father Carter helped to evacuate us.

I spoke up. "It can't be that serious. Why attack a research station and a monastery?" The loud, persistent blaring of the alarms drowned out my question. I was pulled out of the station. Father William placed his hand on my head and pushed down while shoving me inside of a roller. He and Father Carter sandwiched me into the front seat while the guys crammed into the back or held onto the sides. I was wondering what Winks had done to create such a distraction when I glanced up. My heart sank down into my hips, and bile rose in my throat. "It's the fucking Alux! We're out here without a warship!" The wind caught my words and blew them back.

Father William had wasted no time. The roller he was whisking us all away in was surrounded by a thick cloud of dust. He sped toward the monastery which was receiving the brunt of the attack.

Father Carter yelled, "Defensive shielding is holding!"

Taking us from the research station and to the monastery which was the apparent target of the attack hadn't seemed like the brightest idea to me at first, but now I saw their weaponry. From the grounds around the perimeter, massive blaster cannons had risen. Their barrels rose and swiveled as they targeted the Alux warship. Then, a series of powerful blasts from the weapons caused the ground to shift making the roller lift and slam back down with jarring force. My teeth clacked together painfully. Dust filled our eyes and noses.

"Shit!" Gripping the bar over my head, I stared through gritty, streaming eyes at the sizzling energy field in front of us. We were speeding straight toward it.

At the last possible moment, a section only large enough for us to pass through opened before shutting behind us. It made the hairs on my arms stand on end. Relief washed over me as I released the breath that I hadn't realized I'd been holding. Reaching down, I used the neckline of my shirt to wipe the dirt, dust, and tears from my eyes. Dirt and rocks flew from the roller as he steered it into an opening.

Emergency lighting cast a yellow glow at forty-feet intervals as Father William sped us along the narrow access tunnel. The loud rumble of sound didn't provide us with enough warning. The ground beneath us shook. Above us small bits of debris fell, tinging against the roller. The shifting ground beneath us sent the front driver's side of the roller into the side of the tunnel. Sparks flew as metal scraped against stone. Binder's shoe hit me hard in the head as he was flung from the roller. Cedrenus got tossed out with him as the roller's back end lifted. Father Carter disappeared from beside me as his robe tore free of my grasping fingers.

Stuck, I ducked and held on while the roller flipped. The tunnel's grey concrete rushed to meet the windshield. The two slapped together. Plasti, metal, and concrete screeched against each other as momentum carried the roller forward. I hoped against hope that the guys had had time to get out of the way. The roller slammed to a stop. Father William's shoulder was gouging me between my shoulder blades. My face was squished against the roller's rollbar. The metal was hot from friction.

"Pull them out!" Stayton yelled.

From the level of commotion, it sounded to me like everyone had survived. Without, sounds of battle boomed. The heavy priest was pulled free which gave me the opportunity to breath. Pushing my hand against the cement, I managed to get my face away from the rollbar. Then, another boom rattled me around inside of the crumbled roller. Hands reached down, grabbed me, and pulled me out. Cedrenus' eyes met mine. The relief initially in them was replaced with warning. When the two priests saw me, their eyes darkened with anger.

"We can explain," Stayton said.

"There is no time. Follow us." Father Carter was livid, and it didn't seem to be all due to the Alux.

Reaching up to my face, I felt the rip in my disguise. My mask had torn away from where it met my hairline.

Cedrenus said, "It's also your nose." Taking my hand, he urged me into a run.

We followed after Stayton and Ross. With my free hand, I reached up and felt my face. My fake nose had torn during the accident. Pulling it off, I flung it aside.

Up ahead, a male voice yelled, "Why have you brought them here?"

"They would have been killed!"

The argument raged between two inner factions of the cult while outside, the Alux hammered away at their defenses. Quickly, we realized that the explosion which had caused us to wreck had been a side effect of far worse devastation. A surface attack had begun. The Alux had breached the monastery's defenses. Now, permitted to enter, we were jostled around. Someone stepped on me and pushed me into one of the pewter walls. High-pitched screaming sent a twinge of fear through me. The priests were fighting back.

"This way! This way! Hurry!" Father Carter was leading us away from the fighting. The chamber he was attempting to get past was filled with whirling blades and frantic motion. The tops of the monks' robes had been dropped to hang from their waists leaving their arms and torsos bare and freeing them to fight. They'd paid attention to the reports of previous attacks. Not bothering with blasters, they fought with swords, pole axes, and katanas. "Hurry! You should be safer in here!" He tried to lead us into a saferoom.

"Safer?" Cedrenus asked.

No planet was safe from the Alux. The monastery's security system was state-of-the-art. We'd known for months that we wouldn't be able to breach it without drawing attention to ourselves. However, the Alux weren't trying to finesse their way in as we had been. Our goal had been to come, get what we wanted, and leave with none the wiser. A smash and grab would have been simple even for us. The Alux had compromised the monastery in a matter of seconds. They'd done the same thing to our security defenses on Earth which had been installed by teams of experienced Inquisitors, not to mention what their warships had done on Parvac.

Father Carter didn't understand our hesitation. He and Father William knew we weren't being completely honest, but did they not realize who we were? I reached up to touch my fake nose which had been partially ripped off and took a moment to be relieved that it hadn't been my real nose. Maybe our cover wasn't completely blown.

Glancing innocently around, I spoke up. "If it's all the same to you, I'd prefer to get some weapons and help defend ourselves."

Ross, still in character and messing with his ear, said, "Hiding is pointless."

Cedrenus said, "We practice with blades."

I couldn't help quietly snorting at the understatement. We had sparred so much while trapped aboard the *Empress* that I was eager to see if I could hold my own against Kaoti.

"This is not some role-playing game! This is real! Don't you understand? You could be dead in the next seconds! Obey me!" Father Carter's eyes were as wide as they could be. He was honestly trying to save us.

Staring the man in his eyes, Stayton said, "It is better to die fighting than to be killed while cowering in fear."

Father Carter grimaced, torn as he fought an inner battle between right and wrong. What should he do with us? The death screams of one of his brethren prompted his decision to turn and run toward the battle. We stayed close behind, and when he made a hasty turn, we kept with him. His feet slid on spilled blood as he stopped and turned to enter an armory. Not wasting time, each of us grabbed what was available. Accepting my strength and stamina for what it was, I took two matched long knives. Each blade was as long as my forearm. I would be able to use them for quite some time without tiring, and the blades had been sharpened with precision. Even Kaoti would have nodded in approval. Armed, we followed after the priest to join in the monastery's defense. The Alux hadn't bothered to be neat. They had blasted through the roof and dropped down through the ceiling in their transportation spheres.

"I count five. One is dead," Cedrenus said.

Amid the piles of concrete, wood, pewter, plasti, and broken furnishings, were bodies. Only one of the bodies was that of an Alux. The first one of them to enter had been the first one of them to die.

Unfortunately, the evil alien had taken out three of the monastery's defenders with it. I continued to survey the carnage. "Half a dozen of them was all they thought it would take. Let's prove them wrong."

Stepping over the wreckage, we made our way toward the fighting. Avoiding the stares of sightless eyes, but unable to remain clear of their spilled blood, we converged on one of the vile creatures who crouched over the body of a priest who had died with his features frozen in a rictus of fear. Lifting its doll-like face, it smiled. As always, the beauty of the Alux struck me. Pale skin so white as to appear slightly blue, eyes that seemed sleepy and relaxed, like calm, blue water, were tinged with red at the corners before fading into a purplish-blue at the lower and upper lash lines, and lips that were perfectly formed and painted a smokey-blue were all designed through evolution to draw in prey. The designs painted on this one's face matched the ones we'd seen on all of the others' faces. On the forehead, down the nose, and across both cheeks under its eyes were the dark line-like designs decorated with gold. The design above its nose on its forehead looked like an inverted triangle from a distance. The pale-colored, ethereal hooded robe it wore was splattered with the red blood of the fallen.

It lifted its head and spoke to us in its beautiful voice. "Humanoid fear tastes better to me than their adoration. Love me. Fear me. I care not." Extending its hand to me, it pulled at my heart with its eyes. "I have come for you, my child. Come. Bask in eternal... love."

The draw was strong. A few steps would have us together. All of the worry, fear, pain, and longing would end. None of this mattered. All that mattered was to love and serve our creators. Love and acceptance floated over me like a cool veil, like the ethereal robe of the beautiful being who beckoned me forward. It could all be over, all of the struggle and hardship. The promise was a soft, cool breeze. It was a splash of freezing water against my brain.

I gave myself a shake as its spell broke. Around me, my full-blooded Parvac teammates seethed with rage. The Alux didn't have the same effect on Parvacians as they did on most other non-telepathic species. Whereas they inspired feelings of intense reverence and adoration in them, they inspired hate and battle-lust in my Papa's species. It was something Parvacs had in common with Arachnean Silk spiders.

Stayton struck.

A deep, long gash of torn flesh appeared on the Alux's outstretched arm. Beads of blood formed. Withdrawing the appendage, a hiss of breath escaped it. Gone now was the sweet, serene expression. Now, in its eyes was a look filled with calculative, murderous intent, and all of it was focused on Stayton.

Ross asked, "Does anyone see any reason for a fair fight?"

"Nope," Cedrenus replied.

"No way," Binder seconded.

They all converged on the alien.

From behind, I heard an inarticulate sound of breathlessness and an almost squeaky gasp for air. Turning, I saw the shocked eyes of Father Carter, wide with pain. Blood gurgled from his lips. His hands, fingers splayed, were at either side of his ribs as he looked down at the tip of the blade poking out through the center of his chest. As the killer withdrew his weapon, Father Carter slid free and fell dead at my feet.

Over his lifeless body, I stared into a pair of calm, blue eyes. The lips smiled serenely. "It seems we have come searching for the same guide to the ascended ones. Did you think to take it for yourself, Princess? Once we find them, we will take their knowledge for ourselves."

A few feet behind me and moving farther away, metal struck metal as battles raged. It seemed that I had this one all to myself. It bubbled up within me, and it wasn't fear. No, it was hours, days, weeks, and months of frustration, anger, and rage. Before me was a monster upon whom to unleash it all. "What knowledge?" Blades held ready, I stepped carefully away from the body of Father Carter and prepared to attack. "Do you want to transcend? You and your people? I'll go ahead and speak on behalf of the Cosmos Coalition and say we support the shedding of your corporeal, soul-eating forms."

The sneer looked out of place on its doll-like face. "Our ultimate goal is transcendence. However, until then, we require sustenance. Those we seek have amassed knowledge of worlds and species innumerable."

My thoughts clarified. "Shit. You want to find them to steal their knowledge so you can use the sentient species of the universe as your own personal buffet. Their knowledge would be like a menu for you."

It smiled. "Once we kill the ascended ones, there will be no way to stop us."

Smirking, I said, "They're ascended. You can't kill them."

Its laughter tinkled. The sound was in blatant contrast to the macabre scene around us. "Death may not be an option. However, splintering an ascended being into multi-fractional oblivion will render them as helpless as dead. By the time even one of them is able to reform their splintered being, we will be a force far greater than anything they managed to achieve. The Pariea will be forced to accept us as their masters."

Shocked, everything I'd assumed to be true broke apart and reformed in my mind. The alien consciousness I'd found in a bit of metal had been there as a result of an Alux attack? What all was Stig keeping from us?

Muscle memory had me taking a step back and lifting my blades higher to parry the attack when it came. The Alux's blade dripped with Father Carter's blood. Our blades met and scraped together making a sound which matched the sharp coldness in my opponent's eyes. Battle screams broke our stare. A fence of weapons came between us. The guys had ended the Alux they'd been fighting and had come for mine. They maneuvered me out of the way and attacked like a pack of wolves against an ice bear, striking, drawing blood, darting away, and letting a brother have his turn. They moved with deadly grace.

As I backed away, I heard sounds from another area.

"Where is it?" The fury in the Alux's tone had an element of fearful desperation which sounded foreign to my ears.

I could see them through a crumpled wall in another room, one that mere hours ago had had intense security but now was in ruin. It had housed one of the monastery's treasured book collections. The Alux held a priest by the neck. He was in the Alux's thrall, unable to think for himself, much less gain his freedom. If he couldn't fight for himself, I would.

The priest said, "I don't know. It is gone. I love you. I would never lie to you, nor would I ever hide from you that which you seek. Forgive me."

"Lies!" The Alux picked up the priest and hurled him against a shielded plasti shelf of books. The force shield sizzled when the priest's back struck against it. Electric fire washed over him before letting him drop to the floor. The fabric of his habit smoked as it tried to ignite. Stepping over to him, the alien grabbed him by the shoulder with one hand and held a weapon to his throat with the other. "Open it." He hauled the priest up to his feet.

Hunched over in pain, the priest stared at the Alux with defiance. Its spell had been broken. "Never." In a surprising burst of strength, the priest ignored his painful electric burns and grabbed the Alux by the shoulders of its robe and tugged it around shoving it into the same force shield with which he had just been tortured. He held it there while it screamed and sizzled.

Fearing the priest would sacrifice himself as well, I ran, jumped into the air, and knocked the priest away from the alien. I landed on top of the battered priest which knocked the air out of him. Pushing down with my knee, I bolted upright, blades drawn, and rounded on the Alux. It had fallen free of the energy field. Before it could strike, I slashed with my blades. On its feet now, it parried my strikes. Above my right knee, I felt a burn. It was the unmistakable pain of a blade slice. Using my left blade to defend my torso, I slid my other blade through to the Alux's undefended neck. It gurgled in shock. Then, its body dropped as it slid free of my blade. Certain it was no longer a threat, I tried not to limp as I hurried over to the priest. He was on his side, gasping. "Oh, good. You're alive."

His look was acerbic.

"Father William! I didn't realize it was you! All of you look alike, and your voice didn't quite sound like yourself." I held a hand down to him.

He took my hand and let me help him up to his feet. "My breath was knocked from me, but who needs CPR when a knee to the nuts will do?" He was obviously in pain.

I scrunched up my face. "Sorry." Then, I shrugged. "You're a priest, so it's not like you use them anyway, right?"

All expression left his face.

A series of hard blasts made the surface shake. We held onto each other's arms to keep from losing our balances.

"Everybody out!" a male voice yelled.

Hurrying to act on the warning, I grabbed Father William by the hand and tugged him along with me. He stumbled. Taking a sideways step back, I put his arm over my shoulder and helped him. The structure was crumbling. From out of the rubble, I looked out and saw Militia soldiers who were dressed in full combat gear. They were working to evacuate everyone onto shuttles.

I yelled, "Where did they come from?"

One of the soldiers came over, took stock of our visible injuries with a glance, and took the priest from me. Through his helmet's visor, I looked into his solid black eyes. Shock robbed me of words. The soldier was an Eriopis male, and I knew him. I didn't wait for anyone to help me. It was easier to climb free of the rubble on my own. Finally, outside, I looked up and saw *Teagan's Treasure* firing her blaster cannons at an Alux vessel. It wasn't even a warship.

"I guess we were lucky it was just a scout ship."

"Just a scout ship?" Father William, bloody and battered, stared aghast at the vessel as it broke apart in the dim atmosphere above. "They destroyed our monastery with a scout ship! Our security was unrivaled! We have been here, guarding sacred knowledge for decades! The knowledge had survived for centuries...."

"Not all of it is lost." I kept my tone carefully conciliatory. "Much can be salvaged."

"No, six of them and a scout ship was all it took. Don't you understand?"

Turning, I met his eyes and let him see that I did understand. I could see the question that he was about to ask, but I turned away before he could. Instead, I worked to help load survivors into the shuttle. All the while, I turned over in my mind what I'd learned and repeatedly came to the same conclusion. To save ourselves, we'd first have to save the Pariea. However, to save them, we'd have to find them first. Certainly, by now, the one Eddie had captured had been able to return to his people and warn them about the energy splitting weapon that the Alux had used against it. If that was even truly what had transpired.

"No! No! Do you understand what you ask?" A furious elder priest shoved away from a soldier who was trying to assist him into a shuttle.

"If he doesn't want to leave, we can't force him," one of the soldiers said.

Stumbling back, the priest's eyes were filled with rage. "I refuse to leave!" Lifting the arm which wasn't in a tourniquet, he jabbed at the air in an accusatory fashion. "Would you all leave?" he asked of his brethren.

One of the priests lowered his head in shame. "It is only for medical attention."

"Excuses! Our own medical facilities remain functional. Those amongst you who want to leave may do so if you deem it necessary for your survival. However, you," he turned and stomped over to Father William. Blood loss had made the elder priest's skin turn pale, but his eyes burned with a feverish light. "You brought them inside of our sanctuary, outsiders." His tone was like water in a kettle roiling around right before it began a full boil. "You have betrayed your vows. You have betrayed your brothers. You have betrayed our cause."

Father William stared at him with horrified intensity.

Stayton spoke up. "It was a matter of life and death. He and Father Carter saved our lives by bringing us here. The observatory has minimal defenses." He gestured over toward it. It proved his point, having been reduced to rubble.

The priests acted as though nothing had been said. They spoke without words, without telepathy. Each of them shared an unspoken truth with each other through no more than their eyes, something to which none of the rest of us were privy. The elder priest reached out and tore Father William's robe. "You are banished from our order."

The other priests lowered their heads and as one turned their backs on him.

The elder priest spoke. "You others, who wish to do so may go from here. The Galaxic ship will take you. I will remain." He turned and slowly walked back into the rubble. Most of the blood-stained warrior priests followed sedately behind him. A smoldering page from a book floated up and away from his robes as he led the way.

"Come on." I reached out and tugged on Father William's sleeve. He followed my lead into the shuttle. With my team aboard and accounted for, I told the pilot to take us to the ship.

"Does that hurt?" Cedrenus gave a nod toward my knee.

Scowling, I shook my head. It was just a minor slice from an Alux. They didn't frighten me as much now, not when there were alien apes with which to attend. It always seemed like the same fucking knee that got hurt. Realizing it was a weakness in my self-defense which an opponent could exploit in a fight, I decided to work on it. Glancing around the shuttle cabin, I realized that I wasn't the only one who needed medical attention. We were all stuffed to capacity within the compartment, but our thief was nowhere to be seen. My scowl deepened. Then, the priest caught my attention. His eyes held a distant, vacant look. A slight jostling as the pilot docked in the bay shifted my attention from the despondent priest.

As the shuttle hatch was opened, the first sight to greet us was that of the medical team. On the deck, they surrounded us. Glancing at his scanner's readout, one of the doctors decided to see to Ross first. Ross mumbled something.

The doctor said, "That's an order," and pointed where he wanted him to go.

Instead of arguing, Ross climbed onto the anti-grav stretcher.

The doctor turned his head and stared each of us in the eyes. "I expect the rest of you in the medical bay within the next half hour." He turned his back and followed the team with the stretcher into a lift.

"It was the roller that got him, not the Alux," Stayton told us.

"Where are we? What sort of ship is this?" Father William, dazed, glanced about.

"This is my warship, *Teagan's Treasure*. Welcome aboard."

Time slowed to a stop as he stepped from the lift. He was more breathtakingly handsome than I remembered. A fierce power radiated from him. Tall, blond, muscular, and with eyes appearing solid-black, he stood in uniform with his hands clasped behind his back. I knew why. He didn't keep his thoughts away from me, but he desperately needed to keep his hands away or risk embarrassing us both in front of everyone. Captain Quaid Bosh stood mere feet away from me. Hot need tore through me.

Another shuttle docked as we stared at each other. The soldiers who stepped out of it began removing their helmets. I recognized them all. Quaid had managed to get them assigned to his ship. Rafe, Oren, Levi, and Sebastian had always been his team. Now, he had them back. Quaid had more sway with the Militia than I had realized.

To Father William, Quaid said, "Go with the others to medical. The *Hadrian* will arrive soon to return you to Galaxic space." He gave the priest a nod of reassurance. Quaid's team urged everyone into the lift, everyone except me. Quaid was clenching his sexy jaw with such force that I feared it might break. When the lift doors closed, leaving us alone on the deck, his control broke rather than his jaw.

In his arms, I forgot all of the words I'd been about to say. When his lips met mine, all else was left behind. His arms were steel around me, caging me as if he feared I might slip once more away. He stole not only my breath, but also the tight control under which I'd been keeping myself since my ship had been captured in the wormhole anomaly in Parvac space in what now seemed like a lifetime ago.

Through our lips, he sent a thick cord of pleasure of blinding intensity winding through me. Each brush of his skin against mine twisted me into aching need and then unwound me into exquisite pleasure. When he parted my thighs and entered me, my thoughts shattered before I could wonder where my clothing had gone. He sensuously moved his hips forward and back drowning his body and his mind within me. Instinctually, he reclaimed me, binding our minds firmly together once more. Finding Stig in his territory, he tried to eradicate the male from my consciousness. However, Stig refused to leave. As if to punish the other male, Quaid did what Stig could never do, he had me drowning in pleasure, unable to think and only able to feel.

When my senses returned, I found myself gazing up at the ceiling of the flight bay. The heat of embarrassment from my cheeks did nothing to warm my extremities. Turning from my back to my side on the cold, hard deck, I found Quaid beside me. His chest heaved as he fought to regulate his breathing. Smiling and very pleased, I ran my fingers through his chest hair. It was luxurious. His heart pounded against my palm.

Eyes wide and now surrounded by white sclera, he incredulously asked, "You're ready to go again?" His thoughts became confused. "After all of that?"

Delighted, I smiled and nodded. "Yes! Again, and again. However, let's go to your quarters. I've got a bruised spine from this flooring." I found my undies, but he'd ripped them to shreds, so I stuck them into a pocket of my clothes as I got dressed. Then, I nudged him with my toe to get him moving.

Once his mind cleared, he insisted on a quick trip to medical for my battle injuries. Quaid had my senses singing in pleasure, but beneath it all, he knew the blade slice above my knee was hurting me. Quaid's crew had seen to my team, our priest, and had collected Clark and our shuttle. With all things being managed by others, we decided to sequester ourselves alone together in his quarters for the return trip to Chione.

Alone and in private, I drew him along with me into his bathroom. While he undressed and entered the shower, I stared at my unfamiliar reflection. Only a telepathic husband could have recognized me, even with my disguise ripped in places. Carefully, I began removing my torn mask.

As his senses cleared, Quaid started to slowly skim through my recollections of what had transpired while we'd been apart. He hissed in anger when he encountered the huge blue alien ape in my mind. Quaid detested monkeys of any sort. "Your memories of that horrid creature will give me nightmares."

"Oh, yeah? You didn't smell his breath."

By the time we arrived on Chione, I was feeling much better, even though my Parvac hormones continued to rage. However, now, after my ordeal in unfamiliar space, I had learned to manage it well enough to put it aside in my mind so I could focus, but it didn't go away. Like my past trauma, it was a part of me, and I now knew that I was strong enough to deal with all of it. However, Quaid wasn't able to do the same with my Parvac hormones at least. His Eriopis crewmen weren't doing very well with my hormones either. Hopefully, they were trying to be respectful of our privacy. However, somehow, I doubted it. They would probably tease Quaid for weeks.

He was obviously "love drunk," so Rafe, his second-in-command, was serving as captain. Even in his intoxicated state, he knew what had to be done. He had to reach Earth as soon as possible to help in the investigation into the medical space station and the abduction of Dr. Crispus.

After seeing us safely aboard the *Empress*, he spent a few hours with Neema and me. Cupping my cheek in his palm, he gazed lovingly into my eyes. "The last thing I want to do is leave you."

"I don't want you to leave. Now that I'm back in your arms, I feel there's no place else where I can find such peace and safety." A tear slipped from my eye. I didn't bother trying to hide it. He knew my thoughts.

His smile was fueled by joy, love, and something else. "Lady Bosh, you have always intrigued and fascinated me. However, now, I truly respect you as an equal captain."

Blushing, I said, "Quaid, I'm not a captain. I'm an ensign."

Grinning, he shook his head. "Lady Bosh, you can hold your own with any captain with whom I've ever served." We kissed once more. "This time, I'll wish you the best, but I won't worry about you. I'm too impressed by you to do anything but say, until I see you again, I bid you well, my lady."

It was a painful, but necessary parting, but I knew that soon we would be reunited. Quaid had given me something openly which he'd never before fully given me. He'd given me his respect.

Into my thoughts, he said, "You've earned it."

Chapter Twenty-Two

Alone in my quarters, I went to shower. Without Quaid to distract me, I was free to think. While on the miserable little research location, we'd fulfilled our greater obligations to protect the inhabitants. However, we as students had failed to complete our Academy mission. Opening my mouth to one of the water sprays, I was unable to wash the bitterness from my mouth that was disappointment. Without bringing home the book containing possible clues as to the location of the Pariea, we wouldn't be graduating. Instructor Rovek would have no choice other than to hold us back. "Damn it!" I slammed my palm against the shower wall. Everything had gone sideways when the Alux had attacked. How could we have better prepared for such a contingency? Surely, Rovek would be telling us. "Fucking hell."

As the water beat into my tired muscles, I scrubbed at my scalp and began plotting what to do to Colwyn Winks Taylor. "That fucking asshole!" I'd set up surveillance on his home world, find him, and slowly teach him to regret disappointing me.

Still steaming after I wrapped myself in a towel and left the bathroom, I stomped over to my closet. There, I froze. My safe was open. Propped up on the stand where the necklace my momma gave me should have been was a book. The cover was a simple one of black leather. On the cover, embossed in its center was a simple golden infinity symbol entwined with leafy green vines.

Reaching out, I took it and carefully opened it. The pages were ancient. It was written in a language that I had never before seen. However, the pictures told me everything I needed to know in order to confirm what it was. Instinctively, I knew it was true. This was the book we had set out to find. Each page of the text had been carefully transcribed and adorned with either a gold letter to begin the page or an illustration. Tracing a symbol with the tip of my index finger, I could feel a minuscule hint of what I'd felt from the piece of alien metal which had led us on our mission to Earth. That mission seemed like a lifetime ago.

"Stars. He got it."

Quickly dashing over to my wall-mounted vid-screen, I called my team. Each of their sad faces appeared on my screen as they answered my call, like stars appearing in a night sky.

Before anyone could ask, I held up the book. "Mission complete."

"Yes!" Cedrenus exclaimed.

Ross lifted his fist to punch the air above him and instantly cringed in pain. Even after receiving medical attention, he'd need time to fully recover.

The door to my quarters opened as Clark rushed inside. I handed the book over to him. Opening it, he looked up at the others. "We'll have to decipher it."

"Yes, we will meet in a few hours. Bye." I waggled my fingers at them, ended the call, and turned to Clark.

"A few hours? Don't you want to get to work?" His tone was incredulous.

Letting the towel drop, I loosened my control and watched his eyes darken. Taking the book from his hands, I returned it to the necklace stand in the safe, but left it open. I reentered the room to find him struggling to get off his pants and boots. "I love it when you stand at attention." Smiling, I wrapped my hand around his manly appendage, enjoying the way he pulsed and throbbed with need. Lowering myself to my knees, I winced. My knee still hurt. Fucking Alux.

Clark trembled as he sank his fingers into my damp hair. He held his breath as I touched his rim with my tongue. When I began doing other things, he groaned, "Teagan."

Letting him pop out of my mouth, I grinned up at him. He lifted me to the bed. His eyes were dark with passion as he knelt upon the bed. Taking each of my ankles into his strong, large hands, he slid his rough palms up my legs to my thighs. He lowered his lips to my womanly center. "Oh, Clark." It was my turn to groan and tremble.

We'd showered together and were dressing by the time our privacy came to an end. "Not that again, Mommy. Ugh." Neema, wearing a pink dress with blue polka-dots, sneered at my uniform and went into my closet.

Clark and I locked eyes and suppressed our laughter. She'd been criticizing my attire.

Then, she screamed. It wasn't a hurt scream. No, it was one of unbridled fury. "Where is the most sparkly of sparkles? Mommy?"

Entering the closet, I took out one of my favorite tiaras and placed it on her head. "It seems that I have temporarily traded it. Don't worry. Winks knows he can't keep it. This is just his way of letting us know how much fun he had and that he wants to play Inquisitors with us again." I gave her my sweetest smile.

Aghast, she stammered, "You traded it for a book?"

I shrugged. "This book is going to help us defeat the Alux." I pointed. "He didn't take the crown or anything else."

She let her shoulders drop and straightened her tiara. "Oh, well, okay." Scrunching up her nose at me and observing me with her pale, jade-green eyes, she pointed at one of the dresses hanging in my closet. Taking it down, I changed. She nodded in approval. "Better. Okay. Bye."

"Where are you going?"

"To play." She turned her back and left.

Smoothing down the full, floor-length skirt of the grey dress with its metallic green flowers, I sighed and took out a pair of grey flats to match. Then, with the stolen book held to my chest, Clark and I left our quarters and walked to the lift. Neema was sitting alone in the living area having a tea party. She was smiling and giggling, so I shrugged and followed him into the lift.

As we were entering the conference room, Clark asked the guys, "Where is Winks?"

They didn't interpret it as a question awaiting answers. They took it for what it was, an assignment. They were like a pack of wolves that had scented an injured ice bear. However, after hours of searching for biological signatures on our ship and the planet, we came up empty.

"He's vanished." Cedrenus had difficulty admitting it.

"When was he aboard? How did he get the book into my safe?" I groaned, and not in pleasure. "Momma is going to be furious with me."

"Teagan, it's a small price to pay if it leads us to the Pariea." Stayton, hands covered by white gloves, held the book open while Tyler scanned its pages with meticulous care.

Binder and Levi were running decryption programs on the pages they'd already uploaded. The rest of us were in the way at the moment.

Leaving the ship, I made my way to Chione's land port offices where I made arrangements to have the *Empress* refueled and for a ship wide resupply. Then, I called Clark to see if everyone wanted to take a break and meet me at the food court. They all arrived a few minutes later and had brought Neema with them. "Did you enjoy your tea party?" I asked.

Her eyes danced with joy as she nodded. "Daddy will be here soon!"

"What did you talk about?"

Her smile became wider. "We're going to play in the bouncy house and in the pool! And, we're going to order all the pizzas!"

I grinned at her excitement. It wasn't difficult for them to predict where I intended to go next, Earth. After we had all eaten our fills, we went out to our transport and drove toward the *Empress*.

Neema plastered her face to her window. "Mommy! Stop! Open the door! Let Neema out!" Humoring her, we stopped the transport and parked in front of our loading ramp. Getting out, she pointed up. Around the land port, docking sites were quickly filling with warships. "Daddy's here! Daddy's here!" Her voice had taken on a high, excited pitch. Tears leaked from the corners of her eyes. Bending down to her, I waited while she put her arms around my neck. As I stood, she wrapped her legs around my waist. That was how we stayed and waited. From across the land port, a transport sped toward us. "Mommy!" Neema put so much emotion into the utterance. Excitement, joy, the months of lonely anguish and longing, it was all there.

"I know, baby. I know."

Clark and Cormac stood to either side of us, waiting.

As the transport drew nearer, the driver slowed to a stop. The doors flew open. Eight long legs and a blue-grey body leapt from the roller and jumped toward me. Joy bubbled from me in the form of laughter. Neema wanted down. She ran past Thunderdrop who jumped to my arm and shoulder where he nuzzled my cheek and chirped. I lifted my hand to rub one of his long black legs.

Neema's shock stick thumped against her leg as she ran to the incredibly handsome male who stepped from the transport. Bending, he caught her as she leapt into his arms. He spun her around and laughed while Neema gave him kisses all over his face. Our eyes met. Yukihyo's eyes were a brilliant and joyful white. His arms were huge. It was as if he had muscles on top of muscles. The short sleeves of his black shirt looked ready to burst apart at the seams.

"Stars," I mumbled. He'd been exercising. He'd been exercising a lot. I looked up from his muscles to his face and blushed. He'd been watching me and had a pleased expression on his face. He knew exactly what I was thinking.

"Mommy!" The desperate cry tore at my heart. Niklos ran to me, knocking into my legs, and throwing his arms around my waist.

"Oh, my baby! My boy!" Running my fingers through his hair, I bent and kissed the tears from his cheeks.

Itsy chirped from his back and crawled from him and up to Thunderdrop.

It surprised Niklos when I picked him up and spun him around. He laughed while Thunderdrop chirped from where he balanced on my head and back. Nico climbed from the driver's seat, strode over, picked up all four of us, and spun us around.

Meanwhile, a dozen transports had converged on our location. From Nico's arms, I watched as Yukihyo, who still held Neema, shook hands with Clark and Cormac. Reluctantly, Nico put us down, but his eyes spoke volumes. He wouldn't be putting me down tonight. However, this moment was about our children.

From the next transport, Dario and Fitz brought out Marielle and Tabitha. Nico took Niklos from me. Lifting my hands to my face, I sobbed and stumbled toward them. All of the misery that I'd walled up within my soul poured out. Holding a daughter in each arm, I cried and cried while soothing their emotions so that they wouldn't start crying. I kissed them each and smelled their hair, luxuriating in the way they felt in my arms and in the bonds which I felt with each of them.

"Ma!" Through blurry eyes, I watched my youngest son run from Eli and Farowyn to me. At his side, Flake ran. Happy barking and laughter filled our ears.

With the girls in my arms and their hands affixed in my hair, I knelt. Peter slowed and stopped once we were face to face. With each breath we shared, he calmed. His big brown eyes grew clear.

Then, Neema was on the ground and hugging her brothers. She got knocked onto her butt by Flake who eagerly licked the happy tears from her face. "Yay! We're all back together!" she yelled. "Let's go camping!"

"Yeah!" yelled Niklos.

"Wait until you see what we got you!" she said to her brothers. She hit a command on her wrist and vanished.

"Neema!" Yukihyo screamed in a panic.

"Oh, it's okay, babe. It's a toy we picked up from the Durhcu."

Horrified, he said, "I can't sense her." His handsome face was scrunched up in anguish.

"Neither can I," Zared said.

Seeing him, I became still. The bonds between us seemed to thicken. He and Izaac were each in my mind and eager to be alone with me. I smiled and rocked back and forth on my feet. "It's a toy for their children whose true purpose is protection against the Alux. If you could sense her emotions or thoughts, it wouldn't be working. Neema, show yourself."

She appeared behind Niklos. "Boo," she whispered.

He jumped which made her laugh.

"Come on! I'll teach you both the rules!"

I nodded to her guards. Then, I focused my attention on Eli. "Inquisitor Beck, I formally request the debriefing of my crew and a secure data transfer. The *Empress* and our fighters have undergone several Durhcu repairs and modifications which are not regulation."

"Or even within our technological abilities it would appear. The species has superior defensive capabilities." He'd ordered scans of my ship the moment we'd been within range. Meeting my eyes, he gave a nod of his head. "At ease, Ensign Probus."

There. I'd done everything by the book. Beside me, Clark's shoulders visibly relaxed. Perhaps, we'd be able to salvage our grades. Narrowing my eyes at a drone, I turned with my daughters in my arms and strode up the ramp for the privacy of my ship.

When we entered the Imperial Deck, it was quite the changed scene from when last I'd been there. Before, there had been a quiet, solemn stillness. Neema had played with adults who had done the best they could to alleviate her loneliness. Now, the laughter of children, the chirps of spiders, and the barks of a snow fox bounced off of the walls. Chef added deep belly laughs to the cacophony of joyous sounds.

Seated around the room were Cormac, Drex, Eli, Nico, and Dario who were discussing the treaty we'd made with the Durhcu. "It is imperative that we offer them military support."

Eli stared at him. "I will send my own ship along with the weaponry I have aboard. She can leave once she is refueled. All I request in return is passage aboard the *Empress*."

Looking up from where I played blocks on a blanket with Marielle and Tabitha, I grinned at him and winked. "Your request is granted, Inquisitor Beck." I gave him my sweetest smile. "I'll even grant you passage on the Princess."

"What about in her?" His voice was a growl.

Oh, he was positively wicked. My smile brightened. "My Inquisitor may travel in whatever way best suits him."

Tabitha gurgled. I handed her a block and hummed happily to myself. I couldn't wait until bedtime.

Eli looked down at his vid-screen. "I've ordered my second-in-command to prepare my ship for the journey. Even now, he charts the quickest path to our new allies."

Dario took out his own vid-screen and began making similar arrangements.

Drex scowled. "We all can't very well send off our warships. Else, we will not be able to effectively protect Princess Teagan and the children."

"Sweetie," I said. Inquisitor Drex Licinius stilled and gave me his focused attention. "You are right, of course. However, if you have any weapons to spare, send them with one of the warships." I could tell that wasn't what was bothering him. It was easy enough to figure out. "Drex, I'd feel safer if you were to travel aboard my ship with us. Can't your second-in-command captain your ship and serve as our protection?"

"Of course, darling. Of course." He stood up and moved to the side of the room to make his own arrangements and coordinate with the other captains.

Marielle lifted her hand to my lips, so I took the opportunity to kiss her fingers.

Pierce and Lorca were happily organizing the luggage being delivered from Dario's warship where they'd travelled with the children.

I sighed and smiled. My family was returned to me. We were all together once more aboard my ship. The lift doors opened. My grin broadened. Standing, I walked around the blocks and extended my hand. Clasping Captain Ricimer's forearm, I said, "I sure am glad to see you. Welcome aboard."

He grinned. "Thanks for the vacation. I was worried for nothing. After inspecting the *Empress*, I can see that you've taken excellent care of her and your crew." His eyes held no flattery in their depths. His praise was sincere.

"Thank you, sir. I'm quite ready to turn the responsibilities of the bridge over to you. As soon as we are able, I'd like for you to set our course for Earth."

He shook his head. "Emperor Probus has given me my orders." His tone and expression made it clear. He'd been ordered to return me to Parvac.

"There's no time for it."

He shrugged, saluted me, and returned to the lift.

While the heavy weight of command had lifted from me, a new obstacle had presented itself. I'd have to convince Papa to let me finish what I'd started. Strong hands settled on my shoulders and began to work away at the tension there. Turning, I smiled and gazed up into Zared's eyes. I knew exactly how to occupy myself on the journey to Parvac.

Grinning, he asked, "How long until naptime?"

Our laughter mingled with that of the children.

The End

A personal note from Wendie:

Thank you for reading *Warlords of the Stars*! If you enjoyed Teagan's story and want to see more, please take a moment to show your support by leaving a review on the product page where you made your purchase. Your reviews are important and help other readers discover these books.

Please, keep in touch!

You can visit my website at www.wendienordgren.com[1] or join my Facebook group, Omnes Videntes, where you can discuss books with other readers and get information about new releases.

---

1.   http://www.wendienordgren.com

www.ingramcontent.com/pod-product-compliance
Lightning Source LLC
Chambersburg PA
CBHW021939120726
47992CB00001B/50